More acclaim for
THE LAST OF THE GOLDEN GIRLS

"Susan Swan has written a brilliant chronicle of Paradise Lost told, perhaps for the first time, from the point of view of Eve."

Alberto Manguel

"Breathless . . . Moving . . . Contemporary literature would be hard-pressed to come up with a more engaging narrator."

The London Free Press

"A frighteningly pleasurable novel that goes far beyond the limited parameters of feminine competition. We cannot resist the implacable seduction of *The Last of the Golden Girls*, a tour de force of writing and a brilliant parable for our time."

Aritha Van Herk

Also by Susan Swan:

**THE BIGGEST MODERN WOMAN OF THE WORLD
UNFIT FOR PARADISE**

THE LAST OF THE GOLDEN GIRLS

Susan Swan

FAWCETT CREST • TORONTO

A Fawcett Crest Book
Published by Random House of Canada, Limited

Copyright © 1989 by Susan Swan

This edition published by arrangement with Lester & Orpen Dennys Limited.

Excerpts from "Goddess of Love" from Sappho: *Poems and Fragments*, translated by Josephine Balmer. Copyright © 1984 by Josephine Balmer. Published by arrangement with Carol Publishing Group

Canadian Cataloguing in Publication Data
  Swan, Susan
    The last of the golden girls
ISBN 0-449-22051-6
I. Title
PS8587.W35L3 1991 C813f.54 C91-093264-6
PR9199.3.S83L3 1991

Printed in Canada

First Fawcett Crest Edition: June 1991

*For Katherine A. and the women who went through
adolescence with me*

This novel has been a long time in the making and has had many helpers. Louise Dennys, Donya Peroff, John Lownsbrough, Mike Kohn, C. J. Dingle, Harold Crooks, Tara McMurtry, Connie Rooke, Karen Mulhallen, Vera Frenkel, Erika Ritter, Anne Fullerton, Rob Read. I'd also like to acknowledge assistance from the Canada Council and the Ontario Arts Council.

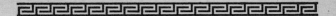

PROLOGUE

WE PLAYED OUR GAMES IN THE HEAT OF SUMMER. IN OUR defence, let me point out that we acted no differently than any of the city dwellers who pack up on the first golden day in July when the temperature soars above 28 degrees Celsius and stream north to the thousands of lakes and bays that turn the heart of my country into a kingdom of inland seas.

We treated our contests like athletic events. And like all good athletes, we shared the illusion that life is a game with rules, that a clear-cut judgment would cure us of our uncertainty about our strengths and weaknesses by dividing us into categories of winners and losers. We didn't fear tests, we yearned for them. There are days I wish we had found other methods of making life knowable. And days when I wish it was summer and we could act out the old contests over and over again.

PART ONE

Losing

Immortal, Aphrodite, on your patterned throne,
daughter of Zeus, guile weaver,
I beg you, goddess, don't subjugate my heart
with anguish, with grief

—Fragment 78, from Section Six,
Goddess of Love

PART ONE

Losing

1 959. JULY 1. UP HIGH, YOU'D NEVER KNOW THE BEACH is the most wonderful place in the world. It looks blank—a line of blond sand, as long and straight as a racetrack until the beach reaches the First Point to the north of U-Go-I-Go Sound where Jay Manchester has a cottage. Then the beach curves into a chunky finger of sand and dock and trees which poke out into the powder-blue water. The Manchester place is the house of logs; it looks small from here but it's as big and round as a giant wooden beehive. Its flagstone walks curve among beds of red and white petunias and Michaelmas daisies. The daisies give off an odour like cat pee when Bobby and I amble past. The flagstone walks slope down to a dock which is the size of a government wharf. The dock houses Jay's speedboat, which takes Jay and his friends waterskiing around the two tiny, wood-crowned islands that lie within swimming distance from his dock.

The Second Point after the Manchester place is the long, spooky bunch of trees with hardly any beach, just rocks and the remains of an old fisherman's dock in the water. You can make out the radar observation dome sticking up beyond the treetops. Some tourists think the dome is a lighthouse. They don't know

5

it's part of the Dew Line. The government put it there for our defence.

Do you see me yet? I am hugging the trunk of Look-Out Pine. See the thin brown foot dangling from the prickly green bough? That's me, Dinger Bell. Contrary to what the adults say, I'm not fourteen years old—I am fourteen summers old. Look higher and you'll see the rest of my skinny body in lime-green Bermuda shorts and matching V-neck sweater—one hand shading my eyes, surveying the horizon the way Cartier does in my grade five history book when the explorer was searching for the route to China through the land mass of North America. Cartier thought the riches of the Orient lay through the Northwest Passage, a few more portages over that-a-way. The trouble with Cartier is that he was just another immigrant who didn't know how to appreciate where he was. It's nicer than China right here on U-Go-I-Go Sound.

Bobby and I never go to the Second Point so I've never seen the dome up close. The Second Point is too far to hike. We're always thirsty by the time we get near the Manchester place, so we usually stop and gulp down our Orange Crush and peanut-butter sandwiches wrapped in waxed paper and hope that Jay will walk down the flagstone path and talk to us. Jay is quite old. He's sixteen. He has hair the colour of wild canary feathers and his body is nothing but right angles. When he stands up in his speedboat and crouches over the steering wheel to watch for sandbars, the spray from the bay glistens on his long, light eyelashes and tanned chest. And on the white-blond hairs on his long, tanned legs.

Of course, I don't look directly at the place between his legs. I wouldn't want him to think badly of me. Bobby says the word "fart", but even Bobby won't look there. I have noticed how he's built, though. Jay's bathing suit bulges like the ones worn by the Italian men we see playing soccer on the public beach. Bobby's mother says they make disgusting spectacles of themselves in their tight woollen bathing suits, bouncing the ball back and forth on their dark heads. Their bodies make me feel scared and excited the same way horror movies do.

Five summers ago, when I found out about the birds and bees,

I was mad at the Brothers until September. It's rude of boys to stick their you-know-whats into girls. Girls can't be that free. So why can boys?

I am telling you this from Look-Out Pine on Poison Ivy Point which is the last point that Jay can see from his cottage. I am the game-maker; I think up the names for our secret spots and the games that Bobby and I play and sometimes the games for the Brothers.

The Brothers are boys we play with when we're bored. It is only an accident of fate that they happen to be related to us. The Brothers are very interested in sex and want to kiss us when we play sardines with them. But they're too young, by half. They are silly with their hairless chests and knobby knees, their little pink fingers hanging down between their legs. The Brothers like to flash open their towels when we take a skinny dip. The Brothers are the first men Bobby and I have seen in the altogether. It's too bad our first penis memory was nothing to write home about, though their bodies look harmless—not like Bobby's body, which has a huge mat of black pubic hair—the most hair I've ever seen. The Brothers and I saw it last night when Bobby came out of the water covered with bloodsuckers and stripped off her clothes so that I could put salt on them.

Bobby has grown up a lot since last summer. I saw high-heeled shoes in her closet this morning and she wears lipstick all the time now. When I noticed the lipstick, I thought she wouldn't want to play with me, but she seems to like me just the same, and invited me to suntan with her at Poison Ivy Point this morning.

Bobby's sitting in the south dune, naked as a jaybird except for the bottom of her two-piece. Bobby wants to get her breasts tanned this summer. She stuck bandages, the round kind, on her nipples so they don't get burnt. I'm a little jealous of Bobby. An eentsy teentsy bit. Bobby got breasts and pubic hair before me—two summers ago—and I felt gypped, but this summer I'm catching up with her: I've got breasts—two bumps. I waited all winter for them to grow before my eyes. I like folding my arms across my chest so I can feel them. I like pressing them together and looking at the cleavage in a mirror. Breasts make me look better. Not that I'm good-looking. This is me: nice, smart (and overly fond of big words), as well as a top golfer who wears glasses and has dishwater blonde hair cut short in bangs.

I wish my eyes were the same colour. My left eye is Gendarme Blue (that's a colour in the Munsell colour chart; it's also the colour the Sound turns in a west wind). My right eye is Sky Blue. It sounds nicer than it is—it's really a blah colour, possessing little value, as Mr. Munsell says, because it has neither hue nor chroma which is the same thing as strength. Fortunately, gold streaks circle the iris of that eye like spokes in a wheel so that helps my light eye to look a little more interesting. I am also tall and skinny and, frankly, still kind of underdeveloped, though pubic hair has sprouted. Bobby's mother told her the hair is there to keep our female organs warm. I wonder what organs she means. There's no room on my crotch for anything the size of a heart or a lung.

Bobby has two nicely coloured brown eyes (Seal Brown on Mr. Munsell's chart and both matching) and common taffy-coloured hair cut short in a duck's ass just like the American movie star James Dean. She also has a smart-aleck way of talking I'd like to copy, and a sexy mouth which hangs open a lot because Bobby's favourite expression is "Duh." Bobby says out loud what people think in secret; sometimes she says what I think which is why I could defend Bobby to the death if necessary.

Bobby's breasts also have cleavage no matter whether she is wearing her two-piece bathing suit top with wired supports or her 36-inch B-cup brassiere. When she's been in the sun, Bobby's acne dries up and Bobby looks beautiful. Her tanned face together with her brown eyes and blonde hair make her look like a sunflower. In the photo on my dresser, she's as tanned as a piece of Scandinavian furniture and winks at me under her velvet riding cap, like the one Elizabeth Taylor wore in *National Velvet* except Bobby's not prissy and gussied up. She's tough as a gunslinger in jeans and a man's shirt and white Bobby (heh-heh, that's a joke) socks and I want to protect and worship both at once because she is brave enough to be a tomboy and not care what people think of her. Of course, it's amazing how plain she is without a tan. And when Bobby gets her period, pimples break out again on her forehead. In fact, when Bobby has her period and forgets to wash her hair, she looks a mess.

Somebody is calling "Dinger! Can you hear me, Dinger? Do you have any matches?" It's Bobby signalling me from the sand dune. My real name is Jude but my last name is Bell, so people call me Dinger. I scramble down the pine's prickly trunk and run so the sand won't burn my feet. In Merton, you can tell when summer is here because the oak leaves grow bigger than mice ears and turn lime green. At the beach, I know it's summer when the sand is so hot it burns your feet and a heat haze bleaches the water and sky to the soft blurry shades that my art teacher in Merton calls pastels. Everything around Bobby and me today is in pastels, especially across the Sound. The baby-blue smudge streaking across the horizon is the Blue Mountains. It's too hazy to see the ski trails on the mountainside—all you can make out is the powder-blue outline of mountains fading into a powder-blue sky and a powder-blue bay.

But the real sign of summer for me is the sight of Jay Manchester's yellow speedboat at the dock on the First Point. When I see his boat's fiberglass hull, yellow as a cob of August corn, I feel happier than when I first see the mice ears on the oak trees in Merton.

"What are you looking at? Something to write a poem about?" Bobby says. I jump into a shady spot on the sand under the juniper bushes.

"What if I am?"

"Just kidding. You don't have to be so sensitive."

"There are matches in the pocket of your school sweater. I saw you put them there this morning."

"Aw, thanks Dinger. What would I do without you?" Bobby reaches out and retrieves the matches from the pocket of her sweater. She shakes out a menthol cigarette from a package of Cameos and I smell sulphur as she puffs dreamily, letting her cigarette dangle from her lips the way the tough guys smoke at the Merton pool hall. "So what are we going to do? I'm bored." Bobby blows a smoke ring in my direction. I watch in awe as the ring floats over the apple-green juniper bushes and disappears beyond a hill of sand.

"We could practise humping."

"You mean the stuff we used to do last summer?"

"You know, practise for the real thing."

"You can't touch my breasts though."

"Why not? You used to let me touch them before."

"Well, you didn't have breasts then and I thought you wanted to feel what they were like. Now you've got them. Now you know."

"I'll let you feel my breasts if you let me touch yours."

"Geez, this is so babyish. It's just like a game of doctor," Bobby says.

"No, it's not. I want to know what to do when it comes to the big clinch."

Bobby sighs. "Okay, Dinger. I guess I don't have anything better to do."

Bobby stands up and drags her towel over to the juniper bush, walking in a funny sort of shuffle because she's stepping on the edge of the towel so her feet don't get hot. I feel excited. Her breasts are still bare. I like kissing Bobby on the lips and squeezing her breasts and praying that nobody will come by and see us. Bobby squats down on the sand. "Okay. I'll be the man. You be the girl."

"No. I want to be the man this time. You lie down."

Bobby lies flat on her back and stares at the sky. She looks totally passive and uninterested. I slowly crawl on top of her until every part of me is covering every inch of her. I stare down into her evenly coloured brown eyes. Bobby giggles. "Don't look so serious, Dinger. This is only a game." I kiss her as hard and tight as I can on her lips. I'm a hard kisser, Bobby says. She smells of Noxzema suncream. Then, very slyly, I begin to feel her breasts.

Bobby's breasts are like fluffy, well-padded triangles ending in huge, round, milky-pink nipples. My breasts remind me of plum pudding with a cherry on top. My nipples are small and dainty; my nipples are also brown, the same colour as my tan. I scoop one of Bobby's breasts in my hands and then release it just so I can feel the soft flesh falling away from my fingers.

Bobby squirms underneath me as if she is distracted by something. Usually, she kisses me back hard and whispers a line from the novel *Peyton Place* in my ear. We both studied the novel and underlined the dirty passages with ballpoint pen so we could memorize them and say the lines to each other when we were practising our clinches. Like the passage on page 303 when Constance MacKenzie's lover surprises her in the kitchen as she's cooking. He says, "Christ, do you know you have the breasts of a virgin?" I also like the part about Rodney making love to Betty on the beach. He's totally carried away. He murmurs, "Please . . . please" against Betty's skin. It's romantic but it's also kind of sad because you know he's going to get Betty into trouble.

Nervously my hand slides under Bobby's back and pushes her breasts against mine. "*Peyton Place*, page 269," I whisper.

"Come on, honey," Bobby says in a fake whimpering voice. "Do it hard honey, bite me a little." Then she arches her body against me. This is one of the old moves. Like doing the tango prone. My hand creeps around Bobby's stomach and explores her hipbone. I place it on her skinny thigh ominously. Will she let me touch her down there? Sometimes she does. Sometimes she doesn't. The folds of skin on her genitals are much thicker than mine. They hang out sloppily. Mine aren't visible although I play with myself a lot more than Bobby. I know just where to touch myself to feel good.

I shift my weight and Bobby groans, "Oh, brother," and I say, "*Lady Chatterley's Lover*, page 270." Bobby says, "What is that? I can't remember," and I say, "It's a new one I just discovered," and I move my hand a little farther up her thigh and whisper the words. "The sun through the low window sent a beam that lit up his thighs and slim belly, the erect phallus rising darkish and hot-looking from the little cloud of vivid red hair."

"Ugh, that's disgusting," Bobby says and giggles and I giggle too and then I move my hand up a little higher. And Bobby's knees buckle and she rolls away from me angrily. "I don't like to be touched there."

"You used to let me do it before."

"That was different. That was before I met Ross. I can't stand anyone but Ross touching me."

"Who's Ross?"

"I told you about Ross last night. We're going steady." Bobby pulls out a Cameo and lights up, squinting her eyes and hunching her shoulders just like James Dean used to do. "I guess you wouldn't understand what something like that means."

"You mean I'm too young?"

"You said it, Dinger. I didn't." Bobby blows another smoke ring and I don't know what to say. No matter how much I think I've caught up to Bobby, she is always a step ahead.

"Jude-ith! Jude-ith!"

Bobby butts her cigarette in the sand quickly and scrambles to put on her bathing-suit top. A moment later, my mother is at the top of the dune looking down at us. My mother is a golden girl, the woman in Technicolor who makes other women feel they are in black and white. Everybody says she should be a movie star, but my mother says her function is to give to others and be appreciated. That's why she never has problems or feels needy—because she is too busy helping people. Sometimes people think she's my sister; I like to point out, "She's my mom." Of course, it's a bit tiresome to hear people talk on and on about how gorgeous my mother is. Mrs. Gallagher says she is better looking than Grace Kelly. It makes my heart sink a little to look at her now. She's beautiful all right, in crisp linen shorts and halter top, and her blonde hair lies in a neat sausage roll across her shoulders. She does wear lipstick above her lip line, though. (Bobby says she does it on purpose because her lips are too thin.)

My mother walks slowly down the path, shielding her eyes against the bright yellow sunlight. She is wearing pretty, toe-less sandals so I guess the sand isn't burning her feet. "So here you are, Jude. Shelly is up at the Big House waiting for you."

"Don't tell me that snob is pestering you again this summer," Bobby says. My mother looks coldly at Bobby but doesn't say anything.

"Bobby, I have to go. Right now."

"Some friend you are."

I put my arm on Bobby's shoulder. "Don't be dumb. Come with me."

"Naw. I've got better things to do." Bobby stands up and runs away, brushing the sand off her thighs. I catch my mother looking at the cigarette butts in the dune. I wait for her comment. No comment comes. "Let's go, Jude." My mother turns and I follow her up the sandy path through the juniper bushes along the Secret Staircase to the Look-Out Pine and then off the Hanging Step into the Unknown Desert.

I stop there for a minute and my mother stops too. She puts her hand on my shoulder. Down on the beach Bobby is throwing a stick for Ben. She's a tiny brown body on the sand, which is white—not snow white, but a chalky ivory hue, I'd say. From Poison Ivy Point the bodies of the walkers look so small they seem out of place. I like it when storms come up and you can see the bodies on the beach start to rush around like bugs and move through the green bushes up to their cottages. When the sun comes out again, dozens of the little pink and white bodies rush back down to the sand. It's like watching migrating insects. The waves are like lace ruffles on the powder-blue bay behind Bobby. And the sun is directly overhead. It beams down on her blonde hair and catches the light of Jay Manchester's speedboat parked at the dock at the First Point. I can see its fiberglass hull as yellow as a plate of butter. Now my mother takes my hand and we walk up the sandy, overgrown path to the barn my family uses for a cottage, and I start to think about Jay.

Does he have any idea how I feel about him? Or what I'd do to get him to notice me instead of Bobby? She likes him, too, but I like him better than she ever could. Besides, I'm smarter and nicer than she is and I can make up poems to tell him how wonderful he is. Bobby wrote him a stupid poem last summer after we saw him waterski. It was copied from a book.

Though I don't often tell you in so many words, Jay,
But I think you're dear and wonderful, and I have right from the start,

You ought to know me well enough, at least, I hope you do,
to know
You come first with me, because I am in love with you.

Isn't that a sickly poem? Here's mine:

JAY THE LIONMAN

The Lionman
Is a face
In dream landscapes.
He rides on a windy plain
And has soft pads for feet
Which is surprising
Considering the length of his claws.

The Lionman hunts me
In thickets on the plain
I cover my tracks with shadows
And borrow time
From Jungle Shamans.

The Lionman is known
To kill slowly.
Entering first by the bowels,
He unpeels a strip of belly—
Then, how the skin unwinds itself,
Ring after ring,
Like a bracelet of silver hoops
Clattering down a spear shaft.

Jay the Lionman is a stalker,
His mane is swept with semen
And the blood of virgins
And he wears the sign of the phallus
As one more unnecessary charm.

Riding on the plains, windy
And thicket covered,

The Lionman
Travels by night
Into the arena of my senses,
Whuh, whuh, whuh,
Hear him coming now
He and his Nuba heart
Will murder me
In darkness.

"Jude, what's the matter with you?" my mother says. "Are you in a trance?"

"I was just thinking about Jay Manchester."

"Oh, the boy who looks like he's going to burst out of his bathing suit?"

"That's a rude way to talk about a man, Mother."

"Well, maybe he'll make you take an interest in your appearance, dear. Those are scruffy shorts you have on." I look down at my baggy, tacky Bermudas and back again at my mother's yellow linen shorts which are creased up the pantleg and my heart sinks a little bit more. I wonder who Jay will pick for his girlfriend this summer. One thing for sure, it won't be me. Another thing for sure: if my mother was my age, he'd pick her.

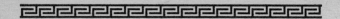

JULY 9TH. THE BROTHERS ARE PLAYING KICK-THE-CAN BY the Polliwog Pond. A bouquet of towheads on top of the sandy hill by the pond. Bouquet—that's a fancy word to describe boys, and I wouldn't say it in front of them, but I like the way the evening sunlight shines right down to the roots of the Brothers' hair, making it shine silver and gold like Peaches-and-Cream corn. Up close, I bet their hair smells hot and sweaty like the hay on the Lefaivres' farm.

The tallest head among the Brothers is Macgregor. Macgregor's hair is dull like a strip of bark from a red cedar tree. Macgregor uses big words like me and if Macgregor wasn't as skinny as a beanpole, he would be cute. Unfortunately his legs look like sticks in his white shorts. That's one thing you notice about Macgregor. He always wears old white shorts with grass stains on his bum. This is the other thing: Macgregor is an expert on sex. He tells the Brothers everything they want to know on the subject, like where to buy condoms at Balmy Beach, so they can put the rubbers in their wallets and feel like big shots. As if any girl would want to go to bed with one of them! Yesterday, Macgregor bought the Brothers a box of sanitary supplies and the Brothers took it to Bobby's sleeping cabin. They shredded

16

one of the napkins as if they expected to find something dangerous concealed in it. All they found were cotton fibres and gauze. The Brothers are very stupid. There are six Brothers in total. Macgregor hangs out with them because he doesn't have anything better to do.

The only time I talk to Macgregor is when I try to stop him from catching tadpoles at Polliwog Pond. I used to collect tadpoles myself which gave us something in common, but I don't do it any more because it is not the sort of thing a fourteen-year-old girl should do.

We are too old for toys and too young for boys, my mother says. It's a helpless age if you ask me. There's nothing to do except walk the beach and put an alert, interested look on your face when boys talk to you. Besides, the polliwogs die if you keep them too long. Unfortunately, Macgregor sticks them in big, slime-coated aquariums so he can study their mating habits. He didn't believe me when I told him it's the frogs that do *IT*, not the little pollies with their squishy, saucer-like bodies. I see the tiny male frogs in the spring climbing up on the backs of their female partners and holding on for dear life while the females float all over the pond trailing long tapioca strings of eggs behind them.

Macgregor is always damming up parts of the pond to catch the pollies who get left high and dry when the water evaporates. So Bobby and I have to dig channels in the sand to let the fresh bay water in from the Sound to save them. We usually do it at night after I've practised on my three-hole golf course. That's where I am now—teeing off for the first hole in the dune. Bobby is sitting on the sand nearby, smoking her twentieth fag of the day. I know because I counted eighteen butts in her cabin ashtray after dinner, each tip smeared with light pink whorls.

"What a die-hard you are," Bobby says as I take a warm-up swing. "You're worse than Macgregor with frogs."

"Your game goes if you don't practise."

"Why don't you ask Macgregor to practise with you?" Bobby points to the Brothers playing by the Polliwog Pond. "I know you're sweet on him."

"I'm not sweet on him."

Bobby laughs way too loud and Macgregor stares our way in

surprise. Bobby stares back with her tough "Duh" expression and Macgregor turns back to the other boys.

"Hey Muskellunge! Hypo! Want to play chuckle-belly?" Oh, no. From the dune the Brothers are pointing at us and laughing. They know they don't have a hope in Haiti of getting us to play chuckle-belly. It's a great game, actually. I wish I could say I made it up, but Bobby's brother Rum Bum showed us how to play it last summer. Everybody lies down on the ground in a row and each person puts his head on the next person's stomach, and then the first person in the line says something funny and everybody laughs and all your heads bounce up and down in a crazy way. It's kind of sexy too—putting your head close to another person's privates. That's why we refuse to play chuckle-belly any more with the Brothers. Unless there's nothing else to do and we're really hard up for new ideas.

"I hate their nicknames for us, don't you?" Bobby says.

"Mine is worse than yours. A fish like the muskellunge is the lowest form of animal life."

"Hypo sounds like hippopotamus. Nobody'd know it stood for hypochondriac," Bobby says mournfully. "I don't care if they think I'm a hypochondriac. I just wish they wouldn't call me something that makes people think of fat animals."

Suddenly, Rum Bum does a war whoop at the top of the dune and the Brothers run down the hill towards us. Now the dune looks like the head of a dummy—a pockmarked Easter Island statue rising out of the sand. The hundreds of footprints of the Brothers make the pockmarks and the tufts of grass on the top of the dune look like the statue's hair.

"Dinger, we were just kidding. We wondered if you'd play Kick-the-Can with us. Or make up a new game. We'll do anything you want. Won't we, boys?" The other Brothers cross their arms on their chests and say, "How, how."

"We don't want to play with you drips," Bobby says. "We've got more important things to do." Bobby hates Rum Bum because he's her brother. His name is Jonathan, but I nicknamed him Rum Bum because he acts crazy, like he's got rum in his bum. For instance, he tries to sneak into our bedrooms at night and we have to kick him out. When he won't go, we have to give him a Chinese wrist burn.

"Got a heavy date tonight?" Rum Bum asks. The Brothers hoot.

"None of your beeswax," Bobby says.

"Don't worry. We know where you're going," Adam says. Adam is one of my brothers; Beckett is the other one. They're twins, blond and totally insignificant.

"Yah? Where?"

"To J-J-J-Jay," the Brothers yell in unison. Then Macgregor scowls and raises both arms to the skies. He says, "Done-done-don-e-da-da! Charge!" A white thing hits Bobby in the ear and then another one hits me on the left breast. I look down at the sand. The white things are the rest of the sanitary napkins Macgregor bought for the Brothers.

I am so taken aback I don't move. Neither does Bobby. We stand, like two dopes, while the white napkins fall like snow. Then Macgregor cries, "The enemy is routed! Retreat, gentlemen!" And the Brothers run off as fast as they can through Dungeon Pines.

"You'll be sorry! You'll see!" I scream. "Adam! Beckett! I'll tell Mom on you!"

"Let's not show them they've got to us," Bobby hisses and walks off as if she doesn't see the sanitary napkins lying higgledy-piggledy on the sand. One of them lies on the juniper bush next to me so I pick it up and stuff it under my sweater. (At my age, you can't be too prepared. I could start bleeding any second.) Then I toss a look of disgust in the direction of the Brothers and run down to the beach after Bobby.

The sand on the shore is starting to cool but at least the waves splashing my feet are warm. And the sun is in its "middle-of-summer" position behind the Manchester place on the First Point.

I usually like walking on the beach from point to point. That's what everyone does up here—old people, kids, and lots of dogs. You never know who you're going to meet. But tonight I feel a little discouraged. The Brothers know Bobby and I like Jay because they read it in my Horse Book. Mom made them give it back, but the damage was done. Creepy enemies of love—that's what the Brothers are. I don't say this out loud because it sounds too high falutin'. I get teased for the way I talk so I try to be polite and not use long words or flowery expressions.

Beside me Bobby starts to hold my hand and all of a sudden I see why. Ahead of us, Bobby's rival for my affections is helping her father pull a Sunfish up on the sand. Her name is Shelly Moffat and she likes me better than she does Bobby. This is Shelly: a private school snob who'd look like a model in *Seventeen* magazine if she wasn't so tubby. Shelly's mother is a distant relative of the Capes who make the pianos my father buys for his refectory in Merton. Shelly says her mother can trace their family connections back to the old country. This is also Shelly: a bit of a pest and a braggart with a friendly way of laughing. I don't say that to Bobby because Shelly doesn't mean to get on your nerves—she just doesn't know any better. I mean, she doesn't understand how to read the signs that say she is crowding you. She used to ask me to play house with her no matter how many times I told her I didn't go in for dolls. Of course sometimes I do play with dolls but not in the summer when Bobby's around. Shelly also has a perfect page-boy hairdo which never gets messy and she acts haughty, as if God has put her on this beach by mistake and she is waiting for him to see he was wrong and put her somewhere else.

I like Shelly but I don't love her the way I do Bobby. For instance, I have never touched Shelly's breasts. She has a gimpy ankle so we don't do sports like me and Bobby. Her main hobby is reading her love letters. Shelly has lots of boyfriends in the city but none up here.

I have to admit that boys don't like me at the beach or in Merton. Not boys that count. Unfortunately, this is the history to date.

"Well, look who's here together again on U-Go-I-Go," Shelly's father says. "The three going concerns. If I was sixteen again, I'd give you girls a run for your money." Going concern is a word for women Mr. Moffat uses to mean the next best thing to sexpot. He calls Marilyn Monroe a sexpot and in our prime maybe he'll call us sexpots too. I'll settle for going concern for now because it's always flattering to be appreciated by a man, even by a creep like Mr. Moffat. It's like having money in the bank you can spend when times get tough.

I'm afraid, though, that Mr. Moffat is a bit on the stupid side.
He doesn't know that U-Go-I-Go Sound is really a bay or that
U-Go-I-Go is not a genuine Indian word but a made-up English
one, even though he writes a sports column for a newspaper.
Mr. Moffat is quite well known although he's a physical disaster.
He looks like the Italian men on the public beach, except he's
much fatter and hairier. He must have been okay once or else
Shelly's mother wouldn't have ruined her family connections by
marrying him. Mrs. Moffat still acts like he's God's gift and so
does Shelly, which makes Bobby and me look down on them.
We think it's sucky to kow-tow to men like our mothers do. Men
are too bossy for their own good and don't seem to catch on that
it's bad manners to rape women one minute and ask us to love
them the next.

As soon as she sees us, Shelly stops pulling the boat and
shrugs helplessly at us behind her father's back. "Dad's trying
to get me in shape for the regatta." Shelly fluffs her perfect hair
and giggles as if nothing could be funnier than making a sailor
out of her. I like the way Shelly sticks out her tongue so a big
whoosh of air escapes from her teeth when she giggles. It's a
friendly noise. I smile at her, and then I see Bobby's frowning.
Right away I stop smiling.

"That's right. I need my little girl to help me bring home a
ribbon from the race this Saturday. Are you two sailors?" Mr.
Moffat asks.

"We think sailing is sissy," Bobby says. "My father owns a
fifteen horsepower."

"Sissy! Don't you know, honey, that sailing is the sport of
he-men?" Mr. Moffat says.

Bobby and I look down at his boat disdainfully. Its triangular
white sail is just like the toy sails on the boats the Brothers used
to float in the bathtub. "Oh, I don't mean this little fella," Mr.
Moffat says. "I mean ocean racing. With three masts and spin-
nakers."

"Dad, don't bother explaining sailing to a tomboy like little
Roberta Gallagher," Shelly says. Shelly pronounces little as if
she means puny. "Roberta only likes masculine sports like field
hockey. You know, the game the big muscular phys. ed. women
play at Huron Ladies' College."

"That's right! You gals all go to school together, don't you?"

"Not me," I sigh. "I'm from hick-town Merton."

"Is that so Jude? Well, have a ball, girls." Mr. Moffat picks up the centreboard and walks on bow legs like a crab into the grassy dune in front of his cottage. From the back, I see tufts of hair growing on his shoulderblades. Mrs. Moffat must feel terrible when she puts her arms around him at night. As soon as he is out of sight, Shelly giggles again and says, "Can I come with you? There's nobody up except me and my dad and I'm going squirrelly."

"Dinger and I are meeting the Manchester boys at the point tonight." Bobby looks at me sternly daring me to call her a liar, but I'm too startled to say anything.

"Will you come over and read stories to me tomorrow, then, Dinger?" Shelly says.

Just as I'm wondering how to answer Shelly's question without making Bobby jealous, a golf ball whizzes over the mast of the sailboat and lands at our feet. The three of us stare at it stupidly.

"It's a hole in one!" Macgregor yells as he struts towards us, my driver slung over his shoulder. Macgregor is still wearing his grass-stained white shorts and my golfing sun visor which the Brothers must have given him. Behind Macgregor come the little twerps waving my golf clubs.

"Ignore them," Bobby says. "If we give them the silent treatment, they'll go away."

"What about my clubs?" I say. Naturally, I can see the wisdom of playing wooden Indian with the Brothers, but it's hard not to run after the little bums and punch them as they march past us with *my* clubs, chanting:

We must, we must, we must improve our busts.
We'd better, we'd better, if we want to wear a sweater!

And then Macgregor yells: "At ease, gentlemen." He takes out a white tee and sets it in the sand. He puts a golf ball on the tee and hits it with a whack, swinging his hips in a simpy way which is how he thinks a girl hits a golf ball. Then he stares off after the ball, looking even more simpy, one knee bent, club hanging over his shoulder. I stare off after the ball too, squinting my eyes into mean-looking little slots.

I'm trying to scare Macgregor but I'm also trying to memorize the spot where the ball landed. It touched down near the barbecue patio in front of the Moffat cottage and it'll be hard to find it because the patio is surrounded by the last of the Dungeon Pines.

Now Macgregor yells, "Battalion one . . . hup, hup . . . battalion two, eyes forward." And right away the Brothers begin to goosestep, like baby Nazis. They point the clubs at us and make machine-gun noises!

"Fall in, men," Macgregor screeches and salutes, looking straight at me.

"See, he's sweet on you," Bobby says.

I clutch my throat and make a throwing-up noise to show Bobby once and for all what I think of Macgregor. But I don't make a move to go after him. Down the beach I see two little stick bodies coming our way.

Jay Manchester is unmistakable even from a distance. His hair is white blond. It's not golden yellow like my mom's hair or taffy-coloured like Bobby's, or dishwater-blonde like mine, or lemon-coloured like the Brothers', but a white blond, the same wheat colour as Mai Britt's hair, the Scandinavian actor who married Sammy Davis, Jr. Jay's body is also easy to spot because it's like a huge inverted triangle; his shoulders are big and his hips are narrow, like he's had an overdose of maleness.

"Look! He's coming to meet you!" Shelly says in awe.

Jay's walking with one of his friends, a boy named Frank who is wearing an orange and black school sweater with Latin words under the name Ashbury College. It's too hot for heavy sweaters but I guess Frank wants to let the world know he doesn't go to just an ordinary high school.

The three of us stop talking. This is a historic moment. The gap between us gets smaller and smaller. Then all of a sudden Jay is right up close and Shelly and Bobby and I smile our biggest smiles which look pretty insincere because we're pretty nervous and Jay smiles a little in return. For a moment, all of us stare really hard into each other's eyes and nobody says a word. This manoeuvre is called "ESTABLISHING EYE CON-

TACT.'' I notice Jay's eyes are Sailor Blue, my favourite colour on the Munsell colour chart. It's grouped under Navy and the closest shade to it is Gendarme Blue, like my left eye. Jay also has long starry eyelashes so his eyes look pretty, like a girl's.

But Jay doesn't say hello. He and Frank just keep walking. I feel disappointed. Is that all that's going to happen? I don't know what I think should happen, but something's got to transpire. After all, Bobby said we were going to meet them and now here they are walking by us as if they don't know us from a hole in the ground. Shelly, the big pest, must be thinking the same thing, because she whirls round and yells, ''Say, aren't you the Manchester boys?''

Jay turns around fast. ''Yeah. Why?'' Even his voice sounds blond, like butterscotch toffee.

''You were supposed to meet these girls tonight.'' Shelly points to us and Bobby grunts ''Yeah'' and pulls a cigarette from her breast pocket. Her matches must be wet because she can't light it. Or else she's stalling for time.

''Need a light, girls?'' Frank walks towards us, flips the top off a silver Zippo, and pushes it towards Bobby. Bobby smiles gratefully, looking at him sexily, head down, eyes up, the way we practise in the mirror.

''You wanted to see us?'' Frank asks while Jay watches, smiling.

''That's right,'' Bobby says and exhales—very suave—through both nostrils. Oh-oh, Bobby's got her courage back. Now she puts on a phony grin and looks at Shelly. ''Her father wanted to invite you to the sailing race this Saturday.'' I look at Shelly to see if she will contradict Bobby, but Shelly is staring at Jay in awe. She's forgotten what Bobby said about meeting them tonight. Up close, Jay looks kind of sleepy, like he's slowly waking up to what he sees around him. If I didn't know any better, I'd say he's not as tough as Bobby.

''Who's he?'' Jay asks.

''Reg Moffat, the sports columnist. He owns the new Sunfish on the beach. The girl with the freckles is his daughter, Shelly, and the tall one is Dinger. I'm Bobby Gallagher.''

''Dinger! What kind of name is that?'' Frank says.

''She's the minister's daughter, stupid,'' Bobby says. ''She's called Dinger because her last name is Bell. Dong dong Bell. Get it?''

"My real name is Jude. It's my mother's name too.'' I smile as if I didn't hear Bobby. The next thing I know she'll be telling Jay I haven't got my period yet.

"Hey! I know you. You're friends of that boy who likes to fish all the time," Jay says.

"That's Macgregor," Bobby says. "He's got a crush on Dinger because she's an egghead. Dinger is also a little prissy. Don't say words like fart around Dinger.''

Jay makes a gasping sound which I think is a laugh but I'm too hurt by Bobby's remark to be sure. Meanwhile, I have to admit Bobby's acting in a way that's interesting. She's got her hands on both hips, one of which is cocked skyward, and one knee is bent, just the way Macgregor imitated a girl's golf swing. Bobby thinks she's so hot, trying to look like Marilyn Monroe. But it's not working. Jay is smiling at Shelly.

"Dinger's father runs the Church in the Pines and Dinger's mother is the best looking woman on the beach.'' Bobby jerks her thumb at me. "Like her, only better.''

This time Bobby has gone too far. She knows remarks about my mother make me feel bad because there's no way I can measure up to her good looks. I step on Bobby's left toe and Bobby jumps up as if I had hit her.

"Is she kicking you?" Jay says and the hushed tone in his voice makes me think he is concerned for me. Then he looks up in the air and yells "Duck! Everybody!" just as another golf ball whizzes over our heads and then plops into the water. Jay scoops it up in his pocket and Macgregor comes panting over, the Brothers following right behind him.

"Did you see what happened to my ball?" Macgregor asks in a fake scared voice that's supposed to sound like a girl. But Jay doesn't smile at Macgregor's joke. He shakes his head slowly from side to side, his arms folded across his triangular chest like he is staring at a smelly fish carcass inside Macgregor's shirt. Macgregor turns and grins a little nervously at me, but I shrug my shoulders as if I don't know where the ball went.

"Keep the ball then, you slime-covered salamander," Macgregor says and without another word runs off up the beach, the Brothers all running after him.

"Hey, what's the matter? Can't you take one of your own jokes?" Jay calls after him.

Jay pulls the golf ball out of his pocket and throws it at Macgregor who suddenly turns and tries to catch it but Jay must have thrown it very hard because Macgregor drops it.

"I think you got to him," Frank says to Jay.

"Come on, girls. We've got better things to do." Frank puts his arm around Shelly and one arm around me and we begin to march off a little foolishly. Jay walks ahead whistling and Bobby saunters along beside him, smoking her cigarette. We go right to the beach by the concession store where Bobby and I like to lie and eat potato chips.

Somebody is sitting in our spot, wearing a pale-blue two-piece like the kind French women wear in the Riviera.

Then a man standing near us suddenly yells, "Hurry up, Mona," and I realize it's Mona Dault. Nobody in my family can say Mona's name right. They pronounce it "dalt", which sounds like dolt, but I say it like dough, the French way, the way it is meant to be said. Mona Dault lives in Merton but her father runs the store at Balmy Beach. It's the Brothers' contention that you can spot a slut by the colour of her skin. And poor Mona's face is as white as a cadaver's. Now she slides off the rock, her breasts jiggling, and Frank makes a sound like the drum roll in stripper music—va-voom, va-voom—as she walks to shore, but Jay doesn't say anything. He just looks and right away I feel ashamed again because my breasts aren't even a quarter the size of Mona's breasts. Bobby's breasts are half the size, which is a little better, and Shelly's breasts are in between mine and Bobby's. Then Jay laughs in his gaspy way and says, "We have to go, girls." And he and Frank walk off towards the First Point. I watch Jay's head to see if he looks where Mona went but he doesn't glance in the direction of the store. Phew! We still have a chance after all.

The leaves of the poplars on the dunes behind us are rustling in the breeze. I can smell the cakey smell of wet sand and shore weeds. It's a wonderful smell. Suddenly, I feel so happy my chest hurts. Bobby, my best friend, is leaning against my shoulder watching Jay walk off and smoking another fag. And Shelly, my second-best friend, is also watching the boys and leaning against my other shoulder. It's summer and anything can happen. Who knows? Maybe Jay will pick me for his girl.

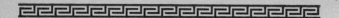

JULY 14TH. THE DRIVE FROM THE BEACH TO MERTON TAKES fourteen minutes. I know the way with my eyes closed. Ahead is Angel's Corners (where people go to heaven in car crashes) and then the hill just before Merton Golf and Country Club. Merton is two miles beyond the ridge; it is the capital of the county, Tecumseh. It is a hilly town settled by a mix of French and English and is located at the bottom of a bay belonging to the largest of the five Great Lakes. That bay is U-Go-I-Go Sound; it is Merton's claim to fame—the largest freshwater bay in the world.

We are beginning the descent into Merton down the long, soft undulating green hill which reminds me of Bobby's mother. I'm serious. Mr. Gallagher is the poor man's Gregory Peck. His dark eyes and equestrian (that's a synonym for knightly) body make women's heads turn when he walks the beach. But Mrs. Gallagher is another story. If you took off Mrs. Gallagher's red plaid skirt and navy Bermudas and covered her round parts with new baby-fine grass, you'd have the Merton Golf and Country Club hill. It's a little steep between the stomach and the breast but luckily Mr. Gallagher changes gears just as we pass by the tall spidery white birchbark arch that spans the driveway into

28

the club. I look blankly at it as if it has no relation to me and I cringe a little when Bobby points to it and says, "There's where Dinger plays golf." Everybody turns to look and Bobby's Aunt Gloria lisps the words on the sign, "Merthon Golf and Country Club". Bobby says her aunt's lisp is an act but I don't see why somebody would talk like a three-year-old unless they had no choice. Now Aunt Gloria turns to me and says, "Are you a golfer, Judith?"

"Is the Pope a Catholic?" Bobby says.

Mrs. Gallagher turns around and scowls at Bobby. "Roberta! Is that any way to talk in front of your relatives?" For a second, I'm confused; then I remember Bobby's aunt is married to a Catholic so she must be Catholic too. The problem with Catholics is they insist on making everybody like them.

Aunt Gloria turns and smiles at Bobby's mother. "We don't eat fish on Fridays. We're not that kind of Catholic." Then she turns around again and giggles at us. "You sinners are forgiven. But I'm only forgiving you because you're so pretty. Which one do you think is the cutest, Wes?" I scowl and sink down into the seat. Bobby sighs beside me and I don't want to look at her. I know Mr. Gallagher will say Bobby is and then I'll have to endure Bobby's triumph. Instead, Mrs. Gallagher says, "Oh, Jude, by far. Roberta ruins her looks with the monkey faces she puts on."

Bobby shifts slightly in the seat. "If you think Dinger's pretty, you should see her mother."

Mr. Gallagher chuckles appreciatively and turns left onto Merton's only respectable road. Our scenic drive runs the full length of the golf course and residential area before it passes Merton's grain elevator and Customs Office at the dock. The Customs Office is in the Post Office. Nobody but me and the Merton librarian knows we still use the Customs Office to handle the American goods, like stone and machinery, which our Canadian freighters bring us. The Canadian National and the old Canadian Pacific Railway also meet in Merton, bringing us grain from the prairies and taking away our exports of flour and feed.

Now Mr. Gallagher drives by a big brick rectangle glimpsed in sections through a row of spreading maples.

"There's where Dinger gets all her A's," Bobby says proudly.

Then she leans forward and taps her aunt on the shoulder. "I wish I had her in my school to talk back to our brown-noses. Dinger would use her big words and put them in their place. They think they're smart. Hah! Dinger is so smart I don't know what she's saying half the time."

Mr. Gallagher makes a choking sound. I know he's laughing because Bobby doesn't realize that if I was really clever with words she'd be able to understand everything I said since I'd communicate it clearly. I frown at the back of Mr. Gallagher's head. I don't care if he thinks Bobby's dense. She's good at breaking the rules and I'm not. I have to toe the line because I'm haunted by the idea of being good. Being Rev. Bell's daughter is something I have to live up to or live down, as my mother would say.

We are in the residential section of Merton now, the part with the town's one genuine mansion. It's brick and drowses like an orange elephant behind a leafy mountain of oak trees.

In the front seat, Aunt Gloria turns around and looks at me. "What a funny little place! Does your family really live here?"

"My father was born here," I say, trying to sound proud. I don't want to be as bad as Joachim Schnell, the famous orchestra leader who pretends he doesn't come from Merton.

"And where was your mother born?" Aunt Gloria says.

"In London." A funny little place—I say the words to myself as we go down the hill to the dock. I know what's coming up next and I don't want to look. It's just ahead through the cedar hedge—our two-storey clapboard house, the manse. Across the street is Dad's office—heh-heh—the Anglican church. Right next to it stands the Roman Catholic cathedral.

"Say, isn't that Jude's father on the steps of that church!" Mr. Gallagher says. He points at a tall, barrel-shaped man shaking hands with a bent-over woman. The man is my father all right—his teeth are long and crooked and yellow and he's wearing his white dog collar. I look away quickly. "No. That's Reverend Charleston from the United Church," I say.

Mr. Gallagher nods, surprised, and we drive on. Bobby turns around and looks at my father through the rear window and I do the same. He's staring after us. I wave just as he becomes a

dark blob against the green lawn of the church. Bobby looks at
me understandingly and waves too.

"Rev. Bell is quite a hero in these parts, Gloria," Mr. Gallagher says in the front seat. I look down at the floor of the car
and don't say anything. I want to shut my ears with my hands
and scream. I've heard it all a googaplex number of times. (Googaplex means infinity, in case you don't know.) How Rev. Bell
talked the mayor and the reeves into putting cable television on
Casaga Ridge. How Rev. Bell coaches the boys' hockey team at
Merton Public School. How Rev. Bell took a sled over the ice
in spring to conduct a funeral service at the Indian reserve. How
Rev. Bell stays up all night playing poker with the men at the
Merton Hotel and then conducts the church service the next
morning. And the most embarrassing part of the story: how
Rev. Bell married a pretty blonde, twenty-six years younger than
himself. My mother figures in these stories as a prize my father
brought home to Merton—as if she was a deer to be bagged in
hunting season. Nobody thinks of it the other way around—i.e.,
my mother sacrificed her beauty to age and decay because she
is a kind person.

My father's figure on the church steps has disappeared. We
are on the Merton dock. A stocky blond man in a white sailor
beanie waves at us outside the fish-and-chip shop. He's wearing
a white short-sleeved shirt, a scarf—like the scarves ladies
wear—around his neck, and a pair of striped Bermuda shorts
that show off his thick muscular legs. I've never seen a man in
a scarf before. I sit up and stare out the window and so does
Aunt Gloria.

"There's my honey!" she squeals. Mr. Gallagher's convertible shimmies to a stop.

The blond man with the scarf walks over carrying a small
duffel bag. His tanned forehead is high and polished like a dome.
A fringe of blond covers his upper lip. He has a moustache too.
He pokes his head into the car window. "Hello! Hello!" he
says. His voice sounds deep and smooth like a swirl of whipped
cream on hot chocolate. "There's my girl! How are you, Heavenly?"

Aunt Gloria giggles and Bobby and I look at each other. What
a name to call a woman old enough to be an aunt. Is he joking?

Mr. Gallagher gets out and puts his duffel bag in the trunk. Then the side door flies open and the hot chocolate voice and the scarf are in the back seat with us. Aunt Gloria turns around and squeals again. "Don't get into any monkey business back there, Michael."

"Ha! Ha! Heavenly knows you can't trust us artists," he says. He laughs, and lifts both of his muscled arms so one rests on the seat behind Bobby and the other rests on the seat behind me. I've never met an artist before, only ministers, lawyers, and shopkeepers—and a few farmers who live outside town.

"Oh, you're so witty, Michael Wadsworth. It's a crying shame you paint pictures. You could make a fortune as a radio announcer!" Aunt Gloria looks conspiratorially at us in the back seat. "Doesn't his voice sound like honey, girls?"

"Listen to that flattery, you two!" He nods at us. "Nobody knows how to appreciate a man better than your aunt, Bobby! That's how she got her two husbands, isn't it, pet? And why she's keeping her third!"

"Oh don't be silly, Michael!" Aunt Gloria giggles.

Bobby and I look at each other. So this is how you get men to like you. You talk with a lisp, you turn Catholic, you exaggerate their good points and pretend you don't have any yourself.

Mr. Gallagher starts the car and we turn left past the fish-and-chip shop and zip out onto the unrespectable road out of Merton. It travels by the motels and junky bungalows with concrete verandas and statues of pink flamingos and black-skinned jockeys on the lawns. I wait for Aunt Gloria to say how ugly it is, but nobody says anything as Bobby's father turns off the ugly road and charges up a tall hill as if we were going to heaven.

The car circles round and round, sailing by birch trees and little stone grottoes where statues of the Virgin Mary sleep standing up with their hands folded across their breasts. Then we come to the parking lot and the cement path leading up to a tall, twin-spired church. That's the Shrine of Martyrs, Merton's famous tourist trap. It was built in the 1930s so it's not old, and it's not even on the spot where the Iroquois slaughtered the Jesuit priests. Father Brébeuf and Father Lalemant were murdered in the woods behind the Shrine at the Village of Saint Ignace. To top it off, the Pope didn't get around to canonizing the poor guys until 1930.

I don't say anything about the fake shrine to the Gallaghers. When people are enjoying an interesting illusion, why spoil it? They can't help it if they're from the city and think like tourists.

Michael Wadsworth comes around and opens the door for Mrs. Gallagher. She looks surprised and I have the feeling he is really opening it to impress Aunt Gloria. Then Mrs. Gallagher smiles and looks happy and I think oh-oh, she's decided it's for her and it's not. Now Aunt Gloria gets out. For the first time I see her pair of brown and white spectator pumps. The toes are perforated like Swiss cheese and so pointed you could kick out the eyes of a snake (as they say in Merton) and the towering heels are as skinny as needles. I don't know how she is going to walk. She must be thinking the same thing because she looks down at her feet as soon as she gets out. Michael Wadsworth comes up and takes her arm.

The six of us begin to march towards the church. "It's the Gloria parade," Bobby whispers to me. Ahead of us Mr. and Mrs. Gallagher goosestep on either side of Aunt Gloria and her husband.

At the door of the church, Aunt Gloria stops and giggles. She looks at Michael Wadsworth and then she turns and winks at us. "Whoever said blondes have more fun?" she says. "Well, they were right." She pulls out a shiny red scarf from her purse and ties it on her head so you can just see her frizzed blonde bangs and not the brown roots at the back. She's wearing a tight white skirt and striped red jersey and is standing as if she can't get her balance. Mr. Gallagher and Mr. Wadsworth are looking at her as if they are seeing her in a movie.

Now we begin the ascent of the steps. Aunt Gloria takes a tiny little step and squeals. The shoes much pinch her. I look all the way up the steps. There are too many to count. I don't know how she is going to get to the top. Luckily, I'm wearing saddle-shoes, white with a navy-blue top section. Bobby has on a pair of penny-loafers. We scuffle and scrape our shoes on the concrete so we don't have to listen to the tiresome sound of Aunt Gloria squealing. I look at my watch. It's taken us eight minutes to do twenty steps. I catch Bobby's eye and she nods. Then we dart around past Mrs. Gallagher and run up to the top. We stand looking down at the adults. They've hardly noticed we've passed them.

I take Bobby's hand and we walk into the dark church where orange lights flicker by the altar, and the rug running up the aisles is not wine red like the rug in my father's church, but the colour of uncooked salmon. There are sputtering candles everywhere you look, plus a priest waving a metal thing that gives out a smoky smell.

I have to hand it to the Catholics—they know how to put on a good show. Things aren't entertaining in Dad's church; there is nothing to do except pray. Now Mr. Gallagher sits down beside us and takes off his dark glasses and bows his head and Bobby and I bow ours. Then I say a little prayer to Mrs. God, who is not the person a minister's daughter is supposed to pray to but I'm sure God's not where he's supposed to be anyway but off gallivanting in the universe while Mrs. God is home polishing the sky so the planets can look shiny when he returns. Heh-heh, I don't say Holy Father, I say Holy Mother or Hi, Mrs. God, I want to save you, I want to take you off to a universe with self-cleaning moons. I know Mrs. God hears me although she doesn't stop scrubbing; she just cocks her head and smiles, "You can't fight the male ego, dear."

I don't know who the devil is. Maybe he's a lecher like Shelly's father with a splendid pair of pointed bat wings and a long, forked penis that curls between his legs instead of the usual old Beelzebub tail. Anyway, Mrs. God is a more understanding deity all around although she doesn't know it because she hasn't taken time out from her cleaning to notice how sweet she is.

I don't have time to say more than how-do-ya-do Mrs. God because Mrs. Gallagher is suddenly standing behind Bobby, one hand on her shoulder, whispering crossly.

"Don't you know any better?" she says. "This is a Catholic mass. Protestants can't pray here."

She grabs Bobby by the shoulder but just in time Aunt Gloria is by her side. "Let them stay, Beth. I'm sure the Father won't mind," she says softly. She is smiling and looking at us as if she really sees us.

Suddenly, Michael Wadsworth is standing behind her. His

chin is directly above her shoulder. He looks like he would like to nuzzle her neck. "What's going on here?" he says.

"Beth wants them to go because the mass is on," Aunt Gloria says. "I think they should stay if they want. It'll broaden their education."

"It's not right," Mrs. Gallagher says.

"Oh, let us stay, Mother," Bobby says. "It won't kill us."

"No. And I don't care what your father says either," Mrs. Gallagher replies. "You're leaving this minute." She takes Bobby's arm again and this time nobody does anything. "Are you coming, Wes?" Mrs. Gallagher asks.

Mr. Gallagher looks down at his hands. He is playing with his sunglasses. "I think I'll stay. I've never been to a mass before," he says quietly.

Mrs. Gallagher makes an exasperated sound and steers Bobby towards the front door. I follow. In a moment we are outside in the hot July sunlight.

"So what are we going to do now?" Bobby asks. That's become her favourite question. She uses it more than "duh" or "oh, really" this summer. It makes me feel tired-out and I guess it has the same effect on Mrs. Gallagher because she looks like she wants to slap Bobby.

"You girls can do what you want," Mrs. Gallagher says crossly. "I'm going to sit down on that bench and knit." She begins to walk down the long steep stone stairs. She doesn't turn back and look at us. Bobby points to the top of the hill and I know what she's thinking. In a minute we run down the steps, past Mrs. Gallagher, and then turn up on the last of the paved road. We walk past another sleeping Virgin and a few more birch trees and then we are at the top. There are no trees or Virgins here. Just a smooth round grassy bump looking out over the countryside. A tall grey metal rail curves around the edge of the hilltop. I don't know why it's there unless it's to stop people from throwing themselves over the hill and killing themselves. And that's a waste of good metal because if you're really determined you can just crawl through it or go around the side.

"I know," I say. "Let's play martyrs."

"Martyrs! What are you talking about?" Bobby says. She looks interested for once.

"You be the Huron who betrayed the Jesuit priests and I'll be Father Brébeuf," I say. "We'll enact his martyrdom right here."

"Sure, you get to be the good guy and I get to be the villain." Bobby makes a disgusted sound and I try again. "I know. You play the Indian this time and you can be Father Brébeuf next time around."

Bobby smokes and doesn't say anything. I wait. Finally, she sighs. "Okay. You win. As always." Then she opens her lips and lets the cigarette drop onto the ground. Slowly, she screws it into the earth.

I take Bobby's hand and lead her to the edge of the railing. As settings go, it's a much nicer place to roast a martyr than the village of Saint Ignace. You can see the Wye River gleaming below like a wet smile in the marshy flats, just the way it did when the Iroquois paddled up it to roast Brébeuf. To the west is Merton. And beyond Merton is U-Go-I-Go Sound. And besides, if you stand straight, people walking down below can look up at you. Who wants to be a martyr in the woods where nobody can see you?

"Okay, Bobby. I'm tied to the stake. You've put on my necklace of axeheads, front and back, and now you're going to pour boiling water over me," I say. I point to the chain she is wearing around her neck. The one with Ross's ring on it. "There's my necklace of axeheads," I say. "Put it on me. Then you have to make as if you are pouring boiling water on me."

"Who am I anyway? Just a dumb Indian?" she says crossly.

"Be quiet, Indians are not dumb, they just don't like to talk in case they end up bragging like white people. Anyway, you're a Huron. You were baptized by Father Brébeuf and you are going back on your word and becoming a savage again." I bend my head so Bobby can put on the necklace. "You call me Echon and you say, 'Go to heaven, for thou art well baptized.' "

"This is the dumbest thing I've ever heard of," Bobby says, but she puts her necklace around my neck and then picks up an imaginary pot and lifts it far above my head and I stare out indifferently across the land of trees and water just the way Father Brébeuf must have stared when they scooped out his skin with clam shells. A finger of sunlight streaks through some thunderheads hanging over the town so the Sound is splashed with bolts of light, like the shafts of sunlight in the paintings in the nuns' house in Merton. I lean a little forward and then I remember I can't lean forward because that makes the axeheads on my back burn my flesh. Now I lean backward a little and I realize I can't do that either because the scorching axeheads on my chest will sear my skin. Rats. The savage has got me every which way. Front or back, there's no escaping my torture. I feel panicky. I don't know what Father Brébeuf said to the Iroquois. But it's too late to find out. I'll have to improvise.

"Forgive them, Father, for they know not what they do," I shout as loud as I can. I hope Jesus won't mind me borrowing his quote. Then I close my eyes. It must be wonderful to be a martyr. They're kind of like golden girls, aren't they, except they don't have to be good looking, just ready to serve. I see mauve lights in front of my eyes. Maybe it's a religious vision. Then I hiss, my eyes still closed: "Say it Bobby, say it."

"Go to hell then, you stupid priest," Bobby says.

"No! No! That's not what you're supposed to say! You're supposed to tell me to go to heaven," I say.

"Go to heaven, you stupid priest," Bobby says.

I open my eyes and sigh. Somehow Bobby never gets it quite right. I take off Bobby's necklace and sit down on the ground.

Bobby stands by the railing, shoulders hunched like the dead movie star James Dean, blowing smoke rings. "I don't like to play kids' games any more, Dinger." She blows a small fat ring and looks at me.

I don't answer.

"What do you think of my aunt, by the way?" Bobby sends a tall, skinny ring over the Wye marsh.

I still don't answer so Bobby says, "I think she's a tramp. That's why she's had three husbands. She just married every Tom, Dick, and Harry she slept with so she could pretend she isn't a slut."

"I think she's kind of interesting," I say before I can help it. Bobby smiles. She's got me talking.

"She's a slut. She's no better than Elizabeth Taylor. And she dyes her hair." Bobby has lit another cigarette. "All fast women have bleached hair."

"They do not!"

"They do too! And pale complexions from staying up late because their mothers don't care about them."

I think of telling Bobby she's a slut because she has pale skin too, but I don't. Martyrs don't say hurtful things. So I look out across the marsh again and try to have a stout heart. Stout is a funny word. It means fat but it also means brave.

Far behind us, a car honks. The adults are waving from Mr. Gallagher's convertible. Michael Wadsworth and Aunt Gloria are smiling but Mrs. Gallagher is yelling at us. Bobby sighs and throws her cigarette over the hillside. That worries me. What if it starts a fire? I look out to see if I can discover a trail of smoke but see nothing.

"It's okay," Bobby hisses and pokes me. "Don't be such a goody-goody."

My head down, I walk back to the car. Mrs. Gallagher gets out and points at the back seat. "Look at that, will you, Roberta? You've got the seat covered in chocolate."

The material of the seat looks exactly like it is smeared with chocolate—except it's not chocolate. Bobby says nothing. She stares at it sullenly. Then she looks at it again. Then she looks at me. I feel the back of my pants. My pants are wet. I'm bleeding. The seat is not covered with chocolate. It's menstrual blood, my first period! Bobby shakes her head warningly and sits down on the chocolate. I sit down—rigid like a wooden soldier—on the other side. Neither of us says a word to Mrs. Gallagher. I feel humiliated. You should be pleased, I tell myself. You're normal. You can have babies. Except I don't want any. Babies mean you have to be unselfish like our mothers who work day in, day out to look after their families. Well, I intend to be as selfish as I can now because I'll have to be a whole lot more unselfish later.

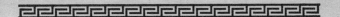

JULY 18TH. I'M LYING IN HAPPY HOLLOW TOUCHING MY-
self. It's a weird place to masturbate, if you ask me. Somebody could walk in. Usually I do it in my bedroom late at night
when my parents are asleep.

Happy Hollow is safe because nobody knows it's here. It is a
circle of sand in the middle of the juniper bushes at Poison Ivy
Point. There are pines to the south and the north, too, which
gives me a little shade, although it's pretty hot lying on the
towel. My body is sticky with sweat already and I haven't even
done it once yet. The first time is always the hardest. It takes
longer. It's all downhill after that, though. The first time you
can't fool around and read while you're doing it. You have to
concentrate and let your index finger do the job. It helps to have
a picture in your mind that's sexy. Like the way Jay looks in his
bathing suit. It can even be a phrase like "thick, hairy wrists".
That line is from a story in my Horse Book, "The Virgin and
the Riding Master". It's about an alcoholic German, Karl Frank,
who tries to seduce an innocent fourteen-year-old blonde named
Monika. (She's a little like me even though authors are supposed
to come up with new characters, but I'm not a real author yet. I
have to build them on people I know, so I've based Frank on

39

Shelly's father. And I have him talk like the Germans who run the camera factory in Merton.)

The line "thick, hairy wrist" is in the opening chapter:

The girls mount the horses and Karl Frank's hoarse laugh rings out in the crisp fall air.

"Don't take any wooden nickels now," he calls.

Monika stands by the old roan, waiting her turn, her heart inflamed with hatred. Then Frank holds out the stirrup. Just as she puts her foot in the stirrup, Frank's thick, hairy wrist grazes her bosom. Monika stiffens, and she strikes him with her rein. "Get away from me, you dirty old man!" she cries.

Karl Frank chuckles, "Oh, Harmonica! [that's his nickname for her]. You just need a good necking to calm you down. You're a real Heller."

I used "thick, hairy wrist" the other day and it made the first time happen a lot faster. I don't have my shorts on or my underpants. Just a halter top with a lace bib over my breasts and two white spaghetti straps to hold it up. It would look a lot better on me if my breasts were bigger, but it serves the purpose.

I'm squinting because it's so sunny. I'm lying on my back. My knees are bent into a bridge that ants can crawl under. Above me, the sky is like a blue friend who knows my secrets. It's a little hard to concentrate out here, though. It's a bit too open, if you know what I mean. It's easier in my bunk bed. There's nothing else to look at or think about except the wood boards under the mattress above me. The boards are scribbled with top secret messages and hearts with arrows drawn through them and smiling cartoon faces. Every summer, Bobby and I marked out heights and accomplishments on the soft, pine boards. Last August, I scratched into one of the unchristened boards the words "First prize for the U-Go-I-Go-Man-Catching Derby: Shelly Moffat." Under that sentence I wrote, in India ink, "Congratulations for being the first girl on the beach to receive ten letters a week from her steady in the city." Then I wrote on another board over my head, "Consolation Prizes to Bobby Gallagher and Jude Bell. To Bobby Gallagher, the Coffin-Nail Medal for inhaling more menthol smoke in one summer than any fag hound would think possible. Also to Dinger Bell, condolences for failing to attract any male other than Macgregor, but warm words of encouragement on her superb performance as a golfer and a brain.''

I didn't think up the part about myself. Bobby penned it in afterwards, laughing. Shelly had nothing to do with the inscriptions and she pretended to be mad when she saw them; but I could tell she was secretly pleased I declared her the winner. Sad to say, the Brothers noticed the writing and put their own version of our contests on one of the empty boards. I tried to cover up what they'd written with nail polish, but you can still make out their insults. ''First prize for never wanting to do anything: Big Boobs Gallagher. Second prize to Ding Dong Bell for having the smallest boobs. Third prize to smelly Shelly for having the worst case of B.O. on the beach. And a big boo for all three, who are the biggest drips and losers any boy could hope to meet.''

The Brothers' joke about my breasts bothers me. I know I'm not much to look at right now, but some day I'll be a blonde goddess like my mother who will inspire men and be loved for it. They will write me scrawly suicide notes, threatening to jump out of buildings or off railway trestles if they can't have my love, and I will smile sweetly and redeem them through the inspirational power of my sexuality.

I am putting my shorts back on. There's no point touching myself out here. I can't concentrate. Besides, the Brothers are playing over the hill. I know they'd never find me here, but just hearing their voices spoils things. They're chanting, ''How, how, how.'' And laughing. Now one of them is saying that stupid rhyme we hate so much. ''I must, I must, I must improve my bust.'' They say it to us all the time. ''I'd better, I'd better, I'd better, if I want to wear a sweater.'' And the others are laughing. I wonder how they'd feel if we talked about the length of their dinks. Somehow it never enters their heads that teasing us about breasts hurts our feelings. How would they like it if we chanted, ''You should, you should, have a penis the size of a . . .'' Drat, I can't think of a word that rhymes with should.

Now I can see them. They're sitting in a circle around the

remains of a bonfire left by the week-end campers. Their dune is much bigger than Happy Hollow. I christened it Hot Dog Hollow, because that's the spot where Bobby told me about sex. "You know what a hot dog looks like?" she said. "Okay, you take the hot dog and put it in the bun." That was all she said. I had to figure it out myself later.

Now the Brothers can't see me because I'm up higher than they are and they are hidden by the pine trees. The sun is shining on their blond heads. Macgregor is sitting near the middle of the circle. He's reading *Peyton Place* to them. I recognize the shiny white cover. I bet Adam and Beckett stole it from my mother's jewellery drawer where she hides it under a layer of cotton batting.

It's thrilling to spy on people. Especially the Brothers. They ask for it. They ask for every mean thing we do. Oh gad. What are they doing now? It looks like some of them have unzipped their pants and are playing with their penises. Macgregor is still reading and not looking at them. But they are looking at each other and snickering. It makes me feel shivery *down there* to see them touch themselves. Bobby and I spy on Macgregor in the outhouse. When he goes to the can, we can look through the knothole in the wood. We can see everything then. Once, Rum Bum caught us looking and acted kind of pleased. Boys are hard to figure out. I'd have died on the spot if I caught the Brothers looking at me peeing.

Now Rum Bum is lying on his back. His arms are out at his sides and he is smiling. I think he is pretending that he had an orgasm, but I know boys don't have sperm at his age. I don't think he can really have one unless he's got sperm. On the other hand, I don't know for sure. Maybe they can. The rest of the Brothers are still playing with themselves and Macgregor is still reading as if he's giving a lecture. How dumb. They disgust me.

"I'm telling! I'm telling! I know who you are and I see what you're doing," I yell out in a kind of sing-song. I sound about ten years old. I don't care. The Brothers deserve treatment like this. Immediately, their heads all turn my way. Even Macgregor looks up. The Brothers begin to run around on all fours like nervous mice. Some of them are struggling to put their shorts back on. Macgregor stands up slowly and stares at me. He looks like he's going to faint. I stick out my tongue and put both my thumbs on the side of my head and waggle my fingers. "Don't tell anybody, Dinger," Macgregor shouts.

"Maybe I will. Maybe I won't. That's for me to know and you to find out." I stand there for a moment longer at the top of the juniper hill. I feel like an avenging angel for all the teased-to-death girls in the world. Then I'm gone. I run down the long, long dune into the Unknown Desert. I know I'm safe here. If I'd stayed up at the point, God knows what they would have done to me. Caught me and tied me to a tree and raped me like foul-mouthed Karl Frank does to my poor helpless Monika.

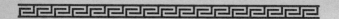

JULY 19TH. MY MOTHER, THE BLONDE GODDESS, AND I, HER flat-chested vassal, walk up the path to the Hanging Step, carrying two trays of food. My mother is stylish in a pair of baby pink Bermudas and a matching baby pink blouse. I hate baby pink. I have on navy blue Bermudas and an olive green shirt and my hair is frizzy from the heat. The Hanging Step is a tree root at the top of Mount Sand and Mount Sand, of course, is the sandy hill behind our cottage. Bobby and I used to jump off the Hanging Step and then run down Mount Sand to the Unknown Desert. My father is installed on an old park bench from Merton just behind the Hanging Step. My father writes his sermons there. He likes the view from Mount Sand.

I reach the Hanging Step first and haul myself up onto the root. Sure enough, Dad is on the bench, in baggy minister-looking flannel pants and a white shirt with rolled-up cuffs.

My father smiles and shows the yellow teeth that make me think of old dogs. "Hello, boys and girls," he says.

"There are no boys here, Slugger," my mother laughs. Slugger is her favourite name for my father. I don't like it to be known too widely but he calls us Big Jude and Little Jude to distinguish us from each other.

44

"Look behind you," my father says. My mother and I both turn and there are the twins, Adam and Beckett. They're not real twins; I just think of them that way. Adam is a year older than Beckett. He came first like the letter A but he's the same height so everybody thinks they are the same age. Beckett is holding something in his hand and grinning uglily. I look again. He is holding my Horse Book up to his chest. It's really my collection of sex stories hidden inside my old orange scribbler with an elephant head on the cover. I've pasted pictures of my favourite palominos on the first ten pages as a decoy to keep the Brothers from exploring it further. Beckett clears his throat the way Dad does before he opens the Old Testament to give us his text for the morning.

"Dear Jay. Do you have any idea how I feel about you? Or what I'd like you to do to me when nobody is around?" Adam says. I don't interrupt him. I feel paralysed. (And a tiny bit curious to hear how my words sound.) "Yesterday on my golf course, I pretended Jay raped me by the third tee. I know rape doesn't sound very nice but it's the only way a man can make love to me without me getting into trouble."

In the open air, my words sound like juvenile descriptions of what I know is real love. The Brothers have unzipped my skin like a jacket so anybody can see my heart is bare. I rush towards Adam but he hands the Horse Book to Beckett and then they run off down Mount Sand howling and laughing. My father frowns and looks at the tray. I wait for him to do something.

"Babe, is there any of your potato salad left?" All my father thinks about is food.

"You ate it all for lunch," my mother says. Then she says to me quietly, "I'll get it back for you, Jude. Don't get into a stew." My mother likes to caution me about stews. I'm prone to them, she says. When she admonishes me to avoid them, I feel hopeless and guilty because I am struck through and through with a stew streak. It's a serious defect in my character.

"I'm never going to write anything again! Never!" I stamp my foot and shout.

My father puts down his book and looks at my mother. "What's the matter with her? How can she be upset in a beautiful place like this?" my father says as if I'm not there.

"It's the summer doldrums, Mac. The children are getting on each other's nerves," my mother says.

I watch a red ant crawling along the sand under my father's park bench. It must be walking in the shadow so the heat doesn't hurt its little feet.

"You haven't forgotten the spoon parable, have you, Jude?" my father asks. I don't say anything. I keep my eyes on the ant. I know what's coming next.

"Well, do you remember it or not? Tell me how it goes."

I look up, eyes staring blankly as if I am blind. That's the face I wear in his church, when I pray to Mrs. God.

"Jude?" my father asks again.

I say quickly, "Heaven is a ballroom where men and women sit eating in beautiful clothes."

"And? What else?"

"Hell is where men and women sit in the same ballroom but nobody is eating," I say. His spoon parable is for babies, like apple juice and arrowroot cookies. I am fourteen years old and in love with Jay whose brown shoulders glisten like the limbs of Mark Antony. (His round arms shone like marble in the sun and made Cleopatra pant with love.)

"And why aren't they eating in hell?" my father asks.

"Because they've got seven-foot-long spoons," I say.

"Oh for goodness sake, Jude, hurry it up," my mother says.

"They're eating in heaven because they're using the seven-foot spoons to feed each other but in hell it doesn't occur to them to help the person across the table so everybody starves." I say it really fast so I can daydream about Jay again. If only Jay knew how deeply I love him. Just seeing him makes me want to write a poem. And that's the acid test, isn't it? Maybe Jay and I will fall in love and I'll let him kiss me in Happy Hollow. It's not too windy there. We'll stand by the charred stumps of old bonfires and he'll take me in his arms and whisper, "Jude, you're the most beautiful girl on the beach." Then he'll put his mouth on mine and I'll show him what a hard kisser I am.

"Dinger? Are you listening? I want you to pick up your seven-foot spoon and try helping your brothers," my father says.

"Yes," I say, and under my breath I add, stick the seven-foot spoon up your ass, you old fart. Then I turn and run up the old wooden stairs into the ugly green barn of a cottage my father's parishioners rent for us each summer because we don't have enough money to buy one. I slam the screen doors behind me. I stomp off to my bedroom. It's the smallest one in the place. It has two bunk beds and a little night lamp with a wrinkled silk shade burnt on one side from the light bulb. I sit down on my bunk bed and read my favourite book, *Pollyanna* by Eleanor Porter. In this chapter, the maid, whose name is Nancy, explains Pollyanna's Glad Game to cold Aunt Polly.

"There you go like all the rest, Nancy." [That's cold Aunt Polly talking.] "What is Pollyanna's Glad Game?"

Nancy lifted her chin and looked cold Aunt Polly square in the eye. "I'll tell you, Ma'am. Pollyanna got a pair of crutches once from a missionary barrel when she was wanting a doll and she cried like any child would. It seems 'twas then Pollyanna's father told her there wasn't ever anything but what there was something about it that you could be glad about.

"And after that Pollyanna made a regular game of finding something in everything to be glad about. She called it the Just Being Glad Game."

I put the book down and sniffle a little. Eleanor Porter puts it so well. Golden girls have to suffer. We have to make the things that hurt us beautiful and encourage others to do the same. Then we get rewarded in the end for being good but we can't think too much about that when we are suffering or our suffering wouldn't be real suffering. I can't wait to grow up and be a golden girl. I'll be a goddess of love and no man will be able to do without me. I will never have problems or feel needy. Men are silly and weak and that is why we have to help them . . . even pitiful excuses for males like my father and the Brothers.

JULY 28TH. I WALK UP THE PATH BEHIND THE CONCESSION store to Shelly's cottage. It's one of the bungalows Mona's father rents to tourists every summer. It's white clapboard, nothing fancy, nicer than ours, but still it must seem like a shanty to Mrs. Moffat, who Bobby says was born with a silver spoon in her mouth. I feel a little guilty going here without Bobby.

In the old summers, Bobby and Shelly used to fight over me. Shelly came to my cottage every morning just before breakfast and sat on my father's bench, eating the Fluffernutters her mother always made for her. Fluffernutters are peanut-butter sandwiches with marshmallow filling. Shelly'd arrive an hour before Bobby did and cry if I said it was my day to play with Bobby. Then I'd feel sorry for her and tell Bobby I'd have to see her later and Bobby would stomp off, swearing. I'd like to be tough like Bobby but I am more like a conqueror with a victim's heart. I fall to pieces when somebody needs me as if their vulnerability gives them a right over me.

So I still feel guilty when I visit Shelly even though I know it's babyish and has nothing to do with being mature the way we are now. I slip in through the old screen door so as not to disturb Mr. Moffat who's typing away on the veranda table, clack-a-clack-clack, like a big katydid. I bet he's not writing at all, he's just typing over and over that silly line, "Now's the time for all good men to come to the aid of the party", to impress Mrs. Moffat. She is sitting near him the way she usually does, white as milk in an old gingham sundress, a sombrero on her head as if she is trying to keep the sun out, inside a cottage. She's reading one of her romance novels and watching Mr. Moffat at the same time. Under the title of her book, "Sprig Muslim", a man in an ankle-length coat is watching a woman stare at herself in a makeup mirror.

"Sssh—genius at work," she frowns at me and Mr. Moffat says, "Aw Betty, it's okay. Shelly tells me Jude's a writer too. So she understands," and then he looks straight across at my V-neck sweater which I've pulled down tight so there's just a hint of cleavage and he grins, leering, "And filling out nicely too," he adds.

The way his eyes keep looking at my breasts makes me feel powerful and humiliated at the same time so before he can compromise me any further, I say "Thanks" and hurry down the hall to Shelly's bedroom.

On Shelly's dresser, I see that Shelly has lipstick too, just like Bobby. Luckily she's still got the doll with a little hole in its lips for the baby bottle, and the Barbara Ann Scott doll whose arms Bobby broke last summer. Shelly has used hockey tape to put a sling on the Barbara Ann doll and Scotch-taped back on the little flaxen wig that looks like a scalp. Seeing Shelly's dolls sitting where they always sit makes me glad; Shelly isn't a real sophisticate yet.

Shelly hugs me and then makes a show of taking something out from under her pillow. It's an envelope with the name Miss Shelly Moffat written in black ink. Underneath her name is the name of Shelly's school, Huron Ladies' College. The "Ladies" is written in capital letters and somebody has underlined it with red pencil. "It's from Roger," she says out of breath. "Want to hear it?" I nod, suddenly out of breath too, and she begins to read.

Dear Shelly,

   I have reneged on writing you because I have been mulling over your hint about sending you a pennant. Really, I was going to send you one but then that is the wrong thing to do to a girl at Huron Ladies' College. Everybody would inquire about it and you would begin to live in a state of symbolism and romanticism. I am serious, Shelly.

Shelly stops reading and looks very solemn. "Imagine, Dinger. He nearly sent me a pennant." She shakes her head and picks up the letter again.

That remark of yours about existentialism, Shelly . . . "It all sounds interesting, maybe I'll take it," is an example. Maybe George Bernard Shaw is interesting too, but he is pointing his finger at you the reader, Shelly, and laughing at your standards. . . .

Shelly stops and looks at me. "What's he saying in this part, Dinger? I don't understand."

"He's being mean," I say. "He's criticizing you for not being serious enough."

"He is?" Shelly looks at the letter again. "You're just saying that because you're jealous. You don't get letters from anybody."

I shrug my shoulders. "You want to hear my latest story?" I say. "It's called 'The Virgin and the Riding Master'." I'm not impressed by words like "a state of symbolism" and "romanticism"! This university man is a worse egghead than me. I pull out my trusty Horse Book.

Shelly sighs and lies back on the bed. She's still looking at her letter.

The two mares cantered slowly around Karl Frank's yard with the relaxed gait that comes from good breeding. It felt, Monika thought, absolutely super to have a horse between your knees again. She expressed her feeling to Betty, who nodded her head happily.

"I guess we'd better pay you," Monika told Frank. "I almost forgot."

"Ha! See! Here's an honest girl! Good girl, nice rider, too," Frank replied. "But you just never mind about it, my girl. Pay me any time you like, see? If you have a bad ride and the horse throwed you, you don't pay me.'' With mounting pleasure, Frank watched Monika's honey-blonde head disappear into the green foliage on the trail. Frank's fingers tightened on the silver dollar in his pocket. The hard coldness of the metal felt good in his hand. I'll give that Monika a good necking yet, Karl Frank chuckled to himself.

"Well, do you like it?" I ask Shelly. Shelly sits up.

"What did you say, Dinger?"

"My story. Don't you like it?

"Sorry. I wasn't listening. I was thinking of what I could say to Roger to make him give me a pennant.''

I sit down on the bed. This has never happened before. Maybe the Virgin and the Riding Master story is no good. Shelly's always liked my stories. I'll rewrite the sex scene so she'll pee in her pants. Shelly will see. Karl Frank will get her—just like he gets Monika.

Suddenly, I hear somebody whistling outside. I jump up. Yikes! Bobby's pouty face is pressed against the screen. I'm caught with Shelly, redhanded.

"I have to talk to you," Bobby says in a self-important voice.

"Not now, Roberta." (Shelly always calls her by her full name to make Bobby mad.) "We're reading one of Dinger's sex stories." Shelly stands up and blocks the screen window so I can't see Bobby. Now I'm really nervous. I'm going to have to choose which one to play with and I don't know what to do. It must be terrible when you're grown up and the choice is between men. But Bobby solves it all for me by saying she just ran into Jay Manchester and he wants to play golf with us tomorrow on the course in Merton.

"Really?" Shelly giggles. "Wait a minute and I'll let you in."

JULY 30TH. BOBBY IS LATE. TEN AFTER NINE AND NO SHOW. Jay and Frank and Shelly and I are in Frank's convertible, waiting in the big U-turn drive behind the Gallaghers' cottage. The Gallaghers live in Trillium Chapel, a big clapboard cottage painted colonial yellow and trimmed with white gingerbread.

Jay sighs and looks at Frank. "Let's bomb off, Frank. We've been stood up."

Frank turns the key obediently. At that moment, Bobby runs out, waving, and her dogs, Joe and Ben, run out after her. Frank doesn't see her as he revs the car and we squeal out of the drive, so I say, "Wait! Bobby's coming!" I don't know why I say that. It would be easier to pretend I didn't see her. But that's me. I can't help shooting myself in the foot.

Bobby walks down the hill to the car. I have to hand it to her. She's walking slowly, as if she knows we'll wait for her. Now she stops by the passenger door and sneers at Jay. That's Bobby's way of smiling. Jay nods and leans forward, flipping up the back seat so she can climb in with me. I look her over carefully. Bobby has on a pair of tight black pedal pushers with white cuffs and a black halter top to match. I've never seen that outfit before. It looks almost feminine. On her feet, Bobby is wearing a pair

52

of sandals. Sandals are not the right shoes for a golf course. She's going to regret her choices. Unfortunately, her hair looks fluffy and nice too—just washed, I bet.

Shelly isn't dressed for the occasion either. I stare thoughtfully at her tightly curled page-boy between Frank and Jay. The heat will make it fall flat by the second hole and she'll get burrs and grass stains on the white flannel trousers she's wearing.

I'm in lime green Bermuda shorts and a plain white blouse. I know I'm going to sweat. My lime green V-necked sweater is draped over my shoulders. It's not angora, but plain wool. Angora makes me sneeze. On my feet are a pair of oxblood golf shoes, the real thing, with a frothy fringe tongue and spikes on the soles to keep me from slipping on the fairway when I swing my club. I'm dressed properly, but Bobby and Shelly aren't. I'm glad. It gives me an edge. With my looks, I need every advantage I can get.

The countryside is still July green through Jay's windshield. The colour hasn't faded to August yellow yet. In a few weeks it will dry up and turn yellow. I like to say it turns blond or blondens. When summer is blondening, it means soon I will have to go back to school.

The beach is far behind us now. There are only squares of barley fields and pine forests and farmhouses like the Lefaivre place where Joachim Schnell, Canada's famous orchestra leader, was born. My uncle, the doctor Charles Bell, took out part of his liver. Every time my mother sees him on TV she says, "There's poor Joachim conducting without his liver."

In front, Shelly is giggling at something Jay said. Bobby pokes me in the ribs and we exchange looks. The lucky so-and-so is getting all the attention.

"Isn't she a snob sitting up there with them?" Bobby hisses in my ear. Shelly turns around. "Pardon?" she says. "Did you say something to me, Roberta?" Bobby shrugs and I pretend not to notice Shelly's worried frown.

Now we sail past the Daults' vegetable booth and there's Mona, smoking a cigarette, and looking a little more white-faced than usual. Jay taps Frank on the shoulder and Frank does a fast turn, skidding to a stop in front of the stand. Mona bends over and pretends to straighten out a basket of corn but I know she is just showing Jay the cleavage in her blouse with puffy sleeves and a low scooped neck. Jay whistles and the rest of us look at her breasts. They're a model of how breasts should be— big and full, like cows' udders.

Mona smiles at me. "Hi Dinger," she says and butts her cigarette.

I nod faintly. Shelly says under her breath, "You know her?" She turns around to hear my answer and I nod again and then Shelly says, "I bet she goes all the way."

"Sssh, she'll hear you," I say very fast, and Mona looks over at me again and I can feel her thinking: you think you're smart— you bunch of stuck-up city kids in a fast red car!

For a minute, I think of getting out of the car and explaining the whole thing to Mona. I could ask her to come and play golf with us. If she got to know Bobby and Shelly the way I have, she'd know they aren't really stuck-up. And if Bobby and Shelly got to know her, they wouldn't look down on Mona either.

Of course, I don't do anything. I just sit in the back seat with Bobby and watch Jay get out and buy a box of raspberries. Mona is smoking another cigarette. Bobby could take a few lessons to develop her expertise. The smoke drifts up Mona's cheeks right past her eyes and Mona doesn't even blink and the cigarette hangs from her bottom lip as if it's stuck there with LePage's glue.

The ash on Mona's cigarette grows and grows until it is quite long but she ignores it and goes about her business at the cash. Suddenly Jay laughs and grabs the cigarette out of her mouth. He makes a show of tapping out the ash.

"Mind your manners, mister." Mona stops what she is doing and looks him up and down. Jay quickly gives her back her fag and then Mona clenches her fist so her bicep pops out. She slaps her bicep with her other hand and it makes a threatening noise. "Or I'll send you on a trip to the moon."

I feel a little thrill and I think Bobby does too, although none of us says a word now. We watch Jay and wait. I expect him to do something impressive. Only he doesn't. He just laughs in his gaspy way. Frank honks the horn and Jay turns, a little sheepishly, and gets back into the front seat beside Shelly. I wave at

Mona and then we're off again, sailing down the old gravel road, a plume of dust in our wake.

Finally Frank turns the convertible into the club, my home away from home. The pro shop is like a Dinky Toy version of the clubhouse. It's smaller and made of black logs too, only its stump ends are painted red.

I smell pine sap when I step out of the car and listen gratefully to my spiked shoes going click-click on the asphalt walk.

Mr. Lando is in the pro shop. He shakes the hands of my four friends. Mr. Lando is my golf instructor. He has a red beet for a nose, and his eyebrows wriggle continually like blond caterpillars. "So the champ is going to take you around, is she?" Mr. Lando says. The boys look up, surprised.

"The champ?" Jay asks.

"Jude Bell is Merton's Junior Women's Champion. She has been for three years." Mr. Lando winks at me. "She'll beat the pants off you boys."

I stroll to the men's tee feeling scared. Ordinarily I don't play with boys in case they get upset at how good I am. Boys are always taken aback by the fact that I play from the men's tee. The ladies' tee is set twenty feet closer to the green. Only sissy women use it. My mother plays from the men's tee because she says she has never felt herself the physical inferior of any man. Off the golf course, Mom acts like she feels inferior, though. She makes excuses about why she goes along with what my father wants, as if that isn't a chicken way to act.

I practise a few swings. Jay and Frank whistle. "There she goes. She's feeling her Cheerios," Shelly giggles. The boys laugh. I jab my red tee into the dirt as if the dirt is Shelly's perfect red page-boy. I set the ball on the tee, step back, do another practice swing, address the ball, and swing again, but I'm not looking at the ball and I fan, missing the ball entirely. The others watch. They don't know that a fan counts on your card as one stroke. I swing again and the ball dribbles along the dirt tee and rolls down the hill, about a yard away. Now Bobby giggles. My face feels hot.

I put another ball on my tee and swing. It connects. It's a long arching drive but it hooks and lands in the woods on the right side of the fairway. The others look impressed. Little do they

know I am going to have a heck of a time getting out of the
woods. What a disgusting start! One shot off the tee and I'm
fifteen strokes on the score card.

I can't stand losing, although I'm a little relieved when it
happens. I want to win but I don't want anyone to lose either.
Usually, a voice in my head says, "Jude's just flashy. She's not
a champion. She doesn't have the guts." Then another voice
yells back, "No! That can't be true. Jude's got to win and demonstrate her natural superiority."

I've known I'm naturally superior to other people since I was
two. Maybe before that even. Crack! My second shot. Another
beauty. No slice this time, either. The boys whistle again. Jay
walks over to where I smacked my ball. He looks at the little
clump of grass I used to tee it up on.

"Can you do that?" he asks.

"A club's length from where you found the ball is permissible."

"Permissible." Frank cracks up. "Hey, Jay! She uses big
words."

"Dinger likes to use big words so people will know she is
smarter than we are," Bobby says.

"I do not, Bobby."

"Dinger *is* smart." Shelly turns to the boys. "She stands first
in her class every year. In Merton, the other kids try, but nobody
can beat her."

"A brain and a golf champion." Jay looks at Frank and shakes
his head. "What is she doing with dunces like us?"

"Some champion. I dribbled off the first tee and you guys at
least hit the ball thirty yards away." Admiration makes me nervous. In Merton, people are nasty to you right after they com-
pliment you for doing something well. So I just look away from
Jay and start to walk down the hole.

It's hot on the course. We are like ants in bright shorts and
tops traversing a bowl of green. The fairway hasn't bleached out
to rust yet. The grass is still the colour of avocados. Overhead
the sun is yellow on my eyelids. Jay is walking beside me. His
face is sweating; his blond eyelashes are down-cast. The two of
us move slightly ahead of the others, swinging our fairway driv-
ers. On the road beside the course, cars leave behind long trails

of dust. I watch Jay hit his ball. It takes him two tries. He says
"fuck" under his breath and I look away so he won't know I
heard him say THE word. Then he strolls off, dragging his golf
cart behind him and staring at the horizon. Jay is mysterious.
It's hard to tell what he's thinking. His look bothers me because
it's not me but something beyond me that makes him happy. I
make my approach and gawk at him as we walk up the little
knoll to the green. He doesn't notice. His tan shows up the
rectangles of blond fuzz under his eyes. The rectangles look as
fuzzy as moth's wings. His tan doesn't go quite all the way
around his arm. The combination of brown skin and white muscle makes me think of marshmallow fudge.

The other little ants are far behind us. Bobby and Shelly and
Frank can't keep up to our pace.

I hit onto the green and land next to the cup. I sink my putt
and then wait for Jay who takes three shots to finish up. Jay is
perspiring slightly and his beautiful golden skin looks shiny.

"What a shot!" Jay says. "I never noticed before, but you're
a pretty kid." He heaves my clubs onto his shoulders and the
two of us walk over to the fifth hole. One hour later, Jay and I
finish the ninth. The others are five holes behind. Mr. Lando is
standing outside his pro shop watching us come in. My golf
shoes go click-click on the asphalt path of the clubhouse.

"Jude looks like the cat that swallowed the canary," Mr.
Lando says as he takes the clubs from Jay.

"She beat me hollow," Jay says. Mr. Lando smiles.

"I'd have been disappointed to hear different," Mr. Lando
says. "She's got a five handicap, you know," he adds. Jay whistles.

"I'm glad nobody told me that when we started out," Jay
says. "But at least now I know why I was beaten by a fourteen-
year-old girl."

Jay and I go and drink orange floats in the dark lobby of the
clubhouse where old men like my father sit around in green
leather chairs and discuss the scores on their golf cards. "How's
the Rev?" they call as we walk in. "Just fine," I reply.

I show Jay the silver cup with my name on it . . . Junior
Women's Champion: 1956–1957, 1957–58, 1958–59. An hour
later, the others straggle in. Jay laughs at how bedraggled they

look. He sticks out his long tanned legs and tries to trip Frank, who grunts and lurches out of the way. Bobby and Shelly's eyes look respectful when they glance at me.

"Are your mom and dad members here?" Frank asks. I nod.

"It's a bit of a dump, isn't it?" Shelly says, trying to sound disdainful. But her dust-smeared face makes her la-di-da manner sound fake.

"I guess it's not as good as the clubs in Toronto," I say. I'm too pleased with my game not to give places in Toronto their due. Once Bobby took me to a clubhouse whose name was a type of rock and I was impressed. We ate good butterscotch sundaes and watched little girls in velvet skating outfits do spirals and spins on a rink as big as the lake in Merton's park. Jay says nothing and sips his orange float with a bored look.

Out on the gravel drive, behind the clubhouse, Shelly starts to climb in the front seat but Jay puts his arm out and stops her. "Winners only," he says and winks at me.

"Never mind, Shelly," I say as I climb in beside him and Bobby and Shelly climb in the back seat. "It's how you play the game that counts."

"Yeah?" says Bobby. "Well it still feels bad to lose, if you ask me." I blush a little; Bobby's honesty makes me feel two-faced. But I've got the honour, as you say in golf. I shot a 42 today—two strokes lower than my game yesterday. Jay shot 78 and Frank 92. Bobby and Shelly didn't bother to count their scores. It's too bad love is not golf.

AUGUST 1ST. BOBBY IS IN THE CAN SMOKING HER BELOVED fag. I'm leaning against the outhouse, standing guard. The outhouse is green but its roof is orange because it's covered in a layer of pine cones. A small screen window has been built for ventilation into the top of its skinny green door. Not that ventilation is necessary. There are so many knotholes in its north wall, Bobby says you can feel the breeze from the bay blow up your ass. Ass, that's Bobby's word, not mine. I use the word "bum". I like to try out crude words to see how they sound, but I want to make it clear they aren't my speciality.

Bobby must be getting her bum blown away today. It's a three-day blow. The branches of the juniper bushes, the grass on the dunes, the little shoots with the striped berries, and the milk-weed plants with their pink star-shaped flowers are all shaking in the west wind. I have on a slicker over my Bermuda shorts and there are goosebumps on my legs. It's cold for August. Maybe it's going to snow. Heh-heh. That's a Canadian joke. We joke about winter the way other people joke about sex. For instance, people laugh when the temperature drops below zero and ask, "Is it cold enough for you?" It's self-congratulatory, my mother says, to take pleasure in the way we endure the cold

59

weather, but I don't see what's wrong with being proud of doing what we do well.

As I said, I'm sitting here beside Bobby and I have goose-bumps on my legs. And on my skinny arms too, underneath my slicker. I know it's not cold enough to snow, but I still don't like the grey cloudbank over the Blue Mountains. It looks like snow clouds to me. Imagine. Snowballs in August. Think of the way we'd brag up in Merton then.

Behind me, the door of the outhouse opens. Bobby pokes her head out. Her hair's in sausage-shaped rollers whose insides bristle with little nylon brushes. Bobby's suffering to be beautiful even though she's lined the rollers with Kleenex so the bristles don't prick her scalp. There must be at least thirty-five torture pieces on her poor head.

"Any sign of the old bag?" Bobby looks like an old bag herself this morning. It's the rollers and the cigarette dangling from her lips. The points of her bra cups poking against her shirt are the only glamorous things I can see about her. You don't see anything sexy like that under my blouse—only two small shadows which aren't enough to stir up anybody except the odd egg-head or weirdo.

I stand up and look down at the Big House, but I can't see anybody through the glassed-in kitchen window.

"Has the old bag got on her how-can-you-do-this-to-me look?" Bobby steps out of the outhouse.

"She looks like she's mad at somebody," I tease.

"Oh, oh. That somebody is me." Bobby pulls a package of Clorets out of her pocket and begins to chew furiously. She reeks of tobacco.

"Do I stink? Smell me, Dinger."

"Where's your hairspray?"

"Oh yeah. The final touch." Bobby hands me a can and I do her from head to toe. A suffocating lacquer smell fills the air.

"Now test me. I'm ready." Bobby throws out her chest and I sniff her up and down. I can see her bra cups clearly now. This is Bobby as I like her best, sexy-breasted and a little nervous. She's going through the motions of her tough-girl act, but it's obvious she's scared and needs me. It's heaven to be needed because I feel superior and humble at the same time.

I am staring down at somebody's feet. The feet are in a pair of old canvas sneakers. They are the feet of an Evil Queen. My eyes slowly climb up from the ankles to the knobby knees and then to heavy, dark thighs the colour of chicken drumsticks. I look still higher. Up across the creases in the plaid Bermuda shorts to the top of the legs, the big, fat tummy, and then higher still—up over breasts that jet out like the Merton Country Club hill and then, alas, into the fierce tanned face of Bobby's mother. "Well, Roberta. Where is it?" Mrs. Gallagher holds out her hand, scowling.

"I haven't done it yet. Sorry, Mom."

"Roberta, what am I going to do with you? Go to your room and don't come out till you've got it in your hand."

"Can Dinger come with me?" Bobby looks at me mournfully and Mrs. Gallagher sighs.

"I suppose she'll go anyway. All right, Dinger."

Bobby and I file by Mrs. Gallagher and walk through the junipers. Now we are standing on the back lawn. You wouldn't think a cottage had a back lawn, would you? But the Gallaghers' place does. The lawn stretches down to a little stream that runs between the parking lot and the cottage. Marsh marigolds and bachelors' buttons grow at the edge of the stream. Up near the cottage, pale pink geraniums and white petunias grow in window boxes and cedar tubs on either side of the front door. I tell you this to let you know where Bobby and I are. We are standing right here—X.

X marks the spot. To the right is a screen window. We can hear the Brothers inside playing a game of Snakes and Ladders. To the left is the clothesline. Mrs. Gallagher's brassieres are drying on the line. The cups of the bras are covered in concentric circles like the armour plates of gladiators. I look slyly at the bras and then follow Bobby inside. We walk along the back hall past the bedroom where the Brothers are playing. They didn't hear Mrs. Gallagher scold Bobby so we're in luck. We can walk by the door without them making fun of us. We go into Bobby's bedroom and shut the door.

Bobby sits down on the bed and starts to weep. Then all of a sudden she jumps up again and shuts the door. Once more—hard. Then she sits back down on the bed and begins to cry again. It's strange to watch Bobby cry. She squishes her nose and mouth and eyebrows together and makes a stuttering, panting sound. The panting sound gets louder and louder and then Bobby's eyebrows fly up and her lips drop apart. She looks like a cowboy in an old Indian movie who has been shot through the chest with an arrow. It makes me feel a little clinical to watch Bobby when she needs me. So I go over and sit down beside her. I pull a Kleenex out of my pocket and hand it to her. Bobby looks at me gratefully.

"Dinger, I don't know how to write a letter."

I nod. It's hard to believe but Bobby is telling the truth. Last summer I watched her trying to write Rum Bum when he was at camp. I finally ended up doing it and I put in lots of Bobby's expressions so he wouldn't realize his sister hadn't written it. I know what to do now. I pull a pencil out of my slicker pocket. And the little notepad I carry with me in case I want to write a poem. Bobby sees what I am doing, closes her eyes, and lies back on her bed like she is dead. I wet the tip of the pencil with my tongue and begin.

Dear Aunt Gloria,

This is just a note to thank you for your being so kind to give me the beautiful sweater. Mustard yellow is my favourite colour. By the way, Jude Bell and I adored our trip to the shrine with you. I've been studying what the mean old Indians did to Father Brébeuf and Father Lalemant at school so you couldn't have picked a better place to take me. Don't you just love the part in the story where the Indian traitor pours hot water over the old priest's head and says, 'Go to heaven, for thou are well baptized'? I wonder how Father Brébeuf could have stood the pain. Last summer I scalded my hand over the electric kettle and I blubbered like a baby.

Well, I'm babbling on. I guess you can tell history is my favourite subject. Many thanks, Auntie dear, for everything. I can't wait for your next visit.

Love,
xxoo,
Bobby.

Bobby sits up and grabs the letter. She reads it again and then hands it to me.

"Read it over once more, Dinger. It's so good," she says. "I think you are going to be a great writer."

I blush and begin to read it again. I told Bobby I was going to be a writer when I was three and I guess she's never forgotten. I read it in a high, screechy voice like a schoolteacher's this time. I want to make Bobby laugh but instead she only smiles and mouths the words as I am saying them. This is one of Bobby's funny habits. She does it when she really likes what you say. It used to make me a little nervous to see her lips moving until I realized it was a sign that I had pleased her.

I finish and Bobby grabs the letter again. She points to the names of the priests. "I think you should spell them wrong," she says. "I'd never get them right." She pauses and frowns. "And don't say history is my favourite subject, because it's not. I like geography."

I rub out the word Brébeuf and respell it. "How's Braybeef?" I ask, and Bobby nods. Then I write in the words "one of" in the sentence about history so I'm not telling a lie about Bobby's preferences. I hand it back to her and she takes a safety pin from her dresser and pins the note onto her pillow. We walk past the door of the Brothers' bedroom and stop simultaneously. Bobby and I look at each other. Then Bobby opens the door and rushes into the room. She kicks over their board and I laugh at their bewildered faces. Then Bobby and I duck out the screen door at the back of the cottage before Mrs. Gallagher can see us. We run up the path to Poison Ivy Point, Joe and Ben barking at our heels. This is one of those days when I love Bobby so much I could marry her.

When we get to Look-Out Pine, Bobby pulls out her package of Cameos. The dogs, Joe and Ben, sit down panting and all three of us watch Bobby as she lights up and says "Ahhh" like she's tasting a delicious chocolate bar.

"Well, now what?" she says and I can tell from the tone in Bobby's voice that nothing but a new game will satisfy her, so I pull out a pocket knife I stole from the Brothers. The handle is fake walnut, but the blade is stainless steel.

"Where did you get the knife?"

"From Adam. He thinks he lost it," I say. I smile. "I'll give it back to him after we're done." Then I point to her matches and she hands them over. I light one and hold it to the tip of the blade for a second. I have her attention now. It's a strain trying to figure out how to entertain somebody as restless as Bobby but somehow I manage.

"There. No germs can hurt us." I stand up and look stern. Then I stamp around Bobby, throwing my head backwards and forwards, howling "U-Go-I-Go! U-Go-I-Go! We makeum big pact. To lastum until eternity. Bobby and I be blood sisters until waters of Sound rise and drown all Balmy Beach cottages." Bobby doesn't know that North American Indians never had blood brothers. In the Merton library, I read about Hollywood borrowing the idea from an African tribe and putting it in the movie *Broken Arrow*. What Bobby doesn't know won't hurt her. I wail, "Wha-wha-wha" and slap my hand across my mouth until my lips sting. Then I sneak a look at Bobby and I can tell by the way she's pretending to scowl that my dancing is impressing her. No matter how indifferent she's trying to look, she can't wait to see what will happen next.

Unfortunately, it's something I'd like to postpone as long as possible: cutting my finger. I take the knife out and hold it above my head so it catches the sunlight. This isn't really happening to you, Dinger, I tell myself. I always tell myself that when something bad lies ahead. Mr. Lando says this is called disassociating; he says all champions have tricks to calm their nerves. My index finger splits open and the blood jumps out as if it's been waiting for the chance. It feels worse than getting a needle and not as bad as stepping on a thumbtack. I hand Bobby the bowie knife.

"It's your turn."

She looks at the knife and take a deep puff on her cigarette.

"What'll this do?" she asks nervously.

"It means I can insult you in public," I say. "It also means I can offer you my boyfriend. And if you are killed, it's my duty to find the murderer," I say. "Blood sisters are the same under the skin."

"Yeah? Does that mean you'll smoke one of my cigarettes then?" Bobby asks.

I hadn't thought about her cigarettes. I shake my head and Bobby frowns.

"Oh. Then I don't want to play this baby's game," she says.

"Okay. I'll smoke a cigarette if you'll cut your finger," I mutter.

"It's a deal." Bobby runs the bowie knife across her fingertip and squeals. "Ow! Goddamn it! It hurts like hell!" she says.

"Hallelujah! Amen! You take my blood, I take yours, how-how-how!" I put her index finger next to my index finger.

As soon as I say this, I sit down on the sand and Bobby does the same thing. I feel a little exhausted. I take out a piece of Kleenex and break it in half. I give a piece to her and a piece to me and we wrap up our fingers. Then she smiles at me and opens her cigarette deck. She passes it over to me and I take one. I roll it around my lips first, feeling the texture. It feels nice. I try it out on the left side of my mouth the way French movie stars smoke, and then I hold it in the V between my first two fingers and make a la-di-da motion with my hand and pretend I am blowing volumes of smoke through my lips. Bobby laughs and lights a match. We are both serious suddenly, and lean towards each other. I put the cigarette into my mouth and she lights it.

Naturally, I'm not going to inhale. I don't want to be a nicotine fiend. So I take a puff and let the smoke out fast. I begin to choke and choke. Bobby laughs and claps me on the back.

"You'll get used to it, B.S.," she says. Then she says the words I dread. "Okay. What are we going to do now?"

"I know!" I start to dig in the sand. A moment later, I bring up the little black cash-box in which I have hidden my Horse Book and my favourite story. I wave *Pollyanna* under Bobby's nose.

She squints through a haze of smoke. "Who's Pollyanna anyway?" she says.

"Somebody you should meet."

"Aw. She's just a character in a novel," Bobby says.

"She's much more than that," I say firmly. I have to encourage Bobby to understand books—or else she'd sit in her room all day with her hair in curlers, smoking and staring at the ceiling.

"Pollyanna is a golden girl. Listen, I'll read you the part where the maid Nancy explains Pollyanna's Glad Game to her cold Aunt Polly." Bobby sighs and stares at a bunch of gnats making little constellations above our heads.

"I'm listening," Bobby says wearily. I wave the smoke out of my face and start.

" ' "Nancy. What is Pollyanna's Glad Game?" ' "

Bobby blows a smoke ring and the gnats break out of the Big Dipper and form the constellation of the Great Bear by Bobby's knee.

" 'Nancy lifted her chin and looked cold Aunt Polly square in the eye. "I'll tell you, Ma'am. She got a pair of crutches once from a missionary barrel when she was wanting a doll. And she cried like any child would." ' "

I stop for effect.

" ' "It seems 'twas then her father told her there wasn't ever anything but what there was something about it that you could be glad about it," ' " I go on.

"Don't tell me this kid is going to be glad she got crutches instead of a doll?" Bobby says.

"Sssh. You sound just like a cold Aunt Polly," I reply.

"Oh, re-al-ly?" Bobby frowns at the gnats floating now over the heads of the dogs, wobbling a little in the smoke from Bobby's cigarette.

"Yes, really." I say really the proper way. "And then Pollyanna gets crippled later in the story, Bobby, so there's irony in her getting the crutches when she thinks she didn't need them."

"Does Pollyanna get to walk in the end?" Bobby asks.

"Just a few steps. But you know she's going to be okay."

"How do you know?"

"Because Pollyanna is a golden girl."

"Is Pollyanna pretty?" Bobby asks. "It doesn't sound like she is, from what you've read."

I hesitate. It's hard to be sure from the author's description. I have the same feeling—that Eleanor Porter is trying to make Pollyanna cuter than she is in real life—but I don't admit this to Bobby. Privately, I am impressed. Bobby put her finger on something that had been bothering me without knowing it.

"Pollyanna is too young to be beautiful, but she's good," I point out.

"So she's not a real golden girl."

"Not yet. But she will be. Pollyanna will be a knockout when she grows up."

"Oh sure, Dinger, just like you and me," Bobby drawls. "And she can't even walk!"

"Golden girls always get their way, but they have to be nice and suffer a lot first. Really, Bobby. A golden girl has to be perfect or else she doesn't get rewarded."

"I wonder what Miss Dalrymple would say about Pollyanna," Bobby says. Bobby's teacher, Miss Dalrymple, is the only adult Bobby has every liked. "She thought Lucie Manette, Dickens' heroine in *A Tale of Two Cities*, was a blonde, blue-eyed simp."

"Be quiet. I'm not going to read any more anyway," I say. I close the book and stand up. I'm mad and I feel like crying. I always want to cry when I get angry. It's a nuisance. "You'll never be a golden girl, Bobby." I shake my head sadly.

Bobby sighs and then she stands right up close and looks into my eyes. Her face has a hang-dog look so I can tell she is sorry from the bottom of her heart.

"Dinger, I apologize for not playing your games any more. Can I still be a golden girl?"

"I guess so," I say sadly.

Bobby puts her hand on my shoulder and looks at me. "I know something we could do."

"Yeah. What?"

"You know when you touch yourself down there. . . . Could you show me?"

"What are you talking about?"

"What you do in Happy Hollow. I spied on you the other day."

"You did?"

"Don't be mad. I just want to know. Do bells ring? Do you see shooting stars?"

"No, it's not in Technicolor, it's just. . . . I can't describe it, Bobby."

"Will you show me how, Dinger?"

"You're kidding."

"No—show me how to do it."

"You sure?"

"Sure, I'm sure. Do I have to ask you again?"

"Okay, okay." I watch dumbly as Bobby takes off her polka-dot bottoms and she frowns and points to mine and I say, "Oh, right," and slip off my panties. I've never shown anyone how to do this before so naturally I'm a little embarrassed. I'm not even sure if I can remember how I learned myself. But I don't tell Bobby this. Instead, I spread my legs and lie back on the sand.

"On your back, see? Now tighten your legs, and think of Jay Manchester's bathing suit. Then say 'thick, hairy wrists'."

There's a silence. "I'm saying it," Bobby says. "But it's not going anywhere."

"Just keep rubbing."

"Rubbing?"

"Yeah, you can't stop, pretend you're under a tap and the water's dripping on you and it won't stop."

"I thought I was supposed to think of Jay Manchester."

"That's just to get you going—now you have to concentrate on the tingling—you want it to get stronger."

"The tingling?"

"Yeah, like you're ticklish and it's getting worse."

"I thought you said tingling."

"Just keep rubbing."

"Oh, I feel something."

"That's it. Rub on that spot."

"What if it gets sore?"

"Rub gently—like you're teasing yourself."

Then I hear Bobby sigh and breathe a little fast and I know it's working and I say, "We are golden girls and men are made to serve us. Our function is to be worshipped. Men must submit to our influence and be transformed. We give men a taste of their possibilities. . . ."

"What are you talking about?" Bobby giggles.

"I'm reciting the words of the goddess—that's what we are, Bobby, golden girls in her service."

"You're crazy, Jude," Bobby laughs. "There's nobody as crazy as you. You know that?"

"There's nobody like you, either." I smile into her Seal Brown eyes just two feet away.

"Are you still rubbing?"

"Yeah—tell me some more."

"Men are silly and weak and that is why we have to sacrifice ourselves to them, but we never have problems or feel needy because we're so busy helping . . . ah . . . ah."

"Dinger?"

"Ah—say ah . . . ahhh."

"Yeah."

Bobby sits up suddenly, puts on her bottoms, and reaches out for a cigarette. "Jude. Jude! I think it worked!"

"If it did you'd know," I say and roll over so my back is towards her. I don't want Bobby to see how red my face is. My upper lip feels sweaty.

"I don't know if you'd call it a real orgasm," Bobby says and I hear the sound of a match striking. "It felt like pins and needles and then it was over."

"Maybe your orgasms are different from mine."

"Oh good—you'll allow it as an orgasm then." Bobby stands up and looks down at me, exhaling smoke. "Hey, you're all sweaty."

"Yeah."

"What did you mean about the goddess stuff? It was really crazy." Bobby points to my shorts. "Hadn't you better put those on? You don't want the Brothers to come along and catch you like that." She blows another smoke ring. "Gee, if anybody saw us they'd think we were lesbians."

"Yeah, that's us." I laugh and pucker up. "Come here, sweetie-pie."

"Jude—be serious. You swear you'll never tell anybody about what we just did."

"We're blood sisters, aren't we?"

Bobby laughs, then looks sombre. "You're my best friend. You know that?"

"You're mine too." I look in awe at her sexy pouting face

and her nicely shaped breasts, wondering how somebody so mature could be interested in a kid like me.

"We are blood sisters," Bobby says. "You'd never do anything to hurt me, like bring somebody else to our secret spots." Her hooded brown eyes are so wide open they look sand-coloured in the sunlight. "And I'd never betray you or tell your secrets like where you hid your Horse Book." Then Bobby narrows her eyes the way I imagine cold Aunt Polly narrows hers when she looks at Pollyanna and Bobby says, "Okay, cut out the mush. I'll race you back to your place."

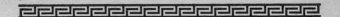

AUGUST 5TH. BOBBY HAS HER PERIOD. SHE HAS TO SIT ON the beach. Her mother said she can't get wet because she is wearing a napkin. The Brothers know and ask her why she won't go swimming to embarrass her. Bobby just smiles and fluffs her hair, which is no longer taffy-coloured but golden blonde. My hair is still the colour of dishwater, but this morning Bobby emptied a brown peroxide bottle on her head while her mother was off at the concession store. The Brothers gawked at her when she walked down to the beach. They whistled and called her "Blondie". She didn't even look at them; she acted so confident they could hardly believe she was my friend. They are still acting a bit impressed this afternoon, but it won't last. Sooner or later they'll go back to their usual creepy selves.

Shelly and I are pretending we can't go in the water either. Shelly is lying beside me on a striped towel and picking at the skin under her bathing-suit straps. "Crumb!" Shelly says. "I've got tan marks!" It's irritating the way Shelly inspects her body all the time, brushing off the sand from her skin, checking her page-boy with her fingers, or smoothing baby oil over her arms. Even for a girl, Shelly is a little bit too concerned about her appearance.

The adults are sitting down the beach from us, about fifty
yards or so. None of the adults has said anything about Bobby's
hair. They are drinking gin and tonics on lawn chairs which they
have set up in the shallow water by the shore. My father's tan
coats the pouches and wrinkles of his stomach like brown shel-
lac, painting it healthy, but misses the back of his legs which
are still white and very wrinkly. Mrs. Gallagher has wrinkles
on her legs too and her large thighs are solid like the thighs of
a football quarterback. "Thunder thighs" is Bobby's nickname
for her mother.

My mother's legs aren't wrinkly, and she doesn't need a tan to
cover up signs of age because her brown body looks young. She
is a thousand times more beautiful than Mrs. Gallagher who is
just lucky her large bosoms balloon over her bathing suit top.
Mrs. Gallagher looks like a fine-charactered Indian when she gets
a tan but even so, she can't compare with my mother. My mother's
hair is a long mane that hangs in the hollow between her shoulder
blades. The sun turns her hair white at the ends so her hairdresser
thinks she has bleached it.

My father tells my mother, "You're the best." Unfortunately,
he doesn't say that to me. He's never told me I'm pretty except
once he said he hated my bangs because nobody got to see my
nice face under all that hair. Sometimes I hate my father. I say
to myself how stupid he looks. He's twenty-five years older than
my mother and he gets mad when he plays sports like tennis that
make him notice he isn't young. He looks okay in the pulpit
when the lectern hides his paunch but he is out of place on the
beach. He has a pot belly and his breasts droop like a lady's. I
turn my head so I don't have to see him. He's the only one sitting
on the sand, curling and uncurling his enormous toes as he reads
over his sermon. He wears a nondescript bathing suit which used
to be gun-metal gray, but it's so old now it's the colour of mud.

Bobby has on her red tank suit. It's stretched out of shape and
has a tear on the seam, starting under her breasts and running
to the bottom of the suit, but I still love how she looks in it. I
have on a green woollen suit with a stupid square boater neck.
It's a sappy suit. Dozens of white ruffles cover the crotch in
place of a skirt. I like Shelly's suit better, too. It's a two-piece
with fat red poppies that her father brought up from the city. It

makes her look older than me even though it's a little tight across her tummy.

We are lying on our backs, screwing our eyes up at the sun, and thinking of nothing in particular. The crickets are noisy in the woods behind the beach; their racket sounds like one long drawn-out collective scream. Macgregor and the Brothers are fishing down by the Polliwog Pond. It's a Methodist Island day, which means a good day for a boat trip because there is no wind. If the water is royal blue in the morning, it means the Sound will be choppy by 2:00 p.m. But if it is bone white like it is now, it means it will stay calm all day.

"Somebody's coming our way," Bobby drawls. Shelly and I sit up. A speedboat is out by the fourth sandbar, making an ache of sound. The monotonous sound gets closer, bit by bit. The Brothers hear it too, and give up fishing to watch it approach. At the third sandbar, I recognize a blond head above the steering wheel. Two other heads are visible through the windshield. Bobby makes an inscrutable face.

"It's Jay Manchester," she says.

Shelly and I jump up and wave frantically. Jay lifts his arms in a leisurely salute. On the shore, the Brothers swarm around us like flies. Macgregor squints in our direction and then turns his back on the boat and keeps on fishing.

"Shame! Shame! Bobby and Dinger are in love!" Rum Bum shrieks.

The corncob yellow boat drifts in over the first sandbar. Effortlessly, Jay hops out and guides the craft to the beach. He smiles at Shelly and me and looks over towards Bobby. She is acting nonchalant, lying on her stomach with her elbows propped in the sand so she can hold up a book. It's a copy of *Peyton Place* she bought herself. Her bum looks round and firm and slippery under her tank suit, like you'd want to reach out and touch it.

"What's the matter, Bobby? Cat got your tongue?" Jay calls. Bobby lifts her head in our direction and then looks back at her book.

Jay grins and goes over and stretches out beside Bobby. "My mother won't let me read that book," Jay says.

"Too bad for you," Bobby says. She turns a page in her book.

Jay laughs and makes a fart-like sound by cupping his hand under his armpit. Then he leaps to his feet again.

"Anybody here want to go to Methodist Island?" he says. On the shore, the Brothers start chattering in excitement. Shelly and I exchange happy little looks. Jay's boat is the fastest on the beach. It goes 18 m.p.h. It has white fiberglass seats and a yellow fiberglass hull inscribed with letters that say "Look Ma. No Hands." I call to Macgregor and we all wade out and get in. The Brothers stand on the shore with the adults watching Jay put on his ski.

To my surprise, Mona Dault is sitting in the front with Frank. "Hi Dinger." Mona gives me a quick glance. She has drawn in her eyebrows with black pencil and painted her lips a typical red. Mr. Munsell says the notion of typical red varies with each person. That's why he made up his colour chart. In Mona's case, I'd say typical red looks like the scarlet colour you see on red jellybeans. Mona also has on a two-piece like Shelly, only hers is so tight it must have shrunk in the wash.

I say, "Hi Mona," and then we all turn and watch Jay put on the slalom ski at the sandbar.

Jay grins and lifts the leg with the ski into the air so the tip rests on the surface. He's getting ready for the jolt when the boat starts up and pulls him out of the water. I feel a pit in my stomach. I always feel a pit when a waterskier starts from the sandbar because you have to have strong arms to hold on while everybody watches you wobble back and forth for the first few embarrassing seconds until you start to plane on one ski. Bobby and I can't start from one ski because our arms aren't strong enough yet.

Today I feel a pit in my stomach worse than usual. I wouldn't want Jay to hurt himself. Now Jay picks up the two-handled tow rope from the water and turns to wave it at the Brothers.

"Anybody who makes it out here can come with us," Jay yells. The Brothers dash into the shallow water, yelling and pushing each other. Everybody in the boat laughs except Macgregor and me. We know what's coming next. Jay makes a circle sign with his thumb and index finger at Frank, who is sitting behind the steering wheel. Frank guns the boat and we take off before they can reach us.

Some of the Brothers stop wading into the water but Adam and Beckett keep rushing towards it. For a second I feel sorry for the twins. Then I think of the Horse Book and put on my cruel look. It serves them right. I shout "Goodbye" and wave at my mother, who has put her arm around one of the Brothers. She is frowning and trying to call something to us but her voice is lost in the roar of the motor. I wave again and finally she gives up and wags her arm back and forth from the elbow in a little movement that Bobby calls her Queen Wave. Then I concentrate on Jay. He is not quite on top of the water yet. He is holding on, crouched down, arms bent into his chest, his ski zigzagging back and forth across the wake as he tries to hang on. I pray, dear Mrs. God, help him up. Jay is strong and blond but he still needs a bit of luck. Then suddenly, Jay is leaning back. His ski has stopped quivering and he is planing nicely. A roostertail of spray shoots out behind him. He looks like a one-legged brown bird flying behind a wall of iridescent spray. The spray falls through the air like sparkling feathers and drips down across his tanned body. Suddenly, Jay jumps the wake and his ski makes a wet, cracking noise on the surface of the water. Bobby and I say "Oh" together and Macgregor, sitting beside me, turns and spits over the gunwale.

"Doesn't that piece of musculature ever tire of displaying himself?" Macgregor hisses in my ear.

"Aw. You're just jealous cuz you're a toothpick," Bobby says.

Macgregor spits again and stares at his long, thin white feet planted on the fiberglass floor of the boat. I can see his feet poking out of the towel Macgregor wears to keep himself from getting sunburnt.

"Shut up yourself," Rum Bum says to Bobby. "Jay is a big hunk of muscle. That's why you girls like him."

I don't say anything; I keep looking at Jay but I am chewing over Rum Bum's words. I don't know what makes Jay so good looking. It's not just his muscles, or his colouring either. Rum Bum has the same colouring, for instance. Of course, Jay also has a small bum and shoulders like a triangle. But there is something sleepy about him that reminds me of a girl. Maybe it's his long starry eyelashes or the slow gaspy way he laughs, as if he's not sure what else to do.

Now we are past the Second Point and heading towards Methodist Island. The radar dome shines the dull white of a ping-pong ball. I imagine the Americans are up there getting ready in case the Russians make a goof. I don't think the Russians would send over a missile in the heat of summer. The Russians have long winters like us and probably get a little crazy around February, waiting for spring. If the world was going to come to an end, it would happen then. The Russians wouldn't be stupid enough to do it on a Methodist Island day. I point it out to Macgregor and he grunts and doesn't say anything. Nobody talks about it. I guess there's not too much to say.

Now Frank turns the boat west and we head towards the lighthouse behind the sandy cove at the tip of Methodist Island. We head straight for the run-down dock, then suddenly Frank swerves and drives back out the way we came. So Jay swings on an arc towards the shore, one hand stretched out in the air ahead of him, the other hand still hanging onto the ski rope. At the last moment in the arc, he planes into the shore, kicks off his ski, and runs onto the sand. Bobby claps and Rum Bum makes a whistling noise. Mona stares a little stupidly at Jay on the beach. I don't think she knows what a brilliant manoeuvre Jay's done for us.

"Our muscled friend knows how to ski all right," Macgregor says.

"Eat your heart out, Professor," Frank says.

We are sitting on Methodist beach, on towels, in two groups, which is a little strange. The groups are the same groups we sat in on the boat. Bobby, Shelly, Mona, Frank, and Jay are in one group—the winners' group. I am in the losers' group with Macgregor and Rum Bum. At least from here I can get a good look at Jay's long, brown body stretched out on the sand beside Mona. Next to Jay, Mona's wan tan looks faded. Jay is as tanned as MacIntosh toffee.

To be frank, I don't know what to do. I don't want to drink beer so that doesn't leave much choice. Now that I'm grown up, I can't do the things that used to be fun. For instance, the last time Bobby and I came up here, I made up a really good witch game. It was so good all the Brothers wanted to play the witch.

Naturally, there's no point showing Jay the witch game. I hope nobody brings it up either. We could play Lawrence of Arabia. It's not babyish. Jay'd be good at portraying Lawrence, the crazed white man who lived among the Bedouins. And I'd be his Bedouin princess who he made love to every night in the sand dunes outside the Sultan's tent, the desert moon burning over his shoulder, coating his long blond body in silver.

"Why don't we play Lawrence of Arabia?" I say, hoping for some interest from the other group.

Mona looks my way and lights a cigarette. "We don't have to be doing something every moment, you know."

"But there's nothing to do," I say.

Jay smiles at me. "Jude's right. Who's going to race me to the old lighthouse?"

"Hardy-har! The big brown piece of muscle wants to neck," Rum Bum says. Macgregor grunts, his head still under his towel.

Shelly makes a whinny noise that's meant to be a sophisticated laugh.

"Does that mean yes?" Jay asks. Shelly swings her head so her page-boy hairdo falls flick, flick into place. She doesn't look as good as she did when we started out. For one thing, it is weird to have perfectly combed hair when you're on a picnic. And for another, she's getting sunburnt across her tummy where the skin isn't used to the sun.

"Wouldn't you like to know?"

"Come on then, Bobby, show me what those legs of yours can do," Jay says. Bobby stares at him for a minute and then she turns and looks at me as if she is looking at somebody she hardly knows.

"Why don't you race the golf champion? She's got longer legs."

Jay looks startled. "Well, I thought I'd race you, Bobby," he says. He stares down at the ground a little sheepishly, and I feel like I want to sink through the sand all the way to China. I hate myself for thinking Jay might like me. He doesn't even want to walk to the old lighthouse with me.

"Well, go on, Dinger. I know you want to kiss him on the top of the tower," Bobby says.

Macgregor pokes his head out from under the towel, scowling. "Shut up, you shivering, six-bellied sidewinders," Macgregor says to Bobby. "Go to the tower yourself with this piece of brown muscle."

"All right, I will." Bobby stands up and then saunters off. Her skinny red bum shifts from one cheek to another in the walk we practised last summer. For a second, Jay stares at her. Then he jumps to his feet and runs to catch up to her. As soon as she hears him behind her, Bobby starts to run; her wild, free run, arms pumping the air as if you are pulling yourself forward on a rope.

Mona watches her go, frowning. And then Frank tugs her arm and says, "It's you and me, Mona baby."

Mona brushes the sand off her thighs and shrugs. "Okay."

"Thank God. Now I can drink in peace," Rum Bum says as they walk off. He sits down beside Shelly and opens his mouth to demonstrate he needs something poured into it.

Shelly opens more beers and hands one to Rum Bum and then one to Macgregor. He shakes his head and slowly stands up, clutching his towel. "Let's go for a walk, Jude, and leave these alcoholics to their vociferous vices." Macgregor looks anxiously at me and for a minute, I think he likes me just like Bobby says he does.

"Hardy-har! Dinger doesn't want to go with you," Rum Bum says.

"I do so." I don't, but I feel an obligation to Macgregor for sticking up for me against Bobby and Shelly.

So I pick up a Coke and walk off, Macgregor scuttling along beside me, one hand holding his towel. He sips from his bottle and I sip from mine but we don't say anything to each other. We just keep walking as fast as we can to the old dock where the Indians live in pitiful little green clapboard houses. Too bad I'm with Macgregor and not Jay. Bobby is probably kissing him on top of the old lighthouse right now and looking down at us and laughing.

I pause and shade my eyes. "What a scenic spot! It's so beautiful it hurts to look at." My mother says beautiful things hurt her to look at. I'm not sure what she means but it sounds very mature.

Macgregor scowls. "You don't have to put on an act with me."

We walk along in silence now. The breeze is rustling the tops of the poplar trees near the beach and the sand is burning my feet. Macgregor saw right through me and now I don't know what to do. All of a sudden, I feel a hand on my shoulder. I stop and clasp my hands behind my back. I don't want to give him any ideas. Because maybe this is it. The big clinch. I turn my head very slowly. Macgregor looks funny. Not the way he usually looks. I think that's because he's smiling.

"I didn't mean to hurt your feelings," he says softly. "But I don't know why you think you have to act like them. You're twice as good as they are." He smiles again and for a moment I think I am with somebody I've never met before.

"I think you're the most beautiful girl on the beach," Macgregor says. "I don't know why I'm telling you this because you'll only use it against me. Girls always do." He looks down at the Coke bottle in my hand whose neck is glinting green in the sunlight. I look at it too. I stare at the white letters scrawled across its dark bumpy surface and I read the words Coca-Cola over and over again. This may seem like a stupid thing to do when somebody's just told you what you've wanted to hear all your life, but I don't know what to say. The trouble is, I never expected the words to come from Macgregor. Drat. Why do the ugly boys always like me? I'll never have a boyfriend like other girls. But I have to say something so I ask him if he's kidding and he shakes his head. He's still staring down at the Coke bottle and I know it's my turn to say what I think of him but I don't know how to described the mixed-up feeling I have of liking him and looking down at him at the same time. You just can't say things like that to a boy. But I have to say something, so I say thanks, and then he says that it's okay and keeps looking down at the Coke bottle.

All of a sudden, I hear Rum Bum. He's standing up on the dunes behind us. Shelly and Frank are with him. He's yelling, "Dinger and Macgregor, up in a tree, k-i-s-s-i-n-g!"

Macgregor looks up and I give him a push, a hard one, and he falls down, kerplop, on his bum on the sand. Then I shake my Coke bottle up and down until I can hear it fizz and I spray

Macgregor's shocked freckled face. He just stares at me with his mouth open, and the beads of Coca-Cola dripping down over his nose and chin, until I'd like to hit his head with the Coke bottle. He brings me nothing but humiliation. It's hell to be a teenager. And being me is worse. Would you want to be like me? Tall and skinny and only attractive to goofs. Go on. Nobody in their right mind would say yes.

I throw down the Coke bottle and then I run off down the beach. I hear Macgregor call my name as if he thinks he's done something wrong but I don't turn around to answer. I sit down on the towel and put my head on my knees. They're coming back talking and laughing. Macgregor goes over to his towel and sits down. It's Bobby, looking sulky, and Frank.

"What's the matter, Professor, didn't she want to see your dick?"

I gasp. Macgregor gasps even louder than me. Dick! What a word to use! Language like that makes me realize Frank is debauched.

"Did I say something wrong?" Frank asks.

"Watch your tongue, Frank," Jay says. Oh no. The golden boy is back too. Mona is standing beside him, smiling, one hand on his arm.

"Ah, what a bunch of sucks!" Frank says, and passes a beer to Mona. She takes one and throws her head back to drink it. I watch Jay watching Mona; her breasts quiver a little as she arches her head in the sunlight.

"I don't know about the rest of you, but I'd like to do something," she says. "I don't want to just sit around here all day."

"So what do you suggest?" Jay says and looks at her with a little smile.

"Why don't we go and dive off the Mabuno?" Frank says, and we all climb in Jay's boat and go.

Jay cuts the motor and we drift up towards the tip of the wreck sticking out of the water. It's part of the captain's bridge. The rest of the old steamer is under water. You have to swim down to the bottom, and then up through the wreck until you hit air in the captain's bridge. You can't enter the room from above because that part of the boat sticks thirty feet above the surface at a ninety-degree angle.

The anchor makes a wet whispering sound as it sinks overboard. Everybody stands up and watches the rope unravel from the bow cleat, coil by coil. Jay whistles. "Thirty feet," he says. He smiles at me and points at the rope which is still unwinding and I squeeze in between him and Frank to have a better look. Now is my big chance to step out of the babies' group. I lean a little to the right and his thigh brushes mine, softly at first, then harder. Is he doing it on purpose? I look at him but he is looking at the rope with the far-away expression I don't like. I stand dead still. The pressure is steady now. It feels dirty but nice. Oh, Jay, I think, drag me off to the bushes and have done with me. I look around quickly to see if anybody has noticed but nobody is paying attention.

Then Frank says, "Last one in is a rotten egg." He does a cannonball into the bay. And Jay jumps in after him. Then Shelly, then Mona and Bobby. And then I fall down into the bottle-green water. I open my eyes and see a doll-sized shadow on the bottom way below me. Hastily, I make sculling motions with my hands, then I do a duck-dive, feet up, sliding, sinking, down, down.

I'm almost on the bottom. I do another duck-dive, a fast one, and then duck through the open door. My chest is getting tight. I spring up, up, up to the surface and look around. I'm in a funny little room, it's the captain's bridge, and it echoes. Then I see a shape in the corner of the room.

It's only Shelly in the corner. I could recognize her strawberry hair anywhere. She looks scared herself. "If you want to go up to the top of the wreck, Jude, you have to take off your bathing suit," Shelly says.

"Come on, Shelly. Stop kidding me." I frown. I don't like the sound of this.

"Mona's orders," Frank says. I turn around and there's Frank, looking through the window of the captain's room. His face is upside down. "All the girls have to strip," he says. "Or they can't come on deck."

"I'm not stripping."

"Of course not. You're too much of a goodie-goodie." It's Bobby's voice this time, not Frank's. It floats in the air above the deck of the old steamship.

"Have you got your bathing suit on?" I lean out the window and look up. The top of Mona's two-piece bathing suit appears above my head. Then I hear Jay's laugh. You know the one I mean, the laugh that sounds like he's gasping for air. In the next moment, I see him. He is standing beside Mona and Bobby, holding up a towel to shield them from my view.

"You'll have to let me come up. I can't get enough power from here to dive back down and out through the wreck."

"Rotsa ruck," Frank laughs.

"Do you have your suit on, Jay?" I call.

"Yeah," Frank says. "Only girls have to strip."

I hear a sloshing noise and Macgregor's head pops up through the surface of the water. He scowls at me and hauls himself up onto a ledge beside Shelly. He's shivering too. There's no sunlight in here except for that shaft bouncing across the ceiling.

"Jude and I have to strip," Shelly says. "Mona says so."

"Strip! What are those sidewinding scallywags up to now?" Macgregor says. He looks at me, very fierce.

"Any girl who wants to go up on deck has to take off her bathing suit," Shelly says.

"I'm not going up there," I say. Shelly shrugs and giggles a little half-heartedly and then starts to wade and crawl over towards the window. When she gets to the window, she turns slowly and looks at me.

"Are you going up, Shelly?" I ask. I feel like I might cry any minute. "I'm only going to take off my top, Jude," she says. "Nobody's going to get me to take off my bottoms."

On deck, the boys start to cheer as soon as Shelly's head appears out the window. Macgregor and I stare at her like dopes. First her head disappears and then her shoulders and back and then her bum and then her legs. Now I turn to Macgregor. "Are you going up, Macgregor?" I say. I don't want Macgregor to go too, but I wouldn't blame him if he left me. Macgregor doesn't say anything. He doesn't look mad any longer, just grave. Then Macgregor points to the window. Frank's staring at us upside down.

"The professor has to take off his suit too because he's only half a boy," Frank calls down.

"Does that answer your question, Jude?" Macgregor looks

sad and I think of putting my arms around him, but it's too late now—he hates my guts. So I don't say anything; I just stare out the porthole at the radar dome sitting like a golf ball on top of the trees. I guess things could be worse. I guess the world could be blown up by the bomb. Then I sigh and lean forward out the window. Legs are all I see. Mona's hairless shaved ones and Shelly's chubby ones and Bobby's muscly ones and Jay's round smooth calves.

"We can always jump out from the window," I say.

"It's too high," Macgregor says.

"No, it's not as far down as you think. I'll show you."

"What are you up to, you shifty swagwoman?" he mutters.

I listen sadly to Macgregor insulting me in Australian. Then I close my eyes and wrap my arms around my knees. I'm on the ledge. Behind me, I hear Shakespearean words start to echo in the little chamber. "Caitliff! Budmash!" Macgregor's using ancient words because he's run out of modern ones. "Whore's son—beetle-headed knave!" Why do most rude names apply to men, not women? Funny, how I can think about words in the middle of a tragedy. I am still on the ledge. Now I open my eyes and just for a sec, I look up. Oh, Mrs. God, help me! A nudist colony stands on the deck! I see Mona's long pendulous breasts, her nipples cherry red in the hot sunlight, and Shelly's bouncing freckled breasts. I check bottoms. They're on. Now I check Bobby's suit. She's taken it off. I see the massive dark shadow spread across Bobby's crotch. Her pubic hair. Oh, Mrs. God, hear your daughter in the wilderness! I close my eyes again and shut back the tears starting up. Then I lean out, and fall into the water.

Augustus 7TH. I'M SITTING IN THE BOUGHS OF LOOK-OUT Pine, writing. Karl Frank is about to ravish Monika but I don't know how to describe his love-making. It's like writing about flying when you haven't flown a plane. You see, he tied Monika up to his bed with a piece of skipping rope he found in her schoolbag. She couldn't fight back because she was stunned from her fall. Maybe if I dwell on the action nobody will notice I am glossing over the important part.

Shelly is sitting down below. I've brought her here to my secret place because Shelly only took her top off on the trip to Methodist Island. I can forgive a top but not bottoms. In case you're wondering, Shelly visited me after the boat trip to Methodist Island and begged my forgiveness. She said alcohol turns you into somebody else. (A line she borrowed from her father.) So I said it was okay, but I can't forgive Bobby. I have taken a vow to hate her the rest of my life. Last night I took out the snap of Bobby in her riding clothes and cried a little because I still like her skinny legs and the way her short, blonde hair pokes out from under her riding helmet. Then I noticed she wasn't really winking at me. I think she blinked because the sun was in her eyes.

Shelly stands up and calls my name. She holds her papers.
"Want to hear?" she says. I climb down Look-Out Pine and I
sit beside Shelly. Her heroine, Lily St. James, is twenty-three,
eons older than Monika, when she meets her fiancé's mother for
the first time.

"It is nice to meet you, Mrs. Ashton-Huston the Third," Lily
St. James said demurely to the older woman with an aristo-
cratic bearing. Then, clucking soothingly, Paul's mother led
Lily into a courtyard where dusk was beginning to dim the
brightness of the flowers and shrubs.

"I'm Mrs. Ashton-Huston, Jr.," Paul's mother sniffed as
she settled herself and her voluminous skirt into a comfortable
rocker. "It's bad taste to call yourself the third unless all three
generations are alive."

"Oh, I'm so sorry," Lily St. James blushed.

"Now, now *chérie*—you must call me *petite mère*, as Paul
does," the older woman smiled. The serving-girl placed a tray
bearing a silver coffee urn and tiny fragile cups and saucers on
a table near the smiling bejewelled lady. As the maid poured
demitasses, Mrs. Ashton-Huston, Jr. said, "Now I ask you,
Lily St. James, if you felt as sentimental about the old family
plantation as I do, would you let my son will it to a north-
erner?"

"It doesn't seem likely," Lily St. James admitted.

Shelly looks up; she's waiting for me to say something. "Go
on." I nod. "That phrase, 'clucking soothingly', sounds very
professional." Actually, I've read it too many times to like it,
but I don't tell this to Shelly.

"That's all I have, Jude," Shelly says.

"That's all?" I ask. "I thought you wrote pages last night."

Shelly nods but she doesn't look at me. "I did and then I tore
them up. This is all I have."

"Well, why don't you write some more here?" I say.

"Oh, I'd rather hear what's happening to Monika."

"Well, she's in a bit of pinch," I say eagerly, and then I
start:

Monika felt the bed sag under the weight of his flabby, pot-bellied form. Then slowly, her loathsome enemy began to crawl all over her like a hairy spider. It was a night never to be forgotten. It would haunt her for eternity. All she could remember afterwards was waking up in the middle of the night and seeing Frank's pot belly rising and falling laboriously under the blanket.

"But what did he do to her, Jude?" Shelly asks. Drat. She would want to know.

I sigh a little and look down at the paper. "I don't know how to write a sex scene."

"You could say something like 'He was a big playful fellow with—' "

" '—an organ as big as a cigar . . . ,' " I add.

"Well, a fully grown man's organ is bigger than a cigar, Jude—much bigger," Shelly says as if she's seen the real thing and she sighs too. "Jude, I have something to tell you." She looks at me and shrugs her shoulders. "Will you still speak to me afterwards?"

"Of course I will. What are you talking about?"

"Promise? You mean it? You won't be mad after I tell you?"

I shake my head and make the sign of the cross in front of my breast. "Cross my heart and point to heaven."

"I copied the Lily St. James story from a book. I didn't write it, Jude. And sometimes I make up the letters Roger sends me too."

I've already guessed that about Roger's letters but I had no idea Lily St. James was a fake. All of a sudden I feel really sorry for Shelly. She copied her stories from a book and I didn't even like her writing. Why didn't she pick a book that was good? I put my arm around her with a little sigh and she collapses against me, half crying and half giggling with embarrassment. It's a good thing Bobby can't see us. Then, lo and behold—I mean, speak of the devil—there's Bobby now. Bobby and the Brothers are carrying spades down by the Polliwog Pond. Bobby yells something and they begin to dig furiously. Macgregor's waving his arms and Bobby's waving her arms. They're going to let out the pond water so Macgregor's frogs will dry up. What's gotten into the Brothers? The Brothers are supposed to be Macgregor's bodyguards.

"Look! They've captured Macgregor!" Shelly whispers. Shelly's a little scairt of the Brothers. Oops. I s̃aid it. Scairt for scared. That's Merton talk; it's as bad as dropping the "g" from your "ing" endings. Unfortunately, Shelly doesn't know she doesn't have to be scared because she doesn't have any brothers, only a dopey father who tells dirty jokes and flirts with us. And Shelly's mother is an untanned weirdo who reads Georgette Heyer romances and who never washes because she doesn't go down to the beach. Everybody knows there is no running water in their cottage.

Shelly takes my hand and I squeeze it hard. It's not the Brothers I'm afraid of—it's Bobby. Bobby's got an Irish streak and the Irish don't know when to quit. I look over again but I can't see her any more. She and the Brothers have dragged Macgregor off into the Dungeon Pines. I hear the war whoops and then silence.

"Jude! They're coming our way!" Shelly says. I look up and there they are, running across the Unknown Desert, yelling their heads off. Bobby is yelling the loudest. "I guess you're too good for me these days, aren't you, Dinger?" she calls. "Well, you'll be sorry for taking her to our secret spot!"

"What do you mean?" I say, trying to look calm but I'm trembling all over. It's true I promised Bobby never to come here with anybody but her.

"That's for me to know and you to find out," Bobby yells. Now she turns to the Brothers and raises her arms. "Okay. Dig Look-Out-Pine." The Brothers raise their spades and yell "Charge!" Yikes! They're going after my Horse Book. I start fighting with one of the Brothers, who pushes me away with one hand and tries to dig with the other. Now Bobby grabs my arms, pins them behind my back. "Keep digging," she yells. Shelly starts to whimper like the old crybaby she is and then Adam squeals. He's found my box in the sand. He opens it and hands my books over to Bobby. She throws Pollyanna down and brandishes my Horse Book over her head. "This is what I think of you, Dinger Bell!" she says. She begins to run down the dune plucking out pages and yelling out phrases, casting my secret words into the open air. I stand very straight and solemn. I feel as if Bobby has pulled out my bleeding heart and showed it to me like the Iroquois did to Father Brébeuf.

"I hate her!" Shelly yells. "She's an old meanie!"

I walk slowly down Mount Sand into the Unknown Desert, picking up what's left of my Horse Book. That's only one or two pages. I put them in my pocket. "Jude! Look over there!" Shelly points suddenly.

I turn around. Macgregor is tied to a rotten cedar tree, his eyes swollen as if he's been crying, although that's unlikely with a boy like Macgregor.

"They've let my frogs go, haven't they?" he says in a flat voice, as if he doesn't care.

I nod my head sadly. I point to the empty bait traps by the pond. Macgregor looks at the traps on the sand beside Mr. Moffat's empty lawn chair, and then stares at the ground. For a minute he doesn't say anything.

"Do you want me to untie you?" I say.

Macgregor nods and Shelly and I run over and fumble with the knots. The rope is hairy and skinny, the kind that skins your fingers when you untie it. I fumble a little more and then Macgregor steps free. He rubs his wrist and looks at me. Cold as cold. Macgregor is not the least bit grateful for being free.

"You told on me. You told her what I said to you."

"No, I did not, Macgregor."

"How comes she knows then?"

"Knows what?"

Macgregor stares at me. Then he shrugs. "I knew you wouldn't keep your word. That's the way women are. If they get something on you, they use it against you." He scowls and spits on the sand. "Sooner or later."

"Somebody must have overheard what you said, Macgregor. I didn't tell."

"Tell what, Jude?" Shelly asks.

Macgregor stares, scowling at her. "As if you didn't know," he sneers. "I don't know why I was stupid enough to talk to the enemy! Get away from me—you verminous vipers!" Macgregor turns and runs off into the pine trees. He didn't even try to find his frogs. Of course, they'll be hard to catch now. They'll be hiding in the black reedy water, sitting on the bottom and sending up little air bubbles to the surface.

AUGUST 20TH. I'M WALKING THE BEACH AGAIN. I'M walking to Bobby's place. It's getting harder to hate her when she didn't get Jay either. I wish it wasn't true, but I'm not good at keeping enemies. No matter how much I try not to let it happen my imagination keeps putting me in their shoes. Besides, there's only eleven days left in summer, and eleven days isn't much time when you live in paradise. I'm wearing a Shetland sweater because it's cool. A west wind is hurling big rollers up onto the beach. The waves bang onto the sand and then fall backwards again, leaving the sand under my bare feet slick and smooth. I'm splashing through the waves foaming on the shore and the water is warm. You see! It's not fall yet. Winter is still something that happens to other people, back in Merton. Not to me. I bet you hardly recognize who's talking. I'm the teenaged girl shining bronze and gold in the light of the setting sun. My hair is shining golden too. I dyed it the colour of sand, like the Valkyrie, the handmaidens of Odin. Rum Bum told the Brothers that Bobby and I dyed our hair. But I explained that we were born blonde and had our hair touched up. If you're a real blonde, people don't see anything wrong with helping nature along. Their scorn is for girls with dark hair who dye it lighter. They are bottle-blondes who don't fool anybody.

It's amazing how childish I sound when I talk about blondeness. I sound about eight years old. But sometimes when you tell the truth, you sound childish because you're saying things other people won't admit. Take, for instance, the joke adults make about gentlemen preferring blondes and marrying brunettes. It's no joke. It would sound bad if they came right out and said blondes are better looking. The truth always sounds crazy, even though it's the truth.

I turn up the cement walkway which runs from the beach to Bobby's cottage. Bobby's note is in the pocket of my Bermudas. It says:

Dear Dinger:
    An urgent matter has arisen concerning somebody you and I like a lot. I, Bobby Gallagher, request forswith [Bobby's spelling, not mine] that you confer with Shelly and I in the jon just as the sun goes down. I heartily recommend that we let bygones be bygones. This is ADULT business. The password is Tonto.
    PUDDLES OF PURPLE PASSION.

On the bottom of the page Bobby has written her name and surrounded it with hearts and arrows. Then she's written in tiny capital letters: "DO YOU LOVE OR HATE ME?" The L's and H's are very neat but the E's look like a stick with a long line in the middle like a tongue. An outline of Bobby's hand has been drawn over the question.

I stop by the juniper bushes near the outhouse. It feels satisfying to have Bobby beg to see me. It reminds me that I am pretty nice after all. "Heigh-ho," I call.

"Come in, Tonto," Bobby says. She's sitting on one of the outhouse holes smoking a Cameo. I'm surprised to see Shelly is sitting on the other hole. "Well, you took long enough," Bobby says. "What were you doing, catching some new frogs for Macgregor?"

Bobby stretches her legs so I can see they are newly shaved and then she leans back against the wall of the outhouse. Her

Bermuda shorts are down by her ankles and I notice cotton undies sprinkled with umbrellas inside the shorts.

"So what's the big deal?" I say in a heartless tone, turning my left (it's my best) side to Bobby.

Bobby blows a huge smoke ring that wobbles by my face. "Tell her about the contest, Shelly," Bobby says sweetly as if she really liked Shelly.

"Well, it's about Jay." Shelly blows out a smoke ring too. Holy cow! Now Shelly's mastered the art. "Bobby went to the drive-in with him."

"I don't believe you."

"He wasn't her date. Jay went with somebody else."

"Who?"

"Your friend with the big boobs," Bobby says.

"Mona?"

"Yeah. The one who gave him a blow job."

"Pardon?" I ask, and Shelly giggles.

Bobby puts her hand on Shelly's shoulder. "It's okay Shelly, I'll talk now." She exhales, eyes closed.

"I didn't want to tell anyone what I saw at Methodist Island but Shelly coaxed it out of me."

"She did?" It's hard to believe Shelly could convince Bobby to do anything.

Bobby nods, eyes still closed. "Remember when I went to the lighthouse with Jay? Well, Mona started teasing him about picking on somebody his own age. She said she'd take him on a trip around the world if he stepped into the bushes with her for a few minutes."

"And Jay went?"

"Mona dragged him off. Frank and I followed. We had to crawl on our knees through some junipers and then we saw them. Mona was kneeling and her head was buried in Jay's crotch. That's when Frank told me the lucky bum was getting a blow job."

"What's a blow job?" I whisper.

"Look it up, Dinger. You're good at that. It's under fellatio in the dictionary."

"Tell me what it means, Bobby."

Shelly giggles again and Bobby elbows her. "I'll tell you what Frank says about them."

"What's that?"

"There's no such thing as a bad one." Bobby snickers.

"Oh, you don't know what you're talking about."

"Oh yeah? Well, if you're such a know-it-all, how come you don't know?"

"I know. I just wanted to hear you say it."

Bobby smiles. "Anyway, at the drive-in, I told Frank how you wrote sex stories about Shelly's father to entertain us."

"You told him that!"

"Uh-huh. He was very interested. Then I told him that you and Shelly and I all wanted to go out with Jay. That we had a kind of competition going to see which one of us he'd pick."

"I don't want to hear any more!"

"Wait. He asked me if I was pulling his leg and I said it was the gospel truth. I said I wouldn't have told him if it wasn't the end of summer and didn't matter any more."

"And what did he say?"

"He said it was never too late. He asked me to wait where I was—that he wanted to talk to Jay. Then he and Jay had a huddle and Frank came back and said Jay would pick one of us as his girl if we all agreed to do something."

"You're making this up Bobby."

"Just wait till you hear the rest," Shelly says.

"What did he say we have to do?"

"He said Jay would pick the one of us who gave him the best blow job."

"The best blow job! I'm not going to blow job Jay! I don't know how."

"You'd better learn. Because Shelly said she'll go along with it. Didn't you, Shelly?"

Shelly nods.

"Shelly? You wouldn't do something like that, would you?"

"Bobby and I agreed this morning to do it."

"I don't believe it."

"Obviously Shelly isn't as prissy as you are."

"I'm not prissy! I hate it when people call me that."

"Yes you are. You never do anything wrong. You always get good marks and win at golf. You're a goodie-two-shoes."

"Are you going to give him a blow job?"

"Yes. Of course I am. I told him that too but I said you'd chicken out."

"I'm not a chicken."

"Good. Frank wanted us to go over to Jay's cottage but I suggested we can do it at a bonfire at Poison Ivy Point."

"I'm not doing it, Bobby."

"Oh—then you don't believe in the rules?"

"Rules?"

"The ones you and I made up last summer. Shelly read them."

Shelly nods. "I know them by heart. Number One: All's fair in love and war. Two: May the best player win. Three: The one who gets the best boy is the sexiest. Four: Look like you don't know or care about the contest. Five: The ultimate way for us females to express ourselves is through our sexuality. . . ." Shelly giggles. "Oh, that sounds like Jude's big words."

"I'm still not doing it, Bobby."

"Well don't then, chicken. It'll be between Shelly and me. And next week one of us will be Jay's girl."

From behind the row of poplars, Bobby's mother calls Bobby's name in a drawn-out wail as if she's about to faint. She sounds too close for comfort but I can't concentrate on anything except Bobby's conversation. Bobby lights another Cameo and gives it to me. "Have a drag. It'll help you think." I take a puff just as the door opens and Bobby's mom falls in on top of me. For a second, her gladiator bosoms hang half a foot from my face. Then she waves wildly at the cigarette smoke and grabs Bobby by the collar and pulls her to her feet. Bobby's undies are still around her ankles.

"Pull up your pants and come with me this minute, young lady. Wait till your father hears about this." Mrs. Gallagher gives Bobby a push—a hard one—and Bobby falls down.

"First of all you failed school and now you're smoking behind my back! What will it be next?"

Bobby scrambles to her feet and pulls up her pants. Then she looks at Shelly and me and runs into the cottage.

"And I thought you two were a good influence. Shelly, you're two years older, and Judith is a straight A student and here you both are smoking with her right under my nose.''

"We're sorry, Mrs. Gallagher," Shelly says.

"I've a good mind to tell your mothers, but I won't this time. Don't let it happen again, do you hear me?''

At the door of the cottage Bobby's waving pathetically at us behind the screen. Mrs. Gallagher sees her and starts to scream again. I wave back and then Shelly and I run off down the cement walk. We look over our shoulders and I start yelling, "Mrs. Gallagher is a meanie! She smokes like a chimney!" I shout all the mean sentences I can think of about Bobby's mother until Shelly and I are laughing so hard I have to stop. Then I say goodbye and walk puffing through the Unknown Desert to the Hanging Step. I'm not going to enter the competition to win Jay but I may have to go to the bonfire. Just to see what happens.

Aᴜɢᴜsᴛ 25ᴛʜ. Nᴏʙᴏᴅʏ ʜᴀs sᴀɪᴅ ᴀɴʏᴛʜɪɴɢ ᴀʙᴏᴜᴛ ᴛʜᴇ contest. I'm glad. I'm not looking forward to it. I want to put it out of my mind the way I shut out the golf championship at the Merton Country Club before I play it.

Rum Bum and I are collecting wood for the bonfire. We're down by the shore, near the Stepping Stones to Eternity. Bobby and Shelly are up in the bushes making sticks out of the poplar branches for roasting marshmallows. They're giggling a lot, as if they're friends—not enemies who hate each other's guts. Getting nervous must make you lower your standards.

"Dumb broads," Rum Bum whispers under his breath, so I can hear. Rum Bum is trying to be nice to me. I'm not impressed, though he's grown this summer; he's an inch taller than me. Mom says he's going to be a big man. His Bermuda shorts are too small and tight. When he thinks nobody is looking, he tugs at his crotch.

All of a sudden Bobby and Shelly stop giggling. An echo of sound reverberates on the water, then Jay's boat inches into view, trailing a line of white foam. One by one, we file down to the cove. Jay sees us and waves. When the bow hits the sand, Frank jumps out and throws the painter to Rum Bum, who shrugs because he doesn't know what to do with it. "Don't just stand there gawking," Frank says. "Help Jay carry the beer cooler. He doesn't want to get tired out yet." Frank laughs and wiggles his eyebrows knowingly; he's acting like he's a football coach and Jay is his quarterback. As for me, I'm scared to look at Jay in case he knows I'm thinking of the contest, but I look anyway and he takes my breath away. He's put on a lemon yellow sweater that matches his sun-bleached hair.

"Hi, Jude!" Jay smiles sleepily right at me. His Sailor Blue eyes look as if they know there's a triple-A cup Maidenform bra under my sweater. It surprises me that he is not looking at Bobby or Shelly.

He hands us each an opened beer. Behind us, Rum Bum struggles with the cooler. I stop and take a sip. Just to be polite.

"I don't see Macgregor. Good." Frank shows Rum Bum where to put the cooler and Jay laughs like he's gasping for air.

"He's gone back to the city," Bobby says. "To sulk." Jay takes a long swallow and then sits down by the sticks. He tosses his Zippo to Rum Bum, who lights the newspapers he's placed under the kindling. Then Frank pats the sand beside Jay and points to me as Jay laughs nervously again. Bobby and Shelly smile at me as I go and sit beside him. Jay shifts his bum so he's sitting close to my right hip. I smell Old Spice. When my father wears it, my mother says he smells like a tomcat.

"Anybody want me to roast them a marshmallow?" Frank looks around. Nobody says anything, not even Jay. Jay looks as shy as me. I expected him to be more confident.

"Marshmallows! We didn't come here for that," Rum Bum says.

"Shut up, Rum Bum. And do what Frank says," Bobby says. She thrusts her stick in the fire. Its three marshmallows catch fire instantly. Jay gasps and chokes. He's laughing a lot tonight. My hands are shaking. I drink my beer and stare at the Sound. The sun is setting, with a smudge like blood, uncomfortably close to its Back-to-School position on the horizon. I don't like to think about the fall back in Merton where nothing happens except spelling tests and snowstorms that toss the dead buds of the lilac bushes so they rattle against my bedroom window.

I sneak a little look at Jay. He is drinking his third beer, lying on his back. The bulge of his crotch in his yellow pants looks soft and hard at the same time and I can't help wondering what it would be like to touch. The idea of kissing him on his zipper is impossible, especially because of the way Jay is acting now—shy and embarrassed. There's not going to be a contest. Just a bonfire like all our old, boring bonfires, only Jay is sitting beside me. Shouldn't he get up and sit beside Shelly or Bobby? It shocks me to think a real man might like me. It's such a responsibility.

My God. Something brushed against me. Jay's hand. Uh-huh. Jay takes my hand and squeezes it. I shut my eyes. This isn't possible; he lifts my hand to his lips and kisses it. Then he carefully places my hand on his lap. Over his penis. I try to jerk my hand away but he holds it gently and presses it down on him. He shivers. What kind of girl does he think I am? Under my fingers, his thing twitches like it's alive. Everything is sliding out of control.

"I hope you win the contest, Jude. I'm a little nervous," Jay whispers. Then he sticks his tongue in my ear. Ugh. That felt awful. He sighs and kisses the tip of my nose.

"Hey, you two lovebirds. Show me how you smooch. Is it like this?" Rum Bum calls across the bonfire. Rum Bum suddenly grabs Shelly and tips back her head. Shelly laughs in surprise as Rum Bum squashes his face against hers and makes a wet slurping sound like Ben, Bobby's dog, eating his dinner.

"You're a disgrace to the male sex," Frank laughs. Jay moves my hand off his leg and holds it tightly between us. I'm scared I might die if I have to touch him again. Please Jay. No more scary stuff.

"Well, we've had the marshmallows," Bobby says. She lights a cigarette and lets it dangle from her lips. She's got on her sneer—the look that says "Duh, what's it to you?" "Who's going to be first?"

"Jude," Frank says. He nudges Jay and Jay opens another beer and hands it to me without looking at my eyes. I look away.

"You're going to do it, Jude?" Shelly asks.

"Of course she is. She's used to contests," Bobby says. She laughs and I tip up my beer bottle so the beer pours down my throat in a rush. Jay looks around, and then lies back on the sand. His eyes are half-closed, but he's watching me and smiling an anxious little smile. Bobby and Shelly are quiet. Rum Bum whistles and stares up at the stars, only there aren't any. The Big Dipper isn't out, not even the Little Dipper. The night sky is turning Absolute Black, the colour Mr. Munsell says is of lowest value. It possesses neither hue nor chroma. The closest thing to it is what you see when you look through a small aperture into a velvet-lined box.

A few minutes go by. Nobody moves. Frank says, "Come on. Let's get this show on the road." Jay stands up and begins to undress. He takes off his yellow slacks, carefully folds them and looks around nervously. Frank grabs them and hands them to Rum Bum.

"What am I supposed to do with these?" Rum Bum says.

"Eat them," Frank says. Jay has nothing on now but a jockstrap. It's white and mesh. You can see through the holes and the skin of his penis and balls looks very hairy. I don't want to look there.

"Ready to tee off, Jude?" Frank says.

I stare blankly at Bobby and she smiles and nods. I don't know how to give a blow job. I want to giggle. But I think of something really terrible like Ben, Bobby's dog, getting hit by a car so I don't laugh.

"It's better if you get on your knees," Jay whispers.

Knees? I thought he would be on his back and I would crouch over him the way Bobby said Mona did in the bushes. I don't move and Jay places his hands on my shoulders and pushes me gently down on the sand until I'm kneeling in front of him. He's standing very close. My head is level with his jockstrap. Then he takes my hands and puts them around his balls. He shakes my hands and makes them tug off the jockstrap. His penis springs out like a cuckoo bird. It smells sickeningly sweet, like armpit sweat covered up with Old Spice. I should jump up and run away but I can't leave now. I've gone too far.

Jay puts his hands under my chin and lifts it so my lips touch IT. I shut my eyes and he puts his hand behind my head and pushes my face into his crotch. I hear Bobby gasp behind me.

"Jude. Open up."

I don't know what Jay's talking about. Gently his fingers pry my mouth open. Oh. My mouth. He runs his fingers in and out over my teeth so I can feel the whorl of lines on his fingers. Suddenly his penis fills my mouth. I jerk away but Jay grabs my ears and holds my head tight against him. Shelly is screaming and Rum Bum is laughing hysterically. I hear their shouts like background music. Jay pushes his penis back and forth in my mouth as if he wants to come out of the other side of my head. I try to move my head but Jay's holding onto my ears. I stare up at the bottom of his chin.

Jay is sighing and saying words under his breath, as if he's talking to himself while he's sticking his penis down my throat. It's choking me. I didn't think it would be this bad. I put my hands on Jay's knees and pull away with all my might. He lets go of my ears and his penis falls out of my mouth. It sprays my face with icky stuff which sticks to me like glue. Jay falls to his knees making funny sounds as if he can't talk very well. He puts his hands on his crotch and sits back on the sand with a thud. Then somebody says, "Jude fell for it," and everyone laughs. I look up. The sticky stuff is starting to dry on my face. It makes my face tight like the beauty masks my mother puts on.

"What do you mean?" I hear myself say.

"There was no contest. Everybody knew you'd do it cuz you like to win," Bobby says. "You had it coming. You're getting too big for your britches." I sigh a little and put my face down between my knees. I can feel my shoulders shaking so I know I'm crying. I'm making a howling noise too but it feels like it is coming from somebody else—not me. Then I feel a hand on my shoulder.

"Get out of my way," somebody says. A knee brushes my back and Shelly walks over to Jay and puts one leg on either side of his waist. Her bare bum gleams in the moonlight. Shelly has no pants on. No—it is not Shelly! It is Bobby! I pull up onto my elbows and look over at them through the bonfire. The sticky stuff is cracking now over my face and some of the stuff's in my hair.

Bobby is sitting on Jay. She's bouncing up and down like a yo-yo. Jay's hands cup Bobby's bottom and help her bounce. Then his hands lift her off him and move her up his chest and onto his face. Bobby makes a funny panting noise and all of a sudden I can't watch any more, I run off into the bushes, throwing up all over the sand, all over me. The bushes shake but it's only Ben, Bobby's dog, come to find me. Ben licks my face and I pull him close and hide my face in the fur by his neck.

I walk slowly up the path to my cottage. The others have gone home and Jay's boat is a droning sound in the distance. In the living room my mother is playing solitaire. The reading lamp makes a halo of light around her, and my mother's voice floats out through the screen. She's singing her favourite tune—the answer to "Daisy, Daisy, give me your answer do!"

> Charlie, Charlie,
> Here is your answer true—
> I'm not crazy—
> All for the love of you.

It's very quiet in the shadows. A mosquito hums over white geraniums at the end of the flowerbox. I'm sweating, and I smell of beer and sex.

My mother lifts her head and looks out at me although I know she isn't really looking at me. She can't see me but I draw back just the same and she looks down again at her cards. She is smiling as she turns over the Queen of Spades, crooning the last few lines which I used to like to sing so I could say the word damn without her getting angry:

> I do want a stylish marriage.
> I also want a carriage.
> And I'll be damned if I'll be crammed
> On a bicycle built for two.

Before I can stop myself, I make a little sobbing noise and Mom looks into the darkness again. I hold my breath and then she dips a silver spoon into a little bowl of strawberry jam and spreads jam on a saltine cracker, smiling with her red smudged lips. Maybe Bobby is right. Maybe she puts it on that way on purpose.

Then a door opens and my father walks into the room. He

has on his old blue terrycloth dressing gown with the terrycloth tie. It's just like the one Karl Frank wears when he ravishes Monika. Only my father isn't wearing the tie tonight. The robe is open and I can see his privates even though they are in shadow. I don't know why I say "they," as if privates are plural. He's only got one basic thing.

I feel very hot. My cheeks are hot, my hands are hot. What is he doing home, tonight of all nights, when I need my mother? And why is he walking around our house like that! He looks like the dopey safe man I call Dad from the neck up. But from the waist down, he looks like an old spider dragging its hairy wrinkled sac across the sand to the blonde and perfect goddess of summer.

I suck in my breath and will my mother to rebuke him. Wheel around and sock the wrinkled spider in the heart of his wrinkly old sac! My mother turns slowly and lifts her head and then my father bends over and presses his mouth against hers. Then he places his hand just where I don't want him to place it, on my mother's breast. Suddenly, my father looks out the window as if he's heard me.

"Jude! Are you out there?" His shadow looms out through the screen, three times as long as me.

"Yes," I answer. I walk up the steps slowly as if I'm just coming in the door.

"You're home early," my mother says as I walk through the living room. "Did you have a nice time?"

"Nothing special," I answer. I walk quickly into the dim kitchen so they can't see my face. Some of Jay's stuff is still in my hair. I pray it's not noticeable to the human eye. Mom waves at the tray of cheddar cheese and Saltine crackers and jam. She smiles with her vermilion lips.

"Do you want a snack, dear?"

"No thanks."

"Is anything wrong, Jude?"

"Not especially." I walk into the bathroom and pick up the jug of water and start to scrub my face as if it will never be clean again.

SEPTEMBER 1ST. THE BEACH IS BLANK AGAIN. EVERYBODY has gone except the Gallaghers, who are leaving in a few hours. Bobby sent me a note saying she is coming to say good-bye, so I'm hiding at Look-Out Pine. I want to be by myself.

I take out my Karl Frank story and begin to write:

"Aha," Frank cried gleefully. "I see you wanted to come in after all. Don't try to run away from old Karl now. You love old Karl Frank, don't you?"

He bent over her and Monika's eyes rolled in terror; she looked for some way of escape but there was none. She could only lie sprawled on her back and hope Frank would leave her alone.

I feel mean putting Monika in a compromising position, like I'm twisting off the arm of my doll. But I have no choice; I have to boss poor old Monika around. Call me cruel if you like.

Down the beach, the breeze is still warm but the Sound has turned its silvery fall colour. It looks like the colour Mr. Munsell calls Steel Grey but it's really Smoke Grey if you examine it closely. Last night I watched the sun set from here. It set far out on the open water, in the Back-to-School position behind the Second Point. And today the wiggly golden brown lines of the ski trails are visible on the Blue Mountains behind the Sound. It's the first time the air has been clear enough to see the trails. The air is so sharp I can also make out the speckled coats of the baby gulls standing with the grey and white adult birds on the deserted sandbar.

Summer has fooled me again. When I'm in the middle of it, it will last for ever. I get sick of it and wish it was over. Then it's gone and I feel a thousand echoey pains inside me. Pains that are too old and sad to belong to the heart of a teenaged girl.

Wait. There's somebody on the beach now. I see Bobby by the Polliwog Pond. She's wearing a low-cut yellow sundress, and her bleached hair is combed back in a ponytail. She looks older, standing there emptying sand from a pair of high-heeled shoes she's carrying in her hand. I long to run and throw myself at her feet, to admit defeat to my rival, my enemy, and only great love, but instead I start to write again.

When Monika saw escape was impossible, she began to cry. Her whole body was racked with violent sobs.

"Please Frank," she implored, "don't touch me. Oh, oh—oh—oh!" Her voice broke into soft, useless weeping.

The old man in his drunken stupor ignored her plea. He'd no call for pity. He never had. His fleshy arms encircled the taut young body, drawing it off the damp ground. Plod, plod, plod. . . . His footsteps sounded grimly on the soggy leaf-covered debris as he carried the young girl to his destination—the bedroom of his weatherbeaten old house.

"Dinger! Dinger!" Bobby calls.
I don't look up; I'm still writing.

Once inside his weatherbeaten structure, the old man threw Monika carelessly on the half-made camp cot.

"I'll get us sump'n to drink on, eh Harmonica?" he laughed. "Maybe a little snort of whisky. You'd like that, wouldn't ya? I don't like to drink alone, see." He winked wickedly. "And then you'll be ready to give me the blow job you promised me. Remember?"

Monika, paralysed with fear, said nothing.

I stop for a moment. Why does she just lie there? He hasn't tied her up. Maybe he'd better tie her arms to the bed with skipping rope again.

"Jude? Can you hear me?"

Bobby's voice floats near me on the wind. She calls my name two more times and I close my eyes and count to a thousand steamboats so I won't be tempted to answer. One steamboat . . . two steamboats . . . three steamboats . . . four steamboats . . . five steamboats. . . . When I can't hear her any more, I put down my story and watch her walk off down the shore.

I wave at her even though she is just a speck on the long line of yellow sand and then Bobby disappears and the beach looks blond and straight and still, a blank strip as narrow as a racetrack—the way I always think of it when I am back in Merton.

PART TWO

Winning

"For if she runs away, soon she shall run after,
if she shuns gifts, she shall give,
if she does not love you, soon she shall even
against her own will."

So come to me now, free me from this aching pain,
fulfill everything that
my heart desires to be fulfilled: you, yes you,
will be my ally.

—Fragment 78, from Section Six,
Goddess of Love

1 969. AHEAD ON U-GO-I-GO SOUND A YACHT IS MOVING slowly west to the horizon, where the rock humps of the Watchers lie like fallen Indian gods in the water. The yacht inches towards a cluster of sailboats which billow and flutter like white cabbage butterflies on a plate of fresh water. You see only bare backs and the dark balls of heads sitting on shoulders, but I am waiting for you in that clump of bodies. Your yacht pulls aside mine. You climb noiselessly up the swimming ladder, pad slowly over in your canvas sneakers, and discover me lying on the floor of the yacht offering up my body to you like a prayer. I am lying in legs that grow out of cut-off jeans and diaper-shaped bikinis . . . long brown legs glistening with suntan oil . . . shiny, moist legs covered with light hair like peach fuzz, or red, sunburnt legs peeling with flakes of opaque skin . . . white and dead as old birch bark. I am lying so close to the legs I can peel away the flavourless skin with my teeth and eat it. The striated texture is pleasing to the tongue. And underneath the old layer, the new skin is as pink as a baby tomato.

Near me a slender man stands holding a film camera. I am uncertain of my beauty, but in the lens of his camera I float like a golden-limbed summer creature with masses of long hair as yellow as sand, and eyes that shine like July skies.

I beckon with an oil-creamed arm and you lie down beside me. I want you to stay lost with me in this void of pleasure where we can be as single-minded as insects and not admit that time is creeping by us bit by bit out here in the open, inching in its eternal way like the yacht moving towards the billowing sails of the lasers. At this moment, you are not X years old, you are only X summers old.

Ignore the roar of the launch motor which makes you feel you are inside a giant wooden drum. And let the odour of gasoline drift by your nostrils. It evokes Evinrude motors, mosquito repellent, and the sensual feel of a wet bathing suit. Soon it will become the smell of pleasure. Behind our yacht, the huge funnel-shaped crest of the lake sparkles with diamond slivers of light.

I show you how to grasp the cloudy plastic glass loosely between the thumb and forefinger so it will rock with the motion of the yacht and not spill. The wine in the glass shimmers and quivers in a constant silvery-gold motion. You suspend the glass over me so it swings like a bell-clapper in the air, threatening at any second to discharge icy wine onto my bronze stomach. I could smash it out of your hand but instead I stick my finger into the glass and retrieve a sliver of ice. I trail the ice along your shoulder. Now I dab the ice on your belly button, then run my wet fingers along your bare thigh. . . .

You sigh helplessly and stare up through the frosted bottom of your drink glass. You have no responsibility except to submit to this timeless summer moment when anything is possible.

You are too dazed to notice me roll off laughing into the thicket of legs. The iced wine, the scorching sun, the rocking motion of the boat are confusing you. You realize you can't tell the masculine calves from the feminine. Some calves are clean-shaven and yet plumped out like soccer balls inside the skin. Others are thin but still knotted with muscle. Still others are hairy muscular trunks streaming into stump-like feet with no narrowing at the ankles.

You raise your eyes, but even at pelvis level you can't distinguish the sex of the swaying torsos half-covered with colourful triangles that swell with intriguing bumps and ridges. You notice a fully-packed red triangle stretched taut so the five-pointed shape of a maple leaf is visible over a long cylinder with a bump at one end. You have detected a man. Left dress, you note.

You look higher. Aha. The male stomachs are hairy and flat. The female stomachs are flat and not hairy. Then you realize one female stomach is swollen. But isn't the pregnant stomach a surprise? It is not a shimmying jelly-like growth but a bulge of fluid muscle.

Bewildered, you look up at the faces. Child Cape is the face closest to you—an androgynous sunburnt oval beneath a tie-dyed headband. Child's face makes you think of Struwwelpeter, the naughty boy in the German children's story who was beaten with a birch rod. The tie-dyed band circles like a halo branches of feathery hair that stick out over his head. The face beside Child's makes you think of apes and cylinders. Rubbery ears poke out from a blond, egg-shaped head. The forehead slopes and the deep jaw has a cleft in the square chin. The owner of the primate's face is Bull Cape, Bobby's husband. Bobby's face belongs to the blown-up stomach. You take in the light pink lipstick smeared on the sulky, parted mouth, the tanned honey-brown skin, the hanks of platinum hair foaming out from under a floppy canvas hat.

Then you hear a noise like an explosion. Surging through the billowing sailboats is a new boat. The name Jonah Prince is spelled out in gold letters on its bow. A blur of heads bobs behind its spray-soaked windshield. Is it two heads? Or is it three?

The racing boat surges closer, weaving left and right like a demonic waterskier inside the sparkling crest of our wake. Then slowly, out of the thicket of our bodies, an apelike hand uncurls and points a pistol at the heads behind the windshield of the other boat. You wait for somebody to do something. You stare at the gun. The sun gleams on its barrel. You hear the thunk of the bullet as it hits the fiberglass hull of the racing boat. You are surprised that nobody says anything—a yell, a gasp, some-thing—but nobody does. Our brown heads swivel slowly on brown necks and stare at the intruder, our mouths open, our faces constricted in fear.

Bobby screams, "Look out!" as the racing boat surges closer

and almost touches our stern. Child Cape lifts his camera to his shoulder and now a man's exulting face peers through the shimmering windshield. Then the boat veers left and flies thirty feet through the air, landing with a smack near the sailboats and throwing them into confusion.

"Three of our boats have dumped," Bull says into a radio phone. "We'll have to cancel the race."

The intruder picks up speed and roars north. For the first time you notice you are wet. Rivulets of yellow wine stream across your abdomen down into the cloth of your suit. In the fracas, you spilled your glass. You turn and spy me again standing next to Child Cape. My narrow brown face looks at you menacingly, half in sunlight, half in the shadows cast by an inky blue ball of cloud that has drifted across the sun. You blink at the vision of my long blonde hair and eerie dappled face. You will not forget that vision—I promise you. Then the clouds float away and sunlight floods the deck again and you laugh and raise your glass for a fresh charge of wine. There is only summer and it is fat and wide and huge and hot and you are lost in the middle of its stretchiness, spinning and dreaming in hot air and hot water and hot rock and hoping you won't have to come to your senses again.

Friday, 2:15 p.m.

The ride home was over before you knew it. It took less than eight minutes for our yacht to leave behind the milling sailboats and head for our island, slicing east past Sauna Island through the sparkling waters of Laughing Dog Channel. You are standing on the old dock at Good Cheer. Its sagging timbers feel springy under your feet. The island is before you, but squinting into the sun you see just the water-stained timbers of the old dock, sagging under the weight of the plastic-coated chairs and chaise lounges. The ochre planters drip coral pink geraniums. Behind the water-stained dock sits the clapboard boat house where bats cheep in the rafters.

Then you hear voices. A man and two women are lounging in chaises and canvas director's chairs under a red and white Coca-Cola umbrella. The man is talking in a too hearty voice.

The women sip from crystal goblets red with sangria. Up on the pine-lined bluff, workmen are hammering on a huge white dome that looks like a splintered Easter egg. The top half is missing. A half-built frame of wooden dowels covers its base. Bodies hang off the scaffolding shouting at one another.

Their voices irritate you. You resent being back on dry land, in the midst of human activity. The wine has left a grapy ache in the back of your throat and your sunburnt back feels itchy. You walk groggily over to where we sit under the Coca-Cola umbrella. You stop and put on your sunglasses. Ah, that's better. You recognize me by my red bikini and then you spot Bobby sunning herself beside a pair of mustard-coloured dobermans. Isn't it surprising the way her stomach surges over the triangle of her bikini like an astonished chocolate face? The belly button sticking out in a point is the nose. The orange V of the bikini bottom is the mouth. The two circles of cloth on the breasts, puffy orange eyes. You are a little astonished at how virginal I seem next to Bobby, who looks like a vixen in a B movie. You gawk at her breasts shaped like plump zucchinis and her tanned globular belly.

Bobby bespeaks activity behind closed doors while I project innocence. Go on. Don't stop. Compare Bobby and me, body part by body part. We are all objects who come in different shapes and sizes. And I take pride in the part of my being that is pure objectness. My wrists and ankles are as slim as the forelegs of a deer. I have no stretch marks but I have borne no children. And my breasts are as small as a boy's. That's a strike against me. I am also slightly horse-faced with big, sincere eyes. My left eye is a shade more blue than my right. That's another defect. Still, I have a good face as faces go. Sometimes I forget that I have become what is considered good looking. At twenty-four, I still think of myself as a sexual loser.

This is also me to the extent that I can know myself: intense, disarmingly candid, a newspaper journalist with a hesitant speaking manner that doesn't hide a nature inclined toward dichotomies. There is I the iconoclast who never wants to hurt anyone's feelings, and I the doer and I the dreamer. Not to mention I the theoretician or I the lotus-eater and I the Puritan—and, of course, I the truth-teller and I the liar. You motion me to be quiet. You have already picked up on my habit of telling you more than you want to know.

And this is Bobby: moody, generous, a maverick who seeks the setting of a conformist to express herself. At twenty-six, Bobby is the mother of Neil (seven) and Shasta (three). Bobby had a shotgun marriage at nineteen but she still thinks of herself as a sexual winner despite the role of matron she plays in her family. She is the second wife of James Bill (alias Bull) Cape who doesn't look the part but whose father is one of the richest men in North America. The Cape manufacturing firm produces pianos internationally acclaimed for their craftsmanship, and a postage-sized photograph of Sir James can be found in the navy blue encyclopedia that lists important Canadians. It sits above paragraphs strung with initials like a moronic alphabet, listing the radio station and newspaper he owns as well as the charity and business organizations his wife persuaded him to join. Lady Cape is not in the encyclopedia, but it mentions her father, Theodore Lefroy, who turned the old Lefroy Carriage Works into an automobile manufacturing plant and then sold it to General Motors. Today Lady Cape runs the Lefroy Foundation established by Theodore to promote the development of peace and stable government, a mandate with a sentimental resemblance to the founding mandate of Canada.

I am sitting close enough to the son of Sir James and Lady Cape to pinch the hairy, brown stomach bulging over the top of his fully packed Speedo bathing suit. Of course, I'd never interfere like that, but I feel the impulse to tell him to sit up straight for you. With a background like his, he should watch his posture. Nobody would guess we are looking at the remains of a gold medal winner who once rose like a grimacing Captain Marvel out of an Olympic pool—his teeth bared and his eyes glittering like a ferret under an egg-shaped white bathing cap.

He must sense us watching because he picks up a magazine so it blocks the view of his stomach. It is *Time* he's reading? No. The name says *Maclean's*. Isn't it odd? An American newsmagazine has a name that denotes urgency and the Canadian newsmagazine sounds like a brand of Scottish cough drops. One name suggests historical context and the other announces the imminence of the present moment. The names represent strategies for leaving behind our ancestors in the Old Country. Americans pretend there is no past to lose and Canadians ward off the hurt of separation by evolving the past through nostalgic gestures.

You amble over to where I am sitting only to see me lean forward and peer at something skimming the pale blue surface of Laughing Dog Channel. Is it a log or a buoy marker? You look again. I am watching a yellow head skimming the pale blue surface of the channel, neck extended the way water-snakes swim.

Frustrated, you turn to Bobby, who yawns in your face and picks up a hot dog from an ironstone platter. The mustard on the dried-out bun shines like a yellow paint gloss. "It's overcooked," Bobby says in a nasal Ontario accent and tosses it to one of the dobermans whose jaws immediately turn brassy yellow. Scowling, Bobby picks up a novel whose title you spy in spidery red letters: *The Great Gatsby.*

Won't anyone notice you? You walk over to Bull, slumped in his canvas director's chair. He tilts his beer can upside down so the last drops sprinkle his tongue. Now he places his right leg across his left knee and begins to poke at the dirt under his toenail with the nail of his index finger. All at once you feel defeated by the indifference of these characters. You step dizzily under the shingled eave and sit down slowly, your itchy back sliding bump, bump, bump, against the clapboard edges of the old boat house.

Good, you are succumbing. The passive quality in your nature is the very reason you are here. I used to think of you as an imaginary friend, but the proper term for you is reader. Old Voyeur Eyes is my name for you. Naturally you have a body and your own sensations. Would I be so insensitive as to consign you to a narrow psychological reality, Old V.E.? You are my ally and necessary witness.

Frankly, I am a little disheartened by the failure of glamour I perceive around me. If only Bull would sit imposingly, like King Canute, and shout, waving his beer can like a sceptre, "Be still!" to the constant lap of water against the dock. And why doesn't Bobby sound like Daisy Buchanan, Scott Fitzgerald's heroine, whose voice tinkled and jingled of money and who cried over Gatsby's silk shirts before she left him in the lurch for her brutish husband, Tom? I am, like you, accustomed to the faces and bodies of the other family of Irish immigrants synonymous with wealth. The bluntly masculine heads of the American Kennedys with their incandescent smiles.

After all, on the level of fantasy, the rich are invincible. And I crave fantasy. I secretly want to believe that young multimillionaires have silver dollars for their nipples and their come tastes like white Swiss chocolate. Or that, when nobody is looking, a man like Bull dives into a room stuffed with dollar bills—like Unca Scrooge in a Donald Duck comic. But I must forgo childish yearnings. At least the self-made rich of the United States don't have mirror images elsewhere. These unimposing characters prove we *do* have an indigenous culture. Anyway, I'm too preoccupied to care about refuting American imperialism. As your narrator, I am obliged to get on with the story and make our unmythical characters talk. And they are doing all they can to look middle class, to prove Hemingway was right when he told Fitzgerald there is nothing different about the rich except they have more money. I stare expectantly at Bull who pushes his sunglasses back on his head so I can see the circles under his close-set blue eyes. Bull looks hung over but he smiles gamely, revealing large, uneven teeth.

I will try to engage his attention. "Who was that man?" I ask, sipping my wine.

Bull opens another beer can and obliges by looking right into my eyes. "It was that crazy kike," he says in a low voice.

As soon as Bull says kike, Bobby puts down her novel and stretches so her stomach bobs before my eyes, vast as a planet. Everybody directs glances of morbid fascination at Bobby's stomach when they think she isn't watching. But knowing Bobby, there is no reason to feel uneasy. I have heard her laugh at the gaping dock-boys in Indian Harbour who have never seen a pregnant woman before in a bikini.

"You fired a real bullet, didn't you?" Bobby groans and puts on a pair of purple sunglasses with a sprinkling of rhinestones spelling out the initials "B.C."

"I have to go to the can," Bull says crossly. His thonged feet slap the dock. Then our unmythical hero stoops and gradually—

ever so imperceptibly—revolves his buttocks in our direction. "Fuck Jonah Prince anyhow." Now—his back to us—he begins to pee into the shallow water at the end of the dock.

Jonah Prince. For the second time you come across the name of the man in the orange boat who has obsessed Bobby the way Daisy Buchanan obsessed Gatsby. Perhaps Bobby is even more obsessed with Jonah Prince. Or is it men who need women to feel complete, while our sexuality ticks on—each female body a self-sufficient universe? No. The more I think about it, the more certain I am that it is a woman like Bobby, not a man like Gatsby, who is the real candidate for fidelity to the past.

If you look closely at the cover of *Maclean's* you will see the deeply smiling face of her idol, Jonah Prince, as merry as a sun god with protuberant eyes floating on a backdrop sprinkled with winged dollars. Jonah Prince is an immigrant whose success was of no interest to the Capes until he purchased One Tree Island and erected a deluxe Panabode—the eyesore, as Sir James calls it—on a piece of rock so small it is hardly more than a shoal. It intrudes on the Capes' once unbroken view of the open.

"The word 'kike' is ignorant and you know it," Bobby says in her nasal voice. "Isn't it, Dinger?"

"I wasn't paying attention," I sigh and light up a cigarette, stalling for time.

Ordinarily, Bobby takes no position on social or political issues. She wouldn't have felt the need to challenge the use of kike if I weren't sitting next to her. She relies on my intellect and I couldn't manage without her blunt talk because I can lose myself in complexities. I need somebody like Bobby, who doesn't mind sounding definite on my behalf.

Meanwhile, I was remembering Child's letter, which I received this week:

Dear Jude,

If you come to Good Cheer for regatta weekend, I promise I will accept your decision to end what you call "our unforgivable situation". The reason for coming up announced itself this morning: Shelly is not feeling well and decided to stay in the city for the weekend.

We don't need to make excuses to go off alone. You can always say you are interviewing me for the book even though I don't give a damn about Mother's little project. (Which isn't to say I'm not grateful to it for bringing you to me.) If you give in to this cajoling, I swear old C.C. will go back to the shoot in Fogo Island a happy man. Do not, though, arrive with a companion. Last night, I awoke from a dream in which you got off the dock arm-in-arm with that old wind-bag, Higgins Rochester.

In my dream, you stood enchanting the group in stony indifference to me while Rochester, the asshole, announced: "Jude and I are spending the weekend together." I'm totalled by this but manage to croak, "Far out! Do you dig him?" You roll your eyes in a way that says, "I just got laid one hundred times in twenty different positions out of the Kama Sutra, including the Chinese basket twirl." I awoke sitting bolt upright and sweaty, not because you were unfaithful (you know yours truly doesn't put lasting stock in sexual fidelity) but because Rochester had captured the permanence and constancy that is denied me.

Your C.

P.S. In my dream, Rochester had on his Chairman Mao cap. (A Mao cap on a charlatan like Rochester is an affront to the great chairman. May a hundred flowers bloom!)

Beside me, Bobby pokes my arm. "Stop day-dreaming," she says. "Isn't kike watchamacallit—anti-septic?"

I pause and inhale a fresh lungful of candy sweet smoke. A myriad of voices are struggling to express themselves inside my boyish bosom. I, the executioner, want me to stab Bull through the heart for denigrating the Jewish race. But, I the merciful, want to encourage Bobby to give her husband the benefit of the doubt.

"Well, nobody says, 'You rotten Christian'. And why does Bull identify his anger at Jonah with his Jewishness?

"On the other hand, I wouldn't call Bull a bigot as I understand the term, but his lack of experience makes him dwell on difference. In a cosmopolitan world, difference wouldn't be worth mentioning." I exhale and look regretfully into Bobby's rhinestone sunglasses. It's hard to be nice these days and get away with it. Thanks to Freud, people think you are disguising an ulterior motive. So I'm nice on the sly and try to treat things with the same know-it-all *savoir-faire* as everybody else.

"Jude, you always stick up for Bull," Bobby groans and I feel a little quiver of betrayal. She was relying on me to help her sabotage her husband.

"That's not because Jude likes me over you," Bull says. "She's just interested in defending the underdog."

Up on the bluff, there is a frustrated sound like a cow bellowing and Bobby calls to a girl eating a hot dog at a discreet distance from us behind an overturned white canoe. The girl is Bobby's nanny, Sally Love—a real angel puss and a vegetarian who is too polite to tell her employer she doesn't eat junk food.

"Tilly is lost again. And find the children too."

When she is out of sight Bull calls over his shoulder.

"Did you know Sally can't swim?"

"What's it to you?" Bobby says. She gestures at my pack of menthols. "Dinger?" she hisses. "Hurry. Before he sees."

Notice how preoccupied I am as I lean forward and light Bobby's cigarette without so much as a glance her way. The gesture looks like an old duty, as if my heart isn't in it. At the end of the dock my object choice is climbing the swim ladder like a shiny wet water creature. Do you frown at the word object? Relax, do not worry. Object choice is an egalitarian term I made up; it means the one you desire. An appreciator of our unique object form exists for each of us. Child Cape is returning from a skinny dip across Laughing Dog Channel. Child Cape is Bull's youngest brother. He makes documentary films about underprivileged communities with a satisfying stuff-it-up-your-ass style that appeals to my radical tendencies. Not that I am political, like others of my generation. The conflict I feel over wanting middle-class benefits and feeling sorry for the disadvantaged fills me with a self-loathing that stops me from acting.

Now the man at the end of the dock turns his back and I see the white gleam of his untanned bum. I stare there, waiting to glimpse what I know so well—the soft dangle of skin between his thighs. Child tosses his feathery blond hair and the silver dog whistle on his green translucent love beads swings crazily in the hollow between his nipples. Grinning, Child swaddles his narrow hips in his terrycloth towel and begins to walk towards me.

The dock shakes slightly under his feet. My love is my height but he weighs a great deal less than me. I turn his way, sighing. No, I can't give him up, not this man with the gauzy lemon hair of an angel. I lean back and only you witness the desperate press of my oiled shoulders against his towelled thigh. The others see me, Jude Bell, smiling a little inquisitively at the renegade of the Cape family, whose apple-cheeked face is as smooth and as bland as a model in a department-store catalogue.

Child returns the pressure of my shoulder with his knee and pulls on a long-sleeved jersey. Child Cape avoids the sun because he doesn't want a tan, the imprimatur of wealth and leisure.

"Jonah Prince is back, everybody," Child says. "We'd better draw up a new sailing race."

"That is if Bull doesn't kill Prince off first." Bobby refills my glass of sangria and smiles at me knowingly. "Did you know he fired a real bullet at the Thunderbird?"

"You fired a real bullet?" Child asks.

"What if I did?" Bull says. "What kind of mother smokes and deprives her child of oxygen? Her own nanny has more sense than she does."

"Leave Sally out of it," Child says. "I want to know why you did it."

"I ran out of blanks," Bull mutters grumpily. "Don't tell Joyce, okay?"

"Oh, let's drop it," Bobby says, exhaling from both nostrils. "I want to hear what *Maclean's* has to say about Prince. Jude, would you?" I open *Maclean's* and wink at Bobby.

Jonah Prince: the entrepreneur whose racing boat design has revolutionized the sport.

Once a hospital orderly who took a second job picking bottles off the street to feed his immigrant parents, Prince now has houses on four continents and a multinational company. Its profit-sharing schemes are making his name synonymous with the new order of business leaders featured in this issue as ''The Young Aquarians''.

I stop and hold up the magazine. "Oh, here's a picture of Prince on One Tree Island. The caption says, 'Prince's high-powered Thunderbird is a familiar sight to cottagers near Indian Harbour. "Being on the water is the only thing that relaxes me," Prince says. "When you're out on the Sound nothing else exists." ' "

"I'm sick of hearing about that phony. He used to run guns to the Arabs with a man named Salomon. What do you think of a man who sells guns to the enemy of his own people, Bobby? Prince doesn't even go by his real name. It's Preischmann." Bull grabs the *Maclean's* and throws it on the dock.

"I think we should ask him to the regatta anyway," Bobby says. "What do you think, Jude?"

"I don't care what you do," I say. "Competitions are boring. Why waste energy choosing a winner from equals?"

"You don't mean that," Bobby says. "I remember the way you used to play golf. You like to win as much as the next person."

Suddenly, from the east, comes a loud drumming sound. The noise echoes back and forth across the channel. We look east past the tip of the boat house. The drum noise swells as two blobs crawl into view at the east end of the channel. One blob is white. It is an old dory. The other blob is orange and shaped like a phallus. Child puts his hand on my shoulder. "The swami must have run out of gas again," he smiles.

"It's the Thunderbird towing them." Bull jumps to his feet and stares at the approaching procession. Heads in the orange boat confer with heads in the dory as the procession makes a U-turn. Two heads . . . there are two heads. One is bald, grinning. The other is brunette, younger, a girl's head. Now the bald man is on his feet. The noise of the motor dies. The bald man walks to the back of the racing boat. The head pauses, confers again with heads in the dory. Then the man hands the painter to a dark-skinned body in the bow.

Beside me, Bobby stretches out a trembling arm. "Hello, Jonah," she calls in a child-like voice.

The bald man in the orange boat waves as the long racing boat drifts in behind the dory. A white-haired woman, her sinewy neck strung with water lilies, is poling in the stern of the dory. Marvellous legs, the legs of a young beauty queen, protrude from under a green chintz bathing suit. Flaps cover her crotch and her bum. Her wiry arms and chest are covered with brown age spots. It's Lady Cape—or Joyce, as her sons call her. She turns and says something to the dark-skinned person.

This is the swami. I am not fond of the swami, even though this morning I dreamt he levitated by the orange calla lilies near the old boat house. In my dream he wore a saffron robe and his soft hands were folded in prayer position as he slowly ascended to heaven. I watched in awe until his peach-coloured soles dangled above my head. The soles were smeared yellow with lily pollen. But this afternoon, as the swami grabs the dock and ties the painter to the ring, he looks like a cheap little Indian businessman in need of exercise. I am repelled by the way his hairy breasts droop over the edge of his pink robe. The swami is a sugar addict who experiments with hallucinogenic drugs. This afternoon Bobby and I saw little cellophane packets of morning glory seeds next to empty boxes of Black Magic chocolates in his cabin. Lady Cape's guru only does his breathing exercises now and neglects his asanas. Long ago he forgave himself for his physical imperfections.

The swami ascends the ladder with triumphant flourishes of his hands, as if he knows all eyes are on him. Then he folds his hands behind his back and tilts his head skyward in studied concentration. He begins to walk back and forth, patrolling the end of the dock. His salmon pink robe billows behind him. Lady Cape ascends the ladder unaided. The swami stops walking and opens his mouth so I see his salmon-coloured tongue.

"Young journalist," he giggles. "Today is another day closer to . . . closer to . . . closer . . . ?" He waits, grinning, for me to answer. I am perplexed by his Socratic method and turn to Bobby.

"To immortality." Lady Cape gives the response for me.

The swami nods. "What must we do if we want to reach the twenty-first century?"

Again I am stumped. Behind his huge domed forehead the racing boat of Jonah Prince is docking by the swim ladder.

"Serve, love, meditate, realize," Lady Cape says, and looks my way gleefully, a full frontal look so I see head-on her bony, red-lipped face. She is Child's mother and the island deity who allows no discouraging words. Who makes the geraniums coral pink instead of vermilion, the wineglasses crystal instead of plastic, and has decreed that there will be no television on the island to distract us from the pleasures of island life.

I detect a fellow optimist in her determined grin . . . a dreamer who sees in us all potential converts to Joyce Truth's (alias Joyce Cape's) view of the world. It's an ideology that involves me deeply because it tries to accommodate the opposing principles of freedom and justice, of tolerance and conviction, lightly topped off with notions of good Christian behaviour . . . in short, the democratic view.

But there is no time left to contemplate Lady Cape. Jonah Prince is climbing the swing ladder. The spray has drenched his gauzy Indian shirt so it clings to him sexily, revealing a tight woollen bathing suit. I spot an orange crown to the left of the crotch. It looks like a designer's emblem but the design is hardly visible through the gauzy shirt. At the top of the ladder, he stops and holds out his hand to his companion. She also has on a thin Indian shirt which comes to her thighs. It is no doubt his. She looks very young, perhaps a year or two older than Sally Love, but she emanates the atmosphere of high fashion. Her mouth is outlined in brown eyebrow pencil. Her short dark hair is combed back like a boy's. The angular planes of her face are charming.

"*Ciao,*" Bobby shouts.

"*Ciao.*" Jonah Prince smiles. He looks like a member of a species more evolved than other men. His hairless body is elegant and he emphasizes its streamlined shape by sucking in his stomach muscles. Up close, I see he has white eyebrows, which make him look like a cat. Nor is he really bald. Silver curls ring the back of his skull. The silver looks glamorous against his tan. I look dizzily into the wise protuberant eyes and reel back from the force of his vitality. It feels like something is going to happen just by being around him.

"Isn't it superb to be here?" he says. I realize with disappointment that he is talking to Bobby. "I miss U-Go-I-Go like a lover." He blinks his cat eyes. " 'How did the Sound look?' That's what I ask people who've just come back. You know, the way you ask a friend who has just seen your old lover? Is she still beautiful? Does she still wear hammered silver earrings?' "

The swami is not as impressed by Jonah Prince as I am. He stops for a minute, then leans suspiciously out over the dock and looks down into the yellow vinyl interior of the racing boat. It is padded with vinyl on the sides, like a child's playpen. I lean over and look down too. The dashboard is an iridescent silver rectangle. I count ten gauges in all. Tiers of buttons and switches fill the bottom half of the rectangle. Two silver sticks tipped with gold enamel balls sprout next to the padded yellow vinyl steering wheel. The little earmarks of ego make me smile: a yellow crown on his possessions; the expensive racing boat; a woman half his age. I feel a little superior to Jonah Prince. Still I'm amazed at the number of gauges. More gauges line the top of the dash along the side of the boat next to the driver's seat.

"For heaven's sake, Ramaji—stop pacing and come here and thank our rescuer." Lady Cape gestures at the swami, who is still walking back and forth on the dock. "We are in your debt, Mr. Prince," she says and turns to us. "Mr. Prince is interested in the Far East, children."

Jonah throws back his head and laughs a golden laugh, the laugh of summer. I can almost see the laugh float off the dock into the pine trees. "We all struggle to fulfil ourselves. And you, Lady Cape?"

Lady Cape looks fondly at the swami. "I am trying to instil spiritual values in the Cape family. So far, I have few converts."

Jonah smiles charmingly at Bobby. "A pity. A pregnant woman would find the tortoise pose beneficial."

"You practise yoga, Mr. Prince?" the swami asks.

"During periods when I was undergoing a great deal of stress," Jonah Prince says.

"Oh, I see," Lady Cape says. "We all suffer great stress in our lives at one time or another, Mr. Prince."

Jonah nods, and I realize with a start that he is looking at me. "And who are the rest of your clan?" He smiles exuberantly. "You are . . . Mrs. Cape the Third?"

"It's bad taste to call yourself the third unless all three generations are alive," I say.

His marble blue cat eyes bulge. "Of course! You want to be called 'Ms.' like the American feminists." He points to Child. "Is this your husband?"

"Ms. Jude Bell is the recording angel of the Cape family," Child says.

"You're writing a book?" Jonah Prince says.

"Yes, she is—*One Hundred Years of Pianos*," Lady Cape says quickly. "In honour of the sale, you know. Who is your charming friend, Mr. Prince?"

"Oh excuse me," he laughs. "May I introduce Katy Hindsmith, my partner's niece?" Then he extends a hand to Bull.

"Katy said I must apologize to you for the fun I had this afternoon. She said I interrupted your race."

"There was no wind anyhow," Bull mutters; he shakes Jonah's hand and then stands, his long, apelike arms folded across his chest.

"I don't blame Mr. Prince. We've been very negligent. We didn't know you were up at the Sound or we'd have asked you sooner," Lady Cape says. She turns to Jonah and smiles. "Will you sail in the Good Cheer regatta this year, Mr. Prince?"

"Is that the race everybody got mad at you for winning?" Katy Hindsmith asks in her high piping voice.

"Only you are guileless enough to say that, Katy." Jonah smiles at her and then turns back to us. "If you will allow me to reciprocate with drinks on my island?"

Before Lady Cape can reply, the noise of a small engine ricochets back and forth across the walls of the bluff. The noise gets closer and then a red-haired man with an eye-patch thunders out of the pines, driving a motor scooter. He is Mister Tom, the Cape butler, who takes charge of the vegetable garden. He gets off and takes out four large white plastic bottles from a cart behind the bike.

"Oh, Mister Tom. Not those old buoys. I want pretty ones. We're going to start the race in the channel this year so the guests can watch it from the dock," Lady Cape says.

"We need a windward start, Mother," Bull says. "How many

times do I have to tell you every boat must get away with a clear wind?''

''Why don't you make Joyce happy for once?'' Child says. He moves over and stands beside Lady Cape. I look at the pair curiously. It's easy to see they are mother and son. The two have the same frank, wide-open blue eyes, the same thin, uncontrollable hair. But Lady Cape's silver hair shimmers like moonlight and the hair of my darling shines blond as the sun.

''Thank you, Dickie.'' Lady Cape smiles at Child and then taps the shoulder of the swami. ''You see, Ramaji? The regatta is a serious event.''

''I see . . . I see,'' the swami laughs. ''Does man who have fastest boat get best-looking woman?''

Jonah Prince looks at Lady Cape as if the swami hadn't spoken. ''Why don't you start it in the open? The guests can watch it from my dock.''

''That won't be necessary,'' Bull says. ''We'll start it in front of the Old Place.''

''What a good idea!'' Lady Cape suddenly turns towards the bluff. A disembodied voice is floating through the trees above a shattering crackle of static. ''Testing . . . testing . . . one, two, three.'' Lady Cape laughs in relief. ''Ramaji, our speakers are working.'' She smiles at Jonah Prince. ''Let one of the boys show you our Aleph Institute for Peace, Mr. Prince. Dickie! You take Mr. Prince for a tour. Bull, I want you to fly into Indian Harbour for more groceries.''

''And what about me, Padmajati?'' the swami asks.

''Why don't you take up more dowels? Mister Tom will help you load them onto the scooter cart.''

''I do not understand.''

The swami pulls out a ridiculous pair of wire spectacles from a saggy pouch in his robe and puts them on. Now he looks exactly like an Indian businessman.

''Tell me. Why are grown men such babies?'' Lady Cape smiles and disappears into the boat house. She reappears carrying a pile of what appear to be small wooden sticks. She hands the dowels to the swami.

''Hurry up, Ramaji—another summer, another heat.'' The swami and Mister Tom begin putting the dowels into the wheelbarrow. Before Lady Cape can give me a chore, I walk off, listening for Child's footsteps on the dock behind me.

"After her, Mr. Prince! Jude will take you up," Lady Cape calls. Then I hear her shout Child's name. "Oh, Dickie, I almost forgot. Shelly called on the radio phone. She's coming up with Higgins Rochester!"

From behind, Child puts a consoling hand on my shoulder.

"I know you'll want to see her but I need Shelly in the kitchen and I'd like you to organize a buoy-painting party to Gull Rock." Lady Cape's voice fades away as Child and I walk gloomily over to a row of scooters standing in front of a railing like horses tied to a hitching post in an old Western. The swami arrives pushing a wheelbarrow of dowels. He frowns at us suspiciously but says nothing. I lean against Child and we stare back at the swami in defiance. Behind him Bobby puffs up the path.

"Give this to His Nibs but don't let anyone see." She hands me a note just as Jonah appears with Katy.

"Is she going to ride a bike in her condition?" Katy Hind-smith says. She points to Bobby standing beside me.

"Why not? Do you think pregnant women aren't healthy?" I grin at Bobby.

"I'll walk this time, thank you," Bobby says.

Child gets on the scooter and pats the seat behind him. I climb on. Beside us, the swami is on his, fumbling with the key.

"Turn it to the left, Swami!" Child says. He looks over his shoulder, winks. "Hold tight."

The bike surges up the path, its engine droning. I lean close to Child. His hair streams into my face, blowing back to me the apple smell of his shampoo. Above us, the sun glints through the tops of the pines. I am in motion on the shores of heaven. Paradise is the body in front of me. Behind us, I hear the roar of the other bikes. I turn and look, my hair blown like a curtain across my face.

Jonah Prince is right behind us. He sees me look, waves, smiles. And you, Old Voyeur Eyes, you follow along behind with the swami. Where else could I put you? If you find this place uncomfortable, I warn you, there are long hours ahead when I will forget you entirely. So pay attention to the buildings on the partly wooden hill ahead where animals stand in stalls that look like giant Christmas crèches. There's the llama with a long skinny neck, and the long-tailed bird on the fence is a peacock. We tear past and the bird flutters off the fence screeching in alarm.

I notice Jonah Prince looking at them too. Then Sir James' private zoo fades in the distance and we pass the Old Place, the gabled farm the Americans built a hundred years ago. The Americans were not extravagant, but practical. They paid a local to live there all year round to mind the cows and chickens because it was an all-day boat trip into Indian Harbour to buy their groceries. Old timers say that when the wind blew from the southwest you could hear the American cows mooing back in Indian Harbour. The low, rotted-out rectangle in the clearing is the Americans' barn. Inside it, anchored by a web of ropes, is the Capes' helicopter.

We are in the centre of a new clearing. Child stops our bike. Jonah Prince stops beside him. But the swami doesn't stop . . . look out! Here he comes! We all jump off our bikes and run out of his way. At the last moment, the swami pulls out the key . . . he holds it up in the air, chuckling.

Child ignores him and points to a meadow beyond a long wooden bridge that spans a granite ravine.

"Sally is in the Japanese garden with Tilly! Let's go help her!"

"You lead the way," Jonah calls and we all get back on our bikes.

Just before us is a little island. Sally Love is standing there with Bobby's children trying to pull Tilly into the water. Tilly is a yak the size of a water buffalo.

"Meet Tilly. She's pregnant and subject to strange cravings," Child says. Tilly lowers her head and begins to chew on an iris on the little rock island.

Jonah Prince laughs. "A Tibetan yak in a Japanese garden!" He throws his arms up in a gesture of extravagant appreciation. "I thought we were in the wilds of Canada."

"You are in the Kotu-e, gathering place for angels and holy animals," Child laughs. "It was part of Joyce's Japanese epoch."

"Your uncle Dickie is an ignoramus." Bobby steps out from behind a pine tree. She looks like a young mother instead of a dissatisfied vamp in a B movie. "Quick, behind you! Tilly's been hiding her surprise from us."

A white, short-haired calf staggers towards its mother, who turns sideways so the knobbed little head can disappear under her great coat.

"Hurray! Hurray! Tilly's made a baby!" the little boy shouts, and suddenly we are all shouting too. Child and Jonah and Bobby and Katy and I—we are yelling with joy and pointing at Tilly's calf. For no reason, I look up. I blink. White flower petals are falling from the sky as a chorus of angels high above us play musical instruments. Ah, we are in the Kotu-e! The blessed place, as Child said. There are no contests or rivalries here. Then I look back at us—to earth. And there we are, very earthy . . . Bobby's stomach bulging over her bikini as she stands smiling beside Sally, her arms around Neil and Shasta. Me, I'm on the shore, leaning into Child. Do I never stop touching him? Not if I can help it.

"Are you going to join us?" Jonah yells to Bobby.

"I'll catch up with you later," Bobby calls back, laughing. "The kids and I have to take Tilly's baby to the zoo." Jonah nods and we climb on our bikes and off we go in a rush of noise and wind. Nothing much grows in it. The circular garden is designed to be seen from above. We pass by a statue of a Japanese fisherman and a five-tiered rock cairn. Water shines in a hole in the bottom rock. A long-handled wooden spoon sits beside the hole for aesthetic reasons. None of us would think of drinking from it. We pass the little teahouse with its curlicue roof. And three more large willow trees beside a bed of iris.

And now we are back in the pine woods, going by the Capes' vegetable garden. Orange-red tomatoes grow on stakes next to the vines of the squash plants flowering with yellow star-shaped blossoms. The swollen tubers of the zucchini are already ripening. We burst out of the woods towards the New Place. The New Place is a landmark in these parts. Tour guides whose boats dare to come this far into the open water point it out with a megaphone: "Designed by Frank Lloyd Wright, this organic structure of wood and glass illustrates Wright's belief that a house should be a noble consort to man and the trees. . . ."

The New Place is not really new; it's only called that to distinguish it from the Old Place. Its ceilings are seventeen feet high, and a seventeen-foot stone fireplace opens into the kitchen on one side and the dining room on the other. Jacuzzi baths go with the bedrooms and so do refrigerators that expel contoured ice cubes through chutes in the door.

But we don't stop. We drive on towards the geodesic dome where the workmen are standing on a scaffolding. A small dome sits inside a partially constructed outer dome. The outer dome rests inside three tall prongs like a ball held in three fingers. The domes are made of aluminum tubes connected with wooden dowels. I know from the swami's diagrams that the small dome measures 30 feet in diameter with an area of 706.51 square feet. The outer dome measures 60 feet in diameter with an area of 1413.02 square feet. Oh-oh. The swami is heading straight for us. We are going to crash. Are you ready? The swami screams and falls off the scooter and Child and I fall off too. Behind us the cart turns over spilling dowels onto the rocks where the stiff blond grass blows in the wind. The swami lies on his back bellowing up at the blue sky. The dowels are scattered all about the rock . . . by my head . . . by my hands . . . by my legs. Somebody calls my name and I yell back laughing, "Nothing's broken." I lie length-wise across a fat streak of sparkling mica cutting through granite the colour of elephant skin and wait for Child to reach me. I can see him struggling to his feet between a pair of hairless brown legs. For a moment the legs seem to span the endless expanse of the Sound. Then they move closer and Jonah Prince stoops down and helps me up.

2:23 p.m.

Jonah smiles at me as he puts his arm around Katy.

"You are not married, Ms. Bell?" he asks.

I smile back. "I don't believe in patriarchal customs."

"Stop pestering her, Prince," Child says. "She may be single but that doesn't mean an old satyr like you can flirt with her."

"Ah-ha, will you report me to your wasp tribunal?" Prince laughs his "I'm all right" laugh, his "I'll laugh at anything" laugh, the laugh that is the height of good spirits. "What do you have to say about this, Ms. Bell?" he asks.

"I think you dropped something," I reply and hand him Bobby's note.

His invisible eyebrows rise slightly. "Oh, of course. Thank you," Jonah Prince says and slips the note inside his bikini, with the gesture of a stripper checking her G-string. I pause for a moment and gape at his flat stomach. Is it flatter than mine? I look again. It is. A crescent of reddish-gold hair curves down the right side of his abdomen and disappears beneath the slippery nylon of his bathing suit.

Meanwhile, Child turns and looks at the dome. "Let's get on with the tour."

From inside the egg-like structure, we hear angry shouts. "Imbeciles . . . moronic apes!" The swami appears on the wood ramp leading up to the dome as if he had dropped from a cloud or a spaceship and not arrived by scooter. He ambles slowly down the ramp towards us, his bright orange robe and bright orange shawl floating out gracefully behind him. He looks half ape, half grey-haired matron. One hand holds his shawl demurely. The other brown hand—a simian appendage—dangles at his side, and his long grey hair is smoothed back as if coiffed from his domed forehead. He emits an atmosphere of wonderment—like a magician.

"I'm sorry, Mr. Prince," he says. "The stupid carpenters have put too much water in Big Dome." He waves a pink-palmed hand. "It is a disgrace—no good to see yet." Then he smiles. "You will see it at regatta dinner, when Padmajati and I demonstrate how we will live like fishes in twenty-first century."

"Underwater?" Jonah Prince says. "In the dome?"

"Yes. When I first come here, I have vision," the swami says. "I see beautiful light to the west. I feel force pulling me down, down to Atlantis. In the water Krishna and the Gopis dance the Rasa Lila. The lights indicate Good Cheer spot during the time of Atlantis. Mr. Prince—before you is the only chance we have to survive in the twenty-first century. After nuclear holocaust, we live under water in Big Dome in peace and plenty."

Jonah Prince laughs. "Ah—I see! You are building the new spiritual centre of North America! And what better place for it than at the bottom of our great Sound whose waters rise and fall in hydrologic cycles that change from day to day, from month to month, from year to year!''

He walks over to the swami and puts a hand on his shoulder. ''Ha ha. Our future as a race will be as freshwater astronauts whose home is a geodesic dome on a shore lined with pine, spruce, birch, and poplar. And we will feed on fish—yellow perch, smelt, whitefish, pickerel, pike, bass, bullhead, catfish, eel, goldeye, sunfish, turbot, freshwater drum, rock bass, crappie sauger, and the suckers who have survived the harvest of the commercial fishermen. . . .''

The swami bows and claps, giggling. ''Very good, Mr. Prince. You understand without the so-called scientific explaining necessary with Western people. But you make mistake about fish—in Big Dome, we eat only wild rice and vegetables grown in our hydroponic gardens.''

''Can you imagine Father doing that?'' Child whispers in my ear and laughs. I don't laugh; I envy the swami his ability to feel religious conviction. It is hard work to be a skeptic like me, who suspects conviction is an illusion our subconscious chooses for self-serving reasons. Religious belief—despite its time-consuming rituals—is more relaxing. And the swami has a plan for the future, a strategy. I have nothing except desire for a man who doesn't belong to me.

2:39 p.m.

Jonah Prince's ocean racer slowly edges out into Laughing Dog Channel. Then, without warning, it begins to plane high in the water, unleashing a wake that rocks the Chimo inside the boat house. Jonah waves, while the small figure of Katy bounces foolishly on the seat beside him.

''What did he mean—see us tonight?'' Bull slings his free arm around Bobby, his beer can aloft.

''We're all going to his place for a drink,'' Bobby says. ''Your mother's orders.'' She twists away from Bull and for a moment, Bobby and I both stare at Jonah's Thunderbird, the orange blob that hovers on the horizon like the tip of the setting sun between the sky and water.

Now Bobby tugs me into the old boat house. Her touch is

urgent. You hurry after us into the gloom which smells of old bullrushes. Bobby's standing next to an old nautical chart of U-Go-I-Go Sound that is tacked onto the wall.

If you look closely at the curving shoreline on the bottom of the chart, you will see the beaches of our childhood, where middle-class cottagers return each summer to measure themselves against the material success of the other families and to connect with an absolute—the unbroken and linear shoreline. Now look up at the small green shapes floating on the top of the chart: these are the islands where the rich of Ontario go to run their summer kingdoms. The first landscape is a racetrack where cottagers jockey for position. The second is a prize you win for financial prosperity. It says something for Bobby's upward mobility that in ten years she has graduated from beaches to islands. But the measure of Bobby's success is men—not islands. She moved on to become the second wife of Bull Cape after she had won Jay Manchester in a contest so long ago she may no longer remember it. And now she has her heart set on Jonah Prince.

The progress of my success in men or islands is harder to gauge. I have never done well in Bobby's kind of contest. Besides, I have a problem with competitions since I am cursed with the contradiction of wanting to win but never wanting anybody to lose either.

It is safer to watch Bobby play out, with fearsome determination, the old games that maximize her sexual power. Bobby is a pre-feminist, a natural champion of her right to pleasure. She lives out in practice what I contemplate in theory. Of course, I am susceptible to islands—those circular summer worlds where all events fold back in on one another. Strange things happen on islands. Mysterious, unexpected things that nobody acknowledges. The moment you step on an island you are free to re-create yourself and the burden of freedom will make you act in a way you won't recognize. North America is an island and look what happened here.

Suddenly Bobby puts her hand on an island shaped like a boomerang. "We are here," she drawls, bringing me back to real time. Then she points at a pin-sized green dot off the western tip of the boomerang. "And Jonah Prince is here. Do you see how narrow the distance is between our islands? Bull says in the low-water years Good Cheer and One Tree were the same island.''

Bobby snaps her fingers and I light her a fresh menthol. Then she slumps against the wall of the boat house, smoking hungrily. ''The very last time I made love to Jonah Prince I was waiting upstairs for the schmuck in Sally's bedroom.'' (Bobby points to the ceiling above us.) You recoil slightly and say nothing. ''I was lying there thinking you have to shake a man like a piggy bank until you get what you want.''

You frown and here I must step in and prevent Bobby from spoiling her story. Bobby only talks roughly when she needs somebody for something. She doesn't like to admit she is vulnerable. Surely, Old V.E., you understand. Is your nature so different?

Try to understand the un-Daisy-like twang in her speech and put yourself in her place that August night when she was lying on Sally's old bunk . . . she is pregnant with Shasta, only in her fourth month, but on her small frame even a bump is noticeable. And she wore Sally Love's tee-shirt. The one that spells out L-O-V-E. See her now? She is smoking one Cameo cigarette after another. This is one of her thoughts: men are made to serve me. She is smoking and staring out the window . . . waiting for darkness to fall so Jonah Prince can join her. He paddles the Thunderbird over under the cover of night. That summer they shared a private joke: if the islanders listen carefully, when the sun is set, it is not just Tilly the yak they'll hear mooing. They will hear the swish of paddles . . . see a boat cross the gap between two islands . . . behind the silhouette of the landscape, lovers are making the eternal journey to the shrine of each other's bodies.

Bobby can make out the wood rectangle of Jonah's boat house and the bald granite hump of his island. His new cottage isn't built yet. Beyond One Tree, a rosy band of light seeps onto the water where the Watchers sit on the horizon like a school of dark hippopotamuses.

The doorknob moves. Our hero starts. Not that she is frightened. And even if she was a little nervous, remember she enjoys fear . . . fear lets her know she is alive. Now the door moves;

freckled fingers curve around the doorframe. The cuticles of the nails are well polished.

He steps into the room. He carries a bottle of Dom Perignon under one arm; in the other, runny Brie cheese and a stick of French bread. He looks at my champion with his staring, protuberant eyes. He is charmed by her . . . enamored of the figure she cuts in her adolescent tee-shirt . . . her pouty pink mouth . . . her heart-shaped face and its curious expression. He is challenged by the way she looks at him with an "I've-seen-everything-but-go-ahead-and-see-if-you-can-be-attractive-for-me, big boy" look. Go on. Just try. He looks again at the hanging-open mouth, the hooded seal-brown eyes.

He sets down his romantic paraphernalia on one of the lower bunks. Our champion eases herself to her feet. From a styrofoam cooler near her feet she retrieves another bottle of champagne—Dom Perignon, too. A hunk of French stick and Brie cheese less runny than his. The golden laugh fills the bunkhouse and bursts out through the screen window into the evening. The sun has not even set. He dared an early sortie to see her.

He uncorks the champagne . . . his, of course. He removes his cloth shirt of Mexican design, then pauses so my hero can admire his hairless brown chest. She likes his body because it isn't hairy. Then he steps out of his navy blue jeans. He is wearing beige underpants—stretchy, silken. The pants are sexy. Our hero stops slouching and sits up. She is wearing the same make of underpants . . . the same stretchy, silken material. She giggles and hooks her thumb under the waistband, snaps it; he smiles, his face very animated, very flushed.

Now they lie back on the bunk, panty to panty. He slips his hand inside her underwear and pulls it to one side. He inserts himself in her. Our hero sits up and pushes him away. He tries to insert himself in her again. This time our champion doesn't push him away. She takes his cock in her hand and rubs it against her. He watches her, smiling. He is used to her ritual. It is either his cock . . . her fingers . . . his mouth . . . fast . . . firmly. She must be sitting like this too: half erect; legs stretched out straight, horizontal. It won't work for her any other way. He looks at her quizzically, like an attentive and elegant bear.

Bobby can feel her coming start from far off. Like the speck

of his Thunderbird on the horizon. The sensation travels closer
. . . she concentrates on the vision of his approaching boat. She
is grateful for his patience. At the same time, she resents all
men for their easy orgasms—the way they leap on top of her
. . . pump madly . . . stare at her wildly and collapse onto her
stomach. Even in lovemaking—the place where my hero wants
to exult in her sexual power—even here men have an advantage.

Now the Thunderbird rushes towards her. She thinks, "Men
are made to serve me." Then she says the phrase "thick, hairy
wrists". She says this over and over in her mind and the Thunderbird shoots out of the water and into the air . . . the navy bay
. . . the cloud-strewn sky. . . . She says, "Ah" . . . "Ah",
like the sound you make when the doctor presses a flat wooden
stick against your tongue . . . a deeper "Ahh" than the "Ah"
you make when your inboard turns a corner in the wave-wrinkled
channel and you see the open sound for the first time. . . .

A moment later, they are sipping champagne again. His erec-
tion shows through his underpants. He wants her but he is not
grabby. He stares up at the jiggles of yellow light on the wood
wall of the bunkhouse. The west light. Bobby's first memory of
joy is contained in that light . . . summer light . . . she looks
at the light. She looks at him. She is smiling. "I've never seen
a woman have orgasms like you," he smiles back. "That's because most women fake it," she says. What there is left of his
eyebrows lifts slightly. He nods, tears off a small piece of bread,
and eats it with a small piece of cheese. Bobby is cutting herself
a piece of Brie . . . smearing cheese on a much larger hunk and
eating it. When she came, she imagined his cock in her mouth.
Now she is putting the bread in her mouth, remembering.

He is watching her, waiting for her to finish. Then he takes
the champagne glass out of her hand, pushes her gently back
into the bunk, slowly slips off her underpants. His bulging eyes
are fierce. He covers her with his body, enters her, and with his
thighs squeezes her legs together. He moves slowly up and down,
then pumps quickly, and all of a sudden Bobby comes again just
like that. There was no inner picture, no nice slow building of
tension.

Bobby hasn't read Norman Mailer's story *The Time of Her
Time* and she has hardly started on *The Great Gatsby*. So, with-

out me, there is a limit to the literary references she can apply
to situations. She moves away from him and lights a fresh
Cameo. He watches her blow smoke rings, smiling. Of course,
he came too . . . right after her. Now he looks at his watch—a
gesture unlike him. He is not the sort of lover who leaves in a
hurry. He knows better, but she's asked him to go. He kisses
her forehead. He is charmed by my hero; then he leaves. She
watches him walk off through the screen window, sees his shoulders go through the pine trees for the last time that summer.
Then nothing. Perhaps he's coming back. She doesn't hear a
motor or the noise of paddles. At last there is a sound like an
explosion. The Thunderbird streaks down the bay from the north.
For a second the boat points right at her. She holds her breath,
then the boat veers west, drops speed, and slides out of view
into its boat house. All at once Bobby stuffs her smoking cigarette down the neck of the champagne bottle and bursts into
terrible, miserable, sad sobs.

3:17 p.m.

There is a new, pulsing sound that shakes the walls of the old
boat house. Another boat is approaching. Bobby and I walk back
onto the dock.
I shade my eyes and look at the cigar-shaped boat whose
mahogany hull is polished like a mirror. White bumpers bounce
like huge cotton-batting tampons against the boat's side where
the name *"At Last"* is stencilled in gold script on the bow. A
man with the face of an oyster is standing behind the wheel. He
has on a long peaked cap, and lawn green sunglasses. His short-
sleeved Hawaiian shirt flaps in the breeze. He is Doc Lefroy,
Lady Cape's brother. The elegant man in the stern is Sir James
himself. He is dressed in white ducks and a navy polo jersey.
Two passengers sit in the midsection. The first one's face is
hidden by rose-coloured granny glasses and a hideous straw hat
like the kind cruise passengers bring back from the Caribbean.
Swatches of palm fronds drooping over the brim cast barlike
shadows on a nose smeared with Noxzema cream. A camera
hangs around the neck of the second passenger, who wears sideburns, a Chairman Mao cap, and wafer-shaped sunglasses. The

person with the Mao cap and wafer-shaped sunglasses is the
man Child mentioned in his letter—Higgins Rochester. He's a
photographer for the Cape newspaper, *The Herald*. The woman
in the granny glasses and sombrero is Shelly.

"Hi, boys and girls!" About ten yards from the dock, Doc
Lefroy salutes us with his peaked cap.

Behind him, Sir James curses and empties his glass upside
down into the water. He looks like a grumpy Franklin Roose-
velt, the American president. Lefroy, on the other hand, looks
like the perfect summer martinet. "Never mind, Bwana." Doc
Lefroy grins. "I'll make you another one. Just the way you like
it." Doc takes off his aviator sunglasses and looks at Bobby on
her chaise, resting her empty glass on her extraordinary chocolate stomach. Behind Bobby, Sally Love is walking towards us,
almost bouncing on the dock's springy boards. She is wearing
a green nylon bikini and holding a fresh platter of hot dogs.
Bobby yawns and plucks one from Sally's tray, carelessly fitting
it inside a hot-dog bun whose crumbling bread is growing stale
in the scorching sunlight. Bobby stains the bun red with ketchup
and begins to eat it, opening her baby pink lips without enthusiasm. "What are you gaping at?" she says. "Haven't you seen
a pregnant woman before?"

"I'm not looking at you, little mother," Doc says amiably.
You follow the direction of Doc's gaze. His eyes are slowly
travelling across the tiny, pouty breasts and down the streamlined pelvis of Sally Love. Doc has no interest in Bobby's mi-
raculous shape. It is the wrinkle-free prepubescent body he
seeks.

I feel a slight distaste for Doc. It is so primitive: the way his
eyes instinctively seek what he thinks is the best biological
choice. Never mind Bobby's evidence of fertility; he wants the
female with the most breeding years ahead of her. I tell myself
not to be judgmental. Neither sex is the victim of the other.
We are half-victims, compelled to act out predetermined im-
pulses.

The central issue is not the predatory gaze of Doc Lefroy; the
central issue is creation and Doc Lefroy is only a device—a sack
of chromosomes that a female like Sally Love needs in order to
fulfil the reason we are here.

Of course, as a device Doc Lefroy is a little out of control.
His interest in Sally is making everyone uneasy. Sally blushes
under his gaze. She puts down the platter and picks up the jug
of sangria. It is hot on the dock. The wood burns my feet. My
throat is dry. I stare at the tinkling pitcher gripped in Sally's
hands. Something unpleasant is about to happen. Bobby senses
it too and gets to her feet beside me, sternly beautiful like a
warrior. I imagine her right hand gripping a spear while her left
steadies her aegis. It hangs over her pregnant stomach, encircled
by two long, flat-bellied Mississauga rattlers.

Our heads are encased in helmets and I hold a broadsword
but have no shield. Bobby and I stand ready, like Athena and
Diana, to do battle against any man who threatens our gender.
(You see, Old Voyeur Eyes? I think in mythic concepts. I am
superior to Doc Lefroy, who stands in his boat leering at this
angel puss who doesn't smoke or drink.)

"Want to come for a boat ride?" Doc winks at Sally. His
greedy sun-red face is dangerously close to the slick green V
between Sally's slim thighs.

Sally whispers something and Doc rolls his eyes at Sir James
who is drinking rum in the stern. "You don't like boats?"

Sally shakes her head uncertainly.

"Leave her alone. She doesn't know how to swim." Doc
Lefroy stiffens. He isn't used to a woman talking back to him.
Now Bobby lowers her sunglasses into battle position. "I said
fuck off, you old creep." Suddenly Doc Lefroy grins. His hand
moves like lightning. He tugs one of the fine blonde hairs curled
next to the V of Sally's crotch. "What's this?" he snorts. Sally
jumps and in the stern of *At Last* Sir James bangs his cane.

"Lefroy! Stop pestering the ladies and make the landlubbers
walk the plank!"

"Right away, Bwana!" Doc Lefroy holds the dock with one
hand and the passengers disembark.

Higgins takes off his skinny sunglasses and kisses me so
warmly I can feel his sideburns scratch my cheek. "Is this your
photographer, Jude?" Bull says.

"Begging your pardon, old chap. I'm *the* photographer. I do
not belong to anyone." Despite his sideburns, Higgins is thin
and faceless. All photographers look a little alike anyway. They

have surrendered their facial features to the lens of the camera in order to look out on the world. Now Higgins' down-turned English mouth flips up and he points his camera at Bobby. "I say, old girl, hold still, will you?" Bobby obligingly cups her hands around her belly and Higgins snaps a picture.

Behind Higgins there is a dock-quake, a seismic trembling. A natural disaster, like a hurricane, is approaching. The dock creaks, heaves tragically beneath us, and Shelly pads across the wooden boards. Then the sunny-faced simperer laughs in a vapid schoolgirl giggle and takes off her sombrero. Two plaits of red hair uncoil snakily down her milky shoulders.

You stare intently at Shelly—first at her plump, freckled feet, housed in wooden clogs and protruding from under the hem of her ankle-length gown. You notice the oddly painted toes—painted the same brackish purple as the nails on her hands. You look up (how can you resist looking up?) You have a fine view from where you stand . . . your eyes follow the folds of her tie-dyed gown, cut to expose a pair of sumptuous freckled breasts, and up to her puffy upper lip whose babyish droop always makes me want to protect her. As you stare, it occurs to you that this woman is not fat, but voluptuous. My description of a shaking dock was overdone by half. And you are right. Why should I festoon Shelly with flattering adjectives? Isn't it bad enough that she has arrived—ruining my last hours with Child—with her silly, little girl braids and Mona Dault freckled breasts? It is an outrage that I am obliged to watch her reclaim her territory: squeezing Child's arm and applying enough pressure to turn his skin white, as if she is testing for sunburn! If I had my way, I'd call her "O" for Obstacle and ignore her altogether.

Shelly met Child before I did, through her job as Lady Cape's secretary at the Aleph Institute of Peace. At twenty-seven, she looks like one of the beatific long-haired women who bake bread and raise children on farm collectives. But I know who Shelly most resembles behind her wireless spectacles: her mother, who believes women's first loyalty is to men. This is Shelly: a conformist posing as an individualist. This is also Shelly: smart but not ambitious, and easy-going with a self-satisfied expression that makes me think she's got a secret I'd like to share.

The dock shakes again and Bobby's Dobermans run over to

Shelly. "Get down, you beasts," she cries and snuggles close to Child as if he belongs to her. "Did Joyce tell you I have special news?" she asks.

Child shakes his head.

"Oh! I'll tell you later then, when we're alone."

Shelly turns to me and kisses my cheek while I smile ruefully. "I didn't know you were coming up, Dinger—I mean Jude. How good to see you." Now she puts a plump hand on my shoulder. You watch this hand with interest. It spreads over my skin like a ruler's on the orb of state. Of course, it's not only Child Shelly assumes she owns but me, thanks to the summers she and I spent with Bobby. Neither of them thought much about me during my winters in Merton. They just came up at the end of June and expected me to walk out of the pines like the Sasquatch.

"She's researching mother's cream-puff history of the clan," Child says hastily. "One hundred years of unseemly profits."

"Oh, Dickie," Shelly giggles. "You shouldn't say that! Jude, hand me Lakshmi and Durga, will you?"

She points at a gold garbage can in the stern of the *At Last*. A selection of small, dark brown Hindu statues poke out of the can next to several magnums of champagne.

"Sorry, I forgot," she laughs. "How would you know you are looking at the divine mother in two of her manifestations? I left Mother Kali at home. Her negative energy would only bring Joyce bad luck for her regatta. Wouldn't it, Child?"

"All Joyce cares about is the Good Year Regatta cup." Child picks up the golden garbage can, frowning. He puts it down as the disembodied voice of Lady Cape floats through the pines and across the water.

"Attention all idlers! Commence regatta duties at once!"

Now there is another voice shouting and Bull rushes towards us, hurling everything in his path into the water. "Okay everyone! You heard what Joyce said! Last one in is a rotten egg!" He tosses Sally's hot-dog platter high above our heads and the hot dogs fly skyward, bursting open like milk pods and then falling with little plops onto the swells by the dock—floating fat and pinky brown like penises before sinking into the reed-thick depths where water snakes wait to nibble on their soggy meat.

(Remember, Old Voyeur Eyes? Sex was first explained to me in the image of hot dogs and hot-dog buns.)

Meanwhile, you are too entranced with the falling hot dogs to see me grapple with Bull, who pushes me in, and then Child jumps in after, knees drawn up to his chin, arms around his knees, cannonball style. Now Bull grabs Sally and jogs with his wide-eyed burden to the diving board at the end of the dock. You hear the whine of board and rusty nails as Bull bounces, Sally Love's head and upper shoulders hanging sack-like over his apelike form . . . dear, gullible Sally Love who looks like a mermaid but has never learned to swim. She makes a faint wailing noise no louder than a kitten's cry and you smile at the charm of that sound. No harm is being done. Sally Love is safe in the arms of an old swimming champion like Bull Cape. There is a whale-sized splash as two bodies hit the bay. And finally you don't just giggle, you laugh a summer laugh as high and as infectious as the laugh of Jonah Prince. You run across the hot dock and dive in. You are suddenly having more fun than you thought possible.

You drop down, feet first, almost to the bottom, and the pale waters enclose you like a tomb. Then you bob back up again. Your head rises to the surface like one of those burrowing, stone-clinging insects that mature on the bay bottom. This is the gymnastics of metamorphosis. Water streams down your ears. Your eyes fill with light. You are changing into an air-borne creature rushing up like a plume of smoke towards the sky to live out what little life you have—the hours between sunrise and sunset.

3:55 p.m.

Quick. Hurry up the swim ladder, Old Voyeur Eyes. Now kick your foot and shake your waterlogged head to clear your ears of water.

You pause and look around regretfully, trying to take it all in—the other swimmers floating like moments in time, the rustling noise of water against the dock, the laughing voices. It is cooler now. You notice goosebumps on your skin. An easterly breeze is freshening, wrinkling the channel with small waves. Shivering, you walk up to the peephole in the west wall and look through without even wondering how you knew it was there. Bobby and I are inside watching Child pull something out of a long box. He winds it about his neck, and holds it in his arms. Without waiting, you turn and enter the boat house.

There is a flutter above your head. You look up at the ancient rafters stained with bat shit. Then suddenly, the dark shape in Child's arms slides sinuously down his body and slithers your way, weaving its head to the left and right. You draw back, press against the wall. Your eyes are gradually adjusting to the gloom. The shape is a snake . . . huge . . . obese. The triangular head stops by your ankle, darts out its tongue, sniffing the air for your smell. Relax! I said before you play no role in the action. I am the one—not you—who has to worry about snake bite. And no sooner do I speak than *voilà*—Child blows his dog whistle and the boa constrictor turns and slowly weaves its way back to its owner.

Child puts his hand into the wire case and pulls out a white something. Then he puts it down on the floor. The white something doesn't move. I know what's coming next. I don't want to look, but I can't stop myself. I'm waiting for the boa to strike its squeaking victim. I can't bear the thought of the animal's terror as it disappears down the slick throat, trailing pink legs and a tail behind it. But the victim doesn't squeak and the snake doesn't strike. It only slides by the white something and curls around the feet of its master.

"What's the matter?" you hear me ask.

"Pig only feeds in the water." Child throws the white something into the slip. "And stop looking so worried, Jude. The mouse is dead." There is a small splash and then a loud splash as the mouse and snake drop into the boat slip. Suddenly, out of the gloom, Bull appears carrying a white terrycloth robe. He stops and shakes it at Bobby like a voodoo charm.

"Joyce wants you to carry a robe when the photographer is on the premises," he mutters.

"Can't a Cape wife be photographed pregnant?" I put my hand on Child's shoulders.

"It's against family rules." Child shakes his head. "That's why my brother's been confused about the birds and bees ever since I can remember."

"What are you babbling about?" Bull stares at us with eyes not yet accustomed to the darkness.

"Well, I looked enormous as a Buddha in our wedding photographs," Bobby says. "And I don't intend to raise another generation of prudes! It will be good for Neil and Shasta to say—'Tadaah! There's mom—preggers! She's the blob standing next to Dad in his flannels and white blazer. Do you know they had to get married?' "

Bull holds out the robe. "Will you please do us all a favour and put it on?"

"Listen Bull, I'm sick of being told how to act," Bobby says. "If I want to dye my hair orange, I will, and if I want to wear a bikini when I'm nine months gone, I'll do that too. Isn't it enough that I sat for a photograph with that old creep last winter?"

I have a copy of Bobby's portrait by Karsh on my dresser. She is wearing white satin with silver metallic ribbing along the bodice and cuffs. Her face is softly rosy, but her hooded eyes look angry under skinny well-plucked eyebrows and her hair, brushed up and back from her high forehead in a page-boy cut, is not dyed platinum against Lady Cape's wishes; it's brown.

"This is the last time I'm asking you." Bull wraps the robe around Bobby. "Put it on."

"Fuck you, Bull Cape!" Bobby yells, and throws the robe to the ground. "And fuck your stupid old mother. She just wants to get into the swami's pants!"

"Don't you dare talk about Joyce like that!" Bull grabs Bobby by the shoulders and a knee-high shape crouched by the up-turned dinghy rushes out of the gloom. Bull swears and turns sideways so his hip catches the Doberman and Emily bounces off him. Her claws scrabble on the boat house floor and she falls into the slip yelping pitifully.

"You bastard." Bobby sinks to her knees and reaches down into the dark water. In a moment, Child and I are beside her. I put my arms around Bobby's shoulders and Child hauls out a shivering dog.

"There . . . there . . . baby," Bobby croons. Bull says nothing as Emily hobbles towards Bobby, then sits down dripping and shivering by her feet. Bobby bends down and examines her paw.

"Look what you've done." She turns toward Bull. "You hurt her paw."

Bull stares at us, shifting from one square foot to the other.

"Come with me to Indian Harbour?" he says meekly.

"I'm going with Jude," Bobby says and Bull whirls around as if he sees me for the first time.

"We're going to buoy paint. Remember?" Child picks up a paint tin and loads it into the dory. I take two bottles of Chablis from the boat house fridge and a salad of chick peas. We will feast on the remains of the swami's lunch. The bottles clink under my arm. I look matter-of-factly to my left and my right, like a bureaucrat on government business. Beside me, Child goes about his work swiftly. He packs Bobby's easel and box of oil paints into the bow with his film camera and then staggers into the stern carrying the food cooler. Child and I dart a look at the boat house door and then we both smile in relief. Light, sweet summer air billows through the empty opening.

Bobby climbs into the bow of the dory and sits slumped in a heap. Child and I sit in the stern, on each side of the twelve-horsepower motor. I look up as Child pulls the cord. A familiar body in a flowered granny gown stands at the boat house door.

I smile at Shelly and place my tanned, arched foot between Child's legs so my toes graze his inner thigh and all at once we shoot forward out of the dark of the boat house into the sunlight. Shelly runs along the slip, shouting. "Where are you going?" she calls.

I shout, "Gull Rock." You don't know if Shelly can hear my words over the noise of the outboard. You are startled by my bad manners, and I am a little surprised by myself too. Smiling, I turn and wave and slowly Shelly shrinks to a pink dot by the old clapboard boat house.

4:02 p.m.

The heat is baking out here on Laughing Dog Channel. Our procession chugs slowly away from the mysterious shaggy pines growing right down to the edge of the water, their roots sunk deep into slabs of rocks which volcanos left behind millions of years ago. We are heading for the hot, wet nothingness of the open water.

I close my eyes. The sunlight this far out is an ugly mauve red on the backs of my eyelids. I open my eyes and look at Bobby. Why hadn't I noticed before? Bobby is metamorphosing in the white watery heat as we pass Jonah's island. She turns her head towards One Tree Island and smiles, her mandibles twitching, the August light shining strangely in her compound eyes.

4:13 p.m.

In the bow my fecund ant queen sits, her compound eyes fixed with the stupidity of instinct on Jonah Prince's small granite dome receding in the distance. She is oblivious of the danger of the shoals around us. She scratches her thorax and imagines the colony she will found with her new ant husband away from the mess of her old burrow. In the royal apartment, she will hold a party that never ends while an endless procession of workers crawl around her as if going about a mountain, regurgitating honey dew into her open mouth.

Child looks at her adoringly as he paddles the dory, his narrow wings, sticky and shiny, dragging in the water. He possesses absolute faith in Bobby's desirability. He admires the cone-like tip of her abdomen, thirty thousand times larger than his body. From that swollen node, Bobby's eggs will spurt like white pudding—one every ten minutes. Then Child will carry off the egg, lay it with a set of other eggs in one of the hundreds of cavities which he has chewed in the granite—oh, Child will work hard for her later but right now he's glad the all-sensing mind of our ant queen is elsewhere so he can milk me at his leisure. I am round and green—Child's favourite colour. I have almost no head and two small, dark compound eyes like black buttons. My mouth is a beak, a sweet little sucking spear I use for piercing plant tissues. Child's mouth is at my anus. He licks me until I drip helplessly with the sweaty honey he likes.

I crouch motionless. I could flick the drops away with my

hind leg but there is no need to do anything. It's Child's job to dispose of my fluids. In the summer, he carries me from plant to plant for my feedings and when winter comes he will take my aphid babies down into Bobby's new ant burrow.

All at once Child stops stroking me and wraps his four sets of sticky legs about my translucent body. We rise airborne, up the south cliff of Gull Rock. Child's glistening wings are strong and we sail above the horizontal stain of the old waterline that runs from one end of the cliff to the other. We fly up over the deepest edge of the bluff. Seagulls rise into the air around us, screeching and then wheeling off up into the sky, their shadows falling on the stained white granite cliff below. I shudder as I look down at the drop. I would never fly up a cliff this size. My silly wings couldn't manage it. They would beat uselessly as my soft, dripping body tumbled and twisted down to the rocks below.

4:22 p.m.

Bobby is in the dory stuck on a shoal about sixty yards offshore. She is slumped in the middle seat, her legs stretched toward the bow, her head tilted up to catch the sun, her eyes inscrutable behind her rhinestone sunglasses.

Her Doberman, Emily, wriggles out from under the seat behind Bobby and stands up in the dory, her nose propped on the gunwale. She is looking at Child staggering slightly under the weight of the cooler before he deposits it beside Bobby's easel on a waist-high rock the size of a table. Now he and I stand on the shore, ectomorph and mesomorph, waving at our endomorphic champion. "I'm not coming," Bobby calls grumpily. "I'm pregnant, you know. And tired." We wave and shout louder and Bobby clumsily climbs out of the boat. Slowly she drifts in, her belly a wet brown bump breaking the surface like a shoal. Child and I splash back into the water again and help Bobby struggle to her feet on a submerged ledge. She puts her arm around my shoulder and we begin to half slide, half walk. Child follows, half sliding too, his arms outstretched, like a basketball guard on either side of Bobby.

4:38 p.m.

I crouch over my champion who lies naked and spread-eagled on the warm granite, her arms and belly blue for battle, blue for Boadicea, queen of the Iceni. I am adding the last touches of war paint to my warrior queen. I slather the tip of her right nipple red for the battle of Colchester when Boadicea made the seas turn the colour of blood and old men begged for mercy in the council chambers, and daub the bumpy areola pink for the sacking of London when Boadicea killed all of her people who had complied with the Romans. Then I draw a circle around the diameter of the breast to mourn Boadicea's defeat at the hands of General Suetonius who killed 80,000 of her followers.

Child daubs orange paint on Bobby's left nipple. "For Jonah Prince," Child says. "Aren't these his colours?" Then he draws an orange zigzag like the thunderbolt across her belly to the belly button, and heads south. But Bobby sits up and pushes away his hand. "No man touches me there unless he's going to screw me."

I follow Child's course down Bobby's swelling abdomen as she sits—my platinum-haired Boadicea knees up and apart, her belly blooming between the lengths of her thighs. My brush descends all the way down to her pubic hair, which is soft and black-brown like mine. It could be a telltale footnote in our rivalry over who is the real blonde. A real blonde has blonde pubic hair. But we've both dyed the hair of our heads so many times neither of us remembers what our natural colour is.

"Hey!" Child says. "How come you don't push her away? She's not going to make love to you, is she?"

"Women are nicer than men," Bobby says. "You can trust them not to hurt you."

"We share a bond we don't have with men," I say. "We don't rape each other."

"Well, women have rape fantasies," Child says. "It's not all men's fault."

"Female rape fantasies are about sex appeal. It's as if I say to myself 'I'm so sexy, I've made you lose control.' It's not because I really want you to hurt me."

"You mean male aggression proves you're feminine?"

"We seek an expression of desire, not literal consequences. Women understand this distinction. Men don't."

"But women compete for each other's men," Child says, looking at me, and I wonder if he's thinking of Shelly. "That isn't bonding."

"Not Jude or me," Bobby says. "We have an agreement not to lay a finger on each other's men."

"That's possessive, then," Child says. "You don't own those men."

"We've never found each other's men attractive," I say.

"How about Jonah Prince?" Child grins.

"He doesn't do anything for me," I reply.

"Well, there was one guy we both liked," Bobby drawls. "His name was Jay Manchester."

"Oh, he doesn't count. We were just kids then." I quickly draw a half circle to the left of Bobby's mons pubis; then I draw a half circle to the right. I've drawn the top of a heart. Bobby shrieks and closes her legs.

Child stands behind me, places a hand on my shoulder. "I thought you were preparing her for war, not love."

"Is there a difference?"

"Look. It's not our fault if men are violent," Bobby says.

"I give up—make me an honorary woman," Child grins and points to his chest. "Give me breasts like you."

I paint large blue circles around Child's nipples. "It's not the same, is it?" He looks down at his flat chest and sighs. "Oh well. Time to give Pig an airing." He opens the cooler and a shiny triangular snout peers over the top of the styrofoam container. Pig's tongue shivers in the air and her green-black eyes shine. Then she does something surprising: she yawns, a long bored yawn exposing stumps of little half-broken teeth. Child laughs and reaches down to examine her nose. "A little sunburnt," he says. He takes a bottle of Noxzema from the cooler and applies a dab to Pig's nose. The boa executes a sideways coiling movement away from Child's arm and then slips, her wrinkles undulating like the folds in a fat wrestler's arm, over to the shade of an overhanging ledge where Emily chews her stick.

I turn and grab Child's arm, pull him down beside us. "Let's tie Child up and have our way with him," I say to Bobby. "Let's make him submit to the superiority of women."

"Yeah. Let's show him how it feels to be on the other end," Bobby giggles and Child looks tititlated. We seize him, lay him out spread-eagled in the baking sun, just the way Bobby was a few minutes before.

Child doesn't lift a finger to stop us. How can he? We are fierce-hearted Viking goddesses. We bend over and start to molest him and, sighing, Child closes his eyes and touches the small articles hanging from our crystal necklaces—the knives, combs, scissors, needles, keys, even a tiny purse. His hand reaches for the three-armed tortoise brooch fastened to my overgarment and then, ah, his fingers slowly crawl over and cup my breast. "Don't hurt me," he giggles and I say sighing, "Lie down, and be quiet," and Bobby says, "You heard what she said, you son of a bitch."

"Our heads sound different, but we are one woman to you," I breathe in his ear. "We are the daughters of Mimir and Niord."

Cursing, Bobby ties Child's arms with her bikini top and I tie his legs with mine. He couldn't move it he had to—Child is pinned beneath a two-headed woman waving two sets of arms, commanding him to submit. Bobby kneels beside his head, her breasts swaying brown as olives over his open mouth as she smears orange paint on his shoulders and neck. Down below, I slap the paint on thickly . . . wetly . . . fiercely . . . all the way from his instep to his groin, turning him, stroke by stroke, orange.

"Are you going to say uncle yet?" I whisper.

Child says hoarsely, "Not yet," and then Bobby slaps the paint an inch from his balls and he cries, "Uncle! Uncle!" But it's too late. Bobby's head twists round and round and she opens her scarlet beak and Child sees in an instant that she is a great horned owl with teeth like an anaconda. He screams as Bobby tears off his nipples and I insert my spongy reptilian penis into his poor howling mouth. We are not the double-headed Freyja. We are the gripping beast. And this is the day of Ragnarok—the doom of the gods when grizzly bears swallow the sun, and armies of women arise from the sea carrying men's genitals between their teeth like the stalks of roses.

4:40 p.m.

You are sitting off shore in Lady Cape's prize white canoe. You look slowly up at the cliff in front of you. It can't be as difficult as it appears. You saw us climb it slab after slab before we vanished into the crevice of juniper, Emily's stump of a tail the last moving shape you saw.

You put your hands on the gunwales and heave yourself out, fearing the worst. For a moment, the canoe rocks frighteningly, but the water is green and soothingly cool. Feathery green algae on the rocks below flutter up and down in the swells of water. You float onto a slippery ledge, wishing you had on old running shoes—the kind Lady Cape wears when she goes rock climbing.

Then you pull yourself inch by inch onto the dry granite, careful not to scrape your stomach against the stone whose surface feels like frozen sugar crystals. Now you haul yourself to your feet and look around. The soft wind blows you the sweetish odour of decaying seagull feathers. Nearby a tin of orange marine paint sits on the shore. You go to pick it up and then stop yourself. It is not up to you to correct our mistakes. Midway up the cliff, you spy a giant footprint formed by the outpouring of volcanic granite.

You yank down your bathing suit and pee into the giant heel, then pull it back up. You see? The heat is getting to you, too. It is not like you to pee in the open where anybody can see but you are up in the islands where none of us does the expected thing.

Cursing softly, you step off the rock into the bushes where the juniper is prickly underfoot. You are hurrying as fast as you can, but the climb takes you all of eternity. Then at last you're on the top of Gull Rock. You can see 360 degrees in all directions—north to the French River; east to the mouth of Indian Harbour; west to the Watchers which float on the horizon like rock clouds in a sensation-drenched realm of heat. And south to the island of Jonah Prince. It is a view you might see in Iceland or on the Barrier Reef in Australia, a view from the rim of one of the largest freshwater lakes in the world. You feel eerily safe and dangerously alone as you stand, inhaling hot air like a happy mosquito. Then, at the west end of the rock, you notice three people doing something odd to each other's bodies with stick-like things. You start to shout, "Ahoy there," and then you remember we won't look at you. You sit down by a large buoy in the shape of a tripod and squint into the sun. What on earth is going on? Three painted bodies are dancing like savages. The triangles of cloth are gone, so there is no mystery of gender. You miss this mystery a little. Some of the female contours are hidden beneath mats of hair and the male organ with its drooping balls looks frail. We have retained our civilizing traces: Bobby's purple sunglasses with the sprinkling of rhinestones on the lenses, Child's translucent green love beads between his blue breasts, and my silver ankle bracelet with the inscription "Men are made to serve us, love always, Bobby."

4:42 p.m.

I yank Bobby's hand and she pulls Child's. And we go round and round the buoy. Emily drops her stick, starts to bark. "Page 206," I call out.

"Rodney with Betty . . . on the beach," Bobby shouts back.

"His fingers found the tie of her halter and in less than half a minute the garment lay on the sand next to the blanket. Betty's back arched against his arm as she thrust her breasts up to him." I look at Bobby. "What's the rest?"

"She let him do this often, but it never failed to arouse him to near frenzy. Her nipples were always rigid and exciting," Bobby yells.

" 'Come on honey,' she whimpered. 'Hard. Do it hard, honey. Bite me a little,' " I scream.

"Page 269," Bobby shrieks and we sit down laughing by the cooler. Child pours Bobby an ice-chilled vodka, then lights a joint. He passes it to me, his eyes half closed. "Don't stop now," he says. "Go on with you childhood game."

I inhale lazily and begin again. "The sun through the window sent a beam that lit up his thighs and slim belly, the erect phallus rising darkish and hot-looking from the little cloud of vivid red hair."

" 'So proud!' " Bobby says. " 'And so lordly! Now I know why men are so overbearing.' "

"You women think men are supposed to be a constant potent force directed right at you. Look at me, will you?" Child exhales the marijuana smoke and gestures at his penis; it wobbles in the wind, short and pale, almost dainty. "Most of the time the best I can do is manage a semi."

"Where is this quote from, Child?" I say quickly, not wanting to be distracted by his masculine charms. " 'And this time his being within her was all soft and iridescent, such as no consciousness could seize. Her whole self quivered unconscious and alive, like plasma.' "

"Women in Love!"

"Wrong!"

"Lady Chatterley's Lover," Bobby shouts.

"Right!" I shout back.

"Why do you two care about that old fake?" Child grumbles. "Lawrence was a closet homosexual. All his female characters want to control men with their sexuality."

"Well, he was right about that," Bobby says. "But he was too dumb to know women fake their orgasms. Anyway, we like him. Don't we, Jude? For sentimental reasons."

My champion stands up and stretches before her easel. Her stomach flies above Child's head and mine as we sit on the ground, a miniature dirigible. Tiny wormlike lines streak off in all directions from her orange belly button. I turn away as Bobby starts to paint so I don't see her stretch marks.

"All women fake their orgasms, Child. Except for me. I bet Shelly fakes them with you." Bobby scratches her left shoulderblade. It's the spot where the bathing suit strap itches her skin. "Men just don't like to admit it. Even Bull. He thinks it is all in the size of his schlong." Bobby inspects her orange belly button, then pries at the dirt under the nail of her big toe. Now she pulls out a piece of chewing gum from her bag and throws the wrapper into the juniper bush with a gesture of distaste. "Jonah Prince said I don't have orgasms like other women and I said, 'Yeah? That's because other women lie to you.' "

Bobby lights up one of my menthols, her seal brown eyes fastened on One Tree Island to the south. "That was the last time

I slept with him before Bull made me give him up. He said Jonah
Prince was a NOOC—Not Of Our Class. Isn't that ignorant?''

"I bet Jonah Prince had never met a woman like you before,"
Child says. He looks at me mischievously, makes a zipper motion across his mouth with his index finger.

"I guess not," Bobby says proudly. "And I've never met a
man like him, either. He doesn't use dumb words and he
wouldn't use a gun on somebody. Bull fired a real bullet on
purpose, you know. He's just stupid enough to try and kill Jonah."

"You're too hard on my brother," Child says. "It was an
accident."

Child retrieves his long-sleeved shirt and Bobby and I put our
bikini bottoms back on as a concession to mixed company.

"I wonder if I'll get a chance to speak to him when we go to
his island for drinks." Bobby lifts her striped blue stomach above
the wedge of her orange bikini. One side of her belly looks
sticky as if it is melting in the heat. "If so, I'll ask him to Good
Cheer."

"I thought your affair with Jonah Prince was over," Child
says, suddenly stern.

"Jude! Do you hear his tone! Child Cape is male after all!
His first loyalty goes to Bull!"

She turns to Child and he reaches out and takes her blue hand.
He kisses it with eyes half lowered and smudges his thin lips
with blue paint. "I didn't take my brother's side. I used to give
Prince your notes, didn't I?" Bobby smiles and starts to paint
one of her canvases. She strokes in a spidery pine tree and then
splashes on a brown blotch shaped in a hump like One Tree.
"I'm not sure he'll come. He's got that British kid with him.
Besides I don't think he likes pregnant women."

"You could send him one of my poems and pretend you've
turned to writing verse in his absence."

"Why not give him one of your paintings?" Child says. "Like
your version here of Thomson's *West Wind*."

"Jonah only likes European art," Bobby says. "I'd rather
give him one of Jude's poems."

To oblige Bobby, I roll over from where I have been lying
sprawled against Child's chest and fumble in a book. Child takes

the poem from me before I have a chance to hand it over. His hair floats long and silky over his shoulders as he reads:

So who these days
courts her man with poetry
scratching down heaven sent
telegrams, who
throws her sky hook into the
clouds
and grapples for a bit of
the universe? Who else but a soft-spoken
trickster, a third-rate
magician,
would dress her lover
in a suit of words?

Bobby pours herself another glass of vodka and frowns. "That poem doesn't make sense. How can a magician pull down clouds with a hook?"

"Bobby, you have no respect for literature. That's your problem." Child lights us a fresh joint. "Art owes no obligation to reality. It only has to evoke it."

"I have respect for art, don't I, Jude?"

Bobby looks at me lying against the rocks, eyes closed, smiling in the sun.

"You? A Sunday painter?" Child laughs.

"Okay. So I don't understand the poem, Child. I bet you don't understand it either," Bobby says.

"Of course I understand it. She wrote it for me."

Bobby butts out her cigarette and fishes around in the cooler. "I might have known." She brings out the swami's chickpeas, then, scowling, she puts them back.

"You stay away from her, Child Cape. You live with somebody."

"Why do people think you can't cheat on somebody you live with?" Child says. "It's so bourgeois."

"Of course, a love poem could make Jonah Prince feel pressured." I stand up, put my left foot on my right knee, fold my hands in prayer position on my chest, then I stare fixedly to the south—to One Tree. "Ommmm. O mighty Prince! Fulfil Bobby's secret desire and visit her tonight under the cover of darkness." Child laughs and scrambles to his feet. He stands beside me, bends his right knee, puts his right foot on his left leg, one hand in prayer position on his chest, the other hand holding the joint.

"Jude's right—you need to give the Great Prince a chance to get used to you being available again," he says, starting to omm too.

"Sometimes you have to pressure people to get what you want," Bobby says. "Anyway, I want a poem—just not that one." With a grunt of pleasure, Bobby tears open a large blue and silver bag of potato chips and then places a handful of chips in a careful line on the rock beside the easel. "I don't care what the swami says about junk food," Bobby mutters. "I love potato chips." She picks up the first chip and stuffs it into her mouth. Then she picks up the second. Bobby puts a third, fourth, fifth, sixth, and seventh chip into her mouth. Then she picks up a newspaper.

"Hey, this is interesting," she calls out. "Science says the ideal female face includes eye width that is three-tenths the width of the face at eye level; chin length, one-fifth the height of the face; distance from the centre of the eye to the bottom of the eyebrow, one-tenth the height of the face . . . hey, are you listening?"

We, the devotees of Jonah Prince, throw our arms in the air above our heads, omming blissfully. "Come do it too, Bobby. Worshipping Jonah Prince is good for your back."

Bobby stands up, giggling, and leans back, one hand still holding the chip bag. Then she groans and sits down again with a little plop and empties the contents of the bag onto the rocks. "What if he asks me about poetry?" Bobby runs her fingers through the chips, dividing them into little rectangular piles. "You'll have to tell me what to say, Jude!"

"Tell him you burn with a hard gem-like flame." I sit down and assume the cross-legged pose of the swami. I puff Child's joint of marijuana and imagine I have the swami's confidence in a world nobody can see. Dreamily, I put the soles of my feet on either side of my groin. My left hand is on my left knee, my fingers gracefully spread so the thumb and forefinger can hold the roach clip. I stare out across the water at the mainland. "From here, it's easy to see the life I live on shore is only one of many possible lives."

Child squats beside me and takes over the joint. "I know what you mean. We have so many potential selves and not enough time to be each of them."

"I don't know what the two of you are talking about," Bobby says. "I only have one self and it's always the same." Bobby scoops up a handful of chips from the sixth pile. Five piles are gone now . . . three more wait to be eaten. "Isn't that right, Jude?"

There is no answer. The joint is a burnt-out stub in the roach clip and Child and I lie sprawled side by side on our backs, legs shoulder-width apart, hands down, palms up to the sky.

"Jude? Aren't I always the same?" Bobby says.

"Yes, that's one of the things I like about you. You don't change yourself to fit the context. Child and I are chameleons."

"You have to be a chameleon to be a filmmaker," Child says.

"You mean you're deceitful?" Bobby is eating busily now, not stopping to count the rectangles. My voice is just a murmur.

"Yes, in a nice sort of way."

"Do you want to hear more about the ideal face?" Bobby asks. We don't answer. Bobby finishes the last rectangle of chips. She lies back, her head under the newspaper. A moment later she is snoring.

"Now's our chance," Child says softly.

4:48 p.m.

Child curls over me, careful not to crush me, his mouthparts quivering. The pheromone message he is passing me on his sponge-like tongue says: "Our queen is asleep, worn out from her journey. She wants a rest before we start the digging for her new home." He rears onto his hind legs, and I look up in gratitude as his dark tube eclipses the sun . . . huge, fierce—he is a god to me, our insect father Protoptera . . . the beginning of bug life. Gently, his antennae graze my skin and I leak with moisture . . . I feel it seep out of me. My love sap drips onto his mandibles until they shine with the colours of the rainbow . . . ah, thank Protaptera indeed. Child is milking me, his dark bug eyes soft with love and I sit back on my slender legs, push my drooling anus into his mouthpart.

Now Child's antennae stop waving. His head snaps back. He hears a puff of noise. I hear it too. A sound like feathers fanning the air. Then I see the murderous shape tower over us—winged, pop-eyed, snake-snouted, waving its triple-jointed arms. I stare in terror at the hideous face. The noise is coming from the transparent veined wings spreading like sails on either side of its terrible head. Oh, the head is horrible—two intent little pink eyes stare at me fixedly beneath long antennae that curve to the sky like a set of horns.

I scream, "Look out!" but no sound comes out of my mouth. Bobby's head swings back and forth frantically in one of the mantis' triple-jointed arms. And then eggs burst out like foam and spray the head of the murderous bug until all but its little pink eyes are covered with Bobby's babies. My queen's jointed legs stop flailing. Her abdomen is gone and half her thorax is missing. Now the mantis fastens her eyes on Child. I shake my feelers to warn him, but I am helpless as long as Child's feathery antennae stroke my love-sick abdomen. I hear another crunch as the mantis chews into his shell. Oh Protoptera, dear Proppy? Can I call you that? The mantis will eat me too but I can't run away and save myself! Child's strokes are weaker, he bumps my anus once, twice more and I flow on like the waters of the Sound, like a river, milky as a cow only good for dairying, I must hold still and let whoever has need feed on me.

4:49 p.m.

Suddenly it is quiet, dangerously hot. The hands of our three painted bodies stop moving to our mouths. You squint at us, then you blink. You hear a happy drumming sound. Is it a cicada, the heat bug, newly emerged from the earth where it's burrowed as a grub? In the southern United States, cicadas live underground for thirteen years. Here they remain seventeen years in the dark. Which is why Canadian cicadas love heat and sunshine more than cicadas from New Orleans.

And this is the year of the cicada. Hundreds of them are emerging from the ground at this very moment—with little ruby telescopes that explore the air over their heads and big vulnerable eyes, the soft, large, faceted eyes that tell them what happens on the right and left. They are shedding their old skin like car wrecks on the granite rocks. Their eyes give them a slightly paranoid look, and with those eyes, there is good reason to be paranoid. But it isn't an army of cicadas flexing their abdominal segments as they crawl over the rocks to you, drumming for a mate. Bull is hovering directly overhead in the Cape helicopter. It casts a shadow the size of a house on the granite rocks. "Go away," you want to shout but you stop instead and stare at the bodies. Their positions have changed. The swollen body is off by itself, curled on its side under the overhanging ledge where Emily chews her stick and where, deeper in the darkness, Pig sleeps.

Two other bodies, though, are closer together. The head of one is on the stomach of the other. It is more accurate to say the head of one is resting face down on the groin of the other. The hair on this head is long and falls in feathery tufts across the legs of the body underneath. It is unclear where one begins and the other ends.

You feel a cluster of emotions. Fear for the welfare of the group. Then guilt because you can't warn them and anger because they have got themselves into this position in the first place. You are aware emotions come in a cluster like a committee. That is why experience is confusion, as the swami says. But that doesn't make you feel better. You are frustrated at your helplessness. You dread what is going to happen next, but nothing does. The helicopter moves off to the south and then drops down into the pines of Good Cheer Island. You walk to the edge of the cliff to try to see it again and then you notice the Sunfish skimming, its sails luffing a hundred yards from the shoal where the dory crashed. A familiar freckled body is in the stern.

4:50 p.m.

"Dick-ie! Dick-ie! Yoo hoo!" A woman's high-pitched voice is calling Child, calling him by his real name. Child is up in an instant. He wears only his long-sleeved shirt. His painted bum looks oddly clothed, as if he is in orange underwear. Then he whispers, ''Sorry'' and is off, sprinting across the slabs of granite. His thin Struwwelpeter legs pump up and down. He bolts over a boulder and vanishes. He heard the shout the way a sleeping mother hears the cry of her child. I stand up slowly and go to the edge of the bluff. My heart sinks. It's Shelly. She is wading in along the submerged shelf of rock, dragging the Sunfish. Shelly sees me and affects a triumphant pose—the rope over her shoulder like an ancient fisherman bringing in his catch.

''Yoo hoo, Jude!'' she calls again and I wave hello feebly. Beside me a pebble bounces down the cliff and free-falls into the water below. Bobby puts her arm around my shoulder and we stand hip to hip, the way we have stood every summer since I can remember. I lean against her for reassurance. The intruder is down below, looking at us, lifting up her trusting freckled face and waving her hideous wide brimmed sombrero as if we will be glad to see her. The soft wind tugs at her clothes. She is wearing a diaphanous white muumuu which looks out of place in the rocky landscape.

Suddenly Shelly looks down and squeals. Child bends down, pulls something out of her foot. I watch attentively. Nothing is lost on me. Not his concerned smile or the consoling way he puts his hand on her shoulder as they turn to renew their ascent. He looks up, sees me watching, and drops his hand. But it is too late. I saw his protective gesture. Perhaps Shelly is Child's ward, his personal underdog, the way she used to be mine. If so, I'm lost. Nobody leaves anyone they feel responsible for.

''You know what they remind me of, Jude?'' Bobby pulls out a cigarette and I light it. ''Jack Spratt and his wife who could eat no lean.''

I don't answer. The rage I feel over Shelly's arrival is deep and terrible like the light of the setting sun on Gull Rock. If only I had recourse to the swami's perspective. What a relief it would be not to slip under the whirl of sensations . . . to be detached as he is. But I am giving in to the old games of summer. And Bobby's rules are coming back to me. One: always appear unconcerned about the outcome. Two: do not, oh never, grant an identity to the rival.

Down below Shelly has stopped to remove her muumuu which must have been hot in the yellow afternoon sun. Suddenly, her curvaceous white body looks too exposed—a jiggly blur of flesh banded in skinny parallel lines by her bikini.

"Of course, Shelly's never been very athletic," Bobby goes on. "But some men don't like their women to look starved. They like to sink into a body that feels like an air mattress."

I exhale, frowning. "Bobby?"

"Yeah."

"Do you think Child will marry Shelly?"

"He's as good as married, you dummy. He just doesn't realize it."

"But he doesn't love her."

"So what. He needs her to shock his family so he can pretend he's different from them."

"That not true. Child is a renegade—he can't help the family he was born into."

"Then why's he with her?"

"But he's so unhappy!"

"Isn't everyone?"

"No—that's not right."

"Listen. He can be as unhappy as he likes but it won't change anything. Shelly knows her man."

"Not like I do."

"Oh, you think he's interested in you, do you?"

"Maybe."

"Are you telling me you are having an affair with Child Cape?"

"Maybe."

"Well, end it. He's not for you and you're not the type a Cape marries either."

"What type is that?"

"They're either rich so the Capes know that they aren't after their money or dumb so they don't threaten their egos."

"What about you?"

"I'm dumb and rich."

"That's not true!"

"Sssh. They're coming."

Below us, Shelly is limping up the last bit of the climb on her thick-ankled feet. She has the kind of feet it's easy to imagine as hairy. Bobby's wriggly stretch marks prove she is a mother, a real woman. Shelly's soft body is not due to a self-sacrifice she's made to propagate the human race. It is a monument to lack of exercise.

I suck in my stomach, conscious of my physical superiority. Inch by physical inch, I am better. My breasts are pointed and tip-tilted like the breasts of Constance MacKenzie before her Greek lover seduces her in her *Peyton Place* kitchen. The small brown nipples spring erect to the touch at the slightest drop in temperature, my stomach slopes like a sunken floor between the ridges of my hips. I place my hand on my slender pelvis. That's it. Compare flesh. Seek reassurance in the body. My waist can be circled twice round with a pair of hands—hers only by the longest of arms. I spit on my rival's thick ankles. How can I give up my darling to a woman whose breasts swing out of control like sunburnt dirigibles?

Emily drops her stick by Bobby's feet and begins to make little whining sounds in her throat at the sight of Child helping Shelly up the last slab of granite. Bobby reaches down, pats Emily's head. "Child was all over me like a rash last year, you know," Bobby mutters. She moves her hand from Emily's head to the dog's sore paw, and the dog slumps against her. Child and Shelly are only a few yards away now.

My eyes drift sideways to Bobby. "What do you mean, 'All over you like a rash'?" I smile uncertainly.

Bobby stretches . . . yawns. "Just what I said. He wanted me to be a threesome with him and Shelly." Bobby yawns again. "Child's bored. He'd do it with a monkey to get away from his ball and chain. I wouldn't take him seriously if I were you."

The pair is almost upon us. I sigh and walk over to the buoy so I don't have to see Shelly, her hands hanging by her gorilla thighs. Child's face inside the halo of yellow hair looks frightened.

"Hey!" Bobby shouts at me. "He's just a man. We don't expect much out of them. Remember?"

I sigh again and pick up Child's paint brush. I paint a red

stripe down my left cheek. And then slowly another war-like red stripe across my forehead where it belongs.

4:59 p.m.

You are still on the bluff looking down at Shelly and Child. You have just noticed their physical unsuitability. How she towers above the frail fair-haired man, a female gorilla in a crocheted bikini. Her bikini is the colour of pale ice, the same bleached colour as the open water. You are surprised she dares to wear the colour of the sound on her body. You can't see the details from here but you remember how it looks up close . . . the dimpled thighs . . . the over-fed stomach hanging over her pudgy pubic triangle . . . the bloated breasts. . . . Shelly's body is an affront to the natural world. You can't imagine Child fastening himself to her and bobbing up and down, a hapless trifle, a tidbit, pounding away at the enormity of her fleshy ruins.

Of course, Old Voyeur Eyes, you are simply exhibiting human prejudice. No taboos exist in nature against little males and giant females. The common toad squishes himself against the skin of his gargantuan mate, holding fast with small, bulb-shaped fingers. The male of the ladybird beetle is a quivering footnote at the end of a scarlet behemoth.

5:01 p.m.

You are sitting on Gull Rock like the three monkeys, trying to be good. You are doing three postures at once. Mouth shut. Speak no evil. Eyes closed. See no evil. Hands over ears. Hear no evil. You no longer want to hear the narrator who is projecting her inner worlds at you as if you were no more than a screen for her erotic fantasies.

You want to go home. You want to bail out of the action which is taking an ominous turn. You can't say why for certain. Perhaps it is the way the light penetrates your skull through your eyes, driving out your thoughts and activating your sex glands. And you feel helpless in its scorching hold, like the moth in its ever-diminishing spiral path towards the candle flame. Yes, you are getting more and more uncomfortable. Your brains are baking here on the rocks.

You open your eyes a little. This is what you see: a beast in a sombrero hunkering down on her stumpy legs, a huge female gorilla offering her rump to a frail-looking man with a nimbus of golden hair. The blond man stares at her stupidly. You may as well eavesdrop a little. You drop a hand from your left ear. You hear a growl. You drop your other hand so your right ear can hear too. The growl is coming from me. I throw back my head and open my rubbery black lips. My yellow incisors glint in the sun. Shelly looks up just as I run leaping down the rocks and land on her back. She whimpers in fear, but I sink my fangs into her pink pointed clitoris. Blood spills into the air like a thin stream of water from a garden hose and Shelly runs off, her long arms swinging. I lope after her, beating my chest. Emily follows us, leaping up at Shelly and growling, her stick still in her mouth.

5:06 p.m.

"You could get blood poisoning from this, you know."

Shelly shakes her finger at Child Cape, smiling. She is methodically cleaning his chest and torso with turpentine.

Child nods but his eyes look distracted too. Bobby is scowling and smoking like Jack Webb in the old *Dragnet* shows.

Now Shelly makes a wiping motion in the air, as if she wants to clean the sky too, and gestures at me. "Sometimes I feel like a big clumsy ox next to Jude. She's so graceful. I thought that this afternoon when I saw her getting into the dory with you, Child. You know what I mean . . . I wish I was slender like that but it's too late now, Child. You have to love me."

"I don't have to do anything," Child says.

"Oh, isn't he cruel?" Shelly giggles. "He doesn't mean it though, girls."

"You know I always mean what I say," Child says.

Shelly sets down her rag and dries Child's shoulders with a towel. "Okay Dickie. Turn around and I'll do the rest of you." Child shakes his head and sits down against the cooler, his hands on his orange knees, looking up at the sky.

"All right, I'll do Jude." Shelly giggles and turns towards me with an affectionate wink. For a moment, I feel the old love for her. She is a good sport about Child's moods. I would never have the confidence to take them so lightly. Then she puts her hand on my knee and I stiffen. If she so much as touches me again, I, the executioner who waits to do my bidding, will reach out and kill her—strangle her in front of the others. Shelly notices the way I am sitting—ready to strike at the least provocation—and laughs. "Relax! This will only take a jiffy!" She starts to daub my knee. "Sometimes I wonder why Child is with me when he could be with somebody like Jude," she says. "But I've always admired you, haven't I, Jude? Right from the day Mother first pointed you out to me—collecting polliwogs at the pond. I was tubby then; I didn't like to do sports but Jude read me her stories and made me laugh."

"Was Jude tubby too?" Child asks.

"No—Jude was skinny and I wanted her all to myself but she had this jealous friend, Bobby, who stole my dolls and broke their arms." Shelly wipes her forehead with her muumuu and starts in on my ankle.

"What do you mean I broke their arms? You broke their arms," Bobby says. "Have you ever heard of anything so weird? A girl breaks the arms of her own dolls so she can fix them?"

"Who told you that?" Shelly says.

"You did, you dope. When you and Jude tried to get me to play with you. Only I didn't play with dolls."

"And now look at you—the mother of two pups and about to spawn another," Child says.

"Don't knock it. My children are the one thing I've made that I'm proud of," Bobby growls. "I'm not interested in a swinger lifestyle like you and Shelly."

"She doesn't know what she's missing, does she, Child? At our last party, I had the best orgasm of my life." Shelly is cleaning my calf very enthusiastically. "At first, I didn't want to go that route but Child persuaded me. Then I couldn't get enough of it, could I, Dickie?"

"Oh—you're just making that up to impress us," Bobby says.

"Just because you're a stick in the mud." Shelly's hand moves boldly across my thigh. It travels along the inside of the baby skin, moving with determination towards my hip joint. "Bobby should try somebody out besides that boorish husband of hers. Bull doesn't even like women—not like my Dickie.''

I find myself watching Child as Shelly talks, waiting for him to tell her to stop chattering, but he doesn't say anything. He only smiles, his eyes half closed as he strokes Pig's joyful little head, and I feel angry at him for staying silent, for enjoying her bragging.

Suddenly, Shelly's cloth feathers the top of my right thigh and I feel a hotness between my legs. My crotch pulses. Oh God, surely I am not hot for Shelly. Not for her dimpled body. Shelly stops and winks at me.

''Dickie likes open relationships but he'd like to have babies, too. Of course, he'd never admit it, would you, Dickie?''

Suddenly, I sit up gasping. The damp cloth is near my crotch. Already the tender skin is burning. Above me, Shelly is breathing in quick little grunts. Her freckled face is grinning as if she knows she is doing something I like. Behind me, Child jumps up and grabs the cloth out of her hand. ''You don't let turpentine get near the genitals! Do you want to kill her?'' Child's face is perspiring. The strands of fuzzy blond hair stick out stiff with sweat, like candyfloss at a fair. He puts a hand on my shoulder and tears fill my eyes.

''Oh Jude—I'm so sorry,'' Shelly gasps. ''I just got carried away talking about children.''

''And why did you drag up that old business of group sex? You know I don't go in for that any more.'' Child says crossly. ''Nobody wants to hear yesterday's news.''

''Oh, but they do. Especially today, of all days.''

''What do you mean, 'today of all days'?'' Child says.

''Oh Child, stop pretending. We have to tell everybody our news.''

''Oh that. Not now,'' Child says.

Shelly jumps to her feet excitedly. ''Child, I can't wait any longer.''

Bobby reaches into the cooler for more ice. ''For God's sake, what news are you talking about?''

''Save it for later.'' Child's head is bent. He lights another joint and walks towards me, holding it out in front, like a kid in an egg-and-spoon race at a Sunday school picnic. He walks as if the slightest distraction will make the joint tumble out of his hand. "For you, Jude." Child smiles uncertainly. His hand is trembling.

"Well, if you won't tell them, I'll have to do it," Shelly says. "I'm going to have a baby; I've suspected for a month but Child didn't want me to tell anybody, unless I knew for sure. Well, now I do! I'm two months gone." I take the joint from Child. I inhale as if Shelly hadn't said anything. Then I lie flat on my back and stare at the sky. I have fallen down as if somebody's struck me. A shadow moves across my face.

"Aren't you happy for me, Jude?" Shelly asks.

I look up dazed and don't answer. Child is watching me. He lowers his head. "It's Shelly's baby."

"Oh—Dickie! Don't say that," Shelly laughs nervously. "It's your baby, too."

"No. You're the one who wanted it."

"Oh Jude—what'll I do?" Shelly bursts into tears. "Child doesn't want our baby."

"Oh—sure he does," I say awkwardly. "You have to give him time to adjust." I sit up slowly and wait for Child to meet my eyes. "You must admit this comes as a bit of a surprise."

5:13 p.m.

A strange blur is approaching in the silver blue void. It's a man standing upright on a piece of metal curved like a chariot. His object glides across the surface of the sound like a water spider. Behind the windshield, Bull is grinning maniacally.

I saw the same grin on the face of Jonah Prince when he fouled the sailing race. Of course, the expression is transformed on Bull's face. Bull's grin is like the leer of a tiger beetle about to tear open a horsefly. Now Bull cuts the engine. His metal chariot skims on its own momentum into the cove. Just above the submerged ledge, Bull yanks up on the handlebars again and vaults off the side.

I can hear him laughing below. Bull is whistling, thrilled with his daring, and jingling the keys to the ski boat in his hand. Now he assaults the cliff. His long arms seem to drag on the ground as he rushes up the slope, panting and puffing. He knows we are watching and wants to prove he is still an athlete. He disappears into the crevice lined with juniper, his feet encased in the running shoes you wished for just an hour ago. Far behind him to the south, the island of Jonah Prince hovers in the horizon halfway between the water and the sky.

"Dick-ie! Time for happy hour!" Bull calls, grinning as he ambles over to join us. Bull is a long slippery piece of skin in the sunlight, and Child is a half-naked orange Indian. Bull looks at Child's genitals. "I'd be careful if I were you, Child." Bull pokes Child in the ribs. "Remember what happened to Goldfinger?" Then he picks up the paint tin.

"I knew you wouldn't be done yet." Bull smiles at Bobby. "I saw you this afternoon from the chopper."

"You flew over?" Child looks at me.

"Yeah, on the way home from picking up the groceries," Bull says. "The old man is in a foul mood. I asked him to let me run the company but he says the sale has to go through."

"You! Run Cape Pianos!" Bobby snorts. "You should have stuck to swimming."

Dully I listen to Bobby insult Bull. I have only two thoughts: Shelly is winning the competition; today is the last day of summer.

6:10 p.m.

The Capes are posing by the flagpole for Higgins. They look more like potato farmers dressed up for a photograph than Canada's first family—as they are sometimes described in Toronto newspapers.

Even my love, the only rebel among them, stands in the back row like a chastised yokel. His halo of lemon hair is drawn back behind his narrow face in a ponytail. He has also taken off his love beads as a concession to his mother, and who knows what other concessions he will make now that the prospect of fatherhood is before him? At least he looks as miserable as I secretly desire him to feel, frowning unhappily beside Shelly, who is smiling eagerly for the camera in a peasant dress and shawl flung across her freckled cleavage. Next to Shelly, Bobby is smiling out of obligation in a summer dress of nautical white. The mound of Bobby's stomach is only a suspicious bulge under the crisp linen. Mrs. Cape, Jr., is not certifiably pregnant in this photograph. Doc Lefroy and Lady Cape, smiling widely, stand behind Sir James, who slumps scowling at the lens in cream-coloured flannels and an open-necked navy shirt. A wicker table covered with two thousand lead soldiers—all 54-millimetre lead from the British firm William Britains—has been set up in front of Sir James to distract the viewer from noticing he is in a wheelchair.

Shasta kneels in front of Lady Cape in freshly pressed Bermuda shorts and Neil squirms in front of Bull, who has slung his arm like a lasso around his son's neck. Bull, his hair stiffened with Brylcreem, is in creamy flannels like his father.

Higgins' photograph will appear above a caption like "The Capes and friends enjoy a summer evening." The swami and I are not in the picture. We are cultural imports brought into the Capes' summer world and reimbursed for our services. So we are sitting off to the side. The swami, knees crossed in lotus position, meditates solemnly in a small grotto ringed with rubbery blooms of orange and yellow portulacas. On his altar stand Shelly's Hindu statues, Lakshmi and Durga, wearing Shelly's dainty hand-sewn saris. Was it only a few weekends ago that Shelly bathed them in milk and sprinkled them with rice for guru purnima? The swami looks like one of her statues too; he is dwarfed by Big Dome, which rises behind him like a Wizard of Oz bubble cracked in half to reveal Little Dome. Little Dome floats inside, hung with inner tubes which Lady Cape suggested the swami use as dock fenders.

I am sitting in a wicker chair on the screened-in veranda, next to an old radio and an early model of the Cape piano. The Cape insignia—a gold C which I used to see on the refectory piano in Merton—glints above the yellowed ivory keys. On my lap is the first chapter of *One Hundred Years of Pianos*. I know it by heart:

Upper Canada 1869. This was the territory Montague Cape came to conquer. Bounded by U-Go-I-Go Sound to the north and the United States to the south, it was a natural drawing card for the young Irish immigrant seeking a market for the finely crafted instruments that were to earn his grandson one of the last titles of knighthood awarded in Canada. Montague Cape was a Methodist abstainer whose austere personality shaped three generations of Cape men; their conservative business practices were based on their founder's dislike of excessive profits.

I don't like the phrase "natural drawing card" but it is hard not to use clichés when you work in the orthodoxy of fact. Perhaps Child is right. I am wasting my time on a history nobody except the Capes will take seriously. But I wanted the chance to understand Bobby's upper-class world—to penetrate its stereotype—and now I have. I pick up my pen and make an asterisk by the phrase "dislike of excessive profits". Then I begin to write:

The religious background of the Capes encouraged a fear of the wealth that cunning, hard work and a belief in upward mobility would inevitably bring. This belief was to place later generations of Capes in the strange position of holding middle-class values but never fitting into middle-class life. The Capes, despite their inherited wealth, believe the purpose of life is to get richer, but they don't suffer from material deprivation like the poor or experience the same stresses and strains as the middle-class so their continuing efforts to better themselves appear grasping. Their position is similar to the position of the rich elsewhere in North America, people who are not so much unhappy (a myth of the middle-class) as alienated by the social ambivalence toward wealth. To strive for wealth in a democratic society is considered a valuable thing to do, but to be wealthy defeats the premise on which our New World culture rests.

I put my pen down and look back at Child's family. My background helps to create my unfashionable sympathy for the Capes. Of course, their doors didn't swing open the way they do for me in Merton because I am Rev. Bell's daughter. Without my job on their paper, nobody in the Cape family would know who I was.

The truth is, Old V.E., I am a lum—what George Orwell calls the "lower upper middle-class" who serve their communities and don't pass on any inheritance to their children. I have been considered rich by the poor and poor by the rich, so I know the prejudice against both classes and each one's private hurts. But neither class knows how bewildering it is to feel classless or invisible. On the visit home for my father's funeral, my mother and I cleared out the family photographs and I found a snapshot which showed the lum law of relativity at work.

In it, the well-tailored back of Sir James was turned to the camera as he cut a ribbon to open one of the Cape's subsidized summer camps near Merton. My father and the rest of the Merton Rotary Club were the men in the dark suits standing behind Sir James holding homburg hats like fig leaves in front of their trousered crotches. They had been reduced to background by the appearance of the billionaire from the city. Does that make Child and me too different? I refuse to believe it. He is also a victim of class position—an outsider like me, escaping from his ghetto of privilege.

Back at the flagpole, the Capes are growing restless.

"Daddy, I'm tired," Shasta whines. Lady Cape bends down, whispers, "There, there." And Higgins turns my way frowning quizzically. Suddenly a blast of sound from the radio makes everyone look at the veranda and the tableau is over as if a curtain has come down on a performance.

"It is a sad day for Canadian business. Negotiations are under way for the sale of the century-old manufacturing firm of Cape and Son," says a nasal voice in a tone that suggests simultaneous regret and delight.

Lady Cape claps her hands and murmurs something to Doc Lefroy but the noise of the radio broadcast makes her words undecipherable.

"Cape's six hundred employees, who for decades have resisted labour's attempt to organize a union in their factories, are petitioning president Sir James Cape in a last ditch effort to stop the sale. . . ." The radio suddenly dies away. I look up. Doc Lefroy, the consummate flunkey, is hunched over the controls, obeying his sister's orders.

"Thank you, Robin. We don't want to hear about the outside world up here." Lady Cape rings a small bell and Sally Love floats out onto the veranda. The wicker tray in her arms holds a runny wheel of Brie cheese, crystal boats of celery and radishes, and two large ironstone bowls heaped with potato chips and rainbow piles of Smarties. The tray represents Lady Cape's compromise with our polyglot of tastes. Two-thirds is junk food—one-third vegetarian. If you want to be healthy, your sustenance awaits you. If, on the other hand, self-destruction is your path, by all means enjoy yourself on the way down.

"It's happy hour, everyone!" Lady Cape calls and slowly the others drift towards the veranda, careful not to walk in front of Sir James who is wheeling himself slowly up the ramp by the veranda stairs.

"Wait, Lefroy." The gravelly voice of Sir James makes everyone stop talking. "Let us not be frightened to hear what the world is saying about us."

"Allow me, Jimmy." Doc Lefroy reaches for the dial and the radio comes back with its nasal sing-song.

"The brainchild of Montague Cape of County Cavan, Ireland, the Cape company has become a Canadian institution. Its time-honoured tradition of community involvement in the summer camps for under-privileged children and local Santa Claus parades co-sponsored with the T. Eaton Company . . ."

The radio clicks off as the swami slowly materializes behind the old piano. He picks up the hors d'oeuvres tray and empties the cheese and Smarties into a nearby wastebasket. "How can we reach the twenty-first century on food like this?"

"Will somebody stop him! Look what he's doing."

"Robin, it's for your own good. Ramaji thinks you and Jimmy eat too many dairy products."

"Pah! He's a fake! Listen, if you want a swami, I'll buy you a real one from California. Now let me hear my radio program."

Suddenly, the CBC voice is back. All of us on the veranda turn and listen. Doc Lefroy stares sadly at the contents of the wastebasket while we cluster around the radio, as if a bit of machinery can breathe the sound of life.

"Wunderkind financier Jonah Prince told an audience of Canada's most powerful businessmen yesterday afternoon that our banks discriminate against small manufacturers and sales out-fits.''

''I don't want to hear about that crook! Turn it off. Doc, you heard me!''

The radio is hushed. Sir James manoeuvres his wheelchair to the edge of the veranda and stares with a melancholy face at One Tree Island. Down below, Jonah's island shimmers in the heat like a mammoth tortoise.

''Isn't it bad enough I have to look at his dump over there! He's ruining our view!''

''It's not very big, Jim, as cottages go.''

''Who cares about the size! It's the design. He has no business building a modern place on the sound. They wreck the land-scape.''

''Jim, behave yourself.''

''I am. This is how I behave. I've lost my kingdom, but I'm still king of the castle. All the rest of you are dirty rascals.''

At the keyboard of the old piano Sir James begins to sing the lyrics from ''Camelot'', staggering to his feet in the middle of the third verse.

I stare open-mouthed at Sir James, singing on his wasted legs exactly as I would have him do in my secret and guilty dream of the rich. Then from the flagpole Child shouts: ''Three cheers for Father and American imperialism! Hip-hip-hooray! Hip-hip-hooray!''

''Ha-ha! Listen to him, will you, Lefroy? He thinks I should save the company.'' Sir James nods at Doc Lefroy, who is caught in the act of retrieving a pie-sized slice of Brie from the waste-basket. ''Last year we exported nineteen pianos. How can I go on with sales like that!''

''You could go into real estate—diversify, Jim, and keep Cape Pianos as a sideline,'' Lady Cape says smiling.

''A sideline—hell's bells! You and Dickie don't know what you're talking about. Even Steinway has problems. It's the com-petition from the Pacific Rim.''

''You never listen to us,'' Child calls back. ''You're selling out your country. Do you hear me, Father?''

"I hear you all right, but do you hear me? I'll stop the sale if you'll run Cape Pianos with your brother."

"Let Bull run it. He's the one for the job."

"See, Joyce! Dickie just wants to criticize! He's not man enough to take responsibility for his suggestions."

"I don't believe in your kind of capitalism! I believe in a socialist democracy!" Child shouts. "A Marxism for the people!" I look anxiously out towards the flagpole where my darling stands scowling at the veranda. Why don't you listen to your father? Compromise with him? I want to shout, but I don't say anything. I am ill at ease in confrontations. I'm a journalist by profession but a better label for me is observer. I rely on my powers of observation. They keep the world at a distance. The world tries to get closer—to move in on me—so I name and identify to keep it away. Besides, my political confusion makes it hard for me to know what Child should do. I'm too entrepreneurial to be a Marxist although Marxism is an ideology I imagine I'll graduate to one day before I die, when I am less preoccupied with worldly things. That way I'll go to heaven with a clear conscience.

"Do you hear me?" Child shouts again. "I believe in participatory democracy. And consensus!"

"You believe in slogans, Dickie," Sir James calls back. "That's the trouble with you. You don't know anything about real life."

"Real life is your excuse not to take risks! It's an abstraction you use to justify your lack of imagination."

"Pah. Go back to filming your Newfie fishermen. You care about them more than us. Lefroy, let's play war."

Sir James wheels himself over to the wicker table which is set for a re-enactment of Napoleon's victory at Austerlitz on December 2, 1805.

6:35 p.m.

The swami and Lady Cape disappear with the ravaged hors d'oeuvres tray and Neil and Shasta run over to their father who is sitting on a moped. Next to Bull, Mister Tom is watering the tomatoes in the vegetable garden. The arc of falling water turns into a rainbow mist behind their fair heads.

"Daddy," Shasta says. "Neil says he's going to the party tonight and I can't come."

"Don't listen to him. Let's go feed the baby yak, chicken." Bull picks up Shasta and puts her on the moped. A cart containing sacks of timothy hay is attached to its bumper.

"Mommy said I can go with the grown-ups." Neil smiles triumphantly at his sister. She sits behind Bull, her arms wrapped possessively around her father's waist.

"Why should you want to do that?" Bull leans out, ruffles his son's hair. "You don't want to meet a phony? A man who doesn't even call himself by his real name."

Neil looks at his mother. She is posing for Higgins—as I watch—smoking defiantly in her prim white dress. Out by the flagpole, Child is walking with Shelly who is picking flowers for the swami's altar. I can see their bent, intent heads, one yellow, one red, over the top of Higgins' shoulders.

"Mummy likes him," Neil whines. "What's his real name, anyway?"

"Preischmann." Bull nods and turns the key. He bumps off past Mister Tom watering his vegetables and Neil walks back to us on the veranda.

"Why doesn't Daddy like Mr. Prince?" Neil says.

Bobby frowns and drops her lighted cigarette off the veranda to smoulder in a bed of portulacas. "Because he's a Jew," she says softly.

"What's the matter with Jews?" Neil pushes his head into Bobby's swelling abdomen. She rustles in the wastepaper basket and pulls out a handful of Smarties, checking to make sure the swami isn't in the vicinity. She hands Neil the candies. Neil puts the orange Smartie on the tip of his tongue and waggles it at me.

"Jude, do you hate Mr. Prince?"

"I should say not. A man that sexy cannot be all bad." I look over Neil's head at Child. He's scowling at Shelly who is holding out a daisy to him like a peace offering.

"Ha-ha—well put," Higgins laughs. "Neil, without Jews, we would not have modern capitalism."

"I don't understand." Neil opens his palm and lets the rest of the candy fall onto the ground.

"Pick them up, Neil. Don't litter."

Neil kicks at the candy. "But you litter, Mummy. You throw away your cigarettes!"

"Look here, Neil!" Higgins picks up a fallen Smartie and flips it like a tiddly-wink into the wastepaper basket.

"Liberalism, capitalism, Judaism—these are the basis of modern society. The Jews were indispensable to the rulers of the old European states because Jewish bankers supplied the states with loans. And Jewish manufacturers supplied European armies with weapons and food." Neil watches in awe as Higgins flicks another Smartie into his open mouth. "But if I tell you more Jude will call me didactic."

I smile at him but my eyes are still on Child. Shelly is untying his pony tail in order to stick the daisy behind his ear.

Higgins' answer was not what Neil wanted to know. He walks away, dragging his toe on the veranda floor. Suddenly, he looks up and smiles. Lady Cape is coming around the cottage with the swami. I look their way in astonishment. They are holding hands like lovers. The monkey face of the swami is wrinkled in a grin. The freckled face of Lady Cape is smiling too. She walks towards Neil, bouncing a little off the rope soles of her canvas shoes.

"Granny! Granny! Can I meet Mr. Prince?"

Lady Cape sweeps Neil into her arms, laughing. "On Sunday, Bobo . . . on Sunday you can."

"And Shasta can't, can she? She's a baby," Neil says, looking concerned. "She can't meet him at the regatta. It's just me, isn't it, Granny? You have to be old before you can meet a Jew."

Lady Cape frowns and puts Neil down. "Hurry along now, dear. Nanny has your dinner waiting." She pats his ear and pushes him into the New Place where Sally Love stands waiting in the shadows.

7:00 p.m.

Lady Cape steps out of the Chimo, then turns and helps Sir James off the yacht. Bull in his stiff creamy flannels and oiled hair jumps off to help her. Then Child steps off, still wearing Pig like a stole. Shelly's daisy is gone from his hair but his love beads hang back where they belong, in the hollow of his asthmatic chest. Then Bobby in her prim afternoon tea dress, Shelly in her peasant ruffles, and the outsiders—Higgins in his Chairman Mao cap and a pair of white chinos, and me, with Child's daisy poking over the edge of my top, resting between my flat breasts.

We stand for a minute together in the boat house. Then Lady Cape walks off through the door into the sunlight, pushing Sir James' wheelchair.

A wooden walkway stretches like a spine over the hump of Jonah's island. My eyes are fixed on the hump as if I am waiting for my first sight of U-Go-I-Go Sound . . . looking west again and again as I drive north for the shine of blue through the shaggy pines.

And then two figures are suddenly visible against the sky—a bald-headed man of medium height accompanied by a young dark-haired girl. They are walking quickly in our direction. The man has on tight white jeans and a green Nehru jacket. His young companion has on black gaucho pants and a white halter top tied in a knot under her small, firm breasts. She seems to be carrying a frothy white ball in her hands. Halfway down the slope, Jonah Prince raises his hand and waves. A second later Katy Hindsmith raises her hand and waves. She clings to his arm as if drunk.

Ahead, Bull and Sir James are waiting. Jonah Prince reaches them first. He shakes hands with Sir James, looking directly into the older man's eyes.

"So you've come for a look at my little rock," Jonah Prince is speaking in a very loud voice so it's easy to overhear him.

Sir James has on his reserved wasp face, the face he shows in Canada's *Who's Who*. He extends a hand, grudgingly. "I'm told it's the best view in the bay," he grumbles. "But you know, Prince, there was a time when our view was the best."

Jonah chuckles. "And then this fellow you'd never heard of stuck up his boat house and ruined everything." Jonah's laugh floats like a golden bubble above our heads and for a moment I forget the book on Cape pianos . . . I forget Higgins and his

camera sheathed in its case . . . I forget Bobby . . . I forget
Child and our situation . . . I forget Shelly beside him. Behind
the smooth shoulders of Jonah Prince the sun is setting in the
west far beyond the shore of One Tree, over the Watchers. The
western light . . . the golden light of summer floods the island
. . . turning our faces blond . . . making the colours of our
summer clothes blaze like tapestries. It shines on the yellow hair
of the men and in the dark eyes of Katy Hindsmith, making
them all too beautiful . . . all too magical . . . and I feel for all
the world as if the others are not real, not even as characters in
a novel . . . and worse . . . that you are my delusion . . . and I
am instead alone . . . making my voyage through the secret and
terrifying pleasures of summer without an ally . . . then I know
this is nonsense because Jonah Prince is turning now to Bobby
who is waiting in her nautical dress for him to speak to her. All
at once there is silence. There is no sound except the noise of
the water washing against the granite of Jonah's island.

Then Jonah smiles and his lustrous white teeth look as if they
are going to pop from his mouth like kernels from a cob of
sweet corn. "I may have the best view of the open sound, but
Good Cheer has the most beautiful women."

Before Bobby has a chance to reply, Pig suddenly lifts her
head and falls like an arm falling, her jaws open wide. Everyone
laughs and I watch Jonah Prince for a sign of fear, but he doesn't
move. He smiles at Pig who hangs coiled in Child's arm like a
drool of wet, shiny rope. Of course, Pig isn't really wet. It's
only the gloss on her scales that makes her olive green skin shine
in the evening sunlight.

"Oh Jonah! Keep it away from Muff!" Katy cries.

"Pig won't hurt you. She's just yawning to clear her throat of
mucus. She's got a cold," Child says to her.

Jonah laughs and turns to Shelly and me who are standing
very still as if we are auditioning for him. I want him to notice
me first. I want Child to see how a man like Jonah Prince is
bored by Shelly and attracted to me. And now he does. He turns
and looks at me. And suddenly I feel foolish for all of us, lining
up for Jonah Prince like boy-crazy girls. "Oh, you again," I
say before I can stop myself.

And Jonah Prince smiles his fresh-corn smile. "Twice a day may be too much for you, Ms. Bell! But not for me!"

Suddenly Sir James bangs down his cane on the walkway. "The sun is over the yard-arm, boys and girls."

"Jimmy! You'll get your Scotch in a moment." Lady Cape looks anxiously at Jonah Prince.

"I don't serve hard liquor," Jonah Prince says.

"You don't have any booze?"

"Only wine." It is a terrible moment as we wait for the deity of civilization to repair the awkward tension growing in the last human outpost before the open water.

"I'll get some Chivas from the yacht," Bull says to his mother, and we start to follow Jonah Prince up the walkway again. Katy totters at his side, carrying her dog. I see she is not inebriated. She totters because she is wearing high-heeled cork sandals with long laces that run up her legs like the thongs of gladiator boots.

7:10 p.m.

The eyesore that is Jonah Prince's Panabode is in the style of a Swiss chalet. Near it, a Canadian flag is flying at the top of a mast, snapping in the breeze. On Good Cheer, the Capes still fly the British Union Jack. I look at Bobby and raise my eyebrows. Is Sir James going to say something about the Empire? Bobby is thinking the same thing too because she rolls her eyes and smiles. Jonah Prince stands, unsuspecting, surrounded by women.

He gestures toward his cottage. By his door, twelve dripping bottles of white wine sit on an old pine board table. A sailing chart is attached to the cottage wall behind it.

"Mr. Prince is a student of Clausewitz?" Sir James points his cane at a sentence pencilled in on the chart: "Moderation in the field of war is an absurdity."

"Yes," Jonah says and smiles.

At that moment Bull walks back onto the deck, waving two bottles of liquor in the air above his head. "Look after these for me, baby?" he says to Katy. She giggles and walks into the cottage.

"I've always admired you Wasps," Jonah laughs. "The way

you think you are morally right because you were born into a certain geographical area.'' Jonah opens the first of his dripping wine bottles. "And look! Women accept such confidence without question! Katy never waits on me like that.''

"Who is Clausewitz, Mr. Prince?'' Lady Cape asks, smiling at Katy who had come back with a tray of rice cakes wrapped in fig leaves and a glass of Scotch for Sir James.

"A military strategist who said war is like business.'' Jonah pauses. "He said fighting fulfils the same function as paying cash in a transaction. It doesn't happen often but when it does, it must be decisive.''

"And what does Mr. Clausewitz have to do with sailing?'' Lady Cape is still smiling at Katy who is walking slowly, the plate held out in front like a professional waitress, towards Sir James. The older man watches her coming with interest. Both his hands rest on the cane standing erect between his knees.

"Lady Cape, a good skipper is like a general,'' Prince says looking at Katy, too. "He must be able to handle variables he can't control, like the wind, the weather, and most of all himself. It's his decisions—whether he should execute a port tack or give his opponent dirty wind—that will make the difference.''

"Dirty wind? Is that when you sail in front of your opponent's boat and block his wind?''

"Joyce, Lefroy gives it to us all the time,'' Sir James says. "What I want to know is who Prince thinks is going to win tomorrow.''

Jonah Prince looks surprised. "Well, I have a few points in my favour but my love of risk keeps me from predicting my own victory.''

"And what about my son Bull?''

"From what I've seen, your son values stubbornness instead of reasoning. You see, Mr. Cape, the winner will be the sailor who can most successfully avoid the flaw in his character. In sailing, like war, the final outcome is determined by who makes the fewest mistakes.''

"Well said. But nobody calls me Mister. I have a title, you know.'' Sir James smiles and looks down solemnly at the plate of rice balls wrapped in fig leaves. Then slowly, he lifts his cane and bangs it on the wooden deck. "Keep that Jewish food away from me," he says.

Jonah's bottom lip sticks out in a pout. "The rice cakes are from Greece, Mr. Cape," he says coldly.

"Ha—from the Middle East! What did I tell you!" Sir James says.

"Jimmy!" Lady Cape looks at Jonah to see his reaction and the rest of us look at Jonah too, watching to see if Sir James' behaviour will make him think badly of us. Prince clasps one of the sweating wine bottles to his chest and slowly tears off the label, whose lettering looks Arabic. For a second, his protuberant cat eyes appear melancholy. Then he throws back his head and laughs and we all smile in relief.

"Ha-ha! Shall I ask Katy to fetch some gefilte fish from the kitchen? And perhaps some sugary Canadian sherry? Ha-ha!"

"Gefilte fish! I know when I'm not wanted!" Sir James taps Bull on his buttocks with the cane. "Let's go somewhere where they appreciate us, son."

"I'm afraid I'll have to go," Lady Cape says, turning to Jonah and extending a hand. "He's not himself. The American take-over happens on Monday." Jonah nods and Lady Cape smiles jerkily at Child. "You stay, Dickie, and make amends for your father."

"I reckon I'm not going anywhere," Child says and points to the glistening wine bottles. "Now that I'm here, I'm not moving."

Bull jerks his head at the hammock. "Are you coming?"

The hammock rocks slightly. Above its rim, the mound of Bobby's stomach is a dazzling white mountain. A brown arm hangs limply over the side, its fingers trailing on the wood of the dock.

"I think she's staying put too," Child says softly. He nods at his brother.

"It's okay—she's with me," Bull grunts and begins to push his father up the incline.

In the setting sun, Sir James' white head glows faintly pink. For a second, I feel frightened and I think of calling the old patriarch back, of begging him to stay and look after his children, and then Child lifts up his empty glass. "Prince—now you've got to show us why we're staying!"

7:19 p.m.

Jonah Prince's gazebo looks just the way Bobby described it to me during the summer she visited his island every night she could manage it. She used to sneak over after dusk in the old dory, the oars going plonk, plonk in the sound, drip-drip, and then she and Jonah ate out here using his gold-plated forks and two-hundred-year-old porcelain while the kerosene lamps cast shadows across their faces and mosquitoes whined behind the octagonal screens.

Tonight Jonah's gazebo is warm from the coals of his custom-made barbecue. It's built into a table covered in white Delft tiles imprinted with his insignia—the orange crown. It feels cozy now to be inside and not outdoors in the rocks and juniper bushes where bugs of all sizes wait to nip you.

Beside me, Child opens a small suitcase and pulls out a long strip of cellophane packets. I don't know much about drugs. I just take them to be obliging, when circumstances seem to call for it, the same way I'd shake hands or wait for my host to start eating before I do. But the little packets with white pills that look like saccharine tables are likely LSD and the packets with shrivelled dark brown tidbits are psychedelic mushrooms.

Child sees me looking and points to a packet whose contents resemble small, angular apple seeds. "What shall it be? The sacred ololiuqui from the morning glory plant? Or one of C.C.'s special numbers—a joint blended with my favourite hash oil!"

Katy giggles and starts to pass around one of Child's joints. "Don't you know Jonah doesn't do dope? He thinks it leads to heroin addiction."

"Jonah—I didn't know you were a tight ass," Child says.

"My pleasures mustn't interfere with my productivity." Jonah smiles as Higgins passes the joint back to Katy, coughing uncontrollably.

And now he turns his odd cat eyes towards Bobby. "Mrs. Cape, is the view not superb? Even your father-in-law admitted it." Without waiting for her answer, Jonah puts his hand on his sucked-in stomach. "This view helped me to recover from the

break-up of Salomon-Prince," he says slowly. "And the cure
has worked so well I'm thinking of going into politics. I'm going
to start my own movement—the Conservative Maximalist Party
of Canada. More of everything for everyone! Each of us will
become richer not only in goods, but in our personal growth!
Maximalism will mean the end of greed and the beginning of
cultivated pleasure!"

"There you go again," Bobby says. "With your pie-in-the-
sky bullshit about everybody getting richer and richer."

"Well, Jonah is a Libra," Katy says. "He wants to restore
order and harmony and make the best of all possible worlds."

"Ah—a Libra," I say, trying to get his attention too. "The
sign of the opportunist. Child's an Aires—rash, reckless, and
complicated. And I'm a Gemini—the sign of the fickle-hearted.
We're the weasels of the Zodiac."

"I've never heard those signs described like that before,"
Jonah laughs and looks at me as if I'm remarkable. "I thought
the idea is to make yourself as appealing as possible."

I laugh to hide my surprise. "Let me finish, Jonah Prince.
Your aesthetic interests and your love of harmony guarantee that
you are a charming companion. But you're also guilty of artful-
ness, selfishness, and having numerous, but not enduring,
friendships."

"Oh, she just made that up," Shelly giggles. She laughs and
starts to daub oil with a matchstick onto a piece of rolling paper.
"Jude has a great imagination. That's why she always looks as
if she's not paying attention."

9:32 p.m.

The shadows from the kerosene lamps of Jonah Prince are
deepening and across the table Shelly is rolling a new joint for
Child, play-acting the role of devoted wife. To hell with the old
rules about ignoring your rival. Maybe it is important to see
Shelly the way Child does. So I light up another cigarette, but
before I look I remember the description of the perfect female
face Bobby read to us today. The face of Venus is one part baby
and one part breeding machine. The baby part, the large eyes
and small chin, makes a man want to take care of you, and the

mature part, the narrow cheeks and high, wide cheekbones, suggests you can pop out babies as fast as rabbits.

All right, it sounds like sexist propaganda but it makes me uneasy on a level I don't want to admit. The goal of nature is not justice but procreation so maybe it's true Shelly and I are in a race to be selected for the propagation of the species.

If so, Shelly isn't Venus because she's too much baby; she looks like a toddler with her fine red hair and pale freckled skin. And I'm too much maturity, with my narrow face and tomboy body. Oh, I wish I was like Bobby. She wouldn't sit and look at the face of a childhood friend as if she were going to get out a pair of calipers.

Now Shelly giggles and licks the ends of the joint, smiling girlishly like Leslie Caron when she hands Louis Jourdan his cigar in *Gigi*, and suddenly I understand what Child sees in her. Why didn't I see it before? It's what I like about her too—the way she can show her vulnerability. My own vulnerability is something I try to hide.

Child takes Shelly's joint, still staring gloomily out of the window. "What is my Dickie looking at?" Shelly says, frowning, and Child mutters crossly, "Pig."

"She'll turn up when she gets hungry," Shelly sighs and I feel a guilty thrill knowing his tone has made her feel slighted. On an island, the most private of places, we have no privacy from each other's little hurts and triumphs.

Anyway, it's time to do something to help Bobby, so I pull out a poem—not the one Child read on Gull Rock but another one—and say mischievously, "Here's something you inspired Bobby to write, Jonah Prince:

Hold on to your privacy
Libra man
Sunlight will shatter
gossamer things
But if you dare, if
you dare to dream
in steel and glass
Your ideas could blind
the sun.

"Oh Jonah, isn't that cute?" Katy laughs and Jonah laughs too.

"I didn't know Bobby wrote poetry. . . . Wait!" Shelly grabs the piece of paper in delight. "Bobby didn't write that—Jude did. See! It's in Jude's handwriting, the script that looks like chicken tracks! Jude's written poems since she was a kid. Only hers aren't published yet. Do you want to hear one of mine? It just appeared in print. It's titled 'Prayer for Durga':

Om Sri Durgayai Namah!
Oh, how I'd love to send you
The softness of the clouds above,
The lightness of the sky so blue,
The tender cooing of a dove,
The redness of a fresh grown rose,
Thank you for the gift, Mother,
Of your love.

"That hasn't been published anywhere." Bobby scowls knowingly at me.

"It has too. It was published in *Aleph Life*," Shelly says. "The swami's newsletter. Do you like it?" Oh, how she brags. "Do you like it?"

"No," Bobby says. "It's drippy."

"I didn't know the three of you were kids together," Katy says. "Isn't that unusual? Three birds sticking together like that?"

"We spent our summers together," Shelly says. "Now Jude has sold out to the capitalist imperialist press and Bobby has become a bourgeoise society matron."

"I didn't want to get married," Bobby says. "It was an accident. And you're just saying that about Jude because you're jealous of her career."

"I am not, Bobby Cape. I have decided to put my writing aside until after I've had children."

"Bullshit! You want Child to get you a job at the *Herald* and he won't."

"Shelly's father called us the golden girls of summer," I say to distract Bobby.

"Yeah and only two of us were real blondes," Bobby adds, scowling.

"Tell me about your summers together!" Jonah Prince says quickly. "Which one was the most popular?"

"Bobby. She was a rebel, like James Dean in the body of a sexy girl."

"Oh, that's only Jude and her romantic baloney," Bobby says. "I failed school but Jude was a brain and a champion golfer."

"Ha-ha. But which one got the boys?"

Shelly giggles. "Bobby had some luck with a local boy but she had to play a trick on us to do it."

"I did not!" Bobby replies.

"She's telling the truth," I say, suddenly angry with them both. "And Shelly, you went along with it."

"I did?" Shelly looks startled. "Are you sure you aren't getting me mixed up with one of your stories?"

"What trick did Mrs. Cape play?" Jonah laughs. "I want to hear about it."

"Jonah Prince, please! It's ungentlemanly to persist in this indelicate questioning. Here I am drinking wine in bloody paradise with beautiful women and you've got them having at each other like terriers! Child, you tell us about your summers!"

"I was bored a lot, Higgins. I had to sit by the tape deck and change the music while Bull sandbagged girls he picked up from Indian Harbour."

"Bored! I refuse to believe it! You don't know how I envy you Canadians for your lakes where one can go for solace and listen to the call of the whippoorwill. The Americans have their frontier, but you have the wilderness, all of those bloody empty spaces connected up by roads. It's a lot better than we have at home, isn't it, Katy? And you learn to swim at such an early age too! You're all regular water babies."

Higgins waves away an offered joint and lifts his glass as a toast. "Let us drink to the ladies. Aren't they beautiful, Prince? There is no joy in sunrise at dawn. No thrill to watch a spotted fawn, or the brown trout swirl, since I met the golden girls of summer! See—I'm not above a verse or two myself."

"Ha-ha! Thank you Higgins," Jonah Prince laughs. "Let us by all means forget the wounds of our adolescence."

"But you were never a teenager, Jonah Prince!" Bobby says.
"What was I then?"
"You were. . . . It's my husband's term for you."

I hold my breath for half a second in case Bobby says what I think she's going to say. And then she mutters, "A NOOC who runs guns."

"Pardon?" Jonah says. "I've heard allegations of gunrunning before but I've never been called a NOOC—to my knowledge."

"It means 'not of our class'—an immigrant."

Everybody gasps as I knew they would and my heart sinks a little for Jonah and Bobby.

9:38 p.m.

Suddenly Katy Hindsmith points at the ceiling and says, "Jonah, why do you clutter up your place with those old Indian baskets? If I lived here, I'd throw out all your junk and get some nice Eskimo carvings."

"Only the nouveau riche buy those things," Bobby says bitchily and Jonah throws her a sobering look that says, "Take it easy; she's only a child."

Bobby's not doing so well with Jonah this evening. I can tell. She's all sharp edges and Katy's no threat to her, either. Katy is turning out to be one of those dumb British women who only sound smart because they've got an accent.

"Child, tell us how you captured Pig in the jungle. I know it will interest Katy," Jonah Prince says, changing the subject.

Katy smiles. "Oh yes! Tell us how you fought the jaguars and the pythons! I want to hear every juicy detail."

"Ask Higgins—he was along for the shoot," Child says frowning.

"It's not the big creatures like Dickie's snake that you have to watch out for in the jungle, it's the little pests . . . like the chigger flea," Higgins says nodding at Child. "It leaves drops of clotted blood behind that make your skin itch."

"No no, Higgins—that's the pium," Child scowls. "The chigger flea grows inside your skin."

"Oh, don't get them started on bugs," Bobby groans. "I

don't want to hear about creepy-crawlies that lay their eggs in cuts!''

"You wouldn't," Shelly says. "Well, I do, don't I, Higgins?" She grabs Higgins' Chairman Mao cap and puts it on her head.

"It's not the big creatures you have to watch for in the jungle, it's the little pests," she says, mimicking Higgins' cockney accent.

I look at Child to see if he is amused. Child is smiling. And all the others are laughing, even Bobby. Shelly's drunken high spirits have charmed the room. Grinning, Shelly takes a puff from a marijuana joint. Then she bursts out coughing, the way Higgins did earlier. Suddenly everybody is howling. Jonah Prince laughs the loudest. He slaps his hand hard on the ceramic tile in front of him.

9:45 p.m.

I pull a bottle of Dom Perignon out of an ice-filled pail. I don't ask. I just go ahead. I laugh and throw my shoulders back so Child can see my slim tanned breasts press against the thin silk of my top. I say to myself the old words Bobby and I used to invoke our goddess. *Men are made to serve me. I am beautiful. They are lowly. I inspire men and am loved for it. Men can't do without me. I am worshipped . . . my function is to give myself and be appreciated.* The old words tend to go on a little. Child isn't looking at me or Shelly. He is staring out the window, looking morose again.

He must pay attention. Listen. Here I go with the last of our old words. *I give men a taste of their possibilities. I encourage them to be the best of themselves. I never have problems or feel needy because I am too busy helping them. The responsibility lies with men to be transformed—to submit to my influence. They need to change, not me.*

Damn. He is still looking out the window. The dope has made him sullen. But the old words are a little silly, aren't they? I giggle and then brandish the bottle above Jonah's head. "Allow me, sir!" I will win the competition against Shelly. If Child

won't pay attention, I will charm Jonah Prince while everybody
watches.

10:39 p.m.

I stand beside Jonah Prince, tall . . . fair. . . . Oh, Great
Goddess, let him notice this slender muscular body. Let him see
my golden face. I laugh provocatively, hoping Child's eyes are
on me. Then I bend over; my breasts graze Higgins' left ear as
I hand him a plate of flambéed bananas. I feel a secret desire to
enslave all men with my beauty, to make Child and Higgins rise
from their chairs and fall at my feet, babbling their desire for
me so all the world can hear.

So I smile seductively at Jonah Prince who is standing beside
me, parodying the manners of a restaurant chef as he scoops out
the bananas with a silver flipper.

"Is this Bananas Prince?" I ask.

"Bananas Prince! Ha ha ha ha. Bananas Bell, you mean. In
your honour, Jude."

"Notice the flattering twist," I say to everyone. "Jonah Prince
is a supreme diplomat. But even so, Bananas Prince sounds
better."

"Ha ha ha. Of course it does. The writer knows."

Oh, Jonah Prince is so charming. I want my laugh to sound
high, clear, infectious, like his. If Jonah Prince were an insect
his laugh would sound like the katydid. Not the pine tree katydid
which says "s-s-s—s-s-s" or the forktailed katydid which says
"tzit-tzit-tzit-tzit", but the true katydid which says the sound
you were expecting in the first place: "Katy did—she didn't—
she did."

10:45 p.m.

"And how are the bananas? Are they not superb?" Jonah
Prince pours me another glass of champagne.

"EGregious," I answer and drink my glass in two swallows.

Jonah Prince smiles. His mouth is a dazzling cavern of ice.
"The bananas are . . . stupendous. . . . A dessert to write home

about,'' Jonah Prince says and laughs again. His teeth are the teeth of the mongoose as it moves its head from left to right, circling in for the kill, keeping its eye on the white unprotected throat of the cobra.

"The bananas are a nine-day wonder . . . splendiferous . . . as good as they can be . . . ,'' I go on.

"Bananas unparalleled . . . the very best . . . optimum. . . .'' Jonah Prince refills our glasses. He is outdoing me with superlatives. And I am succumbing to the dance of the mongoose. He knows, as I do, that charm is a response to fear, a game to disarm the world before it can hurt you. But I am more charming. Yes, far more. Charming. Than he is.

"The bananas are peerless—unmatchable, unsurpassed—of sterling quality—of the highest type! Of the first water. . . .'' I refuse to stop. I will not surrender. I will defy this sorcerer with the power of my adjectives. "A nine-day wonder! *Prima!*'' I drain my glass in one gulp. "No—Princely!'' I hold out my glass again.

"Aha! Princely! You win!'' Jonah Prince takes my hand. Surely he is not going to kiss it. Has he no imagination? I feel his lips part and the tongue of the cobra darts across the brown skin of my hand once . . . twice . . . so there is no mistake. I look across the table for Child but it is Bobby's eyes I see, burning in the shadows.

11:08 p.m.

An untouched glass of Chablis sits in front of you. On your plate is a barbecued lamb chop. You annoy me, Old V.E. You are a bore, sitting there like a bump on a log and watching me perform. Please! Do something! Save me! Stop me from changing into something I don't want to be! I change my form when I want men to look at me. See . . . it's happening now. . . . I am growing large eyes, small chin and nose, and high wide cheekbones. . . . The eye width three-tenths the width of the face. . . . It's the face of Venus that Bobby read about on Gull Rock. Only something is wrong . . . my face is filling in here . . . collapsing . . . the way channels dug in the sand grow wide and shallow after the waves fill them . . . then the next wave comes and the channel is gone. . . . Oh, the proportions of my face are stretching out of whack—pulling apart in opposite directions like Silly Putty until my head is enormous with huge, dilated nostrils and stump-like teeth. I am a cartoon of desire— a hippopotamus of lust lumbering over to squash you on rotund legs, my belly shimmering slightly in its loose folds of skin.

11:45 p.m.

Child is on his feet, opening the door of Jonah Prince's gazebo. A coiled shape sits on the threshold.

"Oooh—is she slippery?" Katy squeals.

"She's dry as a bone," Child says. "And cold from the rocks. Would you like to hold her?

"Are you sure she won't hurt us?" Katy asks as Child settles Pig's thick heavy-ribbed belly around her shoulders.

"Sometimes a noise—or unexpected emotion—frightens the snake so it constricts around its owner's neck and knocks the breath out of him," Child says. "It can happen with exotic dancers. Then the dancer falls down and that scares the snake so it tightens its hold even more."

"And crushes the ribs," Shelly says.

"No no." Child waves his hand impatiently. "That's a misconception. The snake tightens its hold every time you exhale until you can't breathe, so you end up suffocating."

"I say, don't get any ideas," Katy smiles at Pig.

"Pig's not malevolent." Child smiles too. "The snake only does what comes naturally, out of instinct."

"This winter we planned to visit the tribe who helped Child capture Pig. But things have changed a little, haven't they, Child?" Shelly says.

Child stiffens. "We never know what we're going to do—do we, sweetheart?" He pats Pig's head, frowning.

"You never know!" Katy exclaims. "How frightfully quaint!"

"Dickie and I believe in spontaneity," Shelly says. "That's why we have an open relationship. We are more comfortable without structures."

"Isn't three a crowd?" Katy says.

"Not when you trust each other. If I may quote Fritz Perls—'I am not on earth to fulfil your expectations and you are not here to fulfil mine.' "

"Ha-ha, very nice. But to aim for spontaneity isn't spontaneous," Jonah Prince says.

"Quite right, Prince," Higgins says. "You have to be rich to afford spontaneity. Dickie and his girlfriend couldn't do what they wanted if Dickie didn't have money."

"Hey! Stop ganging up on me," Child says. "I can't help the family I was born into."

"But that's your problem, Child," I say. "People discriminate against you because you are a Cape. No matter what daring or important thing you do—nobody gives you credit for it."

"Ha! Ha! What a speechmaker you are!" Jonah Prince says. "But, of course, I forgot. You are a writer." He comes towards me carrying a bowl of ice cream. "Writers make good *sous chefs*, Ms. Bell." He hands the bowl to me just as Pig shoots forward from Katy's arms and drops her triangular snout into the ice cream.

Katy shrieks. Child blows his dog whistle. Immediately, Pig looks around as if she knows she has committed a *faux pas* and wriggles back to Child.

"You see? Higgins is right," Jonah Prince says. "Who else but Child Cape would have time to teach manners to snakes? But go on, Ms. Bell. Tell us more about your theories on wealth," he says smiling. "What side are you on?"

"I'm on nobody's side. My class position is too ambivalent."

"Aha! An uncomfortable position. So we have more in common than our love of beauty."

"We do?" I look at Jonah Prince in surprise.

"Oh yes," he laughs. "I am—as Mrs. Cape so bluntly put it earlier—an immigrant. Writers and immigrants always hold minority positions."

"And so do filmmakers," Child says. "All artists have to work with the people to destroy the systems of civilization that enable the poor to be disinherited. Or else the poor of the world will rise up and destroy us. They will poison our water systems, they will bomb our airports, they will seize our nuclear power stations—because we were too concerned with our silly material comforts to listen.''

"A pretty speech, Dickie." Higgins says. "But most people have a jolly hard time managing their own lives, let alone enough energy to change the world.''

"I don't accept pessimistic world views, Higgins. They are irrelevant.''

"Ha! Ha! Irrelevant! You can't make the world correspond to an ideal, Dickie. The world will insist on being itself.''

"But what do you do, Prince—if it isn't to make the world conform to your vision? You couldn't build your racing boats without believing that.''

"I make a product out of plastic, Dickie. People are not bent into shape so easily, although I grew up under a government that tried.''

"You tell him, Mr. Prince! Dickie's always looking for role models—for anybody who is different from his family.''

"Oh, be quiet, Shelly. You sound like my father.'' Child scowls.

There is a sudden sizzling noise and Jonah stands before us with another frying pan of flaming bananas. "We are getting too serious," he says disarmingly. "Jude! Pour on the cream! You see, we are each in our own way optimists. Ha! Ha! And what is an optimist but somebody who believes that just around the corner in time everybody will think like us. Ha! Ha!''

12:39 a.m.

The Great White Prince has left us to smoke dope in his boat house. Bobby is with him—three points for her and a minus for Katy Hindsmith, who is sprawled on the floor beside me sucking on Child's hash pipe, her baby-fine dark brows crooked with concentration. She passes the pipe to me and when I take it, she lets her hand drop on my shoulder. "Jonah can be such a bore sometimes," she sighs. "I don't know why he thinks he has to be nice to that silly pregnant lady.''

Katy offers the pipe to Higgins who inhales deeply and then passes it to Shelly who waves it away and staggers drunkenly over to Child. "Darling, let's go home," she says. "We have a lot to talk about."

"Not yet," Child says, swinging back and forth in a white hammock at the far corner of the room. Shelly lets herself half fall, half slide down until she is lying on top of him. The hammock joints creak. "Ooof!" Child says. "What's the matter with you? Stop being such a clinging vine!" The hammock swings back and forth for a moment. Shelly doesn't say anything. She lies face down on Child's chest.

Katy Hindsmith struggles to her feet and walks over to them with the hash pipe. Child looks up, his eyes frightened as if he doesn't know what to do. Katy holds the hash pipe to his lips. He sucks, exhales, choking.

"You're supposed to hold it, silly!" Katy says. She snickers and looks out the screen door of the boat house. We are two floors up. An urban height.

"It's funny we can't hear them," Katy says. "They've been gone a long time." She looks down at the swaying hammock and giggles. "Can I get in too?" Shelly doesn't move and Child's eyes only grow wider. Katy kicks off her gladiator sandals and slides in beside him. She snuggles against his arm and looks up at me. "You don't mind, do you?" she says. "I feel a little lonely."

"I don't mind," I say. I look at Child. If only she knew. Still, I feel a little sorry for her and I can tell by the way Child is smiling at her that he feels sorry for her too.

"I know you all feel sorry for me," she says. "And I feel sorry for myself. I can't deny it. Jonah gets made at me when I'm jealous. He says jealousy is bourgeois. Well, I guess that's what I am. Bourgeois."

"I don't know," Child says. "I don't know if jealousy is the result of lack of a true feeling for the other person or a result of real love."

"Hey! You talk just like her," Katy says and points at me. "How come you two aren't married?"

"Excuse me, ladies, but this is getting a little uncomfortable," Child says. He taps Katy on the shoulder and moves his chin up and down on Shelly's head. The gesture is not without friendly overtones.

"I'm bored," Katy says. "Isn't there something we can do?"

"We could go to Sauna Island," Child says. "We could go there and take a steam bath in the moonlight."

"I don't want to go, Child. I want to go home," Shelly says.

"So we'll drop you off, then," Child says.

A sudden shine of light streams through the boat house window and then we hear the ache of noise that is as familiar now as the lap of waves against the shore.

Katy jumps up and runs to the window. "They're back!" She turns and looks at us. "But let's go anyway! Let's go to Sauna Island. Jonah can come with us if he likes." She smiles at us conspiratorially. "I bet pregnant ladies don't like to steam in the moonlight," she says. She presses her face against the screen. "You're just in time, Jonah!" she calls out. "We're going to Sauna Island."

Child and I look at each other again. I'm touched by her determination to underplay what is going on. It's obvious she is being left out. It makes me want to protect her. Now we clatter down the steps of the boat house. Bobby and Jonah are sitting in the boat at the edge of the dock. Jonah is frowning and Bobby is staring moodily out across the water. We climb into the Thunderbird: Katy Hindsmith carrying her dog, then Higgins and Shelly, then Child carrying Pig, then me. It is after midnight, and we are behaving like a couple. Nobody questions it. Not even Shelly, who has passed out on the seat beside me. She nods against my treacherous shoulder, like a head hitting the pillow. Jonah looks at Bobby. "You want to go to Sauna Island?" he says.

"Two party poopers want to go home first," Higgins says.

Jonah laughs and the Thunderbird slides noiselessly across the silver water. The shadowy fringes of Good Cheer rush by us and the wind whips Child's feathery hair behind him. My darling looks as if he has just suffered an electric shock. The wind blows my hair off my face too and I throw my head back and laugh. Under the cover of darkness, he takes my hand.

1:09 a.m.

You are part of a long brown centipede oozing over benches above and below you, breathing scalding hot air down your dripping back. Just when you think you can no longer stand the heat, a segment of the centipede breaks away. "I can't stand it—I'm going to faint," Katy cries by the first row of benches and opens the door. The centipede jumps and wriggles as the night air blowing over its skin turns to smoke.

"Shut the door, you dope!" Bobby calls. "You don't take a sauna with the door open."

"Katy, Katy! Shut the door!" Jonah Prince laughs. "You're lucky you are not in Sweden where people beat themselves with birch rods for pleasure—ha-ha."

"Jonah, I hate you!" Katy says. The door opens wider and Katy runs out.

On the floor, the tin box under the heap of rocks is red and glowing. Child jumps up, pokes his head out the door, and then turns back, grinning. "She's on the veranda," he says. "She's okay, Jonah." He dips a tin pot into a cedar bucket and sprays water on the steaming rocks. "Let's make this the hottest steam of the summer," he says. The centipede shrieks and then another cool draught of air fills the room.

"Is my wife in there?" Bull walks in and weaves towards the tier of bodies. "There you are! Come down this minute!"

Bobby says, "I'm comfortable where I am."

"I can't trust you for a moment, can I, you bitch?"

"Hey brother! Tie it down. She's your wife," Child says.

"I'm counting to ten and if Bobby's not down by then I'm going up. . . . One steamboat, two steamboats . . ."

"You're upsetting yourself for no reason," Jonah Prince says. "Your wife's behaviour is quite innocent."

"Keep out of it, Prince. Bobby, come down or I'll come up there and get you. . . . Three steamboats . . . four steamboats . . ."

He begins to climb up the tiers of bodies. The bodies refuse to part and let him up and Bobby climbs up another tier.

"You made me burn my leg on the wall, Bull. Stop being such an oaf."

"Well, if you didn't move away, you wouldn't have got burnt. Old Bull wouldn't let his woman come to harm. Get back down here and sit beside me."

"Sit by yourself. You're drunk. I'm going to sit beside Jude."

"I don't think your wife should go anywhere when you talk to her like that," Jonah says.

"You think you're smart, don't you, Prince? You came up this weekend just to get invited to the regatta. Well, we'll see who the real man is tomorrow!"

"Bull. Please. We've had enough."

"Okay, Bobby. You'll be sorry."

At the door, Bull turns and scowls in Jonah's direction. "And you will be too, Prince."

"I apologize for my husband," Bobby says and Jonah nods. He looks pleased Bobby stayed.

"Let's disappear," Child whispers and we rush out the door. You stumble after us. Child and I jump into the water and our bodies disappear into the inky wetness. You take a breath and jump in too. The sensation is indescribable. First the scalding heat and then the scalding cold. You don't know what I'm doing trying to put it into words.

1:30 a.m.

Nobody has any idea where to find Child and me—which is just the way we want it. We are in hiding in a crevice at the top of Gull Rock. On a slick piece of black granite. The granite is marbled with a streak of mica that stands out like a silver vein in the moonlight. Child is lying on the flat part of the rock and I am kissing the line of soft blond hair that runs from his belly button to his cock. There is no time for me to have an orgasm but at least I can give him pleasure. I taste him, hot and thick, his skin sweet from the apple-scented shampoo he uses as soap. His cock fills my mouth. It never fits quite right. It wasn't meant to. I will swallow him anyway until nothing is left, until his slippery male body, the cool and shadowy rocks, the dark triangle of the buoy against the moonlit sky all disappear down my throat.

2:03 a.m.

There are shouts out on the water. The noise of another boat. And Katy's voice. "We know you're out there somewhere! And we're coming to find you!"

We sit up slowly. The Thunderbird chugs into view on the satin void. "We'd better talk," Child whispers in my ear, sighing.

2:15 a.m.

Child and I sit side by side, arms touching, on the furthermost tip of Gull Rock. The cliff here juts out like the nose of an iron and points south, directly at One Tree Island. It is steeper on this part of the bluff, and from the granite wall to the black water beneath us, it's a straight drop.

Over Child's shoulder, a lone figure is climbing the southwest bluff. An animal is barking at its feet. Then Katy disappears behind a jutting crevice.

"I know what you're thinking," Child whispers. "And I've been asking myself the same question." He turns and looks out at the silver water and I sneak a glance at his profile. He slumps, sad and still in the moonlight, his shoulders hunched like a small boy.

"I thought she had miscalculated," he sighs. "I thought it was just a scare."

I wait, afraid to speak in case I find I have no voice.

He throws a pebble into the water. "She wants to get married."

"Oh, don't do that." I lean against Child, pressing his skin for reassurance.

"I need time to figure it out. Now there's somebody else to consider—a baby."

"No! No! You have rights too! So do I!"

"Jude," he begins to sob. "Just don't leave me—don't give up on me. I'll make my way to you somehow."

2:30 a.m.

Suddenly, Child motions me to be silent. Katy is approaching, walking head down, calling "Muff! Muff! Muff! Muff!" but there is no sign of the little dog. It is dark suddenly—without moonlight. We are in a round black void where nothing moves except the water far below, shifting in sighing laps.

The Thunderbird floats offshore; Bobby and Jonah's voices are a restless murmur in the bow.

"Is that your snake?" Katy says. "Oh—it looks so far down."

"Come on!" Child says to me. "Pig's after the dog!"

"You're going to jump?"

"Yes. Pig can't hear the whistle from here."

"You can't jump."

"Why not? We jump from here all the time."

"Not from here. We jump from over there."

"A minor detail. Come on, Katy."

Child grabs Katy's arm and Katy gasps.

"Oh dear! You're right! Your wretched snake is chasing Muff!"

"That's a girl—now like this." Child smiles, holds his arms straight out before him. In the diver's pose.

"Child! The water's too low."

"One, two, three. . . ."

Child swings Katy's arms back and positions them out in front, then he jumps and Katy follows him. I watch Child and Katy falling. . . . Child's hair floats behind him like dandelion fuzz; Katy's dark hair stands up like the wings of a bird.

2:45 a.m.

A snake as long as a canoe slips down the granite slabs, lithe, swollen. The snake is eight feet long with a stomach cavity as large as the womb of a pregnant woman. A dog darts ahead of it. And you thought the granite rock was devoid of life. The snake moves ever so quietly on her legless belly. The dog is running towards the water—away from the heights and their mysteries.

And the snake moves slowly after her, curling and uncurling like a Slinky toy.

It *is* Pig. You recognize her joyful little face with the black stripes like ears on either side of her wide-apart eyes. The scrawly "w" of her mouth seems to be smiling at Muff. In fact, Pig looks shamelessly happy as she slips over the cooling rocks. She yawns uncontrollably and for a moment you imagine yourself slipping head first through Pig's stretchy mouth parts and disappearing down the hot passageway. You are pushed deeper and deeper inside by the contractions of longitudinal muscles which are similar to the birthing muscles on either side of a women's vagina. Of course, you know this is unlikely. Anacondas are capable of swallowing a human but they rarely do. Your nerves are on edge. The sound is dark and silent. Perhaps Pig is merely out for an airing. Perhaps she wants to make friends with Katy's little dog. Anacondas are known to like company. And Pig misses her mate, Arnie, who did not survive the winter.

Oh, it's very odd and exotic to watch a tropical snake wriggle in the moonlight on a barren northern island. Only an hour before, we were eating bananas flambé in the gazebo of Jonah Prince. Now you are a witness to an interspecies encounter, Old V.E. But you don't fool me with your expression of concern. You know you can't do anything except observe the disaster, and you watch anyway. Now Pig moves deliberately, thrusting her head this way and that. She has closed in on the poor little dog and is doing a dance for its benefit. Wait! It is the dog—not the anaconda—who is moving its head this way and that at Pig, and Pig is merely staying away from its jaws. Now the dog curls itself into a hump, head down, tail down, and lunges for Pig's throat. The head of the snake sticks up in the air, its body bent like an elbow, ready to push the dog away. Muff shrieks in fear and runs barking into the water. And then Pig plunges into the water and loops herself around the dog, squeezing it in her strong coils. Pig writhes and writhes. There is no other word for what Pig is doing. Snakes writhe. Pig is a fat long band curled around Muff. Then Pig opens her jaws and swallows Muff, who changes into a wriggling lump inside Pig's throat. The lump wriggles and wriggles and then, finally, stops moving.

3:10 a.m.

Katy lies unconscious in Jonah's arms. Jonah walks ahead over the rocks, slowly. Child follows limping. He only sprained his ankle in the dive but Katy has hurt her head badly. All for nothing. Pig has eaten Muff and has disappeared to digest her

meal. I walk behind Child, my head down. If Child and I had
been watching, Katy wouldn't be injured and her dog would still
be alive. Carefully Jonah lowers Katy into the Thunderbird. He
gets in and turns the key. "I'll come back later to tell you how
she is," he calls to us. His boat heads off down the moonlit
channel.

Suddenly there is a heavy step on the stone beside me. Bobby
pushes by and gets into the dory. It rocks from side to side under
her weight.

"Hey! Remember me?" Bobby says. "I can't go with him to
the hospital."

"Too bad for us," Child says grumpily.

Child settles himself in the bow of the dory, his right leg
stretched out straight on the floor of the boat.

"How's it feel?"

"Oh, it's not so bad, Jude."

"That means it's bad."

Child smiles. Is this what love is? A helpless, undeniable
sensation of vulnerability? Ah, it is. I love Child. And I resent
him for making me feel powerless.

5:45 a.m.

We are stationed in Sally Love's bedroom in the old boat
house on Good Cheer. Sally is visiting her boyfriend in Indian
Harbour. You haven't been here before. Its walls are made of
the same shiny blond logs as the guest cabins up by the New
Place. But there's no fieldstone fireplace or Jacuzzi. Just sturdy
Salvation Army furniture—a coffee table, a bed, and two arm-
chairs. A pot of white petunias hangs beside the door on the
veranda.

I am sitting on Sally's bed, Bobby's head on my lap. Child is
close by in a chair with his legs stretched across the bed, a bag
of ice on his ankle. Beside him is an old pair of crutches we
found in the boat house.

"He's not coming."

"Why don't you give it another half an hour? Jude and I aren't
going anywhere."

"That poor little dog."

"Oh Jude, try not think about it," Bobby says.

"Sssh. There's somebody coming now. Do you hear the noise in the underbrush?"

"I hear it."

Bobby suddenly begins to move. Her hips turn, her feet touch the floor, her face suddenly looks very animated.

"It's him. I can tell by the way he walks . . . heels first," she says.

There are footsteps on the veranda.

"Child, aren't you going to bed?"

Shelly stands before us. She is wearing a floor-length flannel nightgown that makes her look like a little girl. She blinks at us behind her rose-coloured glasses and I feel a mix of guilt and fear. I want her to be O for obstacle, not frail and vulnerable.

"Child, I'm scared in the Old Place without you," Shelly says timidly.

"Let's kip out in Sally's bedroom," Child says to her.

Bobby goes out the door and I turn to follow her.

Child puts his hand on my arm. "Please. Stay with us?" he says. "Shelly's open-minded. Aren't you, Shelly?" She nods her head, smiling nervously, and I look at her in surprise. Is it possible we can include her? Child smiles and I smile back. It is a solution I have not considered before. He hobbles to the door and pushes it shut with his crutch and suddenly the three of us are alone in the room. Sally's vegetarian cookbooks are on the oak dresser next to stubs of old candles in brass containers. On the floor is her green nylon bikini. Her clutter looks like the possessions of an old friend.

Child throws down his crutch and puts his arm around me. I smell his apple-sweet odour. It's marijuana. I smell of it, too. He puts his hand on my breast. "I need you here with me to-night," he whispers. Then he bends over and puts his mouth on my nipple through the material. I pull back because his mouth is rough. He is nervous. Shelly stands just to his left, staring at us in wonderment. I look away and put my hand on his head, bend back. Then his hands wrap around me, holding my shoul-derblades. He bends over and his lips fill my mouth. I shut my eyes as he leads me to bed. His fingers on my arm are plumper than I remembered.

I open my eyes. I expect to see Child. But it's Shelly standing over the bed and undressing me. Suddenly I think of Muff and begin to weep. "The dog," I sob.

"I know," Shelly murmurs. "Child told me." Child stands beside her, one hand on Shelly's shoulder. Ah, what a surprise! They look like a couple.

"It was an accident," he whispers.

Shelly leans close and I feel her tongue lick my nipple. I am surprised at how nice it feels. "I knew you and Bobby did this," she says. "I used to feel left out." Her head inches closer to my face until tendrils of red hair tickle my chin. She looks intense—almost alarmed, her eyes fluttering behind her granny glasses—and suddenly I'm giggling because I'm afraid. In my pride, I never thought of Shelly as sexual, only myself. Tentatively, I touch her cheek and she sighs and takes off her glasses. Then she turns her soft blind face toward my breasts and begins to seek my nipples with her mouth. Suddenly she giggles and takes my hand and places it on her throat, her breasts, then on her genitals, and I feel her, just like me, split, wet, identical. And now I'm weeping again—oh God, why do I have such shame about my body when all women are like me?

And then Child whispers over my shoulder, "Hey, what about me? If I didn't know better, I'd think the two of you wanted to be alone." Child sinks to his knees and begins to kiss the inside of my thigh and little by little I feel one of them and then the other lowering me backwards onto the bed and for a moment, I think it's going to work—that I can have Child because it's possible to share him with Shelly—and I close my eyes waiting for the moment of penetration that always feels like it's happening for the first time, the transfixing moment when one body enters another. Beside me, Shelly is sighing as her hand cups Child's balls. And then Child comes, he pushes her away and lies collapsed on top of me, groaning, his head in my shoulder.

And immediately, Shelly is on her feet by the bed, crying. "I knew it would be like this!" she wails. "You didn't want me here at all!"

Child struggles slowly to his feet, one hand covering himself, and Shelly begins to sob. "I thought you believed in group sex," Child says.

"This isn't group sex—this is making love to Jude in front of me," Shelly wails.

"You'd better go." Child looks at me guiltily and all at once I'm running down the steps by the old boat house. I run across the dock and through the woods until I get to the Old Place. Then I force myself to walk slowly up the stairs and down the hall. At Bobby's door, I turn the knob and look in. Bobby is lying under a mound of bedclothes, her mouth open as if she is exclaiming something to the moon which has turned her platinum hair on the pillow to silver. My chest tightens—she looks so beautiful. Softly, I whisper, "Bobby?"

She stirs and lifts her head half-up on an elbow. "Jude?" she says. "Can it wait until morning?"

Now the bedclothes shift and the mound has a voice. "For God's sake! We're doing the root dance! Can't you give us some privacy?"

And then I'm running again down the old cottage hall, careening like a crazy thing from one side of the wooden walls to the other, my shadow vast and bat-like in the light cast by the kerosene lamps. At the end of the hall, I step out onto the tiny second-floor balcony. I grasp the railing and look out at the silver bay, half expecting Bobby to slip down the hall and join me. But nobody comes. Across the channel, the island of Jonah Prince is a dark bump in the moonlit waters.

Sunday, 10:02 a.m.

There is no wind. But the water on the shore is noisy. Through the screen window, I hear its suck-lap-and-lick on the granite rocks below the Old Place. The Old Place sits partially hidden behind a stand of white pine on the southwest bluff of Good Cheer. It's clapboard, white. The screen veranda runs around the four sides of the house. The Old Place was built out of white pine in 1890. The lumber used in its construction had to be floated out on a barge from Indian Harbour.

I am lying on my back across the old wooden sleigh bed that belonged to the local who worked here. He carved his name on the headboard. Marcel D'Aoust. The date is there too—1888. The bed is made of oak from Good Cheer. It's a handsome thing, its frame curves at both ends like the sleighs of red-cheeked pioneers in paintings by Krieghoff. But it's short, and only wide enough to hold a three-quarter mattress . . . not a double. It is a ridiculous size for a couple.

You are sitting downstairs so you can't see how cramped I am. I have to lie slantwise across the mattress to be really comfortable and even then my ankles hang over the side of the bed. I have asked you to wait downstairs. It would distract me to have you in the bedroom.

You are sitting on the old chintz couch in front of the wood stove. Your legs are up on the coffee table—a single plank stretched across two stumps. The snowshoes of Marcel D'Aoust hang on the wooden wall behind your head. Below the snow-shoes hangs a row of old photographs. There's the founder of Cape Pianos: Montague himself at the helm of the McLaughlin-Buick, a two-seater roadster manufactured in Oshawa in 1908. And there he is again in a Scoter, the runabout designed and built by Lady Cape's grandfather, Jamie McLaren. The man in a light-coloured Packard with a cigar and a homburg as big as Shelly's sombrero is Sir James' father, Roland Cape. Sir James and Lady Cape are trapped by the camera in their phase as a young couple, hatless and grinning on the running board of the Silver Cloud Rolls.

You peer curiously at the photographs. It is gloomy in the living room of the Old Place but there aren't any light switches, just glass-chimneyed kerosene lamps hanging in brackets on the dark brown wood walls. There is no electricity or running water either. Lady Cape wants the cottage to stay the way it was. Remember: you are in Upper Canada where the past is evoked through nostalgic gestures.

You are restless without me around to amuse you. So you stand up and scowl irritably through the front window. The window is Victorian Gothic. Tiny squares with wooden frames divide the glass into dozens of little panes. It's hard enough looking at a view through a rectangular porthole, but it's even worse when the glass is so old and thick it refracts the light. It would be nicer if it were a modern window but Lady Cape won't have the mullions removed.

Through one of the panes a blur of brown and pink figures

lengthens and thickens like the bodies of fish under water. Your eyesight is a little poor this morning but you think you see the Capes setting up picnic tables for the regatta—yes, there's Doc Lefroy carrying an avocado-coloured barbecue shaped like a bee's bottom, and the swami and Lady Cape setting up the red and white Coca-Cola umbrella over the food table, and Shelly slicing oranges and passing the halves to Child who squeezes the sections inside a shiny silver gadget with a long silver handle.

But I don't want to think about Child or Shelly just now. I am doing all I can to forget what happened last night. I am concentrating on something floating above my bed. It is large—virtually the size of a human. It hangs there in mid-air, just above me. Its black, callused feet are trembling and it's wearing a canary yellow robe which flatters its dark monkey face. It's the swami as he looked twenty years ago. His hair is black and nappy and his bushy eyebrows are black too. His body is also leaner. The swami was never muscular like Bull Cape, but when he was a young man, his body was streamlined like Jonah Prince's.

As I watch, the young, yellow-robed swami floats up to the ceiling, his gleaming white eyes shut tight as if he is fast asleep. Perhaps he is dreaming he is back in India. What a nice surprise! Instead of the pale blue sound and its shaggy pines whose boughs are prickly to touch, he is picturing jade green guava orchards and the lifeless dun brown water of the irrigation ditches.

For a moment, the swami's head hovers just below the chimney hole that bisects the water-stained planks of the ceiling. I stare up in fascination. Now's my chance to look under his robe, but a dazzle of yellow light makes me shield my eyes and then ping—he's gone up the pipe hole. The last things I see are the soles of his peach-coloured feet. I wasn't all that eager to see what Indian religious men wear under their dhotis anyway.

Now he is floating high over the roof of the Old Place where Higgins Rochester and I are making love. The wind blows him off course, and for a moment he stops and hangs over the heads of Shelly and Child making orange juice on the beach. His yellow-coloured robe snaps like a sail luffing in the wind. It's a wonder Child and Shelly can't hear him. Then another gust of wind blows the swami south and he floats gracefully, rising higher over the caved-in roof of the barn. Up he goes, over the crèche-like stalls of Sir James' private zoo where the yak lies on her side nursing her baby and the peacock struts on the top rail of the snake-fence corral. Any second he will explode into cosmic dust as yellow and fragrant as the calla lilies that grow by the dock of the boat house. "My fingers are getting tired," Higgins says suddenly and all at once the swami plummets into the sound—bubbles frothing out of his mouth as he sinks cursing into the dark waters, his monkey face scowling with displeasure.

You stop pacing downstairs and frown. You were looking forward to seeing the disagreeable little man disappear for good. And now you have to put up with Higgins talking. But think of me. I am lying earth-bound beside a sleepy lover. He has had his orgasm and is going through the motions so I can have mine. I don't know why it takes a new lover so long to make me come. Perhaps it's because I'm not like a heroine in books written by male authors who comes right after the man penetrates her.

Take, for instance, Maria in Hemingways' novel *For Whom the Bell Tolls*. She only has to close her eyes against the gold red sun in a Spanish meadow and feel the earth move beneath her. Her physiology is so much clearer and simpler than mine. I hear Maria scoff at me from a corner of the bedroom. And I feel implicated; I can't resist trying to live up to a fantasy even if it was inspired by macho literature. I also feel guilt because my fingers work better. I can masturbate in two minutes. Without any foreplay at all. I can lie down on the bed and masturbate and then scramble up again three minutes later and go back to what I was doing. . . . It's a simple mechanical process. I touch myself twenty or thirty strokes with my index and companion finger. A certain pressure on a certain place. Then, presto, I come. And that's what I'm going to have to do now. "Let me try," I whisper. Higgins nods. I rub my two fingers against the delicate fleshy cushion which is still connected by a string of lust to my image of a flying swami. But the swami will not rise. Not even a fold of his yellow robe floats into sight. I lie on the mattress, rubbing furiously. Nothing happens.

"I guess I have to go first or my orgasm feels like a footnote."

"Biologically speaking, it is a footnote. All nature requires of the reproductive act is that the sperm reach the egg.'' Higgins sits up, leans over me, resting on his elbows.

"Higgins—you don't need to be so literal." I sigh and roll out of bed so he can't see my face. I feel relieved that my cunt is less visible than a penis so I don't have the same pressure to perform, but I also feel angry because its lack of visibility means its needs are easier to ignore. And then there is the business of naming. I don't like the harsh sound of "cunt", but I'm stuck with the c-word because I dislike euphemisms. "Down there" sounds as if you are talking about Australia. I'd be happier with an English equivalent to the Sanskrit word "yoni", for female genitals.

Sighing, I walk over to the window and look out. I know what I will see. I will see the same view you saw in my fantasy about the swami. I will see the Capes going about the regatta preparations on the rocks below. And the sailboats of the guests floating towards Good Cheer through the dark green frieze of islands.

From the bed, Higgins says, "You only slept with me because you feel sorry for me."

I look over my shoulder. He is lying in bed with the covers to his chin. "I thought it was the other way around." I turn away so Higgins can't see how unhappy I am. Child and Shelly are there with the others, just as I'd imagined them. Child is standing in his jersey and cut-off jeans, one arm on his crutch, his bandaged leg dangling, as he works the orange-juice maker. Shelly stands beside him in a yellow muumuu covered with sun mandalas. She is feeding him orange slices—doing what I would like to be doing—going through little acts of domestic life with the man I love. Even from here the manner of the proprietor is obvious. I would never treat Child the way she does. As if she owns him. As if he is her thing.

Suddenly Shelly points to my window and Child swings around on his crutch and looks up. I realize Higgins is standing beside me. I draw back. Higgins bends over, kisses my shoulder. If Child could see us, he'd see Higgins' naked chest and my breasts. That is all. That is enough. Down below, Child turns away and looks off towards the open water where the island of Jonah Prince shines sand-coloured in the fragrant morning light. I feel myself turning to wood. Oh, Child, Higgins' kisses mean nothing. I am weak and sensual, but I have pledged my orgasms to you. I can be as pure as Heine's sweetheart. . . . *Du bist wie eine Blume, so hold und schön und rein.* . . .

Now my darling lifts a touchingly thin arm and points at the sound. Lady Cape is suddenly there beside them. They must be talking about the wind. It's a sultry morning. Pinky-blue balls of clouds hang over the land but the sky is clear to the west and there's a stiff sailing breeze, a good omen for the day of the regatta.

Lady Cape is nodding her head and Shelly nods too and reaches out and ruffles Child's hair. Child turns around and looks up again and I move back into the shadows and stare sadly overhead at the pine planks. The planks run in a straight line to the outer wall. Line after line, like highways for insects. Oh, Child, I am too stoical to let you know I am suffering. I only slept with Higgins to up the ante of my sexual power. The rules of the contest are the only rules I know. When I am rejected I take a lover—apply him like a poultice to my pride. You see I fear desire which is Sisyphean and insists on a specific object. (No sooner have you satisfied desire than it calls on you to do it all over again.) I am more comfortable with lust—the quick, democratic urge you can feel in anyone. And now I am a prisoner in a wooden room with a man I do not love.

Suddenly Higgins taps the windowpane. "Here comes a boat." Across the water, the dory is heading our way. Mister Tom, the butler, sits in the back, steering the boat in a peaked cap and sunglasses. Bull is in the front, arms folded across his chest. He sits beside a tall orange buoy. A bulky object is coiled on the seat beside him. The whine of the motor gets louder, then stops. Child hobbles towards the water and tries to grab the bow. Higgins says, "I'd better to down and see if they want help."

Child lifts Pig out of the dory and the snake hangs helplessly in his arms, her mid-section swollen in a squarish bulge. And all at once I feel ashamed to be on this island where the search for love leads to fear and death. Now Mister Tom ties up the boat and the three of them trudge up the path made through the rocks. Their heads are down. From their height, Child looks small and anemic, a boy in men's clothing. I hear Higgins below, telling them I am upstairs in his bedroom. Higgins pronounces my name possessively as if he wants to make sure Child knows we spent the night together. "Jud-dee will be down soon," he says and I cringe at the gloating tone of his voice.

10:37 a.m.

You are a housefly—straddling a crack in the wooden floor, waving your feather antennae at the humans moving their faces in the chairs above. Their discussion sounds like windy noise. You are not fat and clumsy like the common housefly although your speckled grey and black colouring is similar. You are the type who flies tirelessly around light fixtures and human heads, driving everyone to distraction. Your sole asset is that you do not bite. But you'd better fly up off the floor so Lady Cape doesn't step on you with one of her squishy shoes. That's it. Alight on the swami's nose. No, you've gone to the wrong face. That's Child's nose. The swami is sitting between Child and Higgins. Child's bony feet are up on the plank coffee table. His arms are flung on either side of the sofa. If the swami leaned back, he could put his head on one of Child's arms. It's unlikely the swami will perform such an intimate gesture. He is unpredictable, yet there is one thing you can safely assume about him: he will never treat you in a personal way. That is why you must land on his nose. Besides, Child's hand is moving towards you. If you don't fly off this instant you will be squashed. That's better.

The swami's coarse-pored skin feels spongy. Is that a racist observation? No—it's not because he's Indian. You're just tiny. At least your vantage point on the swami's nose is a good place to view the proceedings, even if it is a little too close to the swami's view. You must not hold your size against me. I could make you as big as a bull moose that has strayed from the herd, but think of the nuisance you'd be shambling about the cottage, butting your head against the glass-paned door—rubbing your antlers against the doorframe, searching for a tasty branch of balsam fir. Beneath your proboscis, there is a sound like a thunderclap; your hairy toes quiver.

The swami has cleared his throat: "Will we live on potato chips after the nuclear blast?" The swami smiles, not his pink-tongued grin, but his solemn Mona Lisa smile. "That's it. Child buy a carton of Hostess chips and I buy a case of Coke. Then we sell left-over chips and Cokes to survivors and make profit. That's how we make it in twenty-first century."

"There will only be a nuclear holocaust if we believe there is going to be a holocaust, Ramaji," Lady Cape says. She is sitting on the chair beside the couch and her wet running shoes are up on the plank table too, right next to the swami's.

"Mother's right," Child says. "What people imagine together is as real as something that can be measured."

"Ahha—yes, Child Cape. But what do people imagine? A fairy tale where nice, purring lion lie down with meek little lamb? No—look around you and you will see the evidence of what people imagine. For thoughts are objects, Child Cape. They have a colour and shape and we create the world to correspond to their design."

"Excuse me, Swami, but there is a fly on your nose." Higgins points at the swami's face. "The non-biting variety, I believe. *Fannia canicularis.*"

The swami only laughs. "You North Americans. You get upset over a housefly! See! It doesn't bother me. I will let it stay as long as it wants." Suddenly everyone in the room is looking at you and wishing you harm. For a dreadful second, you see dozens of arms rising—beating the air towards you—falling like clubs on your frail thorax. But the swami raises a hand warningly. You are his fly. He will not have you harmed. Your left wing twitches a little nervously. Like all true flies, you have only one pair of front wings. The halteres, or clublike projections on your rear, don't count. Higgins and Child are still staring at you. Even Lady Cape, the spokeswoman for peace, feels the same impulse to destroy you. She is North American, too. In her Utopia there are no houseflies.

"I can't stand looking at Ramaji with a fly on his nose," Lady Cape says and a rush of wind blows you off your perch. You tumble for a second, then get your air-legs and fly off, your magnificent set of single wings shining in the morning light.

You land on a windowsill in the kitchen and see me—a fair, distracted-looking woman mixing pancake batter in a bowl. Child is standing next to me, washing blueberries in the sink.

Shelly is by the stove, cooking hash browns, and indulging her addiction for fluffernutters. First she spreads a piece of toast with peanut butter. Then she adds marshmallow topping. A fluffernutters has been Shelly's favourite breakfast since she was a teenager. Thanks to our summers together, I can describe Shelly as comprehensively as a naturalist.

The Habits of Humankind's Most Underestimated Foe: The Shelly Moffat Pest (order Diptera, family Culicidae)

The Shelly Moffat Pest is a maggot without eyes or mouth hatched in tire dumps. It lives on Fluffernutters, which it absorbs through its ventricles. If necessary, the pest can go without food for days. In adult form, the mosquito grows to giant proportions and sprouts splotchy-veined wings, a stout proboscis, and extra-long palps. In repose, her body and proboscis make a straight line so the pest appears to be standing on her head.

Her dirty work is done on yachts or patios, where she patrols the environment for mammal life. She whines incessantly on a pitch of middle C and desperation can drive her to feed on birch bark warmed by the sun. She responds to carbon dioxide, heat, and moisture. Once she detects you, she will not let you out of her sight. In my Utopia, there would be no Shelly, only her hash browns resting on the back burner . . . golden brown . . . crispy. . . .

I reach out and taste one. There is no doubt about it, Shelly's hash browns are delicious.

Now Shelly sails out of the kitchen carrying a platter of potatoes and I pour the honey glop of my batter into the black bottom of the iron skillet. The consistency of the batter is lumpy. That's my secret. Lumps in the pancake batter. I empty the bowl of blueberries into the batter. It stains it inky blue. Gently, I turn the pancakes over. They are the size of giant silver dollars. You see, Child! I make better blueberry pancakes than Shelly! It is true she shows skill with hash browns but I am the pancake expert.

Child reaches into his pocket and pulls out a little plastic bag.

"The sacred ololiuqui," he whispers and then he says, "Mama bird to baby bird." I open my mouth and let him feed me. He eats some too and then empties the rest on the congealing pancakes.

"I missed you last night," Child whispers and cups my breast. I stand very still. The pancakes bubble, turn darker navy. Child leans against me and I feel myself going under in the old cottage kitchen, sinking into the water of the navy blue bay seeping under the screen door. I feel it eddying about my ankles, hear its cool trickle through the opening for the sink pipe under the kitchen counter. Paradise is surrendering to the one person who can meet all your needs. Now Child takes my hand and places it on his crotch. I say, "Ah" . . . the sound I make when the islands melt into a tufted green blue behind me and I see the open water . . . ahh . . . ahh and a stream of bubbles escapes my lips. I am floating with Child in the wild bay water . . . drowned . . . drown-dead. . . .

"Excuse me, Jude," Shelly is at the doorway. Her eyes behind her rose-coloured glasses fix possessively on Child. "Joyce wants you and Dickie to serve the pancakes now."

Shelly points at the others grouped around the table, waiting for us to serve them. The swami is reading out the contents on a jam jar to a sleepy-looking Higgins. Then Shelly whispers nervously. "Dickie, you promised there'd be no more monkey business. I'm trying to be a good sport about last night." And Child nods guiltily and follows her out into the living room.

11:10 a.m.

The sailboats are sliding back and forth behind the imaginary starting line, which stretches between the tip of Good Cheer to the west and Jonah's orange buoy to the east. The sun lights up the sails of the Lasers and the white flag that marks the *At Last* as the committee boat. The wind is getting stronger. Fifteen knots at least . . . enough wind to blow the boats easily through the two-and-a-half-mile course. It runs twice around Gull Rock, the same lap each time counter-clockwise, buoys to port. I am sitting beside Lady Cape on the flat rocks in front of the Old Place. Behind us, Mister Tom and the workmen from Indian

Harbour are dragging a line of garden hoses up the cliff from the bay. The men are filling the Big Dome with water so Little Dome will be ready for the regatta dinner tonight.

Lady Cape lifts a pair of binoculars to her eyes. "I see my son but not Mr. Prince," Lady Cape says. "Perhaps he's still at the hospital." A web of white crow's-feet streams off into the tanned planes of her face like cracks in saddle leather. Everyone looks ancient and haggard in the late morning light. Child looks 102—a skinny, peevish old man, in his towel and long-sleeved shirt, nursing a bandaged ankle. His camera is resting in a shady crevice beside him. Even Sally Love looks older, shelling peas into a metal pot. The peas go ping as they fall. Only the swami looks timeless. His dark skin shines like lacquer as he sits eating pancakes on the rocks, the sweat glistening under his woolly hair.

Out on the water, I hear the bang of the five-minute gun. I look out at the sailboats. I see a Laser with an orange crown— then the two-toned Laser of Bull and Bobby. Tan and yellow numbers speckle its sails.

Behind me, the swami raises his hands in the air and says, "Every day is another day closer to . . . to . . . what?"

"To the regatta, Swami," Child mutters and points his camera at the Indian man. A thousand summers ago his boldness could charm me, but this morning his mannerisms fray my nerves.

Lady Cape lowers her binoculars. She frowns warningly. "It is a perfect day for a regatta, isn't it?" she says and turns to me as if she hopes I will say something reassuring. I could say, "Everything feels normal when you experience it. Even unhappiness," or something distracting like, "Let's have orange juice and champagne." A proposal for drinks always invokes enthusiasm.

I could say something, but I feel too jaded. By "jaded" I mean knowing I'm not going to like something that's about to happen but not letting that stop me from experiencing it anyway. I don't want to be here with a group of city dwellers acting out silly competitive games in the countryside. I feel despair coming on like the start of a sunburn.

"What is the goal of life?" the swami says. He is unstoppable this morning.

"The goal of life is . . . is. . . ."

"To forget what you do in the summer," Child says.

"Ha . . . ha. . . . Your son knows how to make the smart answer but does he know how to live the smart life?"

"Ramaji, be quiet for a minute please. There's something going on out there." Lady Cape lifts the binoculars to her eyes.

"What are you talking about?" Child says. He stands up slowly and the swami gets on his feet too, his robe flapping.

"Look! Jonah Prince drop out." The swami is right. The orange crown of his sail is a hundred yards offshore. The wake from his boat glints in the sun, sparkling diamonds.

In a single motion, Jonah Prince leaps off the Laser and ties up his bow line to the steel I-beam beside the ramp to Big Dome. He looks up and points at something.

Beside me Child exclaims: "He's pointing at you!"

Lady Cape turns to me, puts her hand on my arm. "He's lost Katy, dear. He has no crew. You'll have to go." Lady Cape pats my shoulder.

"Go on! Hurry up! He needs you for the race."

Prince calls my name, "Jude! Jude!" I hurry down the pink arm of granite, following the old railway ties. The bluff slopes gently down into the water and then runs for fifty feet below the surface. Prince raises a life-jacket and cheers when he sees me. His eyes are a pair of intense blue dots under feathery white brows.

Child calls from the cliff above, "Jonah, take me!"

Jonah laughs the laugh of high spirits and smiles in Child's direction, but his eyes stay on me. You are watching us too. Glamour is what you see: a blonde woman, a silver-haired man, both with orgiastic grins on their faces, tilting forward, leaning towards pleasure and excitement. The silver-haired man puts his arms around the blonde woman. He ties her life-belt. She stands like a child as he puts the string through the loop at her waist. He holds her for a minute. Suddenly she jerks her head away, as if he has touched a nerve, and looks up—not for you; she is looking at Child.

11:36 a.m.

I haul myself halfway on, stomach first, across Jonah's Laser.
My hipbone hits a cleat.

"Okay. Stop and start again."

The skin on my cheeks burns. I don't like him to watch me
flop about like a fish on his boat.

"How's Katy?" I ask. My voice blown from my lips sounds
as soft and easy as the summer itself. That surprises me.

"She'll be as good as new in a day or two," he says. "She's
more upset about Muff than her concussion. Hurry now! There
bgoes the one-minute gun."

I heave myself up one last time and suddenly we pick up
speed.

We're the first boat across the starting line on a starboard
track. Bull and Bobby follow us about five seconds later, then
Higgins and Doc Lefroy. The sun is directly overhead on the
white sails of our competitors and I feel the competitor's little
lambent ache growing inside me.

I laugh recklessly and make the sign of victory at Jonah, but
his eyes are scanning the water ahead. To our left, Bull's Laser
is coming up quickly.

Now out two boats are neck and neck . . . a hundred yards
apart. Jonah points to Bull's Laser and throws back his head and
laughs his I'm-okay-you're-okay laugh. We have Bull in a trap.
As long as we are on our starboard tack, they are forced to stay
to our left. For a moment, I almost feel happy. We are sailing
west towards the horizon, away from the problem of Child and
Shelly back on Good Cheer. Suddenly in the bow, Jonah points
and yells: "Change your tack!" Bull and Bobby have come
about. They are heading right at us.

"Starboard! Starboard!" Bull yells back. Bobby is crouched
near the centreboard, her arms over her head.

"Bull, don't do it!" I scream. Jonah's face is white. The bow
of Bull's Laser is ten feet away. A collision is unavoidable. Nine
. . . now eight . . . now six. . . . Holy Mother of God, preserve
us from the face of our enemy. We are going to crash. We are
so close I hear the hiss of their wake. We are going to crash . . .

no . . . we miss each other . . . by inches. Bobby and Bull pass
in front of us. For a moment, Bobby and I stand about four feet
from each other—staring eye to eye. She glares at me resentfully.
In her sunglasses, I see a fair-haired woman smiling back at her
like one of those carefree models in yachting magazines, as-
sured that all eyes are on her suntanned breasts.

Then Bull yells, "Get a horse!"

"You anti-semitic buffoon!" Jonah shouts back.

Our boat turns and we head after Bull, reeling on a sea whose
surface is heaving—a blue-green mass fired with iridescent triangles of sunlight. Bull's weight is helping them to sail more
smoothly. Jonah screams at me and I sit farther forward, tighten
the boom vang.

"Flatten the sail! We're bouncing!"

The Laser is five hundred yards from the first buoy.

"Starboard, you suckers!" Bull yells. His Laser comes about,
heads west.

"They set us up!" Jonah points to the buoy ahead. "We have
to honour their tack." Jonah shouts at me. "Did you hear what
I said? Look out—we're going to come about!" The boom hits
me before I can duck. I sob a little in humiliation. Jonah yells
something but I can't hear him in the bubble of sound, of flapping sails and hissing wake. I feel the urge to fall overboard, to
give myself up to the water. A stone-faced Jonah clutches my
arm and yanks me back into the boat. His expression is not
angry or even irritated. It is a strange, harrowing expression of
melancholy and determination. And I think suddenly of Bull's
remark—a Jew with something to prove. It embarrasses me to
think in Bull's terms. Jonah points at Bull's Laser rounding the
buoy ahead. "Centreboard half up," he says coldly. Grimacing,
I lift out the board. I feel ashamed for wanting to give up. At
least our light weight is an advantage. It doesn't take our Laser
as long to climb up and plane on top of the wave.

Now our boats swing around the buoy, heading east towards
the finish line, our sails bang loudly in the wind. Bull's jibe is
sloppy—it's his first mistake. Even so, he's still far enough ahead
to win unless Jonah does something. What we do now will make
all the difference.

"Cross their stern wake! Give him dirty wind!" I call. Jonah looks up in surprise, then moves the tiller and steers our Laser across Bull's wake. Bull stares at us in dismay. His sail is luffing. It's very windy but we are still stopping him from getting enough breeze. The gap between our boats closes. We are bow to bow. Bull swears at the limp sail above his head and turns his Laser to ram us. He's going to try to push us windward off the mark. But it's too late. Our boat bears down. We steal the last of Bull's wind. And now we slide across the finish line.

1:06 p.m.

"Ha-ha, Jude," Jonah Prince says as we pass Sir James scowling in the committee boat. "Did you know you followed an axiom of Clausewitz?" Jonah leans across the centreboard, and kisses me. I stare at him blankly.

"I did?"

"Yes! The dirty wind tactic. Adapt your strategy to your means!"

"You mean the end justifies the means?"

"No-no. That's St. Jerome. Now let us enjoy the spoils of war!" In a single motion, Jonah leaps off the Laser and into the water. He waves at the guests clapping on the bluff of Good Cheer for the Great Prince who has come in first.

Then Jonah guides his Laser to shore and helps me off onto the granite ledge in the noonday sun.

Somebody hands him a champagne bottle. He raises the bottle and pours the champagne over our heads. Jonah laughs and kisses me again, for everyone to see. I feel the foam from his champagne run down my thigh. I throw my head back and laugh too, as if I am a daughter of the sun, a blissfully blonde Aphrodite who puts men in an adventurous holiday mood. Child is sitting on the shore beside Shelly watching me unhappily. Good, I want him to feel as rejected as I do. His pain is the only thing that will make me feel better. I hold out my glass and let the champagne foam over the edges onto my wrist and elbow.

See, Child Cape, Jonah Prince has his axioms of war and I have my axioms of love. And this is one—show the object of my desire that other men long for me as much as you do. And if you will not surrender to the glory of my sexuality, you will lose me to their arms. I close my eyes and suck off the drops of champagne from my wrist, as if I am sucking a man's cock. Bobby is watching us, her hands on her hips, frowning. I know her so well that I know the meaning of her every expression. Bobby is gathering up her nerve to do something.

Then I hear her say, "I have to talk to you, Jonah Prince."

And I walk out of the water obligingly and join the others on the shore. Jonah wades in to meet Bobby. Drops of champagne still run off his balding head. Behind him the other sailors slide in for a landing. There's Higgins and a family from the cove on Rose Island. The sailors are mostly men and a few wives, except for a skinny brunette in a unisex Courrèges bikini. She sailed a Laser by herself. Doc Lefroy is helping the sailors pull or walk their boats into a small strip of sandy beach by the ramp leading up to Big Dome. Jonah touches Bobby on the shoulder once, very gently. She scowls at him, arms folded across her chest, and I want to put my arms around Bobby and say I'm sorry. I was only flirting with Prince to make Child jealous. But now she is walking up the cliff with Jonah.

Behind them the people sprawl on the rocks of Good Cheer like sea lions in the August sunlight. The bluff shimmers white . . . almost phosphorescent. A gull flies overhead, cawing like a crow. A party of men stands by the home-made bar constructed out of planks of lumber. The men stand with elbows bent so their arms form the L of the summer drinker. Bull is mixing viscous yellow drinks, his head turned towards Jonah Prince who is walking up the slope with Bobby.

"Hey, Prince! Want a Harvey Wallbanger? It'll put hair on your chest," Bull shouts. Jonah Prince looks bewildered, then he shakes his head, smiling.

"Aw, don't bother with him; he's a pansy," says Doc Lefroy and makes a funny apologetic bow in case Prince heard what he said. But Prince is too far away now. He and Bobby stand halfway up the bluff—two small figures nearly eclipsed by the huge amphitheatre of water and sky. A minute goes by. Then I hear Bobby's high, quavery shouts floating over the heads of the regatta guests. Nobody hears her except me and Child. He smiles wryly at me. I feel glad. I look down to hide my feelings, and see Shelly's plump feet moving towards me.

Shelly puts her hand to her mouth. "I'd like to make an announcement, folks," Shelly calls, moving her head from left to right like she is saying "no-no", but she is only checking to make sure everybody is listening. "Child and I are getting married. We're going to have a baby," she says. I look at Child. He is looking off at the horizon.

"Why that's wonderful, Shelly!" Higgins says.

"Let's have another bottle of Dom, shall we?" Doc Lefroy says and claps Child on the back. "I never thought I'd see the day when Dickie got hitched. Did you, Sir James?"

Sir James extends a hand from his wheelchair. "When's the little gumper due, son?"

Child hangs his head and mutters something. And my heart drops out of my body. Oh my darling—oh my darling—you are lost and gone for ever. I walk blindly off by myself. Only moments ago I sailed into a rocky bluff with Jonah Prince, self-assured and triumphant. Now I am alone and lost in a wilderness of summer light.

1:15 p.m.

I swim, alternating between a crawl and the sidestroke, and feel my broad shoulders and long arms which exercise has made powerful. Behind me somebody is doing the butterfly stroke . . . splash there he goes out of the water again . . . splash . . . now he hits the surface . . . splash there he goes out of the water again . . . gasp and heave . . . gasp and heave . . . it must be Child . . . Child thinks he must feel pain if he is to beat me . . . he doesn't know harmony will beat struggle every time . . . I begin to do the butterfly . . . strike out . . . gasp . . . heave . . . the other swimmer stops in mid-air . . . mid-arc . . . mid-breath . . . startled to see me move away. . . . "Wait! Wait!" a man's voice shouts but I plunge my face into the water . . . beat my arms against its surface . . . and look down. . . . The sun feels hot on my head . . . the water is clear . . . thirty feet down . . . I see my tiny dark shadow wriggling across the bottom.

And then another shadow wriggles across the lake floor . . . the other swimmer is doing the crawl. Two long, brown, elegant

arms split the water like an axe and Jonah Prince is beside me
in the water . . . he stops . . . rolls playfully over on his back
and I see an arc of dazzling white teeth. "Want to race?" Jonah
Prince says and I feel myself pulled by the currents towards his
glamorous floating mouth which is opening in the sound to receive me.

1:50 p.m.

I beat Jonah to Gull Rock—just. His hand reaches out and
playfully grabs my ankle but I kick my foot free and scramble
up the southwest bluff. The rock pulses with heat under my feet
like a human creature the sun has brought to life. The layers of
lichen are clearer here than on the other cliffs. Orange lichen by
the water. Then older silvery lichen overlaid with the crusty
black spots; next the pale lime-green circles. I stop and catch
my breath. I look out across the water. The sun blazes my cheeks
. . . fires my skin . . . already my red nylon bikini is half dry.
I see Child's blond head out by the ridge of shoals that lies
halfway between One Tree and Gull Rock. He is coming our
way with some other swimmers.

Then I hear the laugh of summer . . . golden, melodious. I
look down at the top of Jonah's bald head. The skin is turning
pink. The golden boy is getting sunburnt. He should have worn
a hat. Jonah looks up and calls, "Wait up!" Now I laugh. I
laugh as hard as I can. As if I want the world to hear me. Of
course it is Child whom I want to hear me laugh.

"Hurry. We don't have much time." I turn and scramble up
another shelf of granite, knowing he will follow. I am panting
shamelessly but I don't want him to see I'm winded. If he catches
me panting, he will think I am weak. He will have an edge on
me and I want to beat him to the top.

I haul myself up onto another ledge, puffing harder. There's
nowhere to go from here except through the crevices lined with
juniper. The bushes are prickly underfoot but they are cool.
That's a relief. The rock is getting hotter as I climb. Luckily,
my soles are hard from walking barefoot on the rocks. Two
weeks of summer. That's all it takes for the soles to toughen.

And now I'm at the top of Gull Rock. I can see the picnic site at Good Cheer, where tiny bodies swarm on the granite bluff. And then I spot Child's pin-sized blond head again and two others still far out in the water. I point them out to Jonah as he joins me on the cliff. He breathes evenly. He isn't worn out from our swim or from the climb. And he is the one who is older. Not me. His fingers press on my shoulder. "Gorgeous view, isn't it?" he says. He puts on his sunglasses, which he's been wearing on a chain around his neck, and looks at me. The same tanned fair-haired woman I saw in Bobby's glasses looks back at me. I stare at this golden-limbed summer creature who seems to have nothing to do with me and let Jonah Prince take her hand. "It's going to take Child and the others longer than you think," Jonah says. "Bobby's a slow swimmer now."

I nod as if I agree but I don't agree. I don't know why I am letting him tug me down the incline, the small slope on the northern side of Gull Rock. It faces the open horizon, out of sight of the others. I pull back and he goes down without me. He stops on a pink ledge and points at his toes, which look pink and swollen. His feet are getting sunburnt too, but he smiles hugely as if that is a private joke between the two of us. Then he steps out of his bathing suit and waves at me to join him. I hesitate. I stop and take another look over my shoulder. I look out over the clear water. The heads are still by the ridge of shoals out in the middle of the channel. I take a breath and walk slowly down the incline to Jonah Prince. I walk slowly. I feel empty, void like the open sound which stretches in all directions around us. Jonah Prince stands with his hands on his hips. His cock is semi-erect; "a semi", I think. "A semi" is Child's expression. All at once I feel heavy with pain and light as air simultaneously. I am walking towards Jonah Prince. Then suddenly Jonah lifts his arm to help me down the last part and I rush into his body. I grab him and he laughs. He pushes me away a little, holds me off from him. His hands on my shoulders, he smiles into my eyes. "Are you frightened?"

I nod and he smiles. He leads me to the wall of the cliff. He begins to take off my bikini. He takes off the top. It peels away from my skin like the rind of an orange. He deposits the top on a small bush covered with the fuzzy white flowers of meadow-sweet. Then he reaches down and gently slides my bikini bot-

toms over my thighs. I cannot move so he puts his hand behind
my knee and lifts my leg. There. One leg is out. He puts his
hand behind my other knee and lifts my right leg. My bikini
bottoms lie like a puddle at my feet. I lean back against the
granite, trembling, and he steps a few feet backward. He stares
at me. Immediately I cover my genitals with my hands. I feel
overweight, foolish. He laughs his laugh of good spirits.

"Don't you know how beautiful you are?" he says.

I don't know. I stare at him blankly. In his mirrored sunglasses, the torso of the smiling fair-haired woman seesaws
against a backdrop of sky and rock. He pushes his sunglasses
back on his bald head as if he knows I'm looking there. "My
dear Jude, let me make amends for embarrassing you. Do you
know where I'm going to kiss you?"

I know. Jonah Prince sinks to his knees on the rock. He buries
his face in my belly, then lower. I stare, still distracted, over his
shoulder out to the horizon which is empty of boats and islands.
I am letting Jonah Prince perform oral sex on me and I am not
letting Jonah Prince perform oral sex on me. I am far outside
the tanned body of the woman I saw in his glasses and I am lost
insider her. This is metaphysical and silly. And anyway, I know
I can't come. I have dedicated my orgasms to Child. Nothing
will happen. And yet, something is happening. I see the swami
the way I saw him yesterday morning, wise and holy rising from
an orange calla lily. Except the flower is pink and purple like
labia. My God. Oh no. Something is happening. I am starting
to come. I have to hand it to Jonah Prince. His tongue work is
dazzling. The swami is rising higher and higher into the northern sky which looks bluer than I have ever seen it before. The
swami rises far above Gull Rock—way over the north group of
the Watchers. He is smiling. He is happy to be rising like a
summer astronaut. Now I am coming hard and fierce against
Jonah's mouth. Above us the swami explodes. Poof! That's a
silly sound. You expected me to come up with another descrip-
tive noise. Then he's gone. Cosmic dust. That is all that's left of
the swami.

Jonah enters me, his face proud and haughty like a Spanish
dancer's. He comes fast and fiercely too and then we droop and
clutch each other like babies. We slide down the rock wall and

stretch out on the granite under our feet. The sun on my face is blinding and excruciatingly hot. The body of Jonah Prince lying across mine is wet and soggy. Something is moving by his left shoulder. It's a cricket, hauling itself slowly across the hot rock to the shade of the fuzzy bushes where my bikini is drying in the sun. I feel a mood of post-coital sadness slide over me as I watch the cricket. It is inching slowly towards the shade just as time is slipping by me: bit by bit, out here in the open sound. Finally Jonah moans a little and shifts his weight off my body. He stands up and grabs his Rolex diver's watch from the branch of meadowsweet where he'd placed it for safekeeping. His sunburnt face shows relief. He hands me the watch. Its black digital dots say 2:15 p.m.

"You know what I'd like?" I murmur.

Jonah sits down and kisses my breast. "Tell me and it is yours."

"I'd like to stay at the sound when the others go back to the city and pretend it will be summer for ever."

"Ahhaha. That is my wish too, but the regatta is over." He sits down beside me and places a hand on my knee.

"Every summer I sail in it to defeat that Southern Ontario boy and then when I do—" He turns to me frowning. "Afterwards I am annoyed that I need to vindicate myself in his eyes."

"Jonah?"

"Yes."

"Do you think the others will find out about this?"

"No," he laughs. "Why should they?"

"What about Bobby?"

"Bobby doesn't even like me."

"Bobby loves you."

"Ha, ha! Is that what you women tell yourselves in order to act out your childhood rivalries?"

"No—no—I love Child!" I stop, shocked.

"And he is getting married to somebody else. Poor Jude. Let me help you put it out of your mind."

He sighs again and turns toward me so his cock presses hard into my side. "Take me in your mouth. Please." Obediently, I roll over and take his cock in my hand. It's shorter and skinnier than Child's or Higgins'. The individuality of men's cocks always surprises me. I thought it was only women whom nature tortured by handing out an assortment of breast sizes and body shapes. He whispers my name and now my cunt is so hot it feels like a swollen triangle rising off the flesh of my body. Gently, I cup his balls in my hands and draw his cock into my open mouth. Jonah shudders as if I'd hit him. He smells fresh, even in the heat, while I can smell the sweat of love-making rising from my own skin as I bend over him, sucking and stroking with an air of reverence which disguises the unlimited curiosity I possess about the behaviour of men's genitals.

Urgently, he begins to thrust himself in and out of my mouth, moaning and panting, while I squeeze his balls and suck harder on the stretchy skin slipping up and down under my tongue and fingers.

I am kneeling over him, drenched in sweat. The breeze fans my hair. Down below, waves suck at the rocks. Suddenly, I feel relief from the sun. I look up. Shelly is standing over me, blocking out the sunlight. Our eyes meet and lock. Her mouth is an empty amazed hole in the blinding glaze of sun and water. My mouth is full of Jonah's come—like a milkweed pod burst at the seams. She says something. I rock back on my heels. Jonah's cock falls out. He exclaims, "What on earth?" I put my hand on his arm distractedly.

"Somebody's here," I whisper. I can't make my lips form her name. Jonah sits up and looks around in a daze like a victim, as if Shelly had hit him on the head with a plank and made him see double.

"Bobby's got a cramp," Shelly says. She is half-sobbing. "Hurry." Jonah jumps to his feet, puts on his suit—one leg in, one leg out, like a crane hopping in the shallow water. I can't move. I lie lifeless, staring at the blue gold sky.

"Hurry! Hurry! She's going to die!" Shelly says.

Jonah touches my shoulder and I haul myself to my knees like a dog. I put my hands on the granite wall to steady myself. Jonah scans the surface below us. Bobby's head is nowhere to be seen. "Oh my God, Bobby's in trouble," I cry. Now I see two heads. Child's head is next to Bobby's. He must be trying to hold her up. Bobby's head disappears again. "Let's go," I say. I put my suit on and begin to run down the rockface, sliding and scrambling. Jonah follows me down, clutching the rocks when the slope gets steep. Shelly scrambles down behind us. I reach the bottom and do a racer's dive—a fast slick skim of the surface. Jonah flails the water beside me. He is doing the crawl, a fast choppy stroke. I gasp for breath. My neck and shoulders hurt but I don't stop. Don't die, Bobby. Don't die. I love you. I love you. Now my legs ache. I can't feel my shoulders and arms any more.

Jonah has fallen back. I can't see him in the range of my vision now. He must be only five yards behind me. I stop, tread water, and look ahead. The two heads are about fifteen yards away. I can see Child and Bobby clearly. Their heads bob as if severed from their bodies. Child's wispy blond hair is matted against his shoulders. Bobby's platinum hair has fallen over her eyes. Her bronze face is shut like a closed-up sunflower. She is either unconscious or dead. Child's right arm is bent around Bobby's neck. "What have you two been doing?" Child shouts. "I've been yelling for twenty minutes." Jonah says nothing.

"Is she hurt?" I shout.

"She got a cramp halfway across," Child shouts and Shelly starts to scream, behind us: "Bobby's going to die. She's drowning!"

Child turns toward her and shouts, "Pipe down! You're hysterical."

"Let me take her," I yell.

"Okay. But we'll do it in relays. She's so heavy," Child shouts. I swim over and extract Bobby's frighteningly white head from Child's arms. Suddenly Bobby's balloon-like stomach bobs up above the surface. Bobby opens her eyes, starts to choke.

"It's Jude, Bobby. I'm going to get you where it's warm and dry. Will you lie still?"

Bobby nods weakly and lets her head sink against my breastbone. I begin to scull backwards, dragging Bobby behind me. Jonah is beside me. "Is she all right?" He peers into Bobby's face and she opens her eyes.

"Here. Let me take her." Jonah reaches for her but I shake my head. I can't bear him to touch her. Not my darling. I cradle Bobby's neck tighter and she starts to choke. Alarmed, I loosen my grip. Behind Jonah, Shelly yells instructions at me. I pretend not to hear. I bend my legs in the frog kick, over and over, careful not to hit Bobby's stomach. The sunlight blinds me as I swim back to Gull Rock, away from Good Cheer. There is no other choice.

2:50 p.m.

The three of us haul Bobby onto the first ledge of Gull Rock. We have brought her here in relays. Shelly climbs out of the water. She sits down on a rock and catches her breath. She is crying. None of us looks at her. We are staring at Bobby. Bobby looks grotesque. She lies slumped on the granite, gasping for air. Her stomach hangs to the side like a wrinkled brown beachball. It is as if I have willed her to look as she looks at this moment . . . ugly, beaten . . . old. I look at her stomach and for a second, I imagine her child's pink, lidless eyes staring at us.

"Do you think Bobby's baby is all right?" I say under my breath. Child shakes his head and frowns.

3:15 p.m.

"Let's talk about what to do," Jonah says. He nods at Child. "I don't think the women should try to swim back. Why don't you and I go?"

"Jonah's right. We'll swim back and get the others," Child says.

Jonah nods. "You sit tight, Jude. Child and I are as good as gone." Child stands up. He looks relieved to have an excuse to do something. The men can't do without the doing. Jonah gets up and dives elegantly into the green-blue surface covered with millions of tiny wave-wrinkles. Child pats my shoulder and dives in too. My fear for Bobby has made me feel close to him again. I stand watching the light distort the men's pink arms and legs under water into gnarled limbs. Slowly, they zigzag off. I sit down and sigh. Bobby slumps against me. "Do you have a cigarette?" she asks meekly. Her Easy Rider sunglasses hang on a chain around her neck. Her shoulder-length platinum hair lies in a wet mat down her back.

I shake my head, pick up her hand. It's limp, cold.

"They really do turn blue, don't they?" Shelly whispers as if Bobby can't hear. I don't reply.

An awkward silence falls over the three of us. I feel too frightened and ashamed to talk. Shelly looks at me strangely and says nothing. When a monarch butterfly alights on my hand, I unhook its black, grasping feet and give it a little push. It wavers for a moment, then flies away.

3:22 p.m.

A brown speck appears a few miles to the east of us. It rolls up and down on the backs of the waves. Shelly and I watch it without speaking. The speck comes into focus, like a detail in a photograph taken with a Polaroid. The detail becomes a boat. It's the *At Last*, Sir James' old Muskoka cigar boat. Doc Lefroy stands in the bow.

Its motor suddenly shuts down with a great sobbing ache of noise and Child and Jonah ascend its swimming ladder. The back of Jonah's bald skull shines like varnish in the August afternoon.

The motor of the *At Last* starts up again and the boat chugs in towards us, banging up and down on the rollers.

"Hi, boys and girls!"

Doc Lefroy pulls off his peaked cap and waves it up and down. His actions look unsteady, as if he is drunk. There is another great sobbing wave of sound and then the *At Last* shuts off a second time. Doc Lefroy crawls out onto its dark mahogany snout, holding a bow line.

I reach over, touch Bobby's thick, wet, matted hair. "We have to go." The hair-stroking seems stagey, as if I want to show Bobby I still care for her. I sense Shelly watching us.

Beside me, Bobby doubles over. "Jude," she mumbles. "I'm having contractions."

3:26 p.m.

Whitecaps bristle like funny, foamy moustaches on humps of navy water. Two figures are climbing down the swim ladder of the *At Last*. Child and Jonah. Child is carrying Doc Lefroy's rubber dinghy. He drops it on the wave surface, then holds it with one hand while Jonah jumps in. Now Jonah hooks up the paddles and begins to row to shore. Bobby looks dopily across the water.

"Oh my God," she whispers. "It hurts." Her chin drops on her chest.

Jonah is on shore now. He hands the bow line of the dinghy to me.

"The rest of you can swim back to the boat. Jude and Bobby will come with me." Jonah stretches his arms out towards Bobby. He is still smiling. "Come along now."

"Not like that! Don't hold me like that! What's the matter with you?"

Bobby pulls back from Jonah and leans against me. Jonah's protuberant marble blue eyes are blank. I realize he is laughing.

"Ha ha . . . she's mad at me . . . that's a good sign."

"She's having contractions," I say warningly.

He puts his hand out again and grudgingly Bobby lets him help her into the dinghy. Then she turns her head, looking for me. I climb into the dinghy too. Now Jonah gets in with a graceful hop, both hands on the swollen rubber gunwales.

"Come on," Jonah says. "You aren't complaining enough. Tell me how to row this dinghy."

Bobby's head rolls listlessly in my arms.

The immense black mahogany side of the *At Last* looms into view, like the side of a schooner in an old adventure movie. The swim ladder hooked onto the mahogany wood is lightweight aluminum with yellow handgrips. It looks frivolous, insubstantial, like our lives. Bobby clings to the ladder. The waves slap against the wooden hull. It's too rough to sail now. The wind must be twenty-five knots. I hear the sound of crashing water, feel the foam on my face as I go up behind her. My God, I feel lonely. I am frightened and lonely. My head is level with Bobby's heels. I stare up at a purple mass of varicose veins on her calf. The splotch of dark arteries runs out in all directions from a hub . . . like an aerial map. A trail of prune-coloured fluid is sliding down Bobby's thigh. Further up, the back of her bikini is wet with blood. I hurry into the cockpit of the *At Last* and grab Doc Lefroy, who stands near the huge teak bar pouring a gin and tonic for Sir James. Together we stretch Bobby across a seat of red foam cushions. She lies groaning, her head rocking back and forth with the motion of the boat. Dark blood is seeping out from under her pelvis.

I feel numb. I lean hard into the mahogany panelling to make the wood pinch my skin. Good—it pinches. I want to hurt like Bobby although I have no idea how much pain she feels. I watch her face for signs but her eyes are closed in a look of self-absorption.

"Will she be all right?" I whisper to Doc Lefroy. He shakes his head as he stands at the helm, trying to attach a bobbing stethoscope to his ears.

Sir James shouts at Doc Lefroy from his wheelchair in the stern. "Lefroy, you horse doctor! Stop playing medico and change course!"

"Wait a minute, Jimmy," Doc Lefroy half-turns and bends over Bobby, one hand still on the wheel. With his free hand, he taps her stomach with his instrument.

"I said I want to go fishing at the Northerlies! Change course! Now!"

"An excellent idea, Jimmy! Just what I was thinking!" I watch helplessly as Doc Lefroy goes back to the helm and the *At Last* circles around, bouncing wildly on the waves. I tell myself to turn and scream at Sir James that he can't go fishing, but no sound is coming from my mouth. I have no will to resist anything that happens. I am as spineless as Doc Lefroy, a true lackey. One: I do exactly the opposite of what I know is right. Two: my lack of control has betrayed the one I love most—Bobby.

Then, over the noise of the engine and the crashing water, Child calls: "Bobby's miscarrying, Dad."

"Fah! I'm sorry. I'm half-cut." Sir James points at One Tree. "We can take Prince home after. There's his runty little island over there."

5:00 p.m.

Bobby lies sleeping—her stomach flatter but still puffy like the post-partum bellies of Egyptian goddesses who represent motherhood and childbirth. She lies in the bedroom off the kitchen on the first floor of the Old Place. She is wearing a heavy flannel nightie with pink-lined ruffles to ward off chills.

Bobby's eyes are closed so she can't see the bouquet of White Ensign petunias I've placed on her lap. The stems are sticky in her hand, a little milky. Already the flowers droop.

"I always liked this bedroom best. I can see his island from here," Bobby says.

"Yes," I say softly.

"Did he look excited when he said he'd meet me tonight?"

"Oh, Bobby. Let's not talk about Jonah now." (Mrs. God, can you hear me? Have mercy upon this miserable sinner.)

"I want to! Don't you understand? I want him to help me leave this hateful island!"

"You're upset. We can talk about it tomorrow." (O Mother in Heaven, I beseech thee to hear me.)

"You mean you didn't tell him I wanted to meet him?"

"No."

"Well, tell him tonight then!"

"I . . . I can't, Bobby."

"Oh, Jude, please. Just do it for me one more time."

I drop my head and look at the bottle of tranquillizers Doc Lefroy left on Bobby's bedside table. What does it matter now? Soon Bobby will be out of commission anyhow. I nod slowly. "All right."

"I don't know what I would do without you, Jude."

"I don't know what I would do without you, Bobby." (Please, Mrs. God, deliver me.)

"Remember how we used to joke that we'd end up living together when we were old?"

"Yes." (Mrs. God, I beseech thee to hear me.)

"I still think we should do that. When we're finished with men."

"Yes." (O blessed and glorious Mother, I beseech thee. Arise and deliver me for they name's sake.)

"I've decided something else, Jude. I can't tell you. Not yet. But I need another poem. One that flatters him."

"Another poem?" (O God the Mother the Daughter and the

Holy Ghost, you take away the sins of the world, take away mine.)

"I don't have a department store of poems, Bobby." (O Mrs. God, hear me. Mother, have mercy upon me.)

"You always say that. Isn't there one about punctuation marks?"

"Yes, maybe." (O Mother, save thy daughter and bless thine inheritance. Give me peace in my time, O Mother. And cleanse my heart within me.)

"Jude, you're not paying attention. Are you trying to tell me something about me and Jonah Prince?"

"No." (O Mother, open thou my lips. And my mouth shall show forth they praise.)

"How does it go, then?"

"I never liked grammar rules
until you schooled me
in the punctuation mark
what bothers me, though,
is this: Are you just an ordinary comma
or a colon denoting ! # ¢ = * ???"

(O Mother, make speed to save me. O Mother, make haste to help me. Glory be to Mother and to the Daughter. As it was in the beginning is now and ever shall be. World without end. Amen.)

"I'll take that one."

The door opens a crack. Doc Lefroy pokes his head in. "Is she awake?" Without waiting for an answer, he walks in. He is sober and dressed for the regatta dinner in navy flannels and a Hawaiian shirt. Reading glasses hang around his neck on a black string.

"My baby. Where did Bull take it?" Bobby mutters from the bed.

"Now Roberta. I told you your little girl passed away." Doc Lefroy checks her pulse.

"You're lying—you old creep." Bobby starts to cry.

"Roberta—sssh. You mustn't blame yourself. A miscarriage is not unusual in the fifth month."

"Was it the swim that did it?" I whisper.

"There's no point in speculating," he whispers back. "We don't really know much about spontaneous abortion."

"Now Roberta, I want you to take something to keep you relaxed." Doc Lefroy shakes the bottle of pills like a maraca. Bobby turns her head away.

"Can I go to the dinner?"

"You're going to stay right here and rest. That's what's important now."

"But I have to go."

"Not this year, Roberta."

Bobby groans again and shuts her eyes. The sound of a gong reverberates over the loudspeaker. Doc Lefroy looks out the window at Big Dome. He checks his watch.

"Jeez. It's meditation time. I told Joyce I'd go too." He looks at me. "Aren't you coming?"

"I don't want to leave Bobby."

"Company isn't good for Roberta now." Doc Lefroy takes my arm cajolingly. "She needs rest."

"Don't talk about me in the third person! You asshole."

"Ssssh. Now don't take it so hard, Roberta." He whispers into my ear theatrically. "A lot of gals won't admit it's happened, you know. They think it means they've failed as women."

Behind us, there is a timid rap on Bobby's door. It swings slowly open. Neil pads in and covers Bobby's bed with stuffed toys. Sally Love follows him in. Her eyes look red; she has been weeping.

"Let's leave the little lady with her family, shall we?" Doc Lefroy says. I follow him out quietly.

5:15 p.m.

I am stumbling through the maze of paths by the Japanese garden, on my way to the dome. Just before the floating bridge, the swami appears on the path ahead. A purple robe is wrapped many times around his womanly body. He folds his hands in prayer fashion and bows.

"Young journalist is unhappy?"

"Yes," I say. I want to say the hardest thing of all—help me—

but I can't ask for something for myself so I say instead, "Swami, I am very troubled. Bobby's lost her baby."

He grins as if I am making a joke. "You and young Cape wife must detach yourself from relationships and attach yourself to God." He puts a pudgy hand on my shoulder. "Remember the sage who went into the forest and renounced his family, his kingdom and his wealth? The sage happened to be present when a hunter shot a pregnant deer. The deer gave birth to a baby and died and the sage raised the deer. It used to stay close while swami meditated. Then when this swami died, he came back in next life as a deer. Why? Because he allowed himself to become attached."

The swami bows again and then walks up the Japanese bridge and vanishes. I start to tremble as I stand in the clearing. There is somebody in among the pines. It's Bull hunched over by Mister Tom's vegetable garden, digging into the earth with a spade. Behind him the ripening tomatoes drip red globes down the fuzzy green stems. Mister Tom's tomatoes are tied to the stakes with string—hundreds of them—waxy, almost synthetic in the light of the late afternoon. As I watch, Bull lowers a small towelled bundle into the sandy earth. He throws in a spadeful of earth. Damn . . . damn . . . he is burying Bobby's baby. I want to grab the spade out of his hand and do the job myself. Now he stops and covers his face in his hands. Why didn't I think he would be affected by the miscarriage? This is the bond he shares with Bobby: their love of children. I feel tears seep onto my own cheeks. Once I thought the love of women was chivalrous, superior—the essence of romance. The love of men, by comparison, seemed primitive and messy, and all too dangerous. I no longer understand my old divisions. Bull has been faithful to Bobby in a way I have not.

5:37 p.m.

I am praying for Bobby's lost child on the weighted floor of Little Dome. Sitting on the weighted floor is like sitting on the old dock, except it's nicer. You don't have to worry about mosquitoes in here.

I chant "Ommmm" out of politeness for the swami's formalities and stare at the doll-sized Krishna figure, one of Shelly's statues, on the altar. It gazes back at me from under heavily fringed eyelashes. The doll is dressed in one of Shelly's hand-sewn saris. It has the same plump womanly body as the swami and its long pointed face with its starry gaze looks female by Western standards. The swami is dressed in a matching purple robe. He sits to the left of the altar. His knees are crossed and his wide-open eyes express amazement, delight at the closed ceiling of Big Dome. The workmen finished it just an hour before. Unfortunately, there is still more water to pump into the outer sphere so Little Dome can float securely. That's the background noise you hear—the racket of the swami's old water pump. Its frayed black belt is running round and round behind a hydroponic flower bed, spraying water from the sound into the bottom of Big Dome, into the moat—or canal, as Lady Cape calls it. Lady Cape is sitting beside Child and me in a white terrycloth jumpsuit, leaning against a wall that holds up another hydroponic planter of trailing purple petunias.

Doc Lefroy is snoring on the other side of her. Strands of brown hair flutter slightly on his forehead each time he exhales. Lady Cape looks at him crossly. Then she looks at the swami but the swami is still admiring the ceiling. He looks as holy and wise as he did in my dream of his rising from the calla lilies.

"Shhh Robin. That's enough," Lady Cape hisses. Doc Lefroy's eyes flip open. He nods consolingly at me as if he is thinking of Bobby, and then slowly his chin sinks back onto his chest. His eyes flutter closed. He starts to snore again and suddenly, he farts—a smelly fart. Lady Cape's face turns mauve, like Krishna's petunias on the altar.

The swami sniffs loudly. Doc Lefroy smiles weakly at Lady Cape who is suddenly on her feet in front of him. He watches open-mouthed, almost boyish as she raises her hand and slaps him hard across the cheek.

"What the fuck!" Doc Lefroy shouts.

"You ought to be ashamed of yourself, Robin. You've spoiled meditation for all these people."

"What have I done?" Doc Lefroy asks.

"You've polluted the air. What a stink!"

"That enough! I leave island! People of Good Cheer not ready for the truth of Ananada!'' the swami shouts. He pivots on his salmon pink heel and hurries towards the door of Little Dome. Lady Cape turns her full-breasted bodice yearningly in his direction.

"Ramaji, wait!"

"In Big Dome, nobody strike anybody else! In Big Dome, we live in paradise on earth! There we free of silly games that say I better person than you! All is peace and harmony here, Padamaji—not slap, slap. You bad, I good!"

"Wait! I didn't mean to hit him, Ramaji!"

"I go. For good.''

The swami walks out the door of Little Dome. Lady Cape clutches up her shawl and runs to catch him. Child beckons, and I follow him. The swami is striding angrily onto the dock that floats across the moat of Big Dome. Lady Cape catches up to the swami and grabs the hem of his dhoti. The swami swirls about, screaming at Lady Cape and flailing his arms as if he is fending off something that's landed on his head. Suddenly Lady Cape unzips her white jumpsuit. She steps out of it and stands in front of the swami in a sturdy white bra and white nylon panties. "Ramaji!" she calls. "Look at me!" The swami turns smartly on his heels and runs up the ramp to Big Dome.

I see all this in a moment . . . the childishness of the swami . . . the ardour of Lady Cape. Child sees it too. He puts his hand on my shoulder, whispers into my ear. "Isn't he supposed to believe in detachment?" Behind us, Doc Lefroy staggers out of Little Dome. His childishness is obvious too. But he is not as theatrical or compelling as the swami.

"What's got into Joyce?" he mutters.

Nobody answers him.

"Ramaji!" Lady Cape calls again. "I don't care who knows!" The swami half turns and she undoes her bra. Now she winds up like a baseball pitcher and lets the brassiere fly. The bulbous white strip lands on one of the hydroponic planters of geraniums, like the breastplate of a Valkyrie.

"Mother!" Child shouts. "Don't!" He runs after her. She is weeping and stepping out of her white undershorts. She is naked just as the swami closes the door. She stands, fragile in her freckled, wiry body, her arms outstretched longingly. She is no longer fifty-six years old but only a young girl without a wrinkle on her aging skin.

"He'll come back," Child says. He rushes across the dock and puts his arm around the naked Lady Cape. He kisses her cheek. She sobs louder. I have never seen her like this.

"Any little thing I could do?" Doc Lefroy calls.

Lady Cape looks up, bewildered, mascara streaking her mauve cheeks.

"You've done enough," Child replies. "Jude, go and tell him Mother needs help with the regatta dinner."

I nod. I don't want to find the swami, but I want to help Child. For him, I would do anything. I feel my lips stretching into a smile. I hear my voice saying, "Of course, I'll go."

I walk out of the door of Little Dome looking over my shoulder at my darling . . . I walk across the plankway . . . across the moat of Big Dome . . . the water makes squishy wet sounds as my feet hit the boards . . . I climb up the ramp to the open doorway . . . I feel Child's eyes warm on my back . . . ah . . . ah . . . I know he loves me . . . the way I want him to love me . . . I reach the doorway . . . pause . . . I do not turn around . . . then I walk out into the evening sunlight.

It is only a two-minute walk to the swami's cabin. Planters of geraniums and white petunias hang from the roof of the porch. The smell of lotus-blossom incense comes through the window. I walk up to the porch. I have no idea what I am going to do. I look through the cabin window. The swami is sitting on a pillow on the floor in a pose of meditation. His hands are folded in prayer position on his chest. When he hears my step on the porch, he jumps up and snuffs out the incense. Now he disappears into another room. I hear his door slam. Is he relieving himself outdoors? O Holy Mother, this is insane. Me, Jude, here to placate an irate swami. Me, whose soul is in shreds.

I go down the steps of the porch and walk to the back of the cabin, ready to avert my eyes if I should catch him performing a bodily function. Or will I interrupt a religious practice he'd rather I didn't witness? But the little terrace behind the cabin is empty. So are the pines behind Mister Tom's plot of tomatoes. He must have gone into the Japanese garden to meditate, but the thought of brushing into him in the woods gives me the willies. Besides, I have done what I said I would do. I cannot do more than that. Not tonight.

I walk back to the front door of the cabin. It is me who has to perform a bodily function. I look around cautiously for the bathroom. The incense stick is still smoking. The pillow still bears the imprint of the swami's buttocks. On the floor by the bed, I see the swami's secret supply of morning glory seeds. He has been grinding them into powder with a mortar and pestle. I take a taste of the fresh powder and quickly scribble a message: "Lady Cape says the regatta dinner cannot go on without you. Please don't let us down. We need you."

This is nonsense. I don't need the swami. But I put the message on his pillow like a good disciple, open the door, stick my head out, call one more time.

"Swami? Swami? Are you there? Lady Cape wants to see you!"

I go back inside and open a door to a closet hung with red, yellow, orange dhotis. Wrong door. I open the door beside it. Thank God, it's the toilet. I walk in, pull down my pants. I hope the swami doesn't rematerialize as I straddle the toilet bowl.

There is a loud rap on the door. I scramble back into my pants and zip up.

"Who's there?"

I'm terrified. I know it's silly. The swami can't behead me for desecrating his holy cabin. I take a breath then peek around the door, expecting to see his dark monkey face staring at me reprovingly.

Instead Shelly is standing before me, dressed for the regatta dinner in a purple sari, just like the swami and her Krishna doll. A vermilion dot is painted on her forehead like an out-of-place red freckle. I want to yank off her sari and punch her in her fat freckled heart. I hate her for tricking Child into getting married.

"Oh, it's you." I pull out my menthols as if I don't have a care in the world and offer her one.

"I'm pregnant," Shelly says. "Remember. No vices now." I look down at her freckled toes without answering. "Jude, I'm trying to be a good sport about last night but there is something I have to ask you."

"What could that possibly be?" My hard voice startles me.

"Are you in love with Child?" She sits down on the swami's bed and looks as if she is going to cry.

I take a breath. "Yes."

"You're doing this to pay me back!" Shelly starts to sob. "For the trick Bobby and I played on you."

I feel myself becoming very still.

"I only went along with Bobby because you liked her better than me. And you still do. You don't take it out on her. Only me. Why?"

"You have no backbone. You put men first, just like your mother. Bobby doesn't."

"Bobby Gallagher puts herself first! All she cares about is what she wants!"

"She does not! She's just honest. Not like you. You said you were against marriage and then you use the oldest trick in the book to get Child! That's deceitful!"

"I wouldn't talk about deceit if I were you." Shelly looks at me intently and I see again the empty amazed hole of her mouth when she caught me this afternoon with Jonah. I start to tremble. Then she sobs: "Jude, Child's not for you. You want him to be somebody he's not."

"I only want him to be happy."

"You want him to rebel against his family, but I accept him as he is. You'd only make him feel guilty for not living up to your expectations."

Shelly stops crying. For the first time her eyes look certain. I feel surprise and admiration for her sudden courage. Shelly has never had any lasting shape for me. She has always been a backdrop to my summers with Bobby. But it is too late to let her into my imagination now. I think instead of Child walking like an angry angel through Lady Cape's beds of portulacas, his lemon yellow hair floating around him. No! No! Never! Child is not like the rest of his family. Neither Shelly nor Bobby can tell me who is right for me! I love Child—heart, cunt, and soul.

"Jude, I know Child will never love me the way I want him to. I know he will never commit himself the way I want him to either." Shelly sighs. "But I accept this. He likes to pretend that life is always open-ended so he is free to go, but in his heart he wants security."

"You are wrong. And I will prove it to you."

"How? By pressuring him to be a man he isn't?"

"No. By loving him. You think you own him. That's the difference."

"That's not the difference! You see him as a character in a story. Yes! This is just a game to you—a contest to see who will win the boy, like we used to play in our old summers together. But Child isn't a prize. And neither is Jonah Prince!"

"Jonah Prince—Jonah Prince! Is he the only thing you women care about?" a voice behind my back says.

"Oh, hello there. We were just waiting for you," I say guiltily.

The swami stands in the doorway, the sunset turning his steel grey hair salmon pink. He bows a little and then opens a drawer of his dresser and takes out a box of burfi. Chuckling, he offers us a piece of the white fudge. I shake my head and Shelly shakes her head too, giggling suddenly, her tongue between her teeth the way she used to giggle when we were girls. I say, "Excuse us," and the swami nods. Then he scoops up the note, chewing thoughtfully. His cheeks go up and down. His wool hair sticks out in spikes. He looks like a feeding llama.

"Tell Lady Cape I have second vision in garden." He smiles as we reach the door. "I see us safe and happy under water, dancing with Krishna."

"We'll tell her," I say and we go out into the twilight. For a moment, we stand in a pretence of friendliness, listening to the crickets whistle in the stiff blond grass. Their pitch is lower than usual, a sign that fall is coming. Then Shelly puts a hand on my arm and I think she is going to draw me close in her old way and tell me she accepts my love for Child. Instead she whispers low so the swami can't hear her: "I saw what you did with Jonah Prince today and if you don't leave Child alone, I'm going to tell Bobby."

My heart turns over but I don't answer.

I pull her hand off my arm and walk away.

7:00 p.m.

I am standing on the old dock in a pair of pleated white harem trousers and a white bikini top. You are here with me, Old

Voyeur Eyes. The evening air against your cheek is soft and cool, almost crisp. An edge is in the evening breeze that wasn't there before.

Along the dock, the racing boat of Jonah Prince is rolling slowly up and down on the swells beside the boats of the regatta quest. Most of the other boats are sleek and tubular inboards but smaller and less ostentatious than his. Schlong boats—as they are called in the vernacular—with walk-through windshields and padded vinyl interiors. The yachts—huge oblong blobs with curtained windows—are anchored offshore.

I walk slowly away from the boat and start to follow the swaying Japanese lanterns through the pine trees. The moon is rising through the massed shapes of the trees and the song "Sugar, Sugar" by the Archies floats on the evening breeze. I stop and stand on the stone meadow just before Big Dome which glows like a white egg in the moonlight. I have a sense of great height and space as if I were alone on a prairie before a tornado. I feel a sense of dread. As if all my life has been building toward this moment and there is still time to avoid it but to act is the very thing I cannot do. I want to divert and be diverted. I look up—and see the nighthawk droning overhead—or is it a whippoorwill? I sigh and head towards the dome whose glowing vinyl skin seems to breathe in and out under its frame of criss-crossed aluminum tubes.

7:33 p.m.

Islanders are swaying around me; their bare or sandalled feet seem to float up off the weighted floor, as if they are obeying dome law. For this is a peculiarity of spheres, which look small from the outside since they present no wall for the eye to estimate. But inside, domes seem larger than they are, making people feel freed up or "decompressed", as Buckminster Fuller put it.

The energy of the dancers frightens me because I feel the same dizzy lightness in myself. As if in one step I will spring up and fly until I hover at eye level with Lady Cape's hydroponic planters suspended thirty feet from the ceiling.

Overhead, hydroponic geranium plants with their lemon-scented leaves swing free . . . lush . . . hot pink . . . not starved like the swami's rice plants in the hydroponic paddies of Big Dome.

Across the room on a huge platform rising out of the dancing bodies, Doc Lefroy is rotating his hips in a lewd Elvis Presley gyration to "Love Me Tender" played by a band of men in blue and yellow tuxedos. Suddenly, Doc Lefroy puts out his hand and for a moment I think he wants to have sex with me. I shudder and feel afraid. I'm afraid if he wanted me, I would submit the way I submitted to Jonah Prince. Then Doc Lefroy shouts something and the walls of the dome seem to shudder from the applause as Jonah Prince, dressed in a white linen suit with a black string cowboy tie, moves through the crowd. Immediately, the band starts to play "For He's a Jolly Good Fellow".

"Ha-ha." Jonah kisses my fingertips and points at Doc Lefroy who is now swinging his hips in wide arcs. "What charming silliness!" Over his shoulder, the tiny figure of Lady Cape floats weightlessly towards us.

"There you are, Mr. Prince," Lady Cape says. She pries his hand free from my elbow. "I want Jude to sit by Ramaji and you to sit by me."

"We must obey her, Jude." Jonah nods solemnly. "She is our only tie with civilization tonight. The energy, can you feel it building? People can't control themselves on islands! Ha-ha! Without her we would be lost." Jonah whispers in Lady Cape's ear. She blushes as I sit down and watch the two of them fly out onto the dance floor. The swami watches too. Very slowly and carefully, he lifts up a leaf of spinach and places it in his mouth. Lady Cape hasn't told him it's rude to start eating before the rest of us. Manners are not an issue to bother your guru over.

I light a cigarette and wish Bobby were with me. I'd revolve slowly in my chair, and say, "I made love with Jonah Prince today." Bobby's lips would fall open and I would say quickly, "It was a mistake and it's over. I'm sorry." This is what the interior me wants to do. And Bobby would wink and let me put a lit cigarette between her fingers. "Sex with men isn't as important as the love between women," she'd say. And before I could whisper another word she'd list the reasons why it doesn't matter. "One: I don't love Jonah Prince," she'd say. "He's only a distraction because I'm bored with my marriage. Two: I know the man I desire is irresistible." Or she wouldn't talk at all. She'd put her head on my chest and let me hug her while she wept about her baby. It wouldn't be necessary to say anything more. Of course, this is only a possibility. I don't know what Bobby would do. Perhaps the real Bobby is not my Bobby of the sultry face longing for Jonah Prince, but somebody else hidden inside her that I don't know, that I have never known, not now or before.

8:03 p.m.

The ruling factions of Good Cheer are sitting at a long head table, like a house of parliament. Only the Crunchy Granola Mothers, co-headed by the soft-breasted swami and Lady Cape, and the head of the Big White Hunters, Sir James, are all staring at each other as if the power of the dome has forced them to converge into a centre. Even our renegade outpost seems to be aligned in a confusing way with them both. I sit between Shelly and Jonah who sits beside Lady Cape. The swami sits next to Doc Lefroy who sits between Sir James and Child. Child . . . Child sits across from Shelly. I'm hesitating. I don't want to go on with this, particularly when I don't feel like I belong to the sunnily smiling creature going through the motions of the evening, as if nothing is wrong. Look, I want to say to the big person who answers to my name, you don't know what you are doing. You're about to betray yourself again. At any moment Jonah will ask you where he can meet you later and you won't know what to say. Or will you, for once, be honest and say, "Look Jonah. I'm in love with Child. I'm not interested."

And now—just this second—Jonah whispers to me, "Where can I meet you later? On my island?"

"Let's meet at the old boat house." I fumble nervously with my cigarette package. For a moment I feel terrible pity for myself. Beside her, Jonah nods and raises his goblet at the swami.

"What will your talk be on tonight?" he asks.

The swami stops chewing his spinach and giggles. "Paradise."

"Paradise!" Jonah laughs. "The swami's going to talk about paradise!" Jonah looks at me and I see nothing but yellow light, as scorching as the glare of August sun. "Paradise is letting the invisible hand of the marketplace bring us unlimited riches. Isn't that right, Jude?"

The tireless performer, my external self, nods and begins to talk before I can stop her. This is what that charming liar says: "My vision of heaven is more seasonal than yours, Jonah Prince. It is always summer and the whole world is living a life of ease on the open sound. Nobody starves because there is enough fresh bass to feed all of India's 613 million and China's 830 million and whoever else of the world's destitute wants to come to the islands." (The smiling liar stops and takes a breath.)

"In the open, we are in the palm of God's hand. Naturally I don't mean God in the usual sense. If there's justice in paradise, God is female and she has a soft spot for bag ladies and Indians. She's a Marxist, too. A female capitalist God doesn't make any sense. Can you imagine a female God saying, 'Okay, you sparrows down there—it's every bird for himself'?"

This woman seems to have caused a sensation. Everybody has stopped talking. Jonah Prince looks at her with interest. Then he throws back his head and laughs.

"A female God! A Marxist God! That is too wonderful," he says.

"Have you become a communist, Jude?" Bull suddenly asks.

"She's a pinko all right," Sir James shouts from the other end of the table. "No doubt about it."

"My dear Jude, wouldn't a life of eternal summer make us all lazy?" Jonah Prince adds, laughing again.

"My God wouldn't want us to get slothful, naturally. She'd be wise enough to realize we need a thunderstorm or two to keep us alert."

You find you are liking this woman even though she is not paying attention to you. She is a charming dreamer, a soft-headed soul.

Down the table, Sir James is looking at me the way he looks at the swami.

"Pah! People are always going to starve," he snorts. "Our world resources can only provide enough for 44 per

ent. The other 56 per cent of our population are dead ducks.
t's a fact of life we all know but none of us wants to admit.''

"Pay no attention to him," Jonah says. "Why is your God
ond of bag ladies and Indians?''

"Because they both try to make paradise in their own way,''
shout.

"Ah, I see," Jonah laughs.

"To a bag lady, paradise is having nobody hassle her. And to
in Indian paradise is the next beer.''

"My dear Jude," Higgins laughs, "paradise is too religious
a word for me. I prefer the word 'Utopia' myself.''

"Fools! Fools! Why nobody listen?'' The swami bangs the
able. "We are in new age of peace on earth! Atlantis is not
ost. I have rediscovered it. I find aura here that indicates Good
Cheer was holy spot during time of Atlantis.''

"Maybe the swami's right," Child calls. "We *are* in a period
of transition. In the Age of Aquarius, nature is recovering her
creative spontaneity. And the citizens of our new Utopia, the
future, will think more about their spiritual welfare than a raise
in their pay cheques.''

"Ah! That will be a good time for the owners of production,''
Jonah Prince laughs. "Perhaps Sir James will be able to buy
back Cape Pianos.''

"Owners of production . . . ha, ha. Nobody own anything.
All resources belong to God.''

The swami laughs and Sir James yells, "Listen to me for
once. Cape Pianos is sold. The new owner can worry about the
spiritual life of his workers for all I care.''

8:17 p.m.

The noise in the sphere is very loud. Local girls from Indian
Harbour run back and forth carrying platters of fried bass with
lemon wedges and parsley. A girl puts down a platter of rare
sirloin steak in front of the swami. Lady Cape motions impatiently and the girl nervously walks down to the end of the table
and puts it in front of Sir James. The band in the blue tuxedos
is playing "Amazing Grace''. There are only a few islanders on
their feet now.

Another girl brings a platter of fresh Ontario corn to our table. Shelly seizes a cob of corn in her soft plump hand. You watch her roll it back and forth until her handiwork leaves a valley in the butter, like a dried-up lake bottom in a geologist's drawing. Shelly starts to eat the corn methodically, row after row, her teeth chattering like a typewriter. You watch her very closely, extremely closely, as if you are a lens focused on Shelly's mouth. The corn moves round and round between her clicking teeth.

You look again. Shelly is not eating corn. She holds a penis, delicately. At both ends. The baby finger on her right hand is crooked. She is playing Child's penis like a harmonica. The last bar of ''Amazing Grace'' rolls out the hole in its tip. And Shelly's mouth opens wide and she chomps down on the soft bald head. Blood streams down over her bottom lip. Now she grins at you and winks. She knows what nobody else knows: this afternoon I sucked the cock of Jonah Prince.

8:30 p.m.

Bull is on the dais, speaking into the microphone. His fair hair is brushed back with Slickum hair oil so he looks like an aging corn god, plump, shampooed—ready for the communal sacrifice. ''Ladies and gentlemen.'' He stops when somebody throws a dinner roll his way. ''It is a great honour for my family to host the thirtieth annual Good Cheer Island Regatta. Tonight we are especially pleased to announce an engagement in the family. May I ask the pair to come up and officially be toasted?'' (He doesn't mention the loss of Bobby's baby. Miscarriages are unofficial deaths.)

The chairs scrape as they stand up. I stare sadly through the brilliant golden light around the head of Jonah Prince, and watch Child and Shelly climb up onto the dais.

My beloved stands small and fragile . . . diminutive like the groom in *Giovanni Arnolfini and His Bride* by Jan van Eyck. The medieval groom in the painting is thin as a twig, in a long fur-trimmed brown gown. He wears a hat that looks like a black box. He stands, his hand raised at the painter in a benediction. His tiny wife in a gown and wimple is by his side.

I see Child (you know me) in the same pose, in the same long fur-trimmed gown. And Shelly swelling in her ridiculous sari, a triumphant freckled hand resting on her pudgy belly.

Oh my beloved, you are lost and gone for ever. Behind the pair, Bull is talking into the mike again.

"Tonight we have the man responsible for the Aleph Institute of Peace here with us. Please welcome Swami Raveshenka, a man of infinite wisdom who can tell you the difference between mediate and levitate without saying a word."

The crowd laughs and the swami walks up the stairs to the dais. Beside Bull's long primate body he looks small and dark. "Thank you, Mrs. Cape's son." The swami pushes Bull off the platform like a performer who wants to have the stage to himself. The crowd laughs. Now the swami puts his hands on his bright purple hips and begins to shriek with laughter. His mouth is a radiant orange circle.

"Friends of Mrs. Cape! Do you have any idea how funny you are?" The swami throws his head back, and begins to rock on his heels. "Ho, ho, ho . . . look at you . . . sitting like children eating pieces of dead cows and fish, waiting to get prizes for the little games you have been playing here all day." The swami suddenly spins around so his purple robe flows out behind him like a wedding train.

"Forgive me, friends of Mrs. Cape . . . I cannot help myself." The swami turns to the band. "Ho, ho, ho. Do you know why I am laughing?" he asks.

One of the musicians puts down his guitar and looks at the swami. "Straight people are funny," the musician says and half turns to grin at the other members of the band. They nod and smile and the swami begins to giggle again.

"And curved people? Are they funny too?" the swami asks. He laughs with delight. The musician shrugs his shoulders and looks puzzled. The swami strolls back towards centre stage.

"Straight or curved—all friends of Mrs. Cape are funny. Why? Because you have the souls of children."

Suddenly a dinner roll flies past the microphone. It strikes one of the band members in the chest. A few of the diners laugh, but the swami doesn't smile or acknowledge the incident. He sits down on the floor of the stage. He crosses his legs and places a foot on each thigh. The candles flicker on the tables of guests sitting beneath the hydroponic planters.

"You know how children love, don't you? A man with the soul of a child walks up to a woman and says, 'Hello. You have a cute nose. I think I want to marry you.' And the woman with the soul of a child says to the man, 'You want to marry me? You better have lots of money if you want my cute nose to be with you the rest of your life.' So the man makes lots of monies and buys the cute nose and they live together and then the man says, 'Hey, your nose is no longer cute. I'm going to go out and buy myself a younger, cuter nose.' "

The swami stops and looks around the room. Nobody is talking now. I look down and see Sir James whispering to Doc Lefroy. The two men are hunched angrily over the table, leaning on their elbows.

"In India man and woman raise their children together, then seek spiritual destiny by living apart," the swami says.

"Man in India do not need to make monies or build weapons to prove they are man. But man in West do not feel like man unless they have the biggest missile. How big your missile?" The swami grins and gestures pointedly to his crotch. "My missile bigger than your missile," he says. "So I can buy a cuter nose than you.

"When somebody say to man in West, 'Hey, if you play with missiles, one billion human beings die, one billion injured,' he says. Oh, that's okay, baby, you will survive in fallout shelter. And listen, you will be okay because paper say so. Paper also say your shelter will be uncomfortable, cold. So wear heavy clothes. What to put in shelter? Two weeks' supply of polyethylene garbage bags. After use of each bag tie at neck. What to do with garbage bags when shelter fills up with them? Never mind. Just be sure to put in two-week supply of water . . . a half to a gallon of water a day for each person. What to do with waste water? Put in polyethylene bags. Ha, ha. One billion dead, one billion injured. What to do next? You make love to cute nose in middle of garbage. Ha, ha. Above ground everything vaporize for three-mile radius . . . in thirty-mile radius survi-

ors will envy dead . . . never mind . . . keep making big mis-
iles, baby . . . keep buying cute noses, baby. . . .''

"Get off the stage—you communist fag!" Sir James picks up
a bun and hurls it at the swami.

"Ha-ha. Now Mrs. Cape husband want to battle me with
buns!" The swami laughs and throws the bun playfully to some-
one sitting near the stage. "But ladies and gentlemen—there is
no need to play my-missile-bigger-than-your-missile games! I
have strategy for twenty-first century. Dome life underwater!
When world above destroyed, we go back to way we began—
on ocean floor. Only in domes.''

The swami makes a circular gesture. "Like this! Look around
you! Is it not paradise on earth? We can see stars in dome sky!
And air pressure keep water out and radiation, too. Garbage no
problem—we put waste on hydroponic rice paddies. Ha-ha. You
see? It is not strongest but the flexible who survive.''

"I don't want to hear any more of your claptrap! Get off my
island, you Paki!" Sir James calls. Now some of the men at
other tables are on their feet hurling buns too. Lady Cape calls
to Child who bangs the table for order. Too late. The swami's
purple robe disappears behind a cloud of buns.

You can't help smiling to yourself. You think of a Magritte
painting—an amethyst sari with a cloud of buns placed on the
shoulders. Bread for a head. The swami is smiling too but he
sits very still amid the rain of buns, his hands on his knees,
palms up to the heavens. Then suddenly he inhales and the radiant orange hole of his mouth widens into the space inside the
dome and all of us are falling through his mouth into infinity
. . . sucked into his wet bright interior through the rapidly ex-
panding hole of his mouth . . . falling past his larynx . . . bumping down his windpipe and then head-first through the intestines
and out his smoky anus, spinning like parachute jumpers . . .
knees bent in free-fall position . . . floating and falling like
pieces of debris. Now the tables and chairs in the dome rush
through the air, heading for the swami's mouth. They fly through
his orange radiant hole driven by a wind nobody understands.

PART THREE

Summer Is Ended

The harvest is past, the summer
is ended, and we are not saved.

Jeremiah 8:20

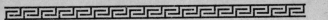

8:38 p.m.

It's the voice I hear first. The big echoey words sound like the Wizard of Oz. The Muzak stops. The newscast is coming through the loudspeakers by the platform where the band is taking a break. Somebody has hooked the speaker up to a radio.

Ladies and gentlemen: we interrupt this program for the following announcement. Terrorists are threatening to explode a three-megaton thermonuclear bomb in New York this evening unless their demands are met. Do not panic. Government sources say high-level officials are meeting with the terrorists and are close to having the situation under control. The terrorists are asking the American government to release three of their members who have been jailed on charges of arson. The terrorists are believed to be a splinter group from the radical underground known as The Weathermen. Please remain calm. We ask you not to try to contact relatives until we have notified you that the crisis has been averted. We repeat: terrorists have seized communications centres in New York, and possibly Los Angeles. Stand by for further instructions. Next broadcast in thirty minutes.

I hear a sound like the wind in the pines. Some of the guests are moaning and crying.

The swami still sits on the floor, chanting, "Ohmmmm." "Let us meditate for one minute. Let us join our spiritual energies . . . let us concentrate and meditate for world peace."

I can't meditate for world peace. Paradise is crumbling. I am dying. Child is dying. We are all dying.

A red-faced man, one of Thomas' workmen, begins to scream and pluck at Doc Lefroy's flowered shirt. Nodding, Doc Lefroy pats the man's shoulder in his best bedside manner.

The swami has stopped chanting.

"Today is another day closer to . . . closer to . . . what?" You are amazed at the swami's persistence, his need to play teacher on the eve of disaster. "Immortality, Swami?" mumbles the man whose head is level with the swami's hips.

The swami claps his hands and runs around the dais in little circles. He executes two short hops, as if he is playing hop, skip, and jump, and then turns once more to the faces in the candlelit dome. The moon suddenly breaks free from behind a cloud and silver light pours over the little dark man and the islanders sitting around the tables at his plump brown feet.

From the back comes a bellow. "It's a hoax!" Sir James is on his feet, waving his cane. "It's a hoax to get us to give money to his survival centre."

For an instant I wonder if Sir James is right. Could it be that the swami has arranged the report of nuclear disaster in order for us to try out Little Dome? It's not that I don't trust the swami. I'd never give him the satisfaction of knowing this, but I respect him for his spiritual prowess.

Bull is tugging at the swami's ankle. At the back, Sir James shouts, "Throw him out, Son! Throw out the bozo!"

The swami lifts his foot delicately out of Bull's hands, like the great blue heron shifting legs in the marsh on Sauna Island. Bull bellows and tries to grab his foot again and the swami dances backwards a few steps. "It is no time for games, Mrs. Cape's son."

"You call this a game? It's no game, Swami!" Bull leaps onto the dais and throws his arms around the swami's knees. The swami has been tackled by the number one quarterback for the

Good Cheer team. I expect the plump swami to bounce back up from the floor and knock into Bull with his soft womanly chest. Instead, the swami lies on the floor, playing possum. Bull crawls to his knees and looks at him. The swami's eyes are wide open and staring up at the ceiling. This is the most devout expression I have seen on the swami's face. Pure reverence. Total detachment. Complete freedom from worldly concerns.

Now Doc Lefroy ascends the dais. His flowered shirt shimmers in the moonlight. He's humming, "By the light . . . by the light of the silvery moon, I'll croon love's tune. . . ." He holds his shoulders a little higher. Something is different this evening if Doc Lefroy has the confidence to take charge.

He walks purposefully over to Bull and whispers in Bull's ear. Bull hands Doc Lefroy the microphone. The body of the fallen swami lies behind the two men like a backdrop. "Ladies and gentlemen, friends of the family, I ask you to stay in your seats." Chairs scrape against the weighted floor of Little Dome. You hadn't realized that people were up and milling about.

"We believe the newscast is a hoax." Doc Lefroy pauses and smiles warmly at the guests.

"All those in favour of carrying on with the regatta dinner raise your hands please?" He looks around the room, nodding as if we need encouragement. There is a sudden silence. The two women sitting at a table near the door into Little Dome put up their hands.

"Very good. I see some hands over there.

"Am I correct in saying we are all in favour of getting on with the prize-giving?" Doc asks. The dome seems to breathe out the collective word "yes". I'm startled by the assent. Many hands rest on table tops or are clasped in laps. Doc notices this too, but he smiles even more deeply and his head swings slowly about the room for a second time. "We have a majority. I repeat, we have a majority. Would the winners come to the platform please?"

Suddenly Jonah puts his hand on my shoulder. "Are you ready, Jude?" He smiles. "They've just called our names."

Over the noise of people talking I hear Bull announce the other prize-winners: "First prize to Doc Lefroy for the Sunfish

derby. First prize to Neil Cape for the canoe race. First prize to
Shasta Cape for the treasure hunt. . . ."

I stand up slowly.

Jonah takes my hand and we approach the podium where Bull
is pouring champagne into the gold regatta trophy. He holds it
out, frowning, to Jonah.

"Jonah Prince and Jude Bell—first prize for the Laser competition. Time: twenty-three point six minutes."

Jonah tries to lift up the garbage can to his lips and laughs as
he staggers under its weight. He turns to me so I can help him
hold it. I look up. Child is watching me. Goodbye, my darling.
The moonlight inside the dome is eerie now, as if the sphere
were submerged in a silver fluid.

Now Bull calls out the runners-up—Sally Love has won second price for pie baking. She steps up onto the podium, smiling
in delight. She is all in white like a fair-haired virgin who holds
candles in Nordic ceremonies. Her slender legs and arms are a
frail pink through the pale gown as Bull takes her hand. It upsets
me to look at her. I want to grab her and hiss, "Smarten up!
Don't let your guard down with that man handing you a cook-
book and squeezing you in a bear hug." Instead I turn and
search for Child in the moonlit sea of bronze faces.

Jonah puts down the garbage can and leads me out onto the
dance floor. The band is playing rock music again. I undo my
hair net . . . shake my long fair hair loose . . . I arch my back
. . . roll my hips . . . toss my head until I can no longer see the
brilliant corona of Jonah Prince or feel the sensory cloud of
Child Cape because I am drowning in moonlight . . . the swami
is walking through the silver sea in his mauve gown . . . the
only man in the primeval world . . . he is walking forwards . . .
his pigeon chest out . . . not minding that the silvery fluid is up
to his waist . . . turning his magenta gown ivory . . . in the
distance I see white-tipped mountains with slopes the colour of
ripe plums . . . their peaks exhaling skinny atomic-shaped
clouds . . . and oh, the clouds are pretty . . . there are bone
white clouds . . . long and funnel-shaped . . . and hellebore red
clouds and marigold and apricot clouds in the form of a mushroom . . . and oyster grey clouds . . . and opal grey clouds in
mushroom shapes too . . . now I point to the clouds so the

swami can see them and he puts his hand on my arm and I'm afraid he's going to ask me what day it is today . . . instead he kisses me on the lips and sticks his tongue into my mouth . . . then he yanks at my halter top . . . he is laughing again . . . "Peekaboo," he says as he grins at my bare left breast . . . he lets the purple robe fall from his womanly body . . . now he is standing in a white loincloth . . . he looks exceptionally well endowed in the strip of cloth . . . he points at his genitals . . . he frowns and points again and I look there but I don't understand his meaning . . . then he takes my hand . . . he wants me to put my mouth on his penis . . . he wants me to suck him off . . . no . . . I can't . . . I can't. . . .

8:59 p.m.

The swami is still on his back. He lies on his back in the corpse position. All this striving for wind is too much for his Eastern soul. It's convenient for the moment to be horizontal while everyone else is dancing vertical in the moonlit sea of jostling bodies. I look around for Child. Where is my darling? Why is he not dancing too?

Then I see Bobby wading towards us. She has come after all. Her stomach protrudes above her orange harem pants. On her platinum head sits an orange turban—as high as a Sikh's. Suddenly she is close enough for me to see her nipples pressed like chocolate rosebuds against her fringed top. She stabs the air with a cigarette. She takes Jonah's hand, her hooded eyes wide open and angry. I would be unnerved if she were staring at me the way she is looking at him. But Jonah throws back his head and laughs. How can he act so calm? He must thrive on danger. I would like to emulate the way he retains his self-composure—his cool.

"Mrs. Cape—how nice to see you're feeling better. Isn't she lovely, Jude? She looks like a midsummer night's dream." He turns to me and for a moment I think I see resentment in Bobby's dark brown eyes but when I look again it's gone.

"Don't give me that bullshit. I waited for you in Sally's cabin—but you weren't there."

Jonah looks surprised. "There must be a mistake."

"Jude told me she'd ask you to meet me there," Bobby says.

"Bobby—I thought you were going to be asleep all night," say softly.

"You didn't tell him?"

"No."

"And I know why!" Now Bobby is angry with me. "You wanted to have Jonah to yourself."

Child is suddenly by my side. He puts his arm around my shoulders.

"I saw how you flirted with him last night." Bobby smiles strangely as if she doesn't believe her own words. "And then you swam off with him and left me all alone."

"That's right, Bobby!" Shelly says. She stands before us with Bull. "She slept with Jonah. Ask her. This afternoon I saw her sucking Jonah's cock at Gull Rock."

Oh Mother of God, do not let Bobby hear what she is saying. Some things aren't true even if they happened. I put one hand to my mouth in horror, and suddenly I'm covered in foul-smelling dark scales from head to toe. I am a catfish. I have no nose, only holes in my skin and gills in my throat.

"Did you sleep with Jonah, Jude?" Bobby's sullen face looks frightened. "Did you, Jude? I want to know."

"No." I lie so easily. Lies are only words. All you have to do is to say them. I smile at Bobby encouragingly. I don't want her to look frightened; I want her to be her old warrior self— the attacker who defends me because I can't defend myself.

"She's lying! She's lying! I saw her! I saw her going down on him!" Shelly screams and tugs Child's arm away from me. "And she's after Child too. She wants to take our men away from us. She wants to pay us back for that summer when we were fifteen!"

"You're crazy!" I shout. "Leave me alone!"

Jonah Prince takes my hand and pulls me away. "We don't have to put up with this, Jude." Nodding, I let him lead me out to the dance floor.

9:01 p.m.

Bobby is yelling at me but it is difficult to dance and tell you what is going on at the same time—to translate what Bobby is saying and intersperse her words with trenchant little observations about our situation. You know the kind of comments I mean: the witty asides you find in stories when the narrator is on top of everything. But here I am, dancing like a maniac and trying to convey the action to you as I am slipping under the course of events without a murmur. I have to dance because I don't want Bobby to know I have lost control. I must shake my breasts and wiggle my hips in order to preserve the me who is dying inside this body of brown skin and blonde hair—the suffering me who smiles instead of screams, who is still observing the forces of her own destruction as they close in over her head. It is all I have left: my ability to see.

"Did you sleep with Jonah, Jude?" Bobby runs through the dancers and throws herself at my feet. "Did you, Jude? I have to know."

"Stop making a fool of yourself! Come back to the Old Place," Bull shouts. "You're overwrought! You should be in bed."

"I want to know, Jude!" Bobby says and starts to weep. Oh no, Bobby—don't cry! Not for the Great Prince. I don't even like him and neither do you.

"No," I shake my head at Bobby. Why is she upset? I didn't mean for her to take it personally.

"She's lying! She's lying! She wants to take our men away from us," Shelly shrieks.

"Jude? This is the last time I'll ask! Did you?"

I'm not sure if Bobby is really asking me the question but I drop my head. I nod slowly. "Yes, I did." Don't you understand, Bobby? I slept with Jonah Prince and I didn't sleep with Jonah Prince. I sucked his cock and I didn't suck his cock. I am guilty and not guilty.

"Oh, Jude! Why did you do that to me? I would never do that to you."

"I'm so sorry! I'm so sorry! I didn't mean to hurt you!"

"She did so! She did it on purpose to get back at you and now she's glad!"

"Bobby! Don't think that! It was a mistake! You know me! I don't like to hurt anybody! Tell her, Jonah! It meant nothing."

"Is this one of your schoolgirl games? You're both hysterical!"

Bobby screams at Jonah Prince, "Answer us, you bastard."

"I don't talk to people when they're irrational. I'm going to get another drink."

"You want a drink? Here's a drink!" Bobby throws her drink in Jonah's face.

"You fucked Jude. Now you better listen to me. I hold you accountable too!"

"I am accountable to no one."

Jonah wades away, sucking in his stomach. Even in a crisis he looks trim, svelte.

Now Bobby turns back to me.

"You're smiling!" she shrieks. "Shelly's right! You wanted to hurt us. Look at you!"

"And what if I did!"

"How could you! How could you do the thing that hurts me most!"

Suddenly, I gloat in my power; yes, Bobby, I wanted to hurt you for not recognizing who I am; you didn't know me and now you must pay, Bobby; you let me worship you, you took my homage without thinking and hurt me when I counted on you to protect me, you hurt me because you only thought of me as your idolater, when I am a goddess; in my arms the heat of sex will transform men; I am powerful. I rise golden brown and burning out of the lake waters, through the peaks of flames my eyes shine with the blue of July skies; I am as white as snow, as timeless as the stone upon which I stand; I steal men from the women who love them, I am the giver of live and the destroyer, I am Aphrodite on the shores of paradise; I alone have the power to bring men to their knees; I walk in their dreams and banish winter from their souls. My hair is as blonde as the sun and flowing like seaweed tresses across the blue and white sky.

09:40 to zero.

Now you hear the Wizard of Oz voice echoing through the dome: *"Emergency bulletin! Emergency bulletin! Prepare to enter fallout shelters or seek protection by lying down near a wall, under a table, close to some exit in case of fire. Again: emer-*

gency bulletin! Blast will occur in 9:39 minutes. Those in the range of ground zero to one mile have three minutes to prepare. Those in the two to five miles from ground zero have fifteen minutes to prepare. All those in outlying areas have thirty minutes.''

09:39 minutes to zero.

The Oz voice says 9:39. You look at your watch just as Jonah Prince presses the weighted door handle, and Bobby runs, arms outstretched, yelling, ''Don't go! If you go, I'm going with you.'' Behind them the sphere rings with the noise of disaster—Lady Cape is on the dais.

''We must prepare! We must prepare! You! That group by the geranium planter . . . you go to the zoo . . . bring back the zebra, the yak. . . .''

The swami is on his feet beside Lady Cape, holding his head, one hand on the side of his darkly scowling face as if he has a toothache. The iron of his hair sticks out behind him like a mat of sheep's wool.

09:19 minutes to zero.

You no longer hear the Oz voice as a distinct voice. The noise of the countdown is only another noise, like the sound of Bull Cape shouting, ''I'll kill him, Bobby—do you hear me? I'll kill him if you go!'' Now you see Jonah Prince climbing into the canoe, now you see Bobby climb in after him; they push off, Jonah paddles wildly, quickly; they reach the door of Big Dome. Bull lurches into another canoe, he unties the rope, then I am at the door of Little Dome, yelling at Bull, ''I want to come too! I want to talk to Bobby!''

Bull waves crossly. I run and step into his yellow canoe.

09:09 minutes to zero.

You are still in the dome. The noise is terrible now. The vinyl walls ring and ring.

09:00 minutes to zero.

I am on fire but my head shoots incandescent flames straight to the heavens, fiery walls of sparks rise from my red-hot charcoal heart, my lungs are nests of oily rags bursting into blood red torches—I am a temple of flames in the bow of Bull's canoe.

08:59 minutes to zero.

Bull is in the stern, paddling like a camper; at the door of Big Dome, Bull ties up our canoe. Bull looks around, he looks at Jonah's empty canoe floating from the metal ring and says under his breath, "I'll fix him! I'll fix him! He'll never know what happened."

"Come back, Bobby! I'm sorry! I love you!"

"Tie it up with the stern rope, will you!"

"The rope won't reach."

"Oh shit. I said to tie it up."

08:50 minutes.

You are still inside the ghostly sphere, the gargantuan globe, watching two men and a woman comfort a hysterical child; the woman strokes its hair, the men stand behind the child murmuring comforting words; the swami and Lady Cape are still on the dais. Doc Lefroy is pushing Sir James into the centre of the dome; the swami is shouting.

Sir James staggers slowly to his feet—it's the second time you've ever seen him stand up; he leans against Doc Lefroy. Sir James grins, the grin looks out of place, a ridiculous grin, would you buy a used piano from a man with that grin?

08:49 minutes.

"You can't stay in here! The water will crush it! It won't stand up." Sir James shouts, "People of Good Cheer prepare! We're going to roll into the water! We're going to submerge!" Waving his cane, one hand is on the arm of his chair, his back is pressed against Doc Lefroy. . . . "Joyce! Listen to me! You're going to drown these people!"

"Be quiet, Jim. We will follow the plan."

"You'll never get this teepee down the hill! You've only got railway ties for runners!"

08:39 minutes to zero.

Big Dome will slide down the old railway ties! You picture it descending slowly, the shafts protruding from each side, encased in the flanges, the water sloshes inside Big Dome, Little Dome floats, moving gently from side to side. Pick a petal off the daisy, the plan will work; pick off another petal, the plan won't work.

"I refuse to go! And so do the rest of these good people!"

"We have no choice, Cape Father."

"Joyce, are you going to let this Paki fag tell you what to do?"

"Jim, what is your alternative?"

"We'll hole up in the root cellar of the old cottage. We'll slaughter the yak and wait it out!"

"There's no room for all of us there. It's safer in the dome."

"I object! I object! Are you islanders a bunch of sheep? Are you stupid enough to let yourselves be led by a yogi?"

Let us ask the people, by all means. Let us ask them. Today is another day closer to . . . closer to. . . ?

Has the swami no sense? If you were a fly now, you'd bite into his nose, deeply, wantonly.

"We'll do it by consensus."

"No. Consensus not let people take their stand. We go by Western custom. Vote better. Vote give everyone chance to register their opinion."

A few of the islanders manage to clap.

08:29 minutes to zero.

Hands shoot up, Lady Cape counts the hands; it's a majority at last, only a man beside Doc Lefroy does not raise his arm; that leaves three objectors, three defectors.

08:09 minutes to zero.

Sir James is screaming, a group of men moves towards him; who are these men? Already they look like Big Dome's army, but it's only Higgins and Mister Tom; they advance on Sir James.

"You never appreciate me! Never! I buy you a yogi fag and what do you do? You fall in love with him! You have to do things your way! You're inflexible! Selfish! You've brought ruin on the Cape family!"

The new military surround Sir James; Mister Tom surrounds the arms of his wheelchair; Sir James' head jerks wildly as they spin him about.

"I'm going to go down fighting! I will stay on Good Cheer until the last mosquito has bit the dust! You'll see! You're all going to drown! You're going to die inside that thing the swami had her build! You're all fools!"

07:59 minutes to zero.

The crowd parts to let Mister Tom wheel Sir James through, the door-flap ascends, making a squeaky sound; men wheel Sir James Cape through the open doorway; you hear the noise of a wheelchair being placed in a canoe, and sloshing water sounds as the paddles dip into the canal in Big Dome, the water sounds go on and on . . . on and on . . . the waters of everlasting life.

07:39 minutes to zero.

I bleed and burn, I run bleeding and burning, deserving to bleed and burn, me, of all people, who thought I would never do anything to hurt Bobby—how did I fool myself? How could I pretend to put others first—I am the game-maker who makes the people up on my own terms and when they don't live up to my fictions, I strike them down with my sword of vengeance. This is also me, Bobby: I, the rejector. Because the wages of idolatry is rejection. And this is also me: the sad dreamer who is afraid to love, who is so sensitive, so candid that she overwhelms people, frightens them so it is easier for her to love in

er imagination than engage with the real thing. And all these
's are burning past the pond with the floating lilies and down
e rock hill beside the zoo where somebody is lassoing the
ak baby. Ah, it's Doc Lefroy, Doc Lefroy is lassoing the calf.
ir James is sitting in his wheelchair, he is holding a rifle and
ointing it at the mother yak.

7:19 minutes to zero.

Bang, bang, you're dead, the female yak is dead, she slumps
orward on her forelegs, bellows in pain, there goes her terrified
aby, I stand, burning in the clearing, the yak is dying, I have
inned again, Holy Mother, forgive me, I did not act to save the
ak and her baby, behind me the rock vibrates with the sound
f marching feet, it's the military recruits, they come quickly,
wo, three, four men, marching in pairs towards the zoo, the
avalry leapfrogs over the snake fence. Charge! I hear shouts,
here will be more blood.

7:09 minutes to zero.

The air is thicker than water, I run so deliberately, I run like
Pegasus and yet I am not there yet, I am moving too slowly, the
ines are silver, silver in the moonshine, the boat house is silver,
he sky is silver with stars, and I am red-hot, glowing orange-
ed in the silvery glade.

7:00 minutes to zero.

Bobby is silver, her stomach is silver, her platinum hair is
ilver, Bobby the moon maiden stands between Bull and Jonah.

"Get off my island, Prince! Now!"

"I'm untying the boat. Leave me alone, Cape."

"Bull! I hate you! I'm going with him!"

"Oh no you're not! Stay here with your husband where you
elong!"

"Take me with you, Jonah! Take me with you please! I love
/ou!"

"If you go with him, I'll shoot you! I'll shoot both of you dead as doornails!"

"We're going to die anyway! For God's sake, Bull! Give up! You've lost me!"

"You're not coming with me! I want to go alone!"

"Please! Please! Don't be cold now, Jonah! It's our last chance!"

"Oh, all right. Get in then."

06:59 minutes to zero.

They do not see me coming, how can they miss me? I am burning my way through the silvery pines, I am a candelabrum of burning branches, my arms are blazing branches too, my feet tree roots, smouldering underground, I run burning to the dock.

"Bobby, don't go with Jonah Prince! He doesn't care about you; he just used you! I love you!"

"No, you don't. Not you. You love your idea of who I am, that's all! Shelly is right! This was just a game to you to even up the score!"

"Oh, don't say that, Bobby. Don't be so cruel. I'm sorry I hurt you."

"It's too late to apologize. And it's too late for me. I'm just a washed-up broad who wants to be with her lover."

Bull yells, "You can't do this Bobby! What about your children!"

"You never thought much of me as a mother so why pretend now? The swami was right. You acquired me like a car and a house! Well, I don't hate you! I feel sorry for you!"

"But your children, Bobby! You can't leave your children!"

"Bull's mother will look after them; she thinks she can do a better job, anyway."

06:50 minutes to zero.

"Oh, what about me? I need you, Bobby, don't die with Jonah Prince, stay here, die in my arms."

"If you're coming with me, untie the rope," Jonah Prince says.

"Bobby, don't pass me over for a man!"

"Jude, you know I put Jonah first! I always put men first!"

"No-no! You don't mean that! It's you and I who love each other—we use men as a way to express ourselves! Bobby! Don't you understand! It was always more important to play the game than win it!"

"Jude, I don't care about your philosophy now. Go die in Child's arms. I'm going to die in Jonah's."

"Bobby, I'll kill Prince before I let you go with him."

"Don't be a fool, Bull!"

"What's going on down there?" It's Sally Love.

"Go back to sleep, Sally Love! The world's just coming to an end, that's all!"

Bobby lights a cigarette in the silvery moonshine, the water is silver, the sky is yellow, there is a strange slow flowing yellow air rushing towards us, Bobby looks at me in the moonlight, suddenly she winks.

"See, I can light it myself."

I fumble in my pockets anyway and then I see Bull raise his old camp paddle, the one with the Ahmek crest, he raises it high, high in the air, I step in front of him but he pushes me down and now it falls slowly, oh so slowly down towards the head of Jonah Prince.

06:49 minutes to zero.

The sky flashes a brilliant yellow, a fiery wind blasts through my body, the paddle hits Jonah's head, Jonah slumps to the dock, his knees buckle, he slumps down like the yak, he is dying, dying silver on the silver dock at the foot of the yellow sky, Bobby shrieks and cries, she falls on her knees and lifts up Jonah's head.

"Speak to me Jonah, I love you!"

Bull stands like a caveman with a club, the paddle drooping in his hand.

"Look what you've done! You've killed him! Well, I'm still going . . . I'm still going with him. . . ."

06:39 minutes to zero.

Bobby, my silver woman, my goddess of the moon, starts to pull Jonah into his boat, first she pulls him by his arms, then she gives up, drops him, his head hits the wood of the dock, clunk, she reaches for his feet, now she pulls his feet, drags her prize along the dock, his head goes bump bump bump on the boards, she steps into the Thunderbird, then reaches back, yanks him by his legs into the boat.

"Don't go, please. I love you."

"That's where you're wrong. You love Child. Oh Jude. All right, come here," Bobby motions me close and I lean toward her. She kisses me on the lips, hard, the way we used to kiss, and whispers, "Look after Neil and Shasta."

She starts the motor of the Thunderbird, Jonah Prince lies on the seat beside her, his head in her lap, the moonlight encases Jonah's face in silver, the bald dome of his head is encased in silver, his golden curls are silver now.

"You can't leave me like this! You can't do it!" Bull screams.

"Just watch me! Goodbye, Jude."

The Thunderbird bumps an inboard, then another, Bobby never could drive the way Jonah liked, then it explodes like a jet, and surges out into the sound.

06:19 minutes to zero.

"Bobby! This is your last warning! Don't go!" Bull screams.

The roar of the Thunderbird grows fainter. It hovers between the tips of Gull Rock and Good Cheer in the silver bay, beneath the yellow sky, a speck on the water. Then it's gone.

"I'll show her! She'll be sorry!"

Bull turns towards the stairs of the boat house. He puts his foot on the first step. I know what he is going to do. Holy Mother, help me!

"Bull! Don't . . . don't . . . go there!"

"Is that you, Jude?" Sally calls.

"Bull, don't do it . . . it won't help! Sally! Come here! There's been a disaster!"

Sally Love stands on top of the staircase in her long flannel granny gown, a silver child against a golden sky. She hangs over the stairs and all her long blonde hair falls forward. Bull takes another step closer to her. The Ahmek paddle hangs from his right hand. His left hand is on the railing. He stretches his left hand up to the silver child. In the yellow light, his right profile is only a silver chin below a clown's blood red lips.

"Don't come down! Stay up there!"

"Jude? Where are you?"

"Stay where you are! Go into your bedroom and lock the door! Hide under a table!"

"No! Come with me!"

Bull's hand touches Sally Love's leg. I rush up the first few stairs, pull on his shirt. Bull's arms swing up. Both hands circle Sally's waist.

"There's been a disaster, Sally. We must hide in the boat house."

Bull scoops the silver mermaid up in his arms.

"No! No!"

I stand on the stairs blocking his way.

"Don't make me hurt you."

"I won't move."

I stand shakily.

"Out of my way."

Bull lifts his leg and points it at me.

I do not feel his foot, only the motion of falling backward and then sideways over the railing onto the dock, the shock of the fall angers me, I struggle to my feet, my left shin is bleeding, Bull is carrying Sally Love into the boat house, I know what he is going to do, the door slams, he flicks the lock in place.

"Bull, do it to me! Rape me! Not her!"

06:09 minutes to zero.

You point to the peephole, you motion to it impatiently, you must have run after me through the silver forest, screaming my name, I am surprised I didn't think of the peephole myself, I stand up slowly, look around, there it is, the knot in the eighth board from the floor, the eighth plank, I put my eye up to the wall and look through into blackness, I can't see Sally Love, I can't see Bull, all I hear is the summery flap of the waves against the dock.

05:59 minutes to zero.

You see me on the dock looking through the peephole, I am bending down, squinting, my hair has turned silver in the moonlight, you see a tall silver young woman bending over to look through a peephole in the wall of the boat house, while behind her a giant eyeball in the sky opens until the fringes of its lashes are the boundaries of the universe, until the lower lash dips deep into the silver waters of the channel and the tips of the top lash curl up and backward into infinity.

04:59 minutes to zero.

I look through the peephole into the gloom of the boat house. I see nothing. Then I hear a loud bumping noise and Sally Love lies in a wet heap on the boat house floor. Bull stands above her. He bends down and scoops her up like a kitten. She is not fighting back. He stands her up and bumps her against the boat house wall. She moans. Her face is hidden under a mat of long hair dripping water onto her shoulders.

"Bull, stop right now! She's just a kid!"

The head of Sally Love lifts slightly, then moves slowly towards her right, towards me.

"Bull! You can't do this! Stop! Stop!"

Bull fingers his crotch. He unzips his pants. For a second, his shadow hangs on the wall of the boat house, caught in the light of the giant eyeball—a stick man with a stick poking out from his groin. Then Bull points his cock like a weapon at Sally Love, Sally Love runs moaning and crying away from him, she runs mewing like a lost kitten, I pound my fist against the wall, I am going to be sick, she screams my name. "Jude!" I pound with both fists, Bull wheels around, I see his cock, thick, stiff, wobble as he takes a step towards her, his cock is as red as a Gertrude Stein rose, his face is as pink

as a Merton peony, he is beautiful and terrible as he grabs
Sally Love, and starts to swear.

"Do you want to go for another swim? Do you want to go
back in? I won't fish you out this time!"

03:03 minutes to zero.

The bumping noises start again, I feel nauseated, I stare
at their shadows on the wall, the bumping noise gets louder
and louder, it's the noise of my head as it bangs against the
boat house wall. My shoulders jerk, my mouth opens, I am
sick all over the place, sick over my halter top, sick over
my feet on the dock, I pull back from the wall of the boat
house and begin to run screaming, "Stop! Stop!" I pause
and pant and the bumping noise starts again, bump, bump,
I turn around and head west, west to Big Dome, to Child.
In the sky above me, the giant eyelid closes slowly like the
shutter of a camera, seamless, like the skin over a baby's
skull, I reach the Japanese bridge strung over the lily pond.
Now I hear snarls and hyena laughter, and clicking sounds
that slither down out of the branches of the pine tree to my
right, the one dripping with human bodies, I look up and
see the figure of Sir James, hanging by his heels from the
longest overhead branch, he's been disembowelled, his
purple-red guts hang out over his cream white flannels, just
hang in the air, even move slightly in the breeze, Sir James
is gnashing his teeth, snarling and snapping his jaws even
though he is dead as a doornail, he has to be dead, he's
disembowelled, and his guts hang out underneath his summer shirt, the shirt blows out in all directions, inverted like
an inside-out umbrella, more guts hang off the rock figurine
of a Japanese fisherman, in the Kotu-e, gathering place for
angels and holy animals, and near the lily pond, the white
heads of the petunias droop under the weight of the slickly
glistening ropes of intestines and spade-shaped hearts, now
the noises grow louder—sharp, rasping squeaks like forks
on a blackboard, and then I see Mister Tom and the military
cadre stringing up Doc Lefroy by the heels—whack, whack,
an axe hits Doc Lefroy in the stomach, shreds his insides

like sauerkraut, Mister Tom hangs him so high I can't see
his face and one of the men says, "You—you're next," and
all the rest of them—whack, whack, then Child, Shelly, the
swami, Bobby, the military want to finish us all off and
scream, "No, not Child," and Mister Tom opens his mouth
so wide the pool of blood under his tongue spills out and
runs down his lips, and he says, "Most of all Child, you
stupid bitch, he was born with a silver spoon in his mouth
and I intend to cut it out"—whack, whack—"You're next
you who thought you were good and pure like Heine's
flower—*du bist wie eine Blume, so hold und schön und
rein. . . .*" And I run stumbling through the bed of white
petunias, I cover my ears with my hands, I scream, and look
down, my feet are moving carefully, so I don't step on the
guts of the yak, there are yak guts for twenty yards to my
right and left, I know by the horns it's the yak, and the
colour of its hide, I mustn't step on its baby, I pick my way
carefully, lifting my foot daintily, now I am through the
bed, past the slaughtering grounds, the petunia-bed massa-
cre, the air smells of copper and cat pee, it's the scent of
blood and petunias. I stagger past the vegetable garden, my
hands on my ears, the orange suns of the tomatoes have
been stomped into the ground, the vine of the squash and
its swollen gourds yanked from the earth, I lurch forward
another step, bend down, there on the wet earth is a tomato,
I scoop it up, put it in my pocket, then I lurch over to the
green plumes of carrots, I kneel, grub in the earth with my
hands, pull out one, two, three, four carrots and stick them
in my pockets, then I see the flat green stems of the onions,
I dig faster now, the noises in the background are disagreeable mutterings, my fingers feel clammy from the earth,
there is soil under my fingernails, I stand up, look around,
the noises are growing again, the sound is rising in waves
through the pine trees. I put the onions in the cups of my
halter top then I start to run again, my hands covering my
ears, I run three stride-jumps at a time up the broad concrete steps of the old path, then I'm out of the woods, the
noises stop, they belong to the trees.

)2:59 minutes to zero.

I run across the concrete path over to the Old Place, I hurry past the barn and the chicken coop, walk up the steps onto the old wooden veranda, look in the window again, I am like a voyeur in my own environment, a midnight archeologist, the orange and yellow chintz sofas glow colourless in the moonlight, a half-full coffee cup sits on the plank stretched across the two stumps, the snowshoes of Marcel D'Aoust are still on the wall, I run upstairs to my bedroom, I open the drawers of my dresser, pull out my sweaters, pull out everything warm I can lay my hands on, then I go to Child's room and do the same thing, now I run downstairs again lugging the suitcases, I stop by the rack and pull off an old duffel coat and a plaid wool jacket, stuff hats and mitts into the suitcases, I look around wildly, what else can I take? Then I grab a novel by Cornelia Lumsden on the dining-room table, *The Alleged Grace of Fat People*, suddenly I want more books, all the books in the cottage, and I remember Chesterton's joke about the book he would take with him on a desert island . . . a book that gave him instructions on ship-building . . . I start to laugh, I whirl around and pull out some of the early twentieth-century novels in the bookshelves on either side of the door going into the kitchen, *Below the Salt*, Thomas B. Costain, *Keys to the Citadel*, A. J. Cronin, *The Magnificent Obsession*, I can't make out the author's name, all the novels are dated, they'll bore us, but they'll do in a pinch, we'll use them for fuel and write new ones, then I grab Bull's copy of *Time*, who cares about American domination under water, I grab the crib board on the bottom shelf, I'm smiling to myself, I'm always good in a crisis, it's something you know about yourself, either you're a screamer or a coper, how funny, to think about leisure time in a holocaust, in the midst of disaster, but I'm not done for yet, not me, I can still rise to the occasion, now I grab the bags, then I clatter across the wooden veranda, oh, I left the door open, the bugs, I turn, it's silly I know, who cares about bugs in the cottage now?

02:00 minutes to zero.

I put down the bags, go back, close the door, then I pick up the bags, walk down the steps, walk through the path of pines, the air is spicy with the smell of cedar, I love the green bowers of pine and the granite rocks and the open sound, ah, you know what I mean, the endless water, I love the sound like a lover, now I'm at the top of the path I feel myself emerging out of the shadows between the rocks into the light, the wind feels lighter suddenly, that's a good sign, it will come our way more slowly, in a plump, plume-shaped cloud, the slower the wind the fatter and shorter the plume, I stride through the stone meadow, past the swami's cabin and then I hear the sound of chanting coming out of his window, I drop my bags and go in.

01:58 minutes to zero.

I expect to see the swami sitting on a pillow on the floor in a pose of meditation, his eyes closed, his hands folded in prayer position on his chest, mumbling some chant, but the swami is in the dome, his incense stick is burning on the floor by his bed, I snuff it out, I don't know why, the pillow on the floor still shows the imprint of his buttocks, and then sitting between his Birkenstock sandals and a pile of carelessly folded orange robes, I see Shelly, she is rocking the Krishna statue in her arms, she's sobbing and crooning to the thing, it wasn't chanting I heard through the window, it was a lullaby and the swami's packets of sacred ololiuqui on the floor by her feet are gone. I put a hand on her shoulder and she stares up at me wildly, she says, "He loves you—he told me he doesn't love me." I make a soothing noise and pull her to her feet, slowly and gently, then we clatter out of the cabin, she's stoned, but she's doing what I say, poor Shelly, she always was a follower.

We are almost at the door of Big Dome, it's rocking slightly in the wind, Shelly and I are standing on the cliff looking west, west to One Tree Island, Jonah's speedboat is in the

lip, Bobby managed the docking, there is a light in Jonah's
'anabode, is she there alone or has she gone back down to
et Jonah's body, she'll drag it all the way up the wooden
ath, ah, a light goes on in the gazebo, she's way ahead of
1e, she is there alone with him the way she always wanted
⊃ be, Bobby is a follower of tradition but I must break my
wn path.

The dome is rocking again, it's not the wind, one of the
ydraulic legs is moving, wait, wait this can't happen.

"Child! We're here! Let us in!"

I run around the dome shouting his name. . . .

"Child! Child! Let us in!"

My words are having no effect on the dark shapes the
noonlight is making visible through the vinyl skin.

Oh Child . . . what can I do to make you hear us? I
push an old ladder against Big Dome, then climb onto the
geodesic wall, and shout again, "Child! Child! Let us
n!" The dome is rocking still more, another leg must be
collapsing, I stretch my arms up, my legs spread-eagled,
push my face and body deep into the vinyl, "Child!" I
shout. "I love you!" My breath is making the vinyl sticky,
ogging the plastic so I can't see through, I pull my head
back, rub the plastic, now I see shapes in the water, ca-
noes floating in the beds of wild rice, new sounds too,
animal sounds, the sounds are coming from the peacock
n the war canoe, Child is on the dock waiting for it to
and.

"Child! Child!"

He looks up, suddenly he yells my name.

"Jude! Jude!"

There's more noise below and the sounds of the Muzak and
hen the door flap rises skyward like a vinyl wing, Child is
suddenly on the ramp below me, he begins to scream, "Get
lown! Now!"

"Child! Get Shelly first! She just overdosed!"

And now Shelly is screaming, "No! No!—I'm scared. I'll
stay here. You two go—go on—you don't want me. I'm better
off here."

00:58 minutes to zero.

Child runs down the ramp and grabs Shelly's arm. "Jude! Jude!" my darling calls up, his eyes don't leave my face as I slide down, then he yanks Shelly up the ramp, his hair floating like a blond nimbus around his shoulders, the door of Big Dome is starting to shut, but Child rushes down the ramp, grabs my arm, pulls me inside and the flap closes behind us, we are inside Big Dome, the woman in the war canoe starts to paddle our way, the poor peacock is still hee-hawing in its bow, we descend down the ladder to the dock; and you climb down too, Old Voyeur Eyes. You get in the canoe right behind Shelly. Shelly sits in the bow holding the frightened peacock, the other woman sits in the stern, Child and I sit in the middle, I reach into my pocket and pull out my carrots, my fingers come out bloody, it's the tomato, it was crushed in my pocket, I wash off a carrot and hand one to the woman in the stern, then you wait, you're not sure what'll happen next, all right, I hand Shelly a carrot, she takes it and smiles at me, I watch her eat it, I eat one too, my function is to imagine paradise, I haven't forgotten the parable of the spoons, the one my father told me, but he didn't understand that in order to create heaven we need the fact of hell.

00:09 minutes to zero.

We are at the dock of Little Dome, the door flap rises, the band leader in his yellow tux calls to us to hurry, then, the Wizard of Oz voice is talking. "Those beyond the hundred-mile radius of the ground burst have five minutes before the second wave of fallout hits," the voice says. "We repeat, five minutes until the fallout reaches you in the outlying areas," now Muzak comes on again, the Barbra Streisand tune "Funny Girl", and we gather by the dais where Lady Cape is standing with the swami, Lady Cape has Shasta in her arms as she shows the islanders how to hang on to the aluminum struts criss-crossing the vinyl and one by one everyone positions himself against the wall of the sphere, holding on to the struts, then Shelly and next

Child and finally I go over to a strut and grab it, and last of all he swami and Lady Cape, and Big Dome begins to rock.

"Hang on to your hats," Lady Cape shouts. "Move in unison so we don't roll over." Now the dome is moving, the shafts are sliding along the track, we are slipping down the granite slope, going over the green lichen and the sparkling streaks of mica, crushing the blond stiff grass growing out of the old volcanic rock, then there is a thud and a sloshing sound as the dome belly-flops onto the hard granite. Big Dome has bounced off the railway ties, and Little Dome starts to revolve, yes, we are turning upside down, Child's face revolves above me, we are spinning in slow motion, spinning round and going down, ah, people are hanging from the rafters of the dome, we're turning round and round and going down and down the cliff into the water, Little Dome rings with cries and the crash of tables, furniture flies through the air, people laugh and scream, the laughers and the screamers, we will all go down together, in the din I hear the sound of Muzak, Muzak and cockroaches are indestructible, we are going round faster now, I hear the plop of bodies falling to the floor, surely, the rolling has got to stop, but no, it's picking up speed, going faster, Child hangs above me, he is looking down at the floor, he is looking for Shelly, she is still in her place, hanging from the strut, oh Shelly hang on, now the dome is stopping, it rocks up and down, then it's still, I hear the far-away sound of waves, we have landed on the water, we are floating on the surface, and now I hear a sound, the noise of rushing water, Lady Cape has ordered the hatches opened, the lake water is pouring into Big Dome, we are sinking, Lady Cape is smiling by the hydroponic garden, she is calling to those of us who are still hanging from the frame to come down, she says we will soon be resting on the bottom, on the floor of the sound, the swami is nowhere in sight, she is alone, a narrow white-haired figure amid the debris of tables and bodies, Child jumps down first, takes my hand, I land on my feet unbruised, Shasta sits nearby in the hydroponic tank, tears dry on her cheeks, she is playing with a piece of broken table leg in the floating flowers, making choo-choo noises as she pushes her makeshift train through the tendrils of geranium roots, Child scoops up Shasta and places her in my arms, immediately she starts to cry and I kiss her forehead, the water thunders around us, we are sinking down, we are almost at the bottom, we have the dead and the badly injured to care for, but we will know what to do, I walk through the survivors smiling and holding the bawling child, Bobby, if you can see me now, take your final look, I am free at last of our old game and the need to play it to the end and damn the consequences. From the shore, you'd never know that Little Dome is the most wonderful place in the world.

About the Author

Susan Swan is a novelist, poet, journalist, playwright, and accomplished short-story writer whose work has appeared in various magazines, including *Maclean's*, *Saturday Night*, and *Chatelaine*. Her first novel, *The Biggest Modern Woman of the World*, was nominated for The Governor General's Award. Her collection of short stories, *Unfit for Paradise*, is a fast-paced look at the misadventures of northerners in the tropics. Susan Swan teaches at York University, Toronto.